THOREAU
AT
DEVIL'S PERCH

THOREAU
AT
DEVIL'S PERCH

B. B. OAK

KENSINGTON BOOKS
www.kensingtonbooks.com

KENSINGTON BOOKS are published by

Kensington Publishing Corp.
119 West 40th Street
New York, NY 10018

3 9547 00386 4878

ISBN-13: 978-0-7582-9023-6
ISBN-10: 0-7582-9023-3
First Kensington Trade Paperback Printing: November 2013

eISBN-13: 978-0-7582-9024-3
eISBN-10: 0-7582-9024-1
First Kensington Electronic Edition: November 2013

10 9 8 7 6 5 4 3 2 1

Printed in the United States of America

Talk of mysteries!—Think of our life in nature,—daily to be shown matter, to come in contact with it,—rocks, trees, wind on our cheeks! the *solid* earth! the *actual* world! the *common sense! Contact! Contact! Who* are we? *where* are we?

—Henry David Thoreau

ADAM'S JOURNAL

Monday, August 3rd, 1846

This morning I glanced up from my search for medicinal plants along the Assabet River and was startled to see the sun-browned face of a stranger appear through a screen of beech leaves. He quickly but calmly communicated that he had found the broken body of a man on the rocks just upriver and sought to alert the local constable.

"Are you certain he is dead?" I said.

"He appeared quite dead to me," the stranger said. "His head had a severe wound, and when I laid my hand upon his shoulder he did not move."

I identified myself as a doctor and urged we get to the man immediately, explaining that I have known cases where all visible signs of life had ceased and the patient was yet revived.

Without further ado we started upriver Indian file, the stranger leading the way. His homespun suit of greenish-brown blended well with the foliage, and it was no wonder he had come upon me unawares. We exchanged few words as we marched, only stating our names and where we resided. Mr. Thoreau's stride was long for his short stature, and within scarce minutes we came to an area beneath the precipitous face of a cliff overlooking the river. We hastened to the body of a man sprawled on the rocks at water's edge, scattering a murder of crows pecking at the back of his head.

The man lay on his stomach, one arm beneath him and the other spread wide and at an angle that led me to conclude it had been dislocated from the shoulder. Both the tibia and fibula of the right leg had thrust clear through muscle and flesh, and the shattered ends showed white where they had pierced the trouser leg. A two-inch-round section of his skull was stove in, and blood had amassed and dried around the wound, with heavy clots clinging to his dark hair. Placed my hand on his carotid artery to check for a pulse. Found none. His skin was faintly warm to the touch, but skin temperature could not help me determine time of death, as he was lying in the hot morning sun. Mr. Thoreau and I turned him over and saw that he was a young Negro.

I bent over the corpse, lifted the arm that had not been dislocated and rotated it. "The body is stiff, but the rigor mortis is fading. This indicates he died sometime yesterday," I told Thoreau.

He glanced up at the high cliff face. "The obvious conclusion is that his death was caused by a fall from up there."

"Obvious but possibly erroneous," said I. "Although a fall from such a height would certainly result in death, I doubt it caused this man's."

Thoreau's deep-set eyes widened. "Do you? Why?"

"There is no blood around the leg wound, for one thing. If such a severe break had occurred when the man was still alive, the severed arteries would have pumped out a profuse quantity of blood."

"Are you proposing, Dr. Walker, that he was already dead when he went over the cliff?"

"I am almost sure of it," I said. "There is clotted blood in his hair from the head injury he received, yet none on the rocks beneath his head, leading me to conclude he was struck a mortal blow elsewhere. The instrument used was round and blunt."

Thoreau nodded and studied the dead man, his gaze compassionate yet probing. "Note how the backs of his fine boots are caked with dirt, doctor. That indicates to me he was dragged with his heels digging into the ground. We will likely see evidence of this atop the cliff. Let us go investigate posthaste."

We made our way up and to the side of the sheer cliff face by way of a steep and narrow path through the woods. When we reached the clearing on top, Thoreau cautioned me to walk no farther.

"Allow me to inspect the ground," he said, "before we tread upon it." He pulled a magnifying glass from the deep pocket of his jacket. "I use it to examine plant specimens," he explained. He then proceeded to hold it over the marks in the damp, bare soil.

After a few minutes had passed I admittedly lost patience. "Well? Did you find any clews?"

He stood back and pointed. "Wagon tracks," he said.

He had stated the obvious, and I was not impressed. But as he elucidated, I grew more so.

"Here the wagon tracks stop," he said, "and two parallel grooves begin. They lead to the near edge of the cliff, and I surmise they were made by the dead man's boot heels gouging the earth as his body was dragged. Between the two grooves are several very distinct footprints, more deeply depressed in the hind than the forepart. These impressions must have been made by the man who was hauling the body. He would have been walking backwards, with his hands gripping the victim under the arms as he pulled him along."

"I can well imagine the perpetrator's actions as you describe them," I said. "Unfortunately, shoe prints such as those could be made by any man."

"Look more closely, Dr. Walker. The soles of the footwear

have the thickness of boots rather than shoes, and there are two deep indentations in the right sole. Should we find the owner of a boot that bears matching marks, we will have found the murderer, or at least the man who threw the Negro's body over the cliff. But how can we preserve such telling evidence?"

"Might not casts of the prints be made with plaster of Paris?"

"An excellent suggestion, if only we had some."

"My cousin Julia Bell does. She had a bag of plaster delivered to her in Plumford just yesterday," I said. "She is an artist and uses it to make face masks."

It was decided that Thoreau would go to Plumford, alert the constable, and obtain the plaster from Julia whilst I further examined the body. I told him where I had left my gig and how to most quickly get to town.

"Look for a big white house with a picket fence overlooking the Green," I further informed him. "It is the residence of Dr. Silas Walker, our grandfather. Both Julia and I are staying with him at present. Pray tell my cousin as little as possible, for I do not want her involved in this foul crime."

"I will be as discreet as I can honestly be," Thoreau said and hurried off.

I descended the cliff path and went back to the dead man to inspect him more closely. His clothing was of cheap quality but of the latest style, more suitable for city than country wear. It was not the sort of apparel I would expect a runaway slave to be wearing. He might have been a freeman from Boston. The pockets of his yellow frock coat, scarlet vest, and boldly checkered trousers were empty of coin, banknotes, or papers of any kind, which suggested to me that his possessions had been taken along with his life. But how had this black stranger ended up at the bottom of a cliff deep in the woods of our township?

Used my pocketknife to slit open his clothes to better examine him for further injuries. He was in the prime of his youth with clean trunk and limbs and no sign of disease or debility. In addition to the broken leg, dislocated shoulder, and head wound I had first seen, one ankle was shattered and three ribs on his right side fractured. As I worked I could not help but be aware of the warm sun on my shoulders, the cliff swallows swooping over my bent head, and the soothing sound of the river flowing beside me. It was altogether too lovely a summer day to be lying broken and dead on the rocks, and I felt deep regret that such a healthy young man had come to such a brutal end in the summer of his own life.

Finding no further injuries or signs of a struggle on his body, I gathered an armful of fresh ferns from the woods and covered his face to keep off the bluebottle flies. I heard a gun go off in the near distance but paid it little mind, for hunters frequent the area. Eventually the town constable found me. Mr. Beers's trudge along the river had caused him to sweat profusely, and his face was so flushed that I sat him down in the shade, soaked my handkerchief in the river, and applied it to the back of his neck.

"I am getting too fat for this post," he panted.

Could not refute him. Eating too much and sitting on a cobbler's bench all day have not made Beers very fit for constable duties. Yet the townsmen reelect him to the office year after year for he is well liked, and his duties are not all that taxing most of the time. Mischief-making boys or an occasional rowdy drunk cause him the most trouble.

He would not go near the corpse nor even look at it. "I'll just set here till the inquest commences," he said. He informed me that the Town Coroner, Fred Daggett, would be along as soon as he found someone to mind his store and he could go round up a jury.

As we waited I asked Beers if he recalled mending a boot with deep cuts on the sole. He did not. I told him about the imprints Mr. Thoreau and I had discovered upon Devil's

Perch. He expressed only the mildest interest. I suggested to him that he should go take a look at the prints for himself. Apparently he did not want to hoist his bulk up the side of the cliff, for he suggested to me in return that I should desist from telling him how to perform his constableship duties.

Before our conversation became more heated, Mr. Daggett arrived with his jury of six Plumford citizens, one of them being the town undertaker. Elijah Phyfe also came. Although he had no legal role to play in this particular proceeding, I suppose he had the right to be present as he is the town's Justice of the Peace and chief magistrate. Coroner Daggett swore in his jury, and they convened around the body.

Mr. Thoreau returned by way of the footpath, and he and I testified. The jury listened to us most patiently and attentively as we presented our evidence. After hearing us conclude that we believed this was a case of murder, they all walked down-river, out of earshot, and conferred with Justice Phyfe. In less than a quarter-hour, they came back, and Coroner Daggett informed us the decision they had reached was Death by Accident. When I voiced my objection, Justice Phyfe raised his hand like a Roman senator.

"Now, Adam, do not be pigheaded about this," he said. "This unfortunate buck, unfamiliar with these parts, couldn't see where he was going in the dark and walked off the cliff. Simple as that."

"But the moon was near full last night!" Henry said. No one paid him any mind.

"A runaway slave in stolen clothes, no doubt," Coroner Daggett said. "No need to make this more complicated than it ought to be. The inquest is closed."

"It is your minds that are closed," Mr. Thoreau declared and without another word marched off.

Justice Phyfe, watching him disappear into the woods with narrowed eyes, asked me who he was. I told him all I knew about Henry David Thoreau was that he came from the neighboring town of Concord. One of the jury members, originally from Concord, commented that the Thoreau family, though respectable enough, was of no major consequence there. Justice Phyfe lost interest.

A moment later the Rev. Mr. Upson came down the cliff path. The fowling piece over his arm, I surmised, was the gun I had heard go off earlier. His satchel looked heavy with game, and I have seen him hunting in the area before. Reckon the poor man has little better to do with his time since losing both his wife and his pulpit.

"Best you move on, Mr. Upson," Phyfe said. "There has been an unfortunate accident here."

Upson gave the corpse a cursory glance. "So I just heard."

"Where did you hear this?" Phyfe demanded.

"Above."

Phyfe raised his eyebrows. "You mean to say God informed you?"

"If I had meant to say that, I would have." Upson pointed to the top of the cliff. "I came across Miss Bell and a man called Thoreau up there, and they informed me that a dead man lay below."

Upon learning that Julia had accompanied Thoreau to Devil's Perch, I drew in my breath but said nothing.

The reverend offered to lead us in prayer, but Justice Phyfe said there was no time for that and turned to the undertaker. "Make arrangements to remove the body as soon as possible, Mr. Jackson, before anyone else from town comes upon it."

"And who will pay for my services?" Jackson wanted to know.

"Oh, what the hell, I will," Phyfe said. "But I'll be damned if I am going to pay for a funeral service as well."

"You are already damned, sir," the Rev. Mr. Upson said, "if you can speak so profanely in the company of a clergyman."

Shrugging, Justice Phyfe looked away without begging his pardon, and Mr. Upson stalked off. It occurred to me that Phyfe would not have risked being so dismissive toward the reverend were he still minister of the Congregational Church. Upson used to hold great sway in town, but times change, even in Plumford. After ten years of hearing Upson preach sin and damnation, his parishioners grew weary of his rigid Calvinist doctrine, and he was voted out of the pulpit, replaced by a Unitarian minister with a more tolerant view of humanity.

The Coroner's Jury having no further use for me, I hurried back up the cliff to find Julia. She was waiting by the gig, eager to hear about the inquest. I told her as little as I could and made it clear that such sordid business was no business of hers. We talked but little on the drive home.

I wonder if I spoke to her too harshly. In truth, I do not know how to communicate with Julia anymore. We have done so little of it over the years. After her father hauled her off to Europe we were forbidden to write to each other, and when we were old enough to post letters on our own, we both wrote in such a stilted, formal style that we left off our endeavor to recapture our childhood intimacy entirely. It appeared that we had simply outgrown each other.

Even so, when I saw Julia alight from the train at the Concord station ten days ago, I was drawn to her as though she were a lodestone. And she seemed just as drawn to me. She had not seen me since I was a boy, yet she headed straight to me without the slightest hesitation and took hold of both my hands. We would have known each other anywhere, no matter how long apart.

"Hello, Lewis," she said.

"Hello, Clark," I replied with a laugh. It delighted me that we had just used the secret names we'd called each other as children.

Julia remained as grave as she'd been as a girl whenever

we'd made plans to follow in the footsteps of our heroes Lewis and Clark. "I have often recalled our grand adventure over the years," she said. "Sometimes I think it was but a dream."

"Oh, it was real enough," I said. "And to think we almost made it to California."

Now she laughed too. "Give or take several thousand miles. I see you have grown up very tall, cousin."

"And you have grown up very beautiful," I told her, for it was nothing but the truth. We stood there and took each other in until the stage driver hollered over to us to get aboard or get left behind.

And now Molly has just hollered up the stairs that dinner is ready. Hope she has prepared a dish more palatable than yesterday's mutton hash. Such hope has no basis, of course. Molly is a most inept cook. No matter. She has a kind heart, and that is the best trait a hired girl—or anyone—can have. Besides, should I crave a good meal I need only ride over to Tuttle Farm and have Gran serve me up a heaping plate of her tasty victuals. But then I would not have the pleasure of Julia's company at table. Thus I shall dine on mutton hash or worse without complaint this noon.

JULIA'S NOTEBOOK

Monday, 3 August

What a remarkable morning I have had. It commenced in quite an ordinary manner, however, with a visit to Grandfather's chamber. Finding him awake, I changed the dressing on his leg. His wound is healing well. Brought him up breakfast on a tray, and he consumed the yolk of a coddled egg and two pieces of milk toast. His appetite is also improving. Offered to read some Poe to him, but he ordered me to take the morning air instead. After asking Molly to keep an eye on our dear invalid, I went across the road to the Green, where I settled myself upon a bench and opened my sketchbook.

Then lo! Grandfather's old gig came to a stop in front of the house, but Adam was not driving it. A man I had never seen before was holding Napoleon's reins. Fearing Adam had met with an accident, I sprang up from the bench and ran to the carriage.

"Calm yourself, Miss Bell. Your cousin has come to no harm," the stranger told me. He jumped off the gig with the sprightliness of a grasshopper and landed directly before me. Our eyes easily met, for he was close to my own height, and his steady gaze calmed me more than his words. "Dr. Walker has sent me to Plumford to fetch the constable. Might you direct me to him?"

I automatically pointed down the road toward Mr. Beers's shoe shop. "Pray why is my cousin in need of a constable?" I demanded. "And how do you know who I am? I am sure I have never met you before." I would not have forgotten such striking features, especially his inordinately large eyes and nose.

"No, we have never been introduced," he replied, ignoring my first question and removing his straw hat. His thatch of light brown hair could have used a good trim and combing. "My name is Henry David Thoreau, and I met up with Dr. Walker this morning by the Assabet River. He informed me that his cousin Julia Bell was an artist." He gestured toward the sketchbook I was clutching to my bosom. "I deduced from the way you hastened to the doctor's gig with such concern upon your countenance that you were she." His intonations had a lofty, educated ring, at odds with his countrified appearance. "Dr. Walker also told me you were in possession of a supply of plaster of Paris you might put at my disposal."

That Adam would suggest such a thing rather astounded me. "For what purpose?"

"One that need not concern you, Miss Bell."

"On the contrary, anything to do with my cousin concerns me, Mr. Thoreau. And if you want me to give you the plaster, you must tell me why he wants Constable Beers."

"The reason may distress you."

"You are distressing me far more by keeping me ignorant!"

"Yes, I believe that I am." He gave me an appraising look, his orbs like luminous convex lenses. "You seem a stable enough sort," he concluded. "Therefore I will be frank with you. Dr. Walker and I discovered the corpse of a young black man at the foot of a local cliff he referred to as Devil's Perch, and I have come to fetch the constable."

"But why the plaster of Paris?"

"To make casts of footprints we observed on the top of the cliff. We believe they were left by the murderer."

"The *murderer?*" I took a step back. My foot landed in a rut in the road, and I stumbled.

"Hold on if you feel faint," Mr. Thoreau said, extending his arm toward me.

Ignoring his offer, I regained my balance and gave him a level look. "I am not in the habit of fainting, I assure you. Tell me more about this murderer."

"I have already told you more than your cousin would care to have you know. Now I must go inform the constable. Might I pick up the plaster of Paris upon my return?"

"Have you ever made casts before, Mr. Thoreau?"

"No, and I would much appreciate instructions from you before I depart."

"Better yet, I will accompany you to Devil's Perch and make them myself," I said. "I am proficient at it."

"I have no doubt you are. But this is no job for a young lady. Just ready the supplies for me if you please." After issuing this curt directive, he turned and walked off in the direction of Constable Beers's shop.

A short time later he came back to the gig and did not look too surprised to see me waiting in it, reins in hand. Neither did he look too happy about it. "I would prefer that you did not come with me, Miss Bell," he said.

"And if I preferred that you did not come with *me*, Mr. Thoreau," I countered, "I could have driven myself to Devil's Perch without you."

"So you could have," he allowed. "I suppose there's no need to waste time discussing it further."

With that, he climbed into the gig so quickly I barely had time to make room for him on the seat. I handed over the reins to him, for in truth I was not sure how to get to Devil's Perch, much less how to drive a carriage. "Huddup!" he told Napoleon, and off we went. A short time later, after taking a meandering country road and then a narrow cart path that wound round and up a steep hill, we arrived at the top of the cliff. Adam was nowhere to be seen.

"Where is my cousin?" I demanded.

"He is with the body below," Mr. Thoreau said. "It would be best if you did not venture to look down there."

Ignoring his advice, I alighted from the gig and went as close to the edge of the precipice as I dared to. Looking down from such a great height made my head all swimmy, but I quashed my qualms as my eyes searched for Adam. When I spotted him I felt the urge to cry out to him, but it did not seem fitting to break the almost palpable quietude. Sunlight lay over the scene below like a glaze of varnish, making the river shimmer and Adam's bared head of auburn hair glow. He was kneeling before the corpse, his broad back blocking my view of it, except for the legs. The sight of the dead man's boots, shiny as seal skin, made me exceedingly sad.

I wondered if Adam was praying over the body. I still do. How odd that I do not know what beliefs my cousin holds concerning God and the Afterlife. As close as we were as children, now we are almost strangers. Even so, I feel as though I know Adam to his marrow and always will. He is, after all, my nearest and dearest kin, and nothing can ever change that.

I left the bluff, and Mr. Thoreau and I unloaded the supplies I had brought: a large bag of gypsum powder, a jug of water, a bowl and mixing spoon, and a small shovel. I then commenced mixing the plaster, stirring the gypsum with water until the composition became as thick as cream, with nary a lump in it.

"I wager you make excellent pancake batter," Mr. Thoreau said.

Had the circumstances been less somber, I would have laughed. "I have no culinary skills whatsoever," I admitted, carefully pouring the mixture into four footprints. "It will take a while for the plaster to harden."

As we waited I attempted to engage Mr. Thoreau in polite conversation. "Where do you reside?" I asked him.

"By a pond," he said.

"You are being very mysterious, Mr. Thoreau."

"I do not mean to be."

"Then pray tell me the name of this pond of yours."

"Walden Pond is not mine, Miss Bell. I do not even own any land surrounding it. I built my cabin on a friend's wood-lot."

"I have never heard of Walden Pond," I said. "Where is it located?"

"In the township of Concord, only a few miles from the railway depot."

"Ah, that I am familiar with. I debarked at the Concord depot less than a fortnight ago," I said. Mr. Thoreau did not ask me what brought me to the area, but I told him anyway. "When I received a letter from my cousin Adam informing me that our grandfather had been seriously injured, I immediately set forth from New York City to help nurse him. Have you ever been to New York, Mr. Thoreau?"

"Yes, a few years ago," he said. "I did not think much of it."

"Most people find it a most impressive metropolis. But I am inclined to agree with you. Too much bustle, too little charm. I prefer Paris. Do you know it?"

He shook his head. "I have never traveled abroad."

Since he did not appear to be more than thirty I ventured to say, in perhaps a slightly condescending tone, "Well, you have time enough ahead of you to do so."

"But not inclination enough," he said. "For me, it would be

a wretched bargain to accept the proudest Paris in exchange for my native village. As much as I might gain from going abroad, I would lose far more from being away. The sight of a marsh hawk in Concord meadows, for example."

Despite his serious expression, I discerned a twinkle in his eye and surmised he was amusing himself by pretending to be more provincial than he actually was. "Whether you are jesting with me or not, Mr. Thoreau, I am disposed to agree with you," I replied. "I am sure I would have been content to stay in Plumford for the rest of my life if my father had not seen fit to take me away when I was eleven. I have traveled the Continent over the last ten years, on account of Papa being a portrait painter who must go to his subjects, but I have always longed to return to America. So I parted ways with him and removed to New York. I teach art there."

"I too have been a teacher," Thoreau said, but he did not elucidate.

Weary of asking him questions, I fell silent, much to his relief I am sure. He looked up to the heavens to follow the flight of an oriole, and I too became captivated by the gorgeous winged creature as it glided past us. Suddenly a gun bellowed, and the bird plunged from the sky, followed by a puff of bright orange and black feathers. I cried out in dismay, and Mr. Thoreau sadly shook his head.

Shortly, a hunter came up the path, clutching the dead bird in one hand. In the other he held a fowling piece. From his smooth stride, superior height, and tall beaver hat, I recognized him to be the Rev. Mr. Upson. He recognized me in return and hurried forth.

"I hardly expected to meet up with you here, Miss Bell," he said, looking from me to the man at my side. His scowl made it clear that he disapproved of finding us alone in such a secluded spot.

I, in turn, looked disapprovingly at the dead bird Mr. Upson held by its feet. He opened the leather sack hanging from his shoulder, and I saw that it was *stuffed* with feathery carcasses and furry pelts. I gasped.

"The necessary means to a noble end," he told me, adding the oriole to his grisly collection. "I need feathers and fur to make my fishing flies."

"You call it noble to slay creatures out of the water to better kill those in it?" Thoreau asked him. They glowered at each other.

I quickly made introductions and gave the reverend a succinct summation of what had brought us to Devil's Perch. We then went to the summit's rim and saw that Adam had been joined by Constable Beers and members of the Coroner's Jury.

"I must go testify," Thoreau said and nimbly clambered down the steep path to join the men below, leaving me alone with Mr. Upson.

Staring down at the group of men who had collected around the body, he heaved a great sigh. I wondered if he was recalling the day townsmen had formed such a jury to view his beloved wife's remains. I could not ask him, of course, since he has never spoken of her tragic demise to me during our conversations since my arrival in Plumford. Indeed, I would not even know of Mrs. Upson's death at the hands of a wretched tramp last summer if Molly had not told me. I glanced up at Mr. Upson's quite distinguished profile and thought I discerned a tear dampening the outer edge of his eye. My heart went out to him, and I touched the sleeve of his black broadcloth coat to comfort him. He covered my hand with his own and pressed it so hard against his arm that I could feel the heat and muscle of his flesh through the woolen cloth.

I tugged my hand free from under his and said, "Perhaps your services as a minister could be of use below."

He looked at me in disbelief. "Are you suggesting I pray over the body of a Negro?"

"Is it not your duty as a clergyman to pray for all souls?"

"Prayer will not help those who have not been chosen," he said gravely.

"I am sure God bestows his love on us equally, Mr. Upson."

"Indeed God does *not*," he replied. But after regarding me most severely for a moment, he offered me a thin smile. "Very well. I will do as you suggest, Miss Bell. My presence will give comfort to the living if not the dead."

He went down the same path Thoreau had taken, and I remained where I was. Should I have been so bold as to join the men below, I would have been asked, politely but very firmly, to leave for the same reason I am not allowed to serve on juries. The Female Sex is far too delicate for such profane proceedings, and men are duty born to protect women from the sordid side of life. I would have accomplished nothing by challenging such humbug. Moreover, I had my own job to do right where I was.

When the casts had set, I took up my shovel, dug them out of the ground, and conveyed them to the back of the gig. My tight bodice hindered my movements, and I rent a seam in the process, but I did not care. That my efforts might help catch a murderer was far more important than a mere tear in my garment.

After the Coroner's Jury had disbanded, Adam came up the cliff trail alone. He told me Mr. Thoreau had tramped off to Concord in disgust because the jury's verdict was Death by Accident and further inquiry was deemed unnecessary.

"Then we must be the ones to probe further," I said.

Adam gave me a look more stern than I have ever seen on his visage. His expression is usually most pleasing, but I did not much care for the stubborn set of his mouth at that moment. I am more accustomed to a smile hovering at the edges of his lips when he turns his attention upon me.

"You must have nothing more to do with this nasty business, Julia," he said. "I am very sorry you came here with Thoreau. You should have stayed at home."

Well! Since when does my cousin tell me how to properly conduct myself? As children we dealt with each other as equals, but it seems the equation has changed. Have I become a lesser person in his eyes since becoming a full-grown woman?

"Come now, Lewis, don't speak to your doughty mate Clark like that," I said, attempting to cajole him. "Have you forgotten how I held my own when we fought wild dogs and bully boys?"

His expression remained stony. "This is not a game, Julia."

"Nor was that! Leastways not for me. I truly believed we would cross the continent together."

"As did I," he said gruffly. "But I was only a boy and did not know the ways of the world yet. Or the proper place of women in it."

"And what is their proper place, pray tell?"

"Home!" he near shouted back at me.

I did not argue with him further. Instead, I left him to his glowering ruminations all the way back to town. When he stopped before the front gate to let me out I cautioned him to be careful unloading the casts.

"The plaster has not yet cured," I told him. "When it does I will clean off the casts with a wire brush."

"I can do that," he said.

"But I started the process, and I would like to see it through to completion."

"You have already seen too much, Julia."

"If you are referring to the body, I barely glimpsed it. Mr. Thoreau told me that the poor soul was a young man of color. What was he doing in Plumford, I wonder?"

"That is what I intend to find out," Adam said, still regarding me most austerely. "Without any help from you, I should add."

No, he should not have added that. It only made me more determined to stay involved in the investigation.

ADAM'S JOURNAL

Monday, August 3rd

It is near midnight, and the only sound I hear is the scratch of my pen nib. I am tired but sleepless as I puff on my father's meerschaum pipe. Julia found it on a high shelf in the study a few days ago, amidst a dusty collection of ivory and scrimshaw carvings. The bowl is burnished gold from use, so it must have been one of his favorites, left here in safekeeping when he went to sea for the last time. Sadly, I lost him too young to have any memory of him, but as I regard the visage of Neptune carved into the bowl and the light teeth indentations in the curving amber stem, I conjure up my own image of him. And as I watch the wafting tendrils of smoke rise and curl away, I imagine they connect me in this world to him in the next.

A sense of disquietude has followed me all afternoon, but I took care to hide it from the patients I attended. As soon as my doctoring duties were done, I headed for Tuttle Farm, hoping to calm my thoughts and lift my spirits with a visit to Gran and then some mild sport. Soon as I stepped into Gran's kitchen, she remarked that I looked peckish and insisted on frying me up a batch of doughnuts. Ate six of them and, thus fortified, gathered my bow and a sheaf of arrows and walked out into the field in back of the barn. Archery proved to be the right prescription for me. As usual, aiming, drawing, holding, and loosing my arrows, then watching their arched, hissing flight into the coiled grass target made me more tranquil.

As I was shooting, I was once again taken unawares by Henry Thoreau. How he just appears as if risen from the grass or dropped down from the tree boughs, I know not. He told me he had first stopped at Grandfather's house and been directed by Julia to the farm.

"I am delighted to see you practice an aboriginal art," he said. As he hefted and examined my bow, he described at some length his extensive collection of Indian arrowheads as well as tomahawk and war club heads.

"How did you come by so many relics from the past?" I asked him.

"Why, I found them."

"But where?"

"Indian artifacts are everywhere hereabouts," Henry said. He glanced around. "Right here would be a good place to look for them. It's a perfect site for an Indian camp or village. Level ground. A river nearby that used to be filled with so many salmon they could be caught by hand before white settlers fished it out. And that ancient stand of oaks just yonder would have yielded acorns to attract the deer that thrived here before the white man killed them all off with his musket."

He kicked about for a moment or two, then stooped and picked up something. He showed it to me, a black granite arrowhead resting on the calloused bed of his palm.

"You amaze me, Mr. Thoreau," I said.

"As I have many a friend on many a walk," he replied with a smile. "It is as if I am a magnet drawing the buried remnants of Indian civilization out of the ground. I do not find it so amazing myself, however. I simply *look*. And the observant eye sees what easily passes unnoticed by most."

He inquired about my yew bow, and when I told him it was of English manufacture, he went into a rather lengthy discourse lauding the power and efficiency of an Indian bow over a modern one. He cited one of elm he had seen in a Harvard collection that he had no doubt would outmatch mine in power and accuracy. But despite his disparaging remarks concerning my English bow, he seemed eager enough to give it a try. We paced off a fair distance from the barn, and I shot several arrows so he could grasp the rudiments of proper form. I then showed him how to hold the arrow on the string by using three fingers.

"But I observed that you use only two," he said. Apparently nothing escapes his notice.

Explained that was a personal preference or quirk I could not account for. I had read that English longbowmen used that grip during the Middle Ages, but it had long fallen into disfavor.

"Perhaps in a past life you went on a crusade as a yeoman archer," he said.

"As no doubt you were once an Indian brave," I replied. We both laughed.

Proceeded to instruct him how to draw, hold, and loose properly. A longbow such as mine requires fifty pounds of effort to hold at full draw, yet he drew it easily. His first arrows flew wildly, but after only a moment's instruction he shot with amazing facility, exhibiting excellent coordination and wiry strength of arm and back. After we shot a dozen arrows each, we seated ourselves upon the stone wall surrounding the farmyard and became better acquainted.

He told me he had attended Harvard, and we established that he had studied there five years earlier than I had. He did not seem to think much of the institution. He claimed that he had as many trades as he had fingers, along with being a transcendentalist and a natural scientist, and that he was presently writing a book in the seclusion of a cabin by a pond. Quite an impressive fellow, this Thoreau, if indeed he is all he says he is.

He asked me where I practiced medicine, and I told him I had been assisting Dr. Holcomb Quincy in Boston for the two years since I had graduated from Medical College.

"But I have taken over my grandfather's practice here in Plumford temporarily, until he recovers from his accident," I went on to say. "He was badly injured a few weeks ago playing town ball on the Green."

Thoreau looked surprised. "Is the play that rough?"

"For the most part, no. But Grandfather was running backwards trying to catch a fly ball and collided right into the town pump. Broke his leg on the base and knocked himself out on the handle."

"I cannot understand why grown men waste their time and strength of mind and body in sport," Thoreau said.

It was my turn to look surprised. "For the joy of it of course!"

"A simple walk in nature can bring joy," he said. "But games of sport can bring out the worst in man's own nature."

"And the best," I said.

"I will gladly argue the point some other time," he offered. "Right now we have more important matters to discuss, however. I am outraged at the decision reached by the Coroner's Jury this morning, and I presume you are too, Dr. Walker."

I assured him that he was correct. "It has disturbed me all day, and I have been attempting to fathom the reasoning behind their judgment."

"Reasoning? There was none! Ratiocination is beyond such fools."

"I have known most of those men all my life, Thoreau, and they are not fools."

"Then how could they have reached the idiotic conclusion that the death was accidental? Did we not present evidence of foul play that was well-nigh unassailable?"

"I agree we stated the case with logic enough to call for a murder investigation," I said. "But such an investigation could arouse fears that a murderer might be loose in the area."

"One *is* loose!" Thoreau said.

"And I do not think Elijah Phyfe wants that made public."

"Do you refer to the pompous fellow in the silk hat and purple cravat?"

I nodded. "Not only is he Plumford's Justice of the Peace. He is also the town's wealthiest citizen. He holds the mortgages on many farms hereabouts, and more than a few town merchants are also in his debt."

"No wonder he held such sway over the men in the jury," Thoreau said. "Still, I fail to understand why he wanted them to ignore our evidence."

"Perhaps you will understand better when I tell you that Justice Phyfe is presently in the thick of persuading several new mills to locate in Plumford," I said. "He is touting our town as a peaceable, conducive environment for trade."

"So that's it," Thoreau said grimly. "Far better to disregard the death of a mere Negro than risk tarnishing Plumford's reputation with a murder investigation. I opine that many of the men on the jury would also benefit from new industry coming to town. Pecuniary interests influenced their verdict."

"This is speculation on our part," I cautioned. "We cannot know for certain what was in the hearts of those men when they considered the evidence."

"I know for certain that self-interest most often supersedes justice," he replied. "Your jury of respectable Plumford citizens acted no better than a pack of slave owners."

I thought that too severe a recrimination, yet it brought us to the sad truth of the matter. Even in Massachusetts, where the abolitionist movement is deemed the strongest in the nation, the death of a black man does not matter as much as would the death of a white man.

"Rather than self-interest, it could have been simple practicality that influenced the jury," I said. "They could have decided that a murder inquiry would lead nowhere. The dead man is unknown, with no identification upon his person, and our constable is a simple shoemaker who lacks both the detection skills and the time to pursue an investigation."

"Thus incompetence and inconvenience were the measures used to determine the verdict." Thoreau heaved a mighty sigh. "Whatever the jury's motivation, it is now left up to us to find the murderer, Adam."

"But whence do we go from here? We do not even know if his victim was a runaway slave or a freeman."

"I am an operative in the underground railway," Thoreau freely admitted to me, "and on my return to Concord this morning I confirmed that no young man of his description has been harbored locally in our houses or hideaways. But I shall investigate further. Someone might have seen our Negro depart from the cars at the Concord train depot."

"And I shall inquire in Plumford," I said. "If we could ascertain what he was doing in this vicinity, that might lead to finding out who murdered him."

We shook hands. Our common determination and shared sense of justice had forged a friendship between us, and we agreed to be henceforth on a first-name basis.

Before we parted, I asked Henry what had brought him to the banks of the Assabet River this morning. He replied he had been in pursuit of a rare climbing fern he had heard grew in the area. He had searched without result for the plant and found the body instead.

"And now you have made your second long hike to Plumford today," I said.

"Not so long. Less than three miles when I cut through fields, which is my preference," he replied. "I am in the habit of walking many hours, day or night, to observe nature and cogitate. I do some of my best writing in my head as I roam. Methinks that the moment my legs begin to move, my thoughts begin to flow."

He politely refused my invitation to sample my grandmother's doughnuts and gave me the arrowhead he had found before going on his way. When I returned to the house, one of Gran's farmhands was waiting for me on the back stoop, the side of his face swelled up and his eyes filled with pain. I took a look inside his fetid mouth and went directly to the gig for my medical bag. When the poor man saw me extract a turnkey, he paled, as it is a dreadful instrument indeed. I assured him he would be feeling better in a jiffy, had him lie on his back, and called for Gran. She came out from the kitchen and cradled his head in her strong, gentle hands as I placed my knee firmly against his chest to keep him down. Told him to open wide, and with one great yank I pulled out a dangerously infected molar tooth. Must say I was so quick about it he barely had time to howl. He felt relief immediately, and for what pain remained I gave him a paper of willow bark powder to mix with water. Gran nodded approval. I was happy she was there to witness that, despite all my fancy learnin', as she calls it, I still use many of the herbal remedies she taught me as a child.

It was nearing sundown when I returned to town. The moment I stepped inside Grandfather Walker's house, I carefully whiffed the air, and kept sniffing all the way up the stairs and into his chamber.

"Any stink?" he asked from his bed in lieu of a greeting.

We both know that the odor of putridity would be a sign that mortal infection had taken hold in his leg wound and the advance of gangrene begun.

"Not the slightest trace," I assured him.

"Good," he said, "as I would not like to give offence to my granddaughter."

He directed his gaze, as I did mine, toward Julia, who was sitting by the window, an open book on her lap. The golden light of the setting sun poured through the panes, making her lovely face and hair glow. And when she looked at me, that very same light seemed to emanate from her golden eyes, as though she were beaming solar rays at me.

"Don't you wish to examine my leg, Adam?" Grandfather said.

How long my attention had strayed from him I know not, but I brought it back and began cutting away the bandages. Grandfather sat up and studied his broken limb with the cool interest of a physician rather than the apprehension of its owner.

"Well, it's healing well enough," he allowed, gingerly touching the crimson scar that extended half the distance between foot and knee. "You did a fine job of mending the tear. I'll give you that much, Adam."

"How fortunate Adam was visiting you the day you broke your leg, Grand-dear," Julia said.

He snorted. "Had Adam not suggested I join him in a game of town ball, I would not have broken my leg in the first place."

"And you will never let me forget it." I smiled at the crusty old man. "I did not expect you to play with such risk to life and limb."

"And I did not expect you to risk my life to *save* my limb, Adam," he retorted. "An open fracture, as you well know, offers a gateway for noxious matter to enter the body. Most physicians, myself included, would have amputated a leg that had a snapped bone piercing through the flesh."

I had been expecting this criticism from him. Until now he had been too weak to make it, and I was pleased that his assertive spirit had returned. But I also felt it necessary to defend myself, especially in front of Julia.

"Of course I considered that danger, Grandfather. But the bone break was not fragmented, and there was a minimum of tissue damage. And dash it all! I could not have you go legless if I could help it. So whilst you were still unconscious, I aligned the two halves of the fibula at the point of breakage and sewed up the wound with cat gut."

"Darn good thing I was insensible to the pain," he grumbled. "So tell me, young doctor. What is your prognosis? When will I be up and about?"

"As soon as a proper knit takes place between the bone ends. And for that to happen, we must keep your leg immobile for a while longer."

He groaned with impatience rather than pain as I replaced lengths of wood to each side of his leg and bound them. Julia brought his pale, bony hand to her lips and kissed it. I could not help but imagine the soft warmth of her mouth against my own flesh.

"Do not fret, Grand-dear," she told him. "You shall be walking about soon enough. And until then I shall stay by your side."

Comforted by her promise, he lay his white head down upon the pillows and closed his eyes. She pulled a light blanket over him, and we both quietly exited the chamber and went downstairs. Molly had gone for the day, and Julia offered to make me supper. I told her I had consumed a hefty portion of Gran's fricasseed chicken before leaving the farm, and she looked relieved. The preparation and consumption of food seem to be of little interest to her. Perhaps she receives her sustenance from her art.

I suggested a stroll in the garden or a walk around the Green, but she declined. Thinking she was perhaps fatigued, I suggested retiring to the parlor where I might entertain her by strumming my guitar. Feeble as my musical talent is, it has entertained her well enough on previous evenings. But again she declined. Stating she had work to do, off she went to the study, leaving me to wonder if she was irked with me. It had not escaped my attention that she had been so this morning. But was she *still?* Decided to find out.

She looked surprised when I entered the study for I have stayed well out of it since she took over the room as a makeshift studio. An unfinished portrait of our grandfather rested upon an easel she had set up by the window. The liveliness of it astonished me.

"I have depicted him as he will look once he recovers," Julia said and gave me an expectant look. "He *will* recover fully, will he not?"

"He is mending as well as can be expected for a man of seventy," I hedged.

"Oh, dear," Julia said, wrapping a long pinafore around her slender frame. "That does not sound an overly optimistic prognosis."

"Oh, I am optimistic," I said to assure her.

"Then why are you twisting your fingers in your palm like that?"

I immediately let go grasping the first two fingers of my right hand, recalling how Julia used to tease me about this telltale sign of apprehension when we were children. She knows me too well. "He will regain his ability to walk," I said. "But he will never regain the youthful vigor you have given him in your portrait, Julia. In truth, I believe Grandfather will need assistance should he continue his medical practice. You might consider staying here in Plumford with him for good."

"For good?" She did not seem too pleased by my suggestion as she turned to the writing desk she had covered with canvas. It was littered with tubes and bladders of oil paints, and vials of turpentine and linseed oil, along with an assortment of brushes. After carefully selecting a brush, she looked back to me. "You might consider staying here for good yourself, Adam. You would be of more assistance to our grandfather than I could ever be."

"But I have my own work to do."

"And I do not?" She slapped the brush lightly against her palm. "I suppose you do not consider me a serious artist because of my sex."

"I am highly respectful of your sex," I replied rather stiffly.

"Even though you think it inferior to yours?"

"You have no reason to believe I do, Julia."

"That you spoke to me as one would speak to a child this morning seems reason enough."

"I knew it," I said.

"Knew what, pray?"

"That you were harboring some resentment toward me. But you should not hold it against me for trying to protect you, Julia. Indeed, that is rather childish, as I am only looking out for you."

My words, unfortunately, did not appease her. Instead, they seemed to perturb her even more. Color rose to her cheeks, and anger flickered in her eyes.

"How fortunate for me that we are reunited, Adam. How did I possibly manage to look out for my own witless self all these years we were apart?"

Do not find sarcasm an attractive trait in women. What man does? Still, I would have been most willing to continue our discussion had she seemed so inclined. But she turned her back to me again and busied herself squeezing paints onto a wooden palette. I left her to her work, and for aught I know she is still at it.

Just heard the tread of her footsteps on the creaking stairs, then the squeak of her chamber door opening and closing. She has finally gone to bed, so I too shall retire, knowing she is safely tucked in. And as I do every night before I fall asleep, I shall imagine how the moonlight shines through the lace canopy above her bed, casting light and shadow upon her face and neck.

JULIA'S NOTEBOOK

Wednesday, 5 August

Early this morning we buried the young Negro. Town officials would not permit him to be interred in the Plumford cemetery, so Adam asked his grandmother to give him a place in the Tuttle burying ground on the farm.

That Elizabeth Tuttle would allow a stranger, and a black one at that, to be buried alongside her kin might be surprising to some, but not to me. During the three years I'd resided in Plumford as a child, I'd never seen her deny Adam anything. I'd thought him a most fortunate boy to have such a doting grandmother and took to thinking of Mrs. Tuttle as my granny, too. Not that I would have presumed to address her as such, for we were not related. Nor had she ever shown the slightest fondness for me. Even so, in my heart she remains Granny Tuttle to this day. I suppose I still feel a strong connection to her because we both care so much for Adam.

Adam, Henry Thoreau, Granny Tuttle, her ward Harriet, and I were the only graveside mourners. How sad to think that the deceased youth's friends and loved ones do not even know what happened to him. After the simple wooden coffin was lowered in the ground, Granny read out some Bible verses, and Thoreau played a poignant tune on his flute.

Adam and I stayed behind whilst the others went back to the farmhouse. We have been cool toward each other since Monday evening, but our warm feelings returned as we stood before his mother's grave and held hands, just as we used to as children. I felt the connection between us once again, as strong as the links in a chain, yet as subtle as a current in the air. The marble marker we gazed upon, carved with an angel's head and wings, was as white and shiny as I remembered it, thanks no doubt to Granny's diligent scouring. I had memorized the inscription as a girl: "Sacred to the memory of Sarah, daughter of Elizabeth and Eli Tuttle and wife of Owen Walker. She was born November 18, 1799, and departed this life June 11, 1829." Seventeen years ago. Adam had been but seven. Two years later, when I removed to Plumford from Boston, we became fast friends, and he would often take me here to admire the marker.

"I have always imagined your mother to look exactly like that beautiful angel," I told him.

"She might well have," he replied. "I remember her voice and laugh and even her touch, but her features have sadly faded from my memory."

"What a pity you have no likeness of her as I do of my own dear mother."

"My father had one, I am told. A portrait miniature painted on ivory. He always carried it on his person. Therefore it was lost with him at sea."

I imagine Owen Walker pressing Sarah's image to his heart as his ship went down in the whaling grounds of the Pacific Ocean. His last thoughts must have been of her and his baby boy.

"Sadly, I have no likeness of my father, either," Adam said.

"Ah, but you do. All you need do is gaze in a looking glass

to see his features. Does not Grandfather Walker claim you are the spitting image of his beloved son?"

Adam smiled at my attempt at a small jest. "I may look like my father, but I have always felt myself more a Tuttle than a Walker."

"Do not let Grandfather hear you say that. He is so proud you followed in his footsteps."

"In truth, I do not intend to follow him but to go my own way," Adam said. "Dr. Silas Walker is of the old school. He still believes in ancient medical theories concerning the body's humors. If purging doesn't do the trick, he is ever ready to use his lancet and his leeches."

"Oh, those horrid leeches! The memory of them makes me shiver," I said. "When I was out of sorts as a child, he would fish them out of the big Staffordshire jar in his office and apply them to my limbs."

"Gran would give me a dose of some bitter herb concoction to cure my ills, and 'twas then I missed my mother most," Adam said. "Ma always dosed me with honey from her prized hives."

It must comfort Adam that when his mother fell off a high tree branch whilst trying to capture a swarm of wild honeybees, she died instantly. When I think of my own dear mother's drawn-out, painful death from Consumption, my only comfort is the frail but persistent hope that a spirit as fine as hers must continue forth in some other blessed form.

Adam and I soon left the little burial ground on the shady knoll and joined the others in Granny Tuttle's kitchen. As she served up gingerbread and chamomile tea, she asked Mr. Thoreau why he had chosen to get himself carted off to jail last month.

"I warrant you weren't fetched up to be a jailbird," she said.

"As the bill, so goes the song; as the bird, such the nest," he replied.

Granny narrowed her eyes at him. "What sort of flummydiddle talk is that? I should think your Aunt Maria was mortified."

"You know my aunt, Mrs. Tuttle?"

"As a girl I was pretty budge with her. And I know all the Thoreaus to be a fine, honest race. 'Tis no wonder then that I was flabbergasted when I heard one of 'em got hisself arrested."

"I preferred that to paying my poll tax," he said.

"Look-a-here, son. 'Tis every freeborn man's duty to pay his taxes. How else can this Great Democracy function?"

"Now, Gran, don't get all brustled up about it," Adam said, falling into her way of speaking as he rocked in the splint-bottomed chair his Grandfather Tuttle had made. "Henry surely had good reasons for refusing to pay the tax."

Granny gave one of her sniffs. "I can think of nary a one."

"Allow me to give you mine, ma'am," Thoreau said, courteous as can be. "I was protesting the Mexican War. I will not pay a penny to support an immoral war designed to spread slavery."

"I don't countenance slavery," she muttered and changed the subject. "Anyways, I hear tell you are now residing in a shanty by some piddling pond, young man."

"Call it a shanty if you like, Mrs. Tuttle, but I live in a good plastered and shingled house entirely of my own building."

"Well, I should think you would feel mighty lonesome in it."

"No more lonely than a loon, ma'am. Nature keeps me company. It is the perennial source of life, is it not?"

"What are you, a hermit?" Granny countered.

"I think that I love society as much as most," Henry replied, but his smile was most ironic.

"So what do you do all day?" Granny persisted. "Anything *useful?*"

"I support myself well enough by the labor of my hands."

"I wager yer family made sacrifices to get you a fine Hahvahd education, young man. What good is it doin' you?"

"I still have the leisure for literary pursuits and the study of nature," he answered. "If a man must have money—and he needs but the smallest amount—the true and independent way to earn it is by day labor. There is no good reason an educated man cannot work with his hands, Mrs. Tuttle."

Adam laughed. "Oh, I am certain Gran agrees with you on that score, Henry. Despite my own fine education, she asked me just yesterday to lend a hand with the apple harvest next month, and I would very much like to oblige her."

I was sitting in the high-back settle by the great fieldstone fireplace, sketching, and my ears pricked up like an attentive dog's. Does Adam plan to stay in Plumford after our grandfather has mended after all? Not that such a decision on his part would change my own plans. Then again, what worthwhile plans do I have? Unless I go along with the terms stated in the letter I received yesterday and commence work within the week, I shall lose the portrait commission I had been promised before departing from New York. But how can I leave Plumford before Grandfather is well enough to do without me? I am afraid I shall have to forego the commission.

Henry got up from the bleached oak table, most likely to avoid further questions from Granny, and strolled over to the fireplace to get a closer look at the old flintlock musket adorning the massive lintel.

"That was my Great Grandfather Tuttle's trusty weapon in the War for Independence," Adam informed him.

"Does it still fire?"

"It does indeed," Granny stated most emphatically. "I recently used it to shoot at a fox sniffin' around the hen house. Just missed the critter, I regret to say."

"Well, I did not regret it," pretty little Harriet said softly as she poured Adam another cup of tea. (She is always right there to serve him when he is in need of sustenance, I have noted.) "I would be greatly upset to see a wild creature killed."

"Then be forewarned to stay away from the Reverend Mr. Upson," Henry said. "I am sure Miss Bell shall do her best to avoid him after peering into his sack of horrors Monday."

I went on drawing in silence, for I saw no reason to tell Mr. Thoreau that I allow Mr. Upson to call on me whenever he begs leave to. How can I be so uncharitable as to refuse a lonely widower such as he?

"What are you scratching away at so industriously?" Thoreau asked me.

"I am *sketching*, not scratching away like some chicken."

He left his position by the fireplace to come look over my shoulder. I did not mind, for my sketch was progressing quite well. I had drawn, with perfect perspective, the yawning hearth outfitted with a lug pole, a chain and pulley, and a long crane. A kettle, suspended by a hook from the crane, hung above a small mound of coals. I had managed, with the adroit use of a mere pencil, to make the coals *glow*.

"Ah, a study of your cousin," Henry said.

Admittedly, Adam was also in the drawing, but well off to the side and sketched in lightly, without any of the attention to detail I had given the fieldstones and brick and cooking implements. He just happened to be in the outer edge of my viewing range, thus I had included him.

"It is a study of a passing way of life," I told Henry, perhaps a little primly. "More and more fireplaces are being blocked up and replaced by cooking stoves."

"You might consider such a convenience for yourself,

Gran," Adam said to his grandmother. "I would gladly buy and install a stove for you."

"You do that, dearie, and I will take a sledge to it, by gory!" she retorted. "There will be no iron monster in my kitchen, saturating the food with poisonous fumes."

Adam, not one to argue futilely, went back to sipping his tea. And Henry went back to studying my sketch. "You have talent enough," he concluded.

"*More* than enough," I said, demonstrating my insufferable lack of modesty concerning my talent.

"More than enough talent to do what?" Henry asked me.

"Why, to make my own way in the world. I barely manage to support myself now by giving drawing lessons to silly girls who do not take art seriously. But my goal is to become a well-regarded and gainful portrait painter."

Henry did not seem too impressed by this ambition. He suggested that I apply my talent to botanical drawings rather than portraits of vain people. Nature, he stated, was a greater and more perfect art than any that man—or woman, he hastily added—can produce. I challenged this, of course, claiming art to be the very measure of civilization.

"It is something to be able to paint a particular picture, or to carve a statue," he allowed. "But it is far more glorious to carve and paint the very atmosphere and medium through which we look. And are we not all sculptors and painters? Our material is our own flesh and blood and bones."

"What sort of flummydiddle talk is that?" I asked him, imitating Granny Tuttle.

He smiled. "At any rate, I am glad to see you are making use of one of my pencils, Miss Bell."

I looked down at the Number 4 in my hand. "You are *that* Thoreau? The one who makes the best drawing pencils in New England?"

"In the world, I venture to say." (Like me, he has no false modesty.)

"Pray why are Thoreau pencils so much better?" I asked him.

"Because of improvements I saw fit to make in my father's established process. Such as using clay as a binder for the plumbago, which produces a better lead."

"Indeed it does," I agreed. "Your lead does not smear as others do. Yet it remains exceedingly malleable. And I like that your pencils come in differing gradations of hardness and softness."

"Produced by varying the amount of clay in the mixture," he informed me. "I also invented a grinding machine that collects only the finest particles of the ground graphite. Therefore, the lead has far less grit. We insert it in a hollowed-out cylinder of wood rather than two halves glued together as our competitors do."

"Well, Mr. Thoreau, I warrant I shall be a lifelong customer of your excellent pencils."

"Allow me to send you a box of them."

"Oh, I am afraid I could not afford an entire box."

"I am offering them to you as a gift, Miss Bell."

Thoreau & Co. pencils are not cheap. In fact, for one such as I, who receives such a meager income, they are very, very dear.

"That is far too generous a gift for me to accept, Mr. Thoreau," I said with regret. "We hardly know each other."

"Then I will renew my offer when we become better acquainted. Unless, of course, you do not wish to know me better, Miss Bell."

Henry Thoreau is such an odd combination of frankness and formality, shyness and boldness, that I confess I am charmed by him. "Of course I wish it," I replied. "And I wish you to call me Julia."

He asked me to call him by his first name too. Thus we are now on easy terms with each other and may be on our way to establishing a true friendship. I would not be so ready to make friends with Henry, however, if Adam did not clearly hold him in high regard. I trust Adam to be a good judge of character. Did he not always know, when we were children, which dogs would bite and which would not?

ADAM'S JOURNAL

Thursday, August 6th

As a physician I heartily subscribe to the notion that men need respite from their daily labors. Vigorous exercise with one's fellows clears the mind, loosens the ligaments, and assists digestion. I vote a game of town ball a fine means to achieve those healthy ends. This evening's game on the Green also showed that little reveals a man's character as clearly as the manner in which he conducts himself at play. I am quite sure Henry would agree with this if nothing else regarding sport.

Espied him striding down the road from Concord and heading toward the Green as we were loosening our limbs to begin our game. He walked with his usual purposeful air, paying little heed to the men on the playing field, as they shouted and ran and tossed and struck balls all around him. It appeared such activity was beneath his notice. When he reached me, he removed his straw hat and wiped his brow with his neck-kerchief, for the evening was close and the sun still shone through the elms.

"I have news," he quietly announced, and drew me away from the other players. "The murdered Negro came from Boston on the cars Sunday last. He sat in the same car as the owner of our gun manufactory and his wife. They remarked that he behaved in a mannerly way, without making eye contact or attempting conversation with them. After stepping down from the car in Concord, he made inquiry with the stationmaster, who gave him directions to Plumford. He spoke to no one else, but he was observed walking over the bridge toward Plumford by the cook at the Middlesex Hotel. He was not seen again till I found him dead."

I was most impressed with his report and had to confess that my own inquiries had resulted in nothing at all. No one I had asked in and around town had seen the man or knew anything of him. "I could go to Boston and inquire at the Causeway Street terminal," I volunteered.

"I am of the opinion such an inquiry would be futile, Adam, or I would have conducted it myself. Hundreds of travelers a day pass through a busy terminal such as that, and it would be like searching for a needle in a haystack to find one who was there four days ago and recalled our Negro. Henceforward we should concentrate our efforts in Plumford and try to discover who he had come to see here."

It was getting on seven, and the men shouted after me to play ball. Henry waved me off, declaring that he would linger awhile and perhaps glean something from the folk milling about.

A goodly number of townspeople had strolled to the Green as it was a fine evening. Families were grouped around the town pump, waiting for play to commence, and patrons of the Sun Tavern had come out to watch with mugs of ale in their fists. They find these weekly games highly entertaining, for the men who play in them, of all ages and sizes and trades, are both enthusiastic and able. However, I have noticed upon my return that the games are much rougher this summer due to the influence of a few coarse players. Indeed, the fierce competition is so contagious the even Grandfather got swept up in it and hence did himself harm.

I allow here that before I removed myself to Boston I was the town's best thrower. I always demur when told so and attribute my results to good fortune, but there is no harm in boasting on these private pages. I have all the required skills, and, in addition, I know all the tricks. A hard and fast rule of town ball is that the thrower must give the striker the chance to hit, the point being to get the ball out into the field so all the players will have opportunity to run, catch, and throw. I try to do a fair job of it and can toss a meaty ball for the striker to take his cut at, but any sensible thrower gives less of a chance to the opposing team's most powerful strikers. No need to let them knock a ball into the high elms and clear the stakes.

There is considerable science in making a tricky throw. One must take care, for if the referee behind the striker determines a fair chance was not given by the thrower, he levies a fine of ten cents to be paid on the spot. To avoid such a penalty, I employ high and low speeds and stealthy forms of spin, confounding a strong striker without the referee knowing quite why it is so hard to make a really good knock at bat against me. Does this make me a practitioner of deception or a proponent of smart play? I believe my mates would call me the latter, for the first side to tally a hundred runs is the side that wins, and it is usually the side I am playing on that reaches the century mark first.

My side of twelve this evening included our blacksmith and butcher, two of the most hale-bodied men in town, but the other side had on its roster several hulking drovers and a former Army sergeant called Rufus Badger, a bellicose lout always ready to participate in any form of mayhem that allowed him to use his fists. Badger is just the sort of man I enjoy confounding. He flailed at my first throw and missed by a rod. My second throw flummoxed him even more, and his lumbering attempt to hit the ball made some bonneted onlookers twitter. He appealed to the referee, who warned me to give the man a meaty ball. So I pitched a ball slow enough for a child to hit. I put a spin on it, however, that broke left as Badger swung, so that his mighty swat only nipped the ball, sending it lamely toward the first stake. He heaved off toward the stake, and I got to the ball. My intention, of course, was to soak the man for an out, but he veered off line to make hitting him difficult. I allow that such a maneuver was within Badger's rights, as a striker has no obligation to run straight between stakes. But he went well beyond the rules of good sportsmanship when he leaped over a seated mother and child, making the poor woman shriek in justifiable fear. Without a glance back at them, much less an apology, he lumbered, with all the grace of a dancing bear, toward the sycamore in front of Grandfather's house. I was in hot pursuit of him, yet managed to observe Julia at the gate, smiling at our manly antics. The air was full of shouts for both Badger and me, and I admit the man showed surprising agility and speed for his bulk. I raced after him, running right between Henry Thoreau and Capt. Gideon Peck. They were having such an intense conversation that neither gave me any notice.

And that was when I perhaps acted a bit hotly. Badger veered toward the stake. I did the same, and from twenty feet wound up and threw the ball with all my strength. The ball hit him square on a buttock so hard it sounded like the tail of a fifty-pound beaver slapping the water. The crowd roared with laughter, and Badger turned to glare at me. The ball is too light to cause physical harm, but his pride had been gravely wounded. He no doubt now harbors resentment toward me, for that and for what soon followed.

We changed sides, and during a short interlude I walked over to Henry and Capt. Peck. The combination of the two appeared most combustible. Peck, as a retired Army officer, is a strong and vocal supporter of the Mexican War, and, sure enough, they were arguing about it when I joined them. Although Henry remained calm, Peck's voice was raised to such a degree that it drew the attention of Sgt. Badger. He came over to his former captain and present employer, towering menacingly over Henry as Peck accused him of being a traitor.

"Captain," I said to Peck, "let us save such hot discussion for the tavern. I am sure the Plumford ladies have come out this evening to be entertained by sport, not loud political debate."

The mere mention of ladies changed Peck's demeanor, and he coolly looked about him. "You are quite right, Doctor," he said in the charming, easy manner he has come to be known for since removing to Plumford. He bowed to me, ignored Thoreau entirely, and strode away, Badger in his wake.

Henry did not seem the least perturbed by his argument with Peck. Perhaps he is used to contentious discussions. "I have gleaned no additional information concerning our Negro this evening," he told me. "Everyone I spoke to expressed mild sympathy that a black man had met with an accident in Plumford and much puzzlement as to why he would have come here in the first place. He was not seen alive by anyone."

I had expected as much. Yet as futile as our investigation has been thus far, we agreed to continue our inquiries rather than give up. I was called to take my turn at bat, and Henry bade me farewell, declaring that he'd had enough of Plumford for the time being. He did not seem to think much of our fair little town.

And he would have thought far less of it had he stayed. It was drawing dark, and the score was ninety-eight to forty-three, with my side ahead, when Rufus Badger came to bat again. Perhaps I was a mite too confident, for I gave the man an easy throw. He struck the ball with such a force it looked to take the leather cover off. It soared far down the Green, but a scout on my team got to it and launched a throw toward mighty Ira Munger, who was in position near third to soak Badger as he rushed toward home stake. Ira stands a good head taller than most of us, and in his high-crowned straw hat he looks a mythical Gigantes. He could well be the strongest man in town. In his butcher shop down below the dam he swings his heavy cleaver so hard through meat and bone I can hear it in the office, and Grandfather has more than once called on Ira to hold down men for painful surgery.

The flight of the ball carried Ira near Sgt. Badger's path, and as Ira extended his hands to meet the throw Badger purposely rammed into him to divert his run. The force of the blindsided collision was most powerful, but as Ira fell backward, he managed to take hold of Badger, twist him around in the air, and smash to the ground on top of him. Hands tight around Badger's throat, he butted his head down on the sergeant's forehead. I calculated another blow like that would open both men's skulls, so I ran to them and pulled Ira off. He looked at me with such blind rage that I should have feared getting the same rough treatment as Badger. But as I have grown up knowing Ira, who often came to Tuttle Farm to slaughter pigs, I was not affrighted.

"Go easy," I told him in a low voice.

Ira nodded, and I saw the ire wane from his eyes. Without another look at Badger, he started to walk away. It was over for him.

Badger, however, heaved himself up and took a blackjack from his coat. In the next instant I managed to divert a crushing blow to Ira's skull with a blow of my own to Badger's shoulder. He glowered at me and raised his weapon again.

"Sergeant Badger! Halt!" I heard Capt. Peck shout with the full authority of a military officer. Badger obeyed the command on the instant and stood stiff and still.

Capt. Peck marched over to us but not with his usual firm stride. Noticing his slight limp, I looked at him more closely than I had earlier in the evening. To my professional eye, he appeared physically deteriorated. Not only was he moving in some pain, but his handsome countenance, usually lit up with a debonair smile, was gray and pinched.

"Pardon Sergeant Badger's hot head," he said to me. "He misses battle and goes looking for it in the wrong places."

"Swinging a blackjack at an unarmed man is in itself wrong," I said.

"Not always," Capt. Peck replied, but he took from Badger the length of leather with a ball of iron wrapped at its tip. "Rufus, go and cool down with a mug of cider." He tossed his man a coin, and Badger lurched off.

The rest of the players resumed their positions, and my team won the game shortly thereafter. But the fight had taken the fun out of the play, and all trudged quietly away, sobered, I think, by this glimpse into the violent side of our natures so easily let loose by just a game. Thoreau's point had been proven without his even being present to make it.

JULIA'S NOTEBOOK

Friday, 7 August

Molly could not be found in the kitchen this afternoon. That girl avoids work like the plague. When first I came to Plumford, she seemed eager enough to cook and clean, but of late she has been so sluggish and tardy-gaited that I am at my wits' end. What do I know about keeping house or keeping servants? Not that I would dare call Molly Munger a servant to her face. She is the "hired girl," free to come and go as she likes. Unfortunately, she likes to go home early and come here late.

But hope springs eternal in the human breast, and with the hope that Molly had not left early and was doing something useful about the house, I went in search of her. I found her in the doctor's office beyond the kitchen, sitting at her ease and tittering whilst Adam amused her by dangling his pocket watch in front of her broad, smooth face.

"Pardon me for interrupting your sport, Molly," I said, trying to sound as sarcastic and scolding as Grandmother Walker used to sound when dealing with her household help (or my own young self, for that matter).

Apparently I lacked sufficient gravitas, for Molly made no

attempt to stifle her glee. "Oh, I don't mind the interrupt, Miss Julia. But Doc Adam might."

"Not at all," Adam assured me. "I was about to end my experiment anyway. Molly cannot stop giggling long enough to focus her attention."

"Well, I can't help but find your notion comical," she retorted, pert as you please.

"What notion is that?" I said.

"Why, Doc Adam thinks he can put me to sleep by waving his watch afore my eyes. Don't that beat all get out?"

I found it quite fascinating. "Did you mean to mesmerize her, Adam?"

"No, I give no countenance to such humbug as the curative power of magnets. It is the curative power of the *mind* that interests me."

Apparently it did not interest Molly. "A good dose of calomel might cure me better."

"Calomel is a preparation of mercury, and mercury is a powerful poison," Adam informed her patiently. "You are too young to habituate yourself to such a strong remedy for such a common ailment as constipation."

"But I am *uncommonly* blocked up, Doc!"

"I shall make you a preparation that can do you no harm, Molly," he said. "Castor oil mixed with cassia, fennel, and half a dram of jalap for good measure. Stop by for the potion before you go home."

Molly thanked him and languidly made her way back to the kitchen.

"She will most likely take her customary midday nap in the buttery now," I told Adam. "If constipation is the reason Molly Munger has been so indolent of late, let us hope your potion works."

"I had hoped hypnotism would."

"But how, Adam?"

"When Molly was in a hypnotic state, I planned to instill in her mind the idea that her bowels would soon perform the desired action." He must have seen doubt in my eyes. "Really, Julia, such a method has been proven to be amazingly effective in curing a great many maladies."

"You have used it before?"

"In point of fact, no. But I have been reading a highly advanced scientific book on the subject. It was published in London two years ago." He lifted the tome off his desk and handed it to me. The title read *Neurypnology; or the Rationale of Nervous Sleep.* "The author is Dr. James Braid. He invented the term hypnotism to describe his method of inducing nervous sleep. He explains his procedure in this book, and I was attempting to follow it with Molly. Unfortunately, she could not take me seriously."

"Nor can I," I admitted, handing back the book.

"I had hoped you of all people would understand, Julia."

He looked so disappointed that I attempted to defend myself. "Why expect me to understand the latest medical methods, Adam? My training has been solely in art."

"And as an artist you must appreciate the mind's ability to produce thoughts of a highly creative nature. Well, the mind has the ability to produce thoughts that control physical functions too."

I considered this a moment and recalled the only time in my life that I had been seriously ill. "I am reminded of Magic," I said.

Adam looked even more disappointed. "What I am talking about has nothing to do with magic, Julia."

"Does it not? Do you remember how ill I became after my mother died?"

"Yes, of course. Grief incapacitated you to such a degree that you could not leave your bed. Grandfather feared that you too had fallen victim to Consumption."

"You would visit me every day, smelling of fresh air and grass," I said. "And one morning you brought me a poor, sickly kitten from the farm. You told me she had been abandoned by her mother and needed my tender attentions or she would perish."

"Ah, yes," Adam said. "You named the kitten Magic."

"And so absorbed did I become in making Magic well that I ceased to dwell on my recent loss and soon became well myself."

"You are right, Julia," Adam acknowledged. "Magic's effect upon you is an excellent example of what I am talking about. The workings of the mind influence the workings of the body, and I would much prefer to induce my patients to use their own thoughts to cure themselves than dose them with harsh drugs. I do not put much stock in purgatives and opiates, but most doctors have great faith in their healing power. Hence their patients do too. Dr. Braid calls this the power of suggestion. When he put his patients in a hypnotic state, this same power of suggestion actuated healing without medicines of any sort. Severe headaches and seizures were cured. Even rheumatic pain and epilepsy."

"That is indeed most remarkable, Adam."

"Furthermore, a good many minor surgical operations have been performed painlessly during hypnosis."

"The more I hear, the more impressed I become."

"Then hark this, Julia. One of Dr. Braid's patients was a young mother who was breast-feeding. She was producing too little milk to feed her babe, and Dr. Braid hypnotized her to secrete more. He began with only one breast, and after it filled with milk she complained of feeling lopsided. So he hypnotized her again and suggested she increase secretion in the other breast. And so she did!" Adam smiled sheepishly. "Forgive me, Julia. You must find such medical frankness indelicate."

I suppose I should have, but I did not. "Please continue," I urged.

"Well, enough about mammary functions. Dr. Braid also discovered that hypnosis produces an extraordinary revival of the memory. He calls this hypnotic hypermnesia. His subjects can recall, in the greatest detail, long-forgotten incidents from their childhoods."

"How pleasing that must be," I said. "My most cherished memories are those of my mother before she became ill. Unfortunately, they have dimmed over the years."

"Perhaps I could help you revive them by means of hypnosis, Julia."

"Can that really be possible?"

"Surely it is worth a try."

I could see how eager he was to experiment. Indeed, I too was eager to give it a try. But I would not give in so easily. "Let us negotiate, Adam. I will agree to be your subject if you agree to be mine. Allow me to paint your portrait."

From the way he winced one would have thought I had suggested pulling out all his strong, white teeth. "You do not want to waste your fine talent on a likeness of me," he said. "Nor can I spare the time to sit for you."

Determined to capture his features before I left Plumford, I persisted. "Then let me at least make a plaster cast of your face, Adam. That would take half an hour at most."

"Very well," he conceded. "But I believe you to be the winner of this bargain. I shall have my poor mug smothered in wet plaster, whereas you shall have pleasant remembrances of your mother."

He sat me down in the consultation chair by the desk and extracted his timepiece from his waistcoat pocket. "Dr. Braid has subjects focus on his lancet case, but I think a watch is less intimidating," he said. He held the watch about a foot from my face, dangling it by its chain. "All you have to do is keep your body relaxed, your eyes fixed on the watch, and your mind riveted on its movement, Julia. You will not lose consciousness. You will simply descend into a deep, restful state of mental concentration. You will hear my voice and obey my instructions. And at the end of this session I will clap my hands, and you will immediately come out of the hypnotic state."

I did as I was told, and it wasn't long before my lids began to close involuntarily. From that moment on I remember nothing till I heard the sharp sound of a clap near my ear. My eyes flew open, and I saw Adam kneeling before me.

"Please tell me all is well with you, Julia," he said.

"Why should it not be?"

"Because I have acted imprudently." He handed me his handkerchief. "Dry your eyes and try to forgive me."

I touched my cheek. It was moist from tears. "Whatever happened?"

"I asked you to go back to when you were a girl so that you could relive happy times with your mother. Instead, you began to relive her last agonizing hours. Go back farther, I kept urging you, and at last you did."

"To before she became ill?"

"Long, long before that."

"Over twenty years ago when I was but a babe?"

"To before you were even born."

"You speak in riddles, Adam."

"I do not mean to. But your recollection was so unexpected and confusing."

"Just tell me what I told you."

"You claimed you were in a garden encircled by colonnades and filled with fig and olive trees. You said it overlooked the Tiber River, and you could see a large amphitheater in the distance. You must have been recalling Rome."

"But I have never been there," I told Adam. "Nor to any part of Italy. My father never obtained a portrait commission there, and we could ill afford to travel for our own amusement. Besides, we speak not a word of Italian between us."

"Yet you speak Latin quite fluently."

"I know nothing of that ancient language, Adam."

"You must have picked up a smattering of Latin somehow," he insisted. "You rattled off a few phrases of it whilst in a hypnotic state."

"Really? What exactly did I say?"

Adam shrugged. "My own Latin is not as good as it could be. I know just enough to understand medical terms."

"Well, never mind about that. Recount more of this vision of mine."

"You said there was a statue of Dionysus in this garden, overlooking a shallow pool."

"Were there other people about?"

He hesitated. "There were a number of them."

"Did I describe them?"

"You said the men were wearing togas and the women stolas."

"How wonderful! Pray, who were these antiquated people?"

Adam looked away from me. "The rest of what you said was rather vague."

"But my description of the garden sounds so explicit. Can you not tell me more details?"

"I cannot," Adam said. "You suddenly started crying again, and I clapped my hands to awaken you."

"Why can I not recall any of this?"

"Most likely because I did not instruct you to. And that was for the best. Otherwise you would have been left with fresh memories of your dear mother's passing."

"But now I am left most curious about my Roman remembrance. Could that too have been dredged up from my past?"

"I thought you said you have never been to Rome, Julia."

"Well, not in *this* life. Perhaps in a previous one, though."

"Nonsense," Adam said. "It was merely a dream made more vivid by your unnatural sleep."

"Well, whatever it was, you must hypnotize me again and bring me back there, Adam. Only this time pray instruct me to remember the visit."

He stood up abruptly and frowned down at me. "I will do no such thing. This experiment should not be repeated. Who knows where it could lead us."

"That is what makes it so exciting!"

"No, Julia. That is what makes it so perilous. Please do not argue with me about it anymore."

I did not. I have found that arguing with Adam only makes him dig in his heels all the deeper. We are much alike in that regard, he and I. But I have not given up trying to persuade him to hypnotize me again. How I wish he would cease being so protective toward me. It can be most irritating.

ADAM'S JOURNAL

Saturday, August 8th

Julia rushed into the barn whilst I was grooming Napoleon this morning. "Come quickly, Adam. There's a badly injured man outside."

Went out to see a lathered nag hitched to a rickety buckboard in front of the house. A farmer I knew to be Mr. Herd was standing by the horse, and his son Hiram was standing in the wagon. They both looked to be all right. Hiram beckoned with great energy, and I ran to the wagon along with Julia. There I saw an insensible man lying on the wagon platform, bleeding from the head. I lifted myself into the back of the wagon and began to examine him. It was difficult to see his head injury through the matted, blood-soaked hair covering it.

"Our bull got loose," young Hiram said. "Found him in the far pasture. This poor fellow was lyin' close by him."

"He was trespassin'!" Farmer Herd shouted.

The boy ignored his father. "Sultan must have gored him, and I fear he is dying."

"Is he still breathing, Adam?" Julia said.

"Yes. Therefore he might still be saved."

Herd and his boy helped me carry the man into the office as Julia cradled his head. We put him onto the examination table and stripped him of his coat, waistcoat, and shirt.

"Looks to be an Injun," Herd said when the man's ruddy torso was revealed.

He bore a few healed scars on his chest, and I saw bruises, most likely from bull hoofs, but no broken bones. His skull, however, was smashed open, and cracked bits of cranial material were pushing against his brain. I deemed him to be young and healthy enough to endure both a gore to the head and my remedy to set him right again.

"I will have to operate," I said.

"Can't you just patch him up, doc?" Herd said. "I ain't payin' for any fancy surgery on some trespassin' Injun. Bad enough Hiram almost kilt our old horse in his haste to get him here."

"Our bull gored him, Pa," Hiram said. "Don't that make us accountable?"

"Injun had no right to be on our land in the first place. Besides which you never seen Sultan attack him. You just supposed he did."

"What else could I suppose, Pa? There was blood on Sultan's horn."

"That don't prove nothin'."

"Enough!" Julia said. "You are wasting precious time with your petty-mindedness, Mr. Herd. Leave the doctor to do what is necessary to save this man."

"Let's go, Hiram," the farmer said, grabbing his son's arm. "We have done our Christian duty by fetching the Injun here and need do no more."

"Wait," I said. "I will need a pair of steady hands to assist me."

Both men shook their heads most vigorously and backed out of the room.

"My hands are steady, are they not?" Julia said. She raised them for me to see. They were already bloody from pillowing the man's head. "Allow me to assist you, Doctor."

I regret to admit that I hesitated before assenting, for it is an accepted belief in the medical profession that women are far too faint of heart and weak of stomach to assist in operations. Yet the idea of having this particular woman at my side made my spirit rise above such a belief. I nodded to her, and we got down to it.

Julia brought me water and a clean cloth to swab the wound site, and, after I cleared out grass, leaf, dirt, clotted blood, and matted hair, I observed the skull fracture more closely. The pericranium was open, and the right back parietal bone stove in. Fragments and spiculae of bone and hair intruded into the cranium, and to determine if the dura mater had been breached I would have to trepan. Before I went ahead with the procedure, I thought best to forewarn Julia.

"I am going to bore a hole right through our patient's skull so I can lift out those broken pieces of bone and relieve the pressure being exerted on the brain tissue," I told her. "Unless that is accomplished with dispatch, he will surely die."

She did not so much as blink. "Then by all means bore away, doctor. And I will pray he survives it."

"He has survived worse," I said, indicating a deep dent on the other side of his head above the temple. "Such a scar as that indicates he was shot in the head."

"How extraordinary." Julia regarded our patient more closely. "What if he awakens during the surgery?"

"He is so insensate that it is most unlikely."

"But what if he *does?*" she insisted. "Will he feel pain?"

"Some," I allowed. "But less than you would expect. The skull has no nerves."

I asked her to shave away the hair around the wound as I laid out my scalpels and tools. She commented that the trephine I would use to bore the skull hole looked much like a corkscrew. I showed her that instead of a screw tip, the trephine had a circular, serrated-edge saw that cut into the bone. This made her shudder only slightly.

And so we began. With Julia at the ready with clean strips of linen, I picked up a scalpel and without hesitation sliced through the flesh and pericranium right to the bone, bisecting the wound indentation. Our patient's legs twitched slightly. Two more cuts at right angles to the first made it possible to fold back the flaps of skin surrounding the wound. As instructed, Julia used the linen strips to press down on the flaps and stanch the flow of blood.

I had never performed such an operation as this before, only observed it being performed in the operating dome of Massachusetts General Hospital when I was a medical student. Yet I proceeded without hesitation or trepidation. I somehow felt in my marrow that I had done all this before in some previous time and place. I realize this makes no sense, but it gave me great confidence nevertheless.

I placed the bit of the trephine a quarter-inch to the left side of the shattered skull opening and began to saw into the raw, white bone, pulling back the instrument occasionally so that Julia could clear away skull fragments. I proceeded with great caution, for I could not allow the trephine to fully penetrate the bone and thrust into the brain, thus instantly killing my patient. When that became a definite danger, I put the trephine aside and cut away the last of the circular piece of bone with the edge of a serrated scalpel. I asked Julia for a beaker of water and deposited the piece in it to keep it fresh until it was time to put it back in place.

I was relieved to see that no part of the crushed cranium had broken through the thin membrane of dura mater surrounding the brain like a protective sack. With firm pressure I used the edge of my scalpel to ease out the loose fragments. I then scraped away all the jagged bits of bone to form a clean edge around the wound. As I worked, a bit of sawn bone slipped between the edge of the skull and the dura mater and alas, out of sight.

Julia had been busy stanching the blood around the wound. I told her to desist for I needed her to perform a more urgent duty. As I pushed down on the dura mater, she must pick out the lost bone fragment with a pair of forceps.

She stared at me in disbelief. "But I have had no training."

"You have the better angle," I explained gently. "And you are so clever with your hands. Just take care not to push the fragment farther out of reach."

She grew pale but bravely took up the forceps. She managed to grasp the bit of sharp bone with them, but slippery fluid kept her from getting a tight hold. Her hand began to shake.

"Steady," I told her softly.

"Do you really trust I can do this, Adam?"

"I trust you implicitly."

Thus encouraged, she tried again and this time succeeded in lifting the bit of bone away from the brain. She cried out in relief.

I acknowledged her achievement with a brief smile before fitting the sawn circular piece back into the skull. Used beeswax to bind it there. As a preventive measure against infection, I washed the wound with red precipitate. Closed the flaps of skin over the incision, sewed them up, and covered the area with linen bandages soaked in diluted honey. Believe in the healing powers of honey almost as much as my mother did.

"That ought to do it," I told Julia.

She gazed down at our patient. "I touched his very brain," she whispered. Overcome by this realization, she began to sway.

I grabbed her arm and led her outside for a breath of fresh air. The Herd men were waiting in the door yard. They expressed relief when I informed them that the Indian was still breathing, and Mr. Herd even offered to pay me for my trouble. Frugal Yankee farmer that he is, he offered me one dollar and two-dozen eggs. I accepted this pittance without the slightest objection. My true reward will be my patient's survival. And the surgical experience I have gained is invaluable.

JULIA'S NOTEBOOK

Sunday, 9 August

I must ready myself for church, so I shall make this entry brief.

Adam saved the life of a mortally wounded young man yesterday, and I had the privilege of assisting him. That I could muster the fortitude to do so might astound some, but we of the Weaker Sex are not so weak as men would have us. Indeed, I see no reason why women should not be allowed to study medicine and become surgeons themselves. But I suppose that is a far-fetched notion.

I have never encountered an American native before. I am familiar with portraits of them by Charles Bird King, however, and our patient has similar features. His face is hairless, and the bones beneath his cheeks are prominent even in repose. He has a somewhat low, backward sloping forehead. His ears have thick lobes and lie close to his head, and his eyelids are ovated, edged with long, straight lashes. His nose is sizeable (indeed, it reminds me of Henry Thoreau's nose), with a predominating aquiline bridge, and his lips are well-formed. His hair is so black it seems tinged with cobalt blue, and his skin is an earthy, burnished shade of reddish-brown that I should reproduce on canvas with a mixture of clay pigments such as ocher, sienna, sinoper, and umber. During the surgery I had opportunity to observe his bare chest, and it is fairly muscular but hairless. I have glimpsed nearly naked men before, models for Papa's paintings of mythic figures, and this Indian would make a good Hermes, the speedy messenger of the gods. Perchance he has come to Plumford as a harbinger—What could he foreshow?

Am I letting my imagination get the better of me? Perhaps I have been reading too much Poe to Grandfather. We both enjoy *Tales of the Grotesque and Arabesque* immensely. Takes us back to the days when I was a child and Grandfather would read macabre tales concerning Bluebeard and the Headless Horsemen and such to me. We have always shared a taste for such fare, which Grandmother Walker, rest her soul, considered quite common. I was never a proper enough girl to suit her, but I suited Grandfather just fine. It pleases me that he still enjoys my company. The more he mends, however, the more anxious he becomes that I shall soon be leaving. I am sorry this disturbs him, but how can I remain here? It is hard enough to make a living teaching art and painting portraits in a metropolis the size of New York; nigh impossible in a village the size of Plumford.

Lo! I have just heard the parlor clock strike ten. That means I am already late for church. It would be of little matter to me if I had not promised Lyman Upson I would attend today. He is supply preaching for the absent parson. If I quickly pin up my hair, tie on my bonnet, and sprint down the Green, I can be at the Meetinghouse within five minutes. Given how long-winded Mr. Upson can be, his sermon is sure to go on for another hour and more. Oh, why did I agree to go and listen to him? Most likely because he looked so eager when he asked me. He does not get many opportunities to preach anymore, and I suppose it would be a pity to miss him. But now more minutes have passed, and I shall be later still. I had better leave off writing at once if I intend to go at all.

It does not appear that I do intend to go, for I continue to write. In truth, I resent that Mr. Upson extracted such a promise from me. I have little interest in hearing more of his bleak views concerning sin and reprobation.

Now Grandfather is calling me for assistance. Surely attending to his needs supplants attending church. I am relieved that I shall be staying at home.

ADAM'S JOURNAL

Monday, August 10th

What might have happened if I had not driven out to the farm this morning makes me shudder to contemplate. I got there just in time to see Gran carrying her musket in both hands and running through the pasture toward the woods. This meant nothing good. I sprang out of the gig and headed after her.

For one her age she was fair flying, apron strings flapping behind like kite tails. I called to her, but she did not hear me, and I finally caught her as she got to the edge of the sugar maple stand.

"Gran, wait," I said, taking her arm to stop her. She was full flushed and puffing like a steam engine. "What's the trouble?"

"Thank the Lord you've come, Adam," she gasped. "I heard Harriet screaming for help up here, and all my farmhands are out mowing the far pasture."

"Where is she?" We looked around, but there was no sign of Harriet. But over Gran's heavy breathing, I managed to hear muffled female cries for aid. "She took cover in the sugaring shed!" I said.

I raced up through the trees and got to the shed just as

Rufus Badger kicked in the door. He plunged inside, and I followed right behind him. Little Harriet was cowering behind a pile of firewood. I grabbed Badger's shoulder and spun him around. He was slobbering drunk, which given his strength and fighting ability, I think now was most fortunate for me. Also, the experience gained at the boxing club in Cambridge stood me in good stead. He came at me faster than I expected, given his drunkenness, and I parried a vicious fist thrust at my head, then dug a blow into his belly that made him gush out air like a burst ball of leather. Even so, he still had strength enough to throw himself at me full force, and we both of us landed in a pile of tangled limbs on the floor. He shot his thick grimy thumb at my eye, trying to gouge it out, but I slipped from his grip, and we were both up in an instant. Harriet tried to scamper to the door, but Badger blocked her. I grabbed a stout length of firewood and brought it down on his head, not intending to kill the man but to stun him to immobility, which I did. He crashed down like a fallen tree.

I swung Harriet into my arms, for she was near fainting, and carried her outside, away from the beast. "You saved me," she murmured into my waistcoat, and I thanked God that I had. I put the poor frightened dear down on a carpet of moss beneath a sugar maple and told her to breathe deeply and slowly.

Gran came running to us, still carrying the heavy musket. Badger staggered out of the sugar shed right then, and wound back his arm to strike me with his nasty blackjack. Gran raised the musket and pointed it at him.

"Don't budge another inch, you soulless villain," she said. Her voice trembled with rage, but her hands were steady. "As a Christian woman I won't kill you, but this load of birdshot will do some damage for sure." She lowered the muzzle and pointed it at a region every man holds dear. "And it will be the last of you pestering girls."

That got Badger's attention. He changed in an instant from a vicious cur into a wheedling conniver. "I meant no harm, ma'am. The miss appeared willing enough when I found her alone picking mushrooms."

"You lie!" Harriett cried out. "I beseeched you to leave me be, and when you wouldn't, I screamed loud as I could."

Badger did not look toward Harriet but kept a bleary eye on Gran's gun. "I reckoned she was just havin' sport with me." He grinned, showing his gums and a few rotten teeth. "Frisky little mares like her like to put up a fuss afore they get broken in."

"Shut your filthy piehole, mister, and get your stinkin' carcass off my property," Gran told him with a wave of her gun.

He snorted. "I wager that old blunderbuss don't even fire, you old hag."

"Either you will lose that wager," I said, taking a step toward him, "or lose a fight to me again."

Badger looked from me to Gran's gun and back to me again. He then whistled for his horse, and it ambled out of the woods to him. He mounted it slowly, and I saw he was in pain from my blows. But he was not yet through making trouble. He unwound a whip from around the pommel of his saddle and raised it to slash down at me.

The next second the air was filled with a roar and choking smoke as the musket discharged and threw a barrelful of shot just past Badger's head into the tree above him. A thick limb was blasted clear and fell down amidst shattered leaves on both man and horse. The horse reared and bolted off through the trees in a panicked runaway that threw Badger sideways one way and then the other, bouncing his hindquarters against the trunks of several maples as he hung onto the saddle. Such a sorry sight it was that Harriet began laughing a bit hysterically until horse and man were out of sight.

After Harriett calmed down and we started toward the

house, I announced that I was going to the Justice of the Peace and have a warrant issued for Badger's arrest.

Gran shook her head. "Don't you do that, Adam. Badger won't come back here. There's easier pickings in town for his lust, and we got to think of Harriet's honor. Don't matter she was innocent of any wrongdoing. Folks gossip most awful about something like this, and them's those who like to lay the blame on the female, no matter what. Harriet's coming of age to marry, so we got to just let this rest."

"I will at least inform Badger's employer Captain Peck of his appalling behavior. I want him to assure me he will keep Badger in line," I said, and Gran did not object to that.

When I returned to town I went directly to the office to check on the Indian. Julia was watching over him, and she reported that he had not stirred at all. As I examined him, she looked most concerned.

"I see no inflammation," I told her. "And although he remains insensible, his heartbeat is much stronger. He appears to be in excellent physical condition, and I am optimistic he will recover."

"Then so am I," she said, yet apprehension remained in her eyes as she studied me. "What has happened to upset you so, Adam?"

I had thought I was hiding my outrage well by keeping my demeanor calm and my countenance impassive, but somehow Julia always manages to perceive my innermost feelings. When we were children, it would annoy me, but now I felt relief rather than irritation. I was in need of someone to talk to. We adjourned to the consultation room, and I told her everything that had occurred at the farm.

"I am still inclined to have Badger arrested," I said in conclusion. "He should be jailed for what he did."

Like Gran, Julia would not hear of it. "If you make the incident a public matter, Adam, it could discredit Harriet's good name."

"Why must women always put reputation before all else?" I said impatiently.

"Because men do," she replied, just as impatient. "With the loss of her reputation, a woman loses the respect of men. And without that, she will never obtain her deepest desire."

"Which is?"

"To marry well, of course. That is the paramount ambition of most women."

"Is it yours, Julia?"

"I am already wedded to my Art."

"Does that mean you would never consider taking a husband?"

"It is certainly not my chief consideration. Indeed, I have not thought much about it since I was a girl and wished to marry my dear cousin Adam." She gave out a short laugh. "How horrified Grandmother Walker looked when I expressed this girlish fancy. She told me that Walker cousins must never, ever marry, but she would not tell me why."

"She must have thought you too young to understand the consequences," I said.

"Well, I should like to hear them now."

"You mean you still don't know, Julia?"

"Know what?"

"The Walker family history."

"Papa never talked of Mama's family to me, except to say they had not approved of him. So it is up to you to tell me of our heredity, Adam. Pray do so here and now."

And so I reluctantly did. "In the past, when Walker cousins married, the offspring that resulted were too unfit to survive."

Julia's expression became most grave. "That is indeed a dire family curse."

"I do not think it so much a curse as a medical disorder. And it is not particular to our lineage. Recent studies indicate children born of first cousins are often physically or mentally unsound. In fact, there is now a movement here in Massachusetts, led by none other than Noah Webster, to make first-cousin marriages illegal."

"And have you joined this movement, Adam?"

"No, no. I do not believe in passing laws that forbid any individual from marrying another. Surely the freedom to chose one's mate is among our unalienable rights."

"And no matter what the law or the consequence," Julia said, "there is no preventing people from falling in love, is there?"

My eyes met hers, but my reply remained mute in my heart. After a long moment she broke our gaze and said she would go see how our grandfather was faring. As soon as she was out of my sight I missed her.

Our conversation has made me recall, once again, what she recounted during her regression. I had hoped to put it out of mind but instead feel a compelling need to record it word for word.

"*I am standing in the warm sun, and the scent of lilies fills the air,*" she began and went on to describe a private garden overlooking the Tiber and an amphitheater on a hill beyond. "*Family and friends surround me,*" she continued. "*We all wear fine woolen tunics, the women's much longer than the men's, draped with swathes of colorful fabric. A woman bearing a bundle smiles at me and then walks toward a young man standing by the pool. He is my husband, and when he looks at me I recognize in the depths of his eyes that he is you, Adam. The woman lays the bundle at your feet and unwraps the swaddling to display a naked boy baby. He is our baby, and he is perfect in every way. You bend down, swoop him up, and hold him over your head toward the sun. With this gesture you formally acknowledge that he is your child and your legal heir, to share your nomen and cognomen. You then declared that his praenomen would be Agrippa.*"

After Julia repeated, in Latin, a string of blessings that those around her were voicing, she went back to speaking to me directly, describing the simple ceremony that followed.

"*You hand me our child, and as I cradle him in my arms our naming-party guests come forth to fasten around his plump neck dainty necklaces decorated with bells and gold objects. You bestow the last necklace, which bears a gold locket containing charms against evil spirits. It is the bulla you wore as a boy, and you beseech the gods to shine as much fortune on our son as they have on you. At that very moment a roar from the amphitheater fills the air. We all laugh and call it a sign of great luck. You smile at me tenderly, and as I look into your eyes and feel the weight of our baby in my arms I am filled with exultation.*"

Tears of joy streamed down her lovely face as she declared this, and it was then that I clapped my hands and awakened her from her reverie. If such happiness as that is not to be ours in this lifetime, I do not want to hear her fantasies about a past life together. And I am sure she would be most disconcerted if I repeated her unconscious longings to her. Hence I shall continue to withhold them.

ADAM'S JOURNAL

Monday evening, August 10th

Completed my afternoon patient calls and drove out to Capt. Peck's. Noticed right off that he has spoilt a perfectly fine old farmhouse, the inheritance of which brought him to Plumford in the first place, by embellishing it as tastelessly as some women ornament their bonnets. The old chestnut siding has been ripped off and replaced with board-and-batten strips, and the simple squares of clear glass in the windows are now diamond-shaped and many-hued. The hipped roof has been dressed up with superfluous gables, and there is enough Gothic fretwork all around to make your head spin. White pilasters run up the two stories of the front, and the rest is painted a yellow bright as dandelion blossoms. All this needless renovation must be very costly, but I am told that spending money is one of the captain's favorite pastimes, along with gambling at the tavern and making himself agreeable to the ladies.

Prepared myself for another encounter with Rufus Badger as I rapped the polished knocker composed of enough brass to forge a small cannon. It rather reminded me of Badger's hard head. But it was not Peck's brutish minion who answered the door. Instead it was the captain himself, his smooth face wreathed in a welcoming smile.

"Why, it is Dr. Walker come to call," said he, sounding as if there could be nothing more delightful than my unexpected presence at his doorstep. "Do come in, sir! No, better yet, let us walk out to the belvedere that I have had built across the field yonder. It commands a fine view of the river, and we can converse in privacy. My housekeeper is a quite a busybody. Come."

As he spoke I observed how pale his complexion was in contrast to his thick black hair. Usually his hair was meticulously brushed and pomaded, with its dashing streak of white artfully arranged along his brow, but today it was dull and disheveled. I noted a small bare patch at the back of the crown, the appearance of which must have brought this vain man some distress. As we began walking through the meadow I became aware that he was having trouble keeping up and slowed to a snail's pace to accommodate him.

"I heard you stopped up a hole the size of a Spanish gold piece in the head of a heathen the other day, Doctor," he said.

"Why do you assume he is a heathen, Captain?"

"Because your hired girl told me he's an Indian."

"You know Molly Munger?"

"Slightly," Peck said. "My housekeeper had the girl here to help with the spring cleaning. Come to think of it, I am not even sure she was the one who told me. There is much talk everywhere in town about him. People are always so curious about Indians, are they not? They are of little interest to me, however. I had my fill of them eight years ago when I took part in the Cherokee removal."

"Down in Georgia?" I said.

"That's right." Peck gave me a sidelong look. "Some think relocating them was unjust."

"And I am one of them," I said. "But I have not come to

discuss the illegality of the U.S. Army's removal of peaceful Indian tribes from their southern homelands."

"Good, for such discussions with Northerners weary me mightily, doctor. So why have you come?"

"I wish to make a most serious complaint against Rufus Badger."

"What has that devil been up to now?" Posing the question, Peck seemed ready to be amused.

"He has terrified the young ward of my grandmother with violent and unwanted attention earlier today. I shall have him arrested and charged with assault should he ever come near her again."

"Now doctor, calm yourself. Did Rufus do her harm?"

"Mental harm most certainly. He near frightened the life out of her. And if I had not arrived in time to put a stop to it, he would have harmed her physically too."

"Are you sure of it? Rufus may be a bit rough in his courting ways, but many a female prefers that." He winked. "We all know how a girl will act up a bit if she wants to heighten our ardor to a fever pitch."

Barely containing an impulse to strike him, I stared at the man, thinking him mad or perverted to the core. "This girl is innocent and not yet fifteen, Captain. She was clearly terrified and just as clearly found Badger's attentions repugnant."

"And you say you put a stop to his amorous pursuit?"

I described how Badger came at me and how I had to bring a piece of cordwood down on his head to cool him off.

Peck looked me up and down. "So you got the better of him, did you? Well, I can only say congratulations, for not many men can make such a boast in regard to Sergeant Badger. He went out on a weekend blow, and I wager he was still drunk as a skunk this morning."

"That does not excuse his behavior."

"No, but it gives reason for his being humbled at your hands."

He seemed to utterly fail to grasp the gravity of the situation. I told him he was missing the point. Badger had been caught in the midst of attacking the girl with the intention of brutally raping her.

"Well, the last part is pure conjecture on your behalf," he said, "since you stopped him well short of that. You know, we go way back, Sergeant Badger and I. He served most loyally and ably under me in the Army, and he serves me most loyally still. I allow he is not entirely trustworthy when he has been drinking. Why, just last week he let me down considerably because of this weakness. It was a far more serious matter than his recent tomfoolery, I assure you. But I forgave him for it." He smiled. "Let bygones be bygones, right, Doctor?"

"Try to hear me, Captain Peck," I said. "I consider what Badger did a most grave offence. And if that brute does not steer clear of Tuttle Farm and my grandmother's ward, I will see to it he ends up in prison. In addition, I take your questioning of the girl's virtue as an insult to her and to me."

Peck stopped in his tracks and gave me a wary look, his smarmy smirk fading away. "Yes, yes, now I understand. You have persuaded me that Sergeant Badger behaved abominably, Doctor. I apologize for his actions and will speak to him directly, although I doubt he will even remember the incident if he was drunk. Even so, you may assure the girl of her future safety from his attention."

This was as good as I could expect from him, and when he offered his hand to seal his promise, I shook it and bade him Good Day.

"Please don't go yet," he said. "There is another matter I would like to discuss with you of a medical nature. Let us continue to the belvedere."

I agreed, and we did not converse again until we reached the octagonal, open-sided wooden structure he referred to as a belvedere. It was located in a secluded spot well hidden from the house by trees, but he still looked about him before speaking. He kept his voice low.

"Your visit today was providential, Doctor Walker. It made me realize that the time has come for me to seek help concerning a growing infirmity. If you can cure me, I will pay any price you ask and follow any treatment you suggest."

I told him to relate his symptoms and that we would proceed from there. I have observed that expressing a long-held fear brings great relief to a person suspecting some dread illness in himself. Often as not, the fear is groundless, and the patient is as pleased with you as though you had just snatched him from the very jaws of death.

"Doctor," he began, "my bones ache, and every night I am awakened by shooting pains in my limbs, like someone is stabbing needles into me. I moan out loud in pain."

I told him I had noticed his limp at the ball game.

"It has gotten worse since, and I fear I am losing control over my legs." He pressed his fingertips to his eyes. "And another thing. I see double sometimes."

I inquired after his digestion and eating habits.

"I eat the same as always, after which I vomit up the most awful bile. I have become disgusting to myself."

I sat him down beside me on a bench inside the belvedere and observed that the pupils of his eyes were small and fixed. I used my knuckles to sharply tap below his kneecap. No reaction. That his reflex system was not normal did not surprise me, for by this time I had surmised what was wrong.

"Do you have difficulty passing water?" I asked him.

His face contorted as though he was about to sob, but he controlled himself. "These last few nights, when I arise to piss, I can barely stay upright. When I finally manage to arrange myself before my chamber pot, I have to wait and wait, and when at last I do piss, there is such pain I cry out. I tell you, my life is a horror. What is happening to me?"

I stood up and motioned for him to rise. "Let me examine your body."

He complied at the cost of some effort in removing his clothes. As I expected, there were telltale lesions clustered on the backs of his legs, along with an ulcer on his left arm.

"When did these lesions appear?" I said.

"Some time ago. But I paid them no mind for they were not like those I had before."

"Describe to me what you had before."

"Well, I had the pox once—a round sore on my manhood and some time later a rash on the bottom of my feet. All went away."

"How long ago was that?"

"Ten years, at least. I underwent the mercury cure. I was out in the field on patrol, hence the treatment was erratic, but the rash and sore went away anyway. So I was healed, was I not?" He looked at me with a pleading expression.

"Mercury is an uncertain treatment for syphilis," I said. "And it is generally agreed that for it to be most effective it must be continued for life."

He groaned. "It was vile to swallow down for even a short time. I sweated profusely, my heart raced, and I could not sleep a wink. My tongue swelled, my saliva was thick and stringy, and my breath stank. I knew a man who lost all his teeth after being treated with mercury, yet if that is the only way for me to be cured, I will faithfully undergo this harsh treatment for the rest of my days. By Beelzebub, I swear I will!" For a moment the fear in his eyes receded and was replaced by hope.

I was obliged to dash that hope with the truth. "There are three stages to this disease, Captain, and you are in the last one. The second stage was quiescence, when your symptoms went away. Some never experience symptoms again, and others, like you, have them reappear years later."

"Will they not just disappear again?" he asked, his voice wavering.

"No. The disease has returned in strength and is destroying your nervous system and organs with apparent speed. That is why your motor skills are deteriorating and every body function is deleteriously affected. You are far beyond the help of mercury now."

Peck sat down in a slump, naked as God made him, and stared dully ahead. "What will happen next? Do not spare me, Doctor."

I told him there would be a continued deterioration until he was completely incapacitated, without control of any body function, and blindness, total paralysis, and insanity might occur.

"How long will this torture go on?"

"That cannot be predicted with any accuracy."

"Come, Doctor. Tell me your prognosis. How long before I die?"

He had a right to know the worst and seemed man enough to hear it. "Six or eight weeks, perhaps less. The symptoms could temporarily fade and give you some days of normal existence, but the disease will return with greater strength after each respite. I would venture you have but a good month before you are incapacitated. After that you will require complete and constant care until death."

"Let death come quickly if I am to be bereft of all dignity and peace of mind."

"If you desire peace of mind," I told him, "you should inform every person you have had sexual congress with since your symptoms returned."

Peck shook his head. "If the women I have lain with have

caught the pox from me, what good would it do to torment them now? They are as doomed as I am."

"They are not doomed if they receive treatment early enough. They must be alerted, Captain, so they can be more attentive to symptoms that may appear and avoid infecting others. Knowing you have done the right thing will surely make the remainder of your life more peaceful."

"But the remainder of my life is so short. And hell is everlasting! God will surely send me there for all my sins." He burst into tears. After a moment, he swiped his hand across his face and regained a modicum of composure. "I was raised to fear eternal damnation, Doctor. But I was also taught that God forgives those who are repentant of their sins. How can I show God that I am repentant?" He looked at me as if I would know the answer to that.

And I believe I did. "Confess to those women you might have infected."

"Will that save me from burning in hell?"

"It very well might," I replied without a qualm. Be there a hell or not, I know for sure it is the only right thing for him to do.

He began to shiver. I helped him dress and walked him back to his house. Before taking my leave I urged him once again to inform his past lovers. He assured me he would do so forthwith.

JULIA'S NOTEBOOK

Tuesday, 11 August

This forenoon the Indian's eyes suddenly opened. His dark irises appeared to be flecked with fire as he gazed at me most fiercely. Although I had been waiting for this moment for three days, I could only stare back at him, dumbfounded. I am grateful Henry Thoreau was present.

"You are among friends," he told the Indian in a soothing voice. "You have been injured. Take care not to move too quickly."

If the Indian understood English, he gave no sign of it. His black eyes darted about the room like frantic flies looking for escape. He attempted to lift his bandaged head from the pillow but groaned from the effort and lay back again. He closed his eyes, and I confess I felt relieved that the wildness I had seen in them was once again shielded from view.

Leaving Henry to deal with our Lazarus, I ran off to fetch Adam at the schoolhouse. There are signs of an epidemic commencing in Massachusetts, and he had gone there to inoculate the children against small pox. That duty done, he was thrumming his guitar for the youngsters as a reward for enduring the needle pricks. Everyone was singing "Turkey in the Straw." I alerted Adam that his patient had awakened, and he immediately took his leave. The students looked most disappointed (as did the young schoolmistress).

When we returned to the office, I was astonished to see our patient propped up with pillows and conversing with Henry. His revival, of course, delighted Adam, who hurried to the bedside to take his pulse. The Indian yanked back his hand.

"This is Dr. Walker," Henry told him. "The very man I was just telling you about. The one who saved your life after the bull gored you."

"I thank you," the Indian told Adam and allowed him to take hold of his wrist again.

"And this young lady is my cousin Julia," Adam said. "She assisted me during your operation."

"Then I thank you too, miss," he said but would not look at me directly.

"What is your name, pray?" I asked him.

"I am called Trump."

"Surely you were not always called Trump," Henry said.

"No, a riverboat gambler gave me the name after fishing me out of the Big Muddy when I was a boy."

"What was your name before that?" Henry said.

"No matter. Trump suits me just fine."

"But you are an Indian, are you not?" Henry persisted.

"I was born a Cherokee." His voice was flat, his countenance devoid of expression. "But that was far away from here a long, long time ago."

"It could not have been that long ago," Adam said. "You look to be no more than twenty."

"Thereabouts, I reckon. How long I been here anyway?"

"Three days," Adam said. "You were brought here in an unconscious state Saturday last. Today is Tuesday."

"I sure didn't plan on such a lengthy stay as that."

"What brought you to Plumford?" Henry said.

"I come lookin' for a fellow name of Caleb. He is near as tall as I am and black as the ace of spades. Sports fine shiny boots and checkered breeches. Have you seen the likes of him hereabouts?"

We were all too stunned to say anything until Henry asked Trump a question in return. "What reason would Caleb have to come here?"

"To do Effie's bidding," Trump said. "That's all he would tell me afore he set off. I would have made Effie tell me more afore I left Boston, but she has gone missin' too."

"Who is Effie?" Adam said.

"A comely mulatto Caleb professes to love even though she works for Mrs. Scudder."

"And who is Mrs. Scudder?" said I.

"I reckon she is someone you will never have occasion to meet, miss. She runs a bawdy house."

"A boarding house?"

"No, miss. A *bawdy* house. Where whores ply their trade," he explained to me most patiently.

"Perhaps you should step out of the room, Julia," Adam said.

I ignored his suggestion and held my ground. But I desisted from asking Trump further questions, for in truth I was out of my element.

Henry took up the inquiry. "When was the last time you saw Caleb, Trump?"

"Over a week ago. That's why I come looking for him." Trump regarded him with narrowed eyes. "When was the last time *you* seen him mister? You must have else you would not be vexing me with questions concerning him."

"I am very sorry to tell you this, Trump," Henry said, "but eight days ago I came upon the dead body of a young Negro meeting Caleb's description. He was lying on the rocks beneath a cliff."

"Caleb got hisself kilt falling off a cliff?"

"That was the verdict of the Coroner's Jury, but Dr. Walker and I believe he was murdered. Was he a close friend of yours?"

"The only one I got. We stowed away on a boat sailing from New Orleans to Boston last winter and have stuck it out through thick and thin ever since. Who would want to murder such a fine fellow as Caleb? Are you sure it was him?"

"The dead Negro was wearing clothes such as you described, but he had no identification upon his person."

"I better take a look at him then."

"He has been buried for over a week now, Trump."

"Then dig him up. That is the only way to be sure it is Caleb."

"You are right," Adam said. "We will exhume the body when you are up to viewing it, Trump."

"I am up to it now."

Adam studied his patient for a moment. "We will go to the burial ground tomorrow," he said.

"We" did not include *me* of course. Adam declared my female sensibilities too delicate to view a corpse. I cannot believe he still thinks me some fragile nincompoop after the staunch way I comported myself during Trump's operation. But in truth I have no desire to see the dead body of that poor young man and did not insist on accompanying them.

ADAM'S JOURNAL

Wednesday, August 12th

This afternoon was gray and the air heavy with damp. A cloud of mosquitoes joined us as we three climbed down from the gig. When I took two crowbars from behind the seat, Henry reached for one and Trump for the other. Since coming to consciousness yesterday, the young Indian has been recovering his strength at a most amazing rate. Nevertheless, I shook my head at him, gave a crowbar to Henry, and kept the other for myself. We all walked to the open grave in the burying ground. At its head stood a simple cedar cross bearing as yet no name. Gran's farmhands had removed the earth atop and around the coffin, but they left it to us to pry up the lid.

The odor of decay permeated the atmosphere. I looked up to see several redheaded vultures circling. "I must warn you that what we are about to do can make even the strongest man qualmish," I said. "And that goes for myself, despite my training dissecting cadavers."

"I inhale the scent as I would a rose, and I am as cheered by the sight of those vultures as by the sight of songbirds," Henry said. "When I was younger I questioned why we cannot depart from Nature more cleanly and gracefully, but now I accept the whole process. I have come to realize the only answer to death is life."

"No, vengeance is the only answer," Trump said.

Henry and I glanced at each other but did not gainsay him. The young man was distraught and no wonder, for we were here to see if he had lost his only friend.

Henry and I stepped down into the grave. There was just room enough dug free of dirt on each side of the plain pine coffin for us to flank it. Without ceremony, we began to pry at the lid with the crowbars. The nails squealed as if in protest at our disturbing the peace of the corpse.

As we each raised the two planks of the lid, a wave of noxious fumes struck us, so pungent my eyes watered, and I had to step back to blink away the tears. Henry too reeled backward for an instant, despite all his talk about roses. We steeled ourselves and stared at a bloated horror. The dead creature before us did not look human but for the clothes it wore, stretched taut to bursting.

"The putrefaction and gases produced by decay can alter features beyond recognition," I explained in a choked voice. "Perhaps you lack the strength to come down for a closer look, Trump."

But he was determined to see if the corpse had been his good friend, and he slid down into the grave and gaped into the coffin. Every feature on the dead man's face was distended to the point of explosion. The eyes were tight slits. The tongue projected out from distorted lips like nothing other than a sickening black leach. The bile of decay had run out of the mouth and nose and congealed on the chin and neck. Insects were already at work under the skin. Their movements made one cheek waver slightly as if from a nervous tick. I sensed the entire corpse was alive with bugs feeding frantically. The head itself moved a fraction. A squirming mass of life had access to the rotting brain through the wound in the back of the skull.

I would not have held it against either man if they had bolted from the spot and not stopped running till they reached town. Henry was flat calm throughout, all alert, studying what lay before him. He glanced at me, and his large, clear eyes seemed to hold a deep understanding of what such decaying mortality meant. Trump looked at the corpse in bewilderment.

"Perhaps you can recognize the clothing?" I said.

Trump nodded and softly said, "Those are his fine boots. I was there when he won them in a game of craps. And he won that yeller coat the same night, the lucky son of a gun. Let me have a knife."

I passed him my pocketknife, and after he felt carefully along the shoulder of the frock coat, he began to slice into the material along the seam.

"Take care," I said. A slip of the knife into the bloated corpse would release enough gas to make us all violently sick.

Trump slowly parted the seam, felt through with his finger, and drew out a gold piece. "Caleb sewed it in there in case he got robbed or cleaned out at dice, so he'd have a fresh stake." He returned the knife to me and slipped the coin into his pocket. "I'll remember him by it."

There was no more to be done, and since the flies had come around in increasing number, we hastily slid the boards back atop the coffin and used the ends of our crowbars to nail it down tight. Henry and I climbed out of the grave, and Henry extended a hand to help Trump out. We shoveled dirt back over the coffin, and I promised Trump I would have the name Caleb carved on the cross.

"I would like to carve Caleb's name on his murderer's chest," he said.

When we got back to town I gave Trump a tankard of cider for his nerves and changed his head bandage. He lay back on his cot and was asleep in an instant.

Henry and I went across the hall to the kitchen and found Julia there instead of Molly, fiddling with the cookstove, which was spewing black smoke in her lovely face.

"Curse this plaguey thing!" she said. "I want to boil water for tea but cannot get the fire to catch."

"Have you checked the dampers?" Henry asked her.

"Oh, what do I know of dampers and such? I am hopeless in the kitchen."

"So you must be," Henry said, "if you cannot even boil water."

"Julia is an artist, not a domestic," I said, and that won me a smile from her. "Leave the stove to Molly."

"That I would gladly do, but she did not even bother to come today."

Henry took up a poker and cleared ashes from the fire in the cookstove, added more kindling, adjusted the dampers, knocked on the stovepipe, and repositioned the kettle. "That should do it," he said.

Julia thanked him and inquired about the disinterment. I told her that Trump had identified the body as that of his friend Caleb. I did not want to offend her sensibilities by imparting further details, but Henry had no such reservations.

"The corpse smelled to high heaven, as to be expected in this heat," he informed her. "The Hindoos dispose of human remains much more tidily by burning them."

Julia did not seem the least put off by such a gruesome topic of conversation. Indeed, she seemed eager to hear more.

"Cremation allows the spirit to ascend pure and fragrant from the tainted carcass to await rebirth," Henry went on to say.

"Do you really think spirits are reborn?" Julia asked him.

"Methinks the hawk that soars so loftily has earned this power by faithfully creeping on the ground as a reptile in a former state of existence," he replied, his own words soaring just as loftily. "And as far back as I can remember, I have unconsciously referred to the experiences of a previous state of existence. As the stars looked to me when I was a shepherd in Assyria, so do they look to me now in New England."

Julia lightly touched her hands to the sides of her high-boned face, a gesture I recalled her making as a young girl when an emotion or notion touched her deeply. "Perhaps I too recalled a former life," she stated in a low, hushed tone and looked at me.

"Never mind about that," I told her brusquely. "It signifies nothing."

Her color deepened. "Such a dismissive response does not delight me, Adam."

"I beg your pardon, but I find it hard to credit the possibility of Reincarnation."

Henry gave me a benevolent smile, as a kindly schoolmaster might give a limited student. "You should read *the Bhagvat Geeta*," he said.

"What is that?" Julia asked him.

"It is a Hindoo book of stupendous and cosmogonal philosophy. I bathe my intellect in it every morning after bathing my body in the pond. *The Bhagvat Geeta* explains Reincarnation as a perfectly natural state. Just as a body passes from youth to old age, the soul passes into another body at death."

I shook my head. "That is a difficult concept for us practical Yankees to accept."

"Why, my friend Waldo Emerson is a Yankee to his core, and he says we do not die, but only retire from sight and afterward return again in some new and strange disguise," Henry said. "Socrates too was confident that we live again. Surely you recall his accounts of Reincarnation from your study of Greek philosophy at Harvard, Adam. And Goethe, if you recall, was certain he had been here a thousand times before and hoped to return a thousand times more."

"I have not read Goethe," I admitted. "Nor do I remember much of the Socratic dialogues I was obligated to translate at school. Rather than philosophy, my interest has always been in the practical sciences, and I am more comfortable discussing the functions of the body than the comings and goings of the soul."

"Yet you were the one who took me back to a past life," Julia reminded me.

Henry's light eyes sparked with interest. "How did Adam accomplish such a feat, Julia?"

"Through hypnosis."

"Hypnosis?" Henry puzzled over this. "In Latin the word *hypnoticus* means inducing sleep. Did Adam give you a sleeping potion?"

"No, he merely dangled a timepiece in front of my face. And that is as much as I can tell you about the process."

Henry turned to me. "Elucidate, please."

"In truth, the journey Julia supposedly took to a past life completely mystifies me," I told him. "But I can explain the process I used to hypnotize her. I simply asked her to fix her complete attention on my watch case. This, in turn, affected the state of her cerebrospinal centers. You see, a continued fixed stare, by paralyzing nervous centers in the eyes, and destroying the equilibrium of the nervous system, produces the phenomenon of hypnosis. Or so claims Dr. Braid, who invented the name. I merely followed the instructions in his book."

"Why, it is a process similar to what the Hindoos do," Henry said.

I tried not to smile. "What *do* the Hindoos do?"

"They sit on the ground with limbs crossed," Henry replied most earnestly, "and fix their eyes steadily on a subject whilst writhing the upper body. Or so I have been told. I have never witnessed it myself."

"I assure you, Henry, that I did not sit with limbs akimbo when Adam hypnotized me," Julia said. "Nor did I writhe." She looked at me askance. "Or did I?"

"No writhing whatsoever," I assured her.

"Can anybody be hypnotized?" Henry asked me.

"If the subject won't take the process seriously, it is near impossible. Concentration of attention is absolutely necessary. Hence, idiots, babies, and the hopelessly insane cannot be hypnotized according to Dr. Braid."

"Well, I am neither insane nor a babe," Henry said. "And although I have been called an idiot by some for my convictions, I can measure a yard of cloth, count to twenty, and tell the days of the week, so I would not be considered one in the eye of the law. And as for taking the process seriously, I assure I would, Adam."

"Are you volunteering to be my next subject?"

Henry nodded most vigorously. "There is nothing I would like better than to experience a past life."

"Oh, I cannot promise to give you such an experience as that. My interest in hypnotism is limited to its use as a healing art."

"Do give it a try, Adam," Julia said. "Just tell Henry to keep going back in time as you did me and see what results."

Of course I knew she was urging me to experiment with Henry so I would be more inclined to experiment with her again, which I had no intention of doing. Even so, I could not resist taking up Henry's offer and the challenge that went with it.

Sat him down on a kitchen chair, pulled out my pocket watch, and dangled it about a foot away from his eyes. Instructed him to look steadily at it whilst keeping his mind free of all other thoughts. When I observed his pupils had dilated, I extended the first two fingers of my other hand and carried them from the watch to his eyes. Just as Dr. Braid had foretold, my subject's lids closed involuntarily, and he instantly fell into a profound sleep, his respiration slow, deep, and sibilant.

"When you hear the clap of my hands, you will awaken and recall everything you experienced whilst in this state," I told him. "Now go back to another life if you can. Take your time."

His face settled into what appeared to be an inward gaze of quietude as his mind oriented itself to this novel commission. Then he jolted in his chair as if struck a blow and appeared wide-awake but for his closed eyes, which moved back and forth with great speed beneath his lids. Of a sudden he commenced to respirate heavily and with alarming rapidity.

"I am taken by surprise," he near shouted. "Two at least pursue me through the trees screaming their war cries."

"Who and where are you?" I quietly said.

His head moved as if to look down at his arms and hands. "I am a red man and wear but a breechclout and moccasins. In my hand I bear my war ax. I race to a jumble of high boulders and bound up them to better defend myself. I whoop in the joy of battle as two enormous foes come at me."

"When in time is this happening?"

He shook his head with impatience. "War paint is smeared across their faces and chests. One has a knife with a metal blade, the other raises a club of wood with a heavy ball that ends in a sharp beak. He swings it at my head."

I tried to ask another question, but Henry raced on.

"I raise my ax, and the wooden ball of his weapon smashes against the sharp quartz edge of it. Bits of pink crystal are broken free and pierce my face. He pulls back his club to strike at me again. Before he can swing I sink my ax deep into his skull with such force that my weapon is wrenched from my hand. He tumbles down into the crevasse between the rocks, my ax still lodged in his head. I feel a searing pain in my side as I turn to take on the other warrior. His knife is dripping with blood—my blood?—and he thrusts it at my chest. I grasp his wrist and twist the knife away. Then I curl my arm around his head and snap his neck. I throw down his dead body. I am invincible!"

Henry's plain face took on an expression of arrogant superiority. Then he tilted his head.

"I hear more war cries. They are from my enemies as they slaughter and maim and scalp my tribesmen. I must go to the aid of my brothers."

Henry swayed back and forth in his chair, working his hands before him.

"But where is my ax? Oh, no! Sunk in my enemy's skull, it is gone down in the crevasse. The ax of my father and his father back in time. The jagged blaze of black stone running through the pink quartz carries great medicine. But I must leave it behind. I hear the enemy warriors rushing toward me through the trees, and I must return to my village to warn my people of their approach. I climb down the boulder. It is red with blood. I feel my side. It is wet with blood. My fingers sink deep into the open knife gash. I try to run, but my legs buckle. I fall, get up, and stumble forth toward a pond I can see through the trees. I fall again. I cannot get back up this time. As I stare at the sky I smell a sweet flower. I believe I am dying."

"Wake him up, Adam!" Julia cried.

I clapped my hands sharply and was greatly relieved when Henry opened his eyes. He struggled a moment, looking about him, shaking off the effects of the ancient reality he had just lived. Then he smiled faintly. "So that is what dying feels like."

"Poor Henry, what a dreadful experience to feel your life waning," Julia said in a quivering voice.

He shrugged off her concern. "There is no value in life except what you choose to place upon it. What mattered most to me at that time and place was having fought bravely and well."

"Do you know what time and place it was?" I asked him.

He sat silent for a moment, considering. "It was in the eastern forests of America. Perhaps right here in Massachusetts. As I was running toward the boulder I passed indigenous oaks, maples, beech, and pine. And when I stumbled toward the water I noted trillium, lady slipper, hobblebush, and Cornell plants amongst the leaves and tree roots."

I shook my head, smiling at him. "Yes, that Indian might well have been you in a former life, Henry. Who else would observe such things as that in the midst of battle?"

"But what was that sweet flower I smelled?" he said, frowning. "The scent is new to my present senses, and I do not know what genus it could have been."

I had little interest in flora at the moment and asked him a more relevant question. "Can you tell me when in history this was?"

"No date comes to mind. As an Indian I would not have known the Gregorian calendar. But one of the men I slew carried a knife with a steel or iron blade. That would have been gotten in trade or war with white men. I saw no sign of a European settlement, however, and no Indian bore a musket. I suppose then it was before Plymouth or Boston existed, but no earlier than fifty years before, for trade had begun." He shrugged. "Two hundred and fifty years ago, perhaps."

He gazed at me in some wonderment, and then his face broke into a smile wider than I'd ever seen on his serious visage.

"An Indian," he muttered in happy amazement. "A warrior at that. How I have longed to be a natural man, to be close to the edge of life, to confront existence without all our endless trappings of today! And so I have been just that, it seems. I must think deep upon it and decide if all this has been a creation of my own mind or, indeed, a recollection of a former life. How can one ever know?"

Without expecting a reply he gave me a most energetic handshake, took up his hat, bid Julia Good Day, and strode out of the house and away to his cabin by the pond.

I looked to Julia. Her fingertips were pressed against her cheeks again. Her face was flushed with excitement. "If Henry truly did go back in time, then so must have I."

"Do not be so quick to jump to that conclusion, Julia. Henry himself expressed doubt, did he not?"

"Even so, I implore you to send me back to Rome. Only this time instruct me to remember what happened, as you instructed Henry."

"I am not some sort of time engine that can transport you backwards," I told her gruffly. "Indeed, I have little or no control over this phenomenon. It might even result in derangement of the mind."

"Hah! It would take more than a swinging timepiece to derange *my* mind."

"Best we forget about it, Julia."

"No! I cannot! Oh, Adam, why are you being so obstinate about this?"

"It is you who are being pigheaded."

"Well, if I am pigheaded, then you are a swine!"

I could not help but smile. "Let us not resort to childish insults, dear cousin."

She smiled back at me. "Indeed, let us not," she said and offered her hand.

I took it and had to resist bringing it to my lips. "And let us not dispute this matter further, Julia."

"Very well," she said, but she made sure I saw the disappointment in her lovely eyes before she turned away from me and busied herself making Grandfather's tea.

If she knew my reason for not wanting to bring her back to Rome again, she would understand. Or would she resent that I withheld much of her remembrance from her?

JULIA'S NOTEBOOK

Thursday, 13 August

Molly's father came by this morning to inform me that she will not be coming to work for yet another day. He is a big, raw-boned man with a plain, honest face, and I did not beat around the bush with him.

"Do you object to your daughter being under the same roof as an Indian, Mr. Munger?"

"I got nothing against Injuns, and Molly don't neither, Miss Bell. Fact is, she was enjoying her proximity to one and the attention that got her from curious town folk. But now she has taken to her bed, and there ain't no budging her out of it."

"What ails her?"

Mr. Munger shrugged his massive shoulders. "She went out for a stroll Tuesday evening and come back looking mighty down. Took to bed, like I said, and there she remains."

"Perhaps Dr. Adam should look at her," I said.

"I suggested just that, but Mrs. Munger does not wish it," Mr. Munger said. "She reckons our Molly's indisposition is minor and will pass shortly."

Let us hope so, for I am left with a persnickety cookstove

and three men to feed. Fortunately, two are convalescents with meager appetites, and the healthy one has his Granny Tuttle and her doting ward to cook for him whensoever he wishes.

After Mr. Munger left I managed to fire up the stove and boil up a pot of coffee, along with an egg. I must say I took a modicum of pride in the achievement, but when I fetched Grandfather his breakfast all he did was complain about the hardness of his egg yolk and the grit in his coffee cup. (I confess I had forgotten to settle the coffee grounds with dried fish skin.) Usually the Old Dear is quite agreeable when he awakens, but he did not seem at all pleased to see me this morning. No matter. I was pleased enough to see him, all bright-eyed and bushy-headed. I smoothed down his unruly white hair with a silver-backed brush that belonged to Grandmother Walker and offered to read him another of Poe's grotesque tales.

"I should like to recount a story to you instead," said he.

My fond childhood memories of his vivid storytelling caused me to believe I would enjoy hearing it, and I nodded for him to go on.

"Once upon a time, long ago and far away," he began, "an able-bodied young man married a beautiful young woman."

"That sounds more like the end of a tale than the beginning of one," I said. "I suppose they lived happily ever after."

"No, they did not. For soon a child was born unto them."

"And this did not bring them joy?"

"It brought them great anguish for the babe appeared to be a monster. It had but one eye located in the midst of its face."

"Is this is a Greek legend concerning a Cyclops?"

"Alas, it is a true story, Julia, that took place in England, not Greece. Shall I continue?"

I nodded although I was not sure I wished him to.

"Above the babe's hideous orb was a tubular appendage, a small proboscis through which it could breathe with great difficulty. Within a few hours it mercifully died. The mother died shortly thereafter, and the distraught father sailed to America, where he had kin in Boston. There he began a new life with a new wife, and in 1645 he removed his family to the newly es-tablished township of Plumford. That man was your thrice-great-grandfather, Hezekiah Walker. And I have yet another story concerning our family history to tell you."

I sensed it too would be a bleak one but asked him to pro-ceed.

"This occurred during my own lifetime, when I was but ten," he said. "In 1786 a babe was delivered of my Aunt Euge-nia in this house, indeed in the very chamber you now occupy, Julia. The women of the family all gathered there to aid her, and the men awaited the blessed event in the front parlor. We could hear Eugenia's muffled screams through the ceiling for many hours, and then we suddenly heard the shrieks of the other womenfolk. The midwife came running down the stairs wailing for God to protect her and fled the house. All became silent, and the men froze in their chairs, except for Eugenia's husband, who immediately ran up to his young wife. I fol-lowed in his wake and entered the chamber without being no-ticed by the adults hovering around my sobbing aunt's bed. I went directly to the cradle, where a small form lay, shrouded by a pillowcase. I drew back the cloth and gazed upon an infant corpse that had hideous facial defects. Where the nose should have been, there was an open eye, big and blue as the sky, and above it a small trunk grew out of the forehead."

I gasped. "No! How could such a thing happen again?"

"Two Walker cousins married again, that is how. Eugenia Walker married her first cousin, just as Hezekiah Walker's first wife was his first cousin. Both unions produced babes with the same tragic birth defects. And because you are my daughter's daughter, and Adam is my son's son, I fear it could happen yet again should you two wed."

"We are not contemplating marriage, Grand-dear. So you have no reason to fear."

"Have I not? I see how Adam gazes at you. And you at him."

"Have you spoken to Adam concerning this?"

"Oh, we have discussed the dangers of close-blooded unions from a medical standpoint many times in the past. But I have not broached the subject with him since you came back to Plumford, Julia. Rather, I have chosen to speak frankly to you instead. Women have more control in love matters than men do."

"Pray do not think I wish to encourage Adam's affections!"

"I do not think you would do so intentionally. But you must be on guard, my dear. Do not forget that you and Adam are no longer children. And what was considered a rash but innocent escapade twelve years ago would be considered a shame and a scandal now."

"I assure you, Grand-dear, my cousin and I have made no plans to run off to California together again," I said and forced a smile.

We left it at that. I did not have the heart to ask further questions regarding poor Eugenia and her husband. It is enough to know that here in this very chamber, with its faded pink toile wallpaper and white dimity window-curtains, a monstrous babe was born and died sixty years ago.

JULIA'S NOTEBOOK

Friday, 14 August

What an odd assemblage our picknick party must have looked gathered 'round a checkered tablecloth beneath a big oak tree—Granny Tuttle in her linen mop cap, Trump with a red bandana wound round his head wound, Harriet in a modest poke bonnet trimmed with green ribbon, me under the wide brim of a battered straw hat borrowed from Grandfather, and the Old Dear himself sporting a shiny top hat to mark his first outing since breaking his leg.

Adam was bareheaded as he so likes to be, the breeze tousling his hair. Not only had he removed his hat, but also his frock coat and waistcoat and neck-cloth to cool off after unloading our grandfather from the wagon, along with a sizeable oak splint hamper. His sun-bleached linen shirt, homespun by Granny, has become soft and flowing from numerous washings, and should I ever convince Adam to pose for me, I would like to paint him wearing it, his strong neck emerging from the open collar. He should be painted outdoors, not in some stilted studio pose, and it is his lively expression I would most like to capture, along with the movement of fabric and hair in the breeze.

Movement! That is what I want to flow from my brush onto the canvas—the movement of energy and light. Some say the daguerreotypist will eventually replace the portrait artist, but I cannot believe it. How stiff and dull and inanimate people look in daguerreotypes. And in many a painting too, if the truth be said. But a talented artist can capture the very soul of the subject. Do I have such talent? Papa once told me that I have far more natural ability than he does. Yet he does not think I can succeed on my own, for men do not take female artists seriously. And it is men, after all, who pay the commissions for portraits of themselves and their kin. 'Tis no wonder Papa always took full credit for the work I did on his canvases. They would have far less value if it were known most of the brushstrokes were done by a mere woman. How that rankles. And how I intend to prove Papa wrong.

But back to the picknick. It was Granny Tuttle's fine notion to have one. "The old doc could use a good airing after such a long spell abed," she told Adam, "and I am all in a pucker to get a look at the redskin."

Granny and Harriet unpacked the hamper and spread out the bounty. There were two good-sized loaves of brown bread baked in Granny's beehive oven overnight, along with a pie bursting with Sheepnose apples that had just come into fruition, a ham cured in the smokehouse last fall, a plump round of Granny's aged, sage-flavored cheese, a slab of sweet butter lovingly churned, I should guess, by Harriet, a corked gallipot of fresh tarragon mustard, and a stoneware jar of fat little pickled cucumbers. All Adam's "favored vittles" of course.

Granny had also stowed deep in the vast hamper two big brown bottles of ginger beer. "Fermented with my good yeast," said she, "so it should have a real nice kick." Alas, the brew was not intended to be sampled by "the wimmen folk," for Granny considers beer a manly beverage. I did my best to hide my disappointment. But I was not to be disappointed for long. Quick as a wink Granny extracted yet another bottle. "Ladies' tonic," she called it. It turned out to be dandelion wine. I have tasted fine wines made from the grapes of Burgundy and Bordeaux, but this particular vintage made from the weeds of Tuttle Farm pleased my palate even more. Sweet dandelion wine is quite delicious when sipped in pleasant company.

Granny had sent over a wagon piled high with fresh hay to transport Grandfather, and Trump had cradled Grandfather's broken leg in his lap so it would not get too jostled during the short journey to the farm. For all his aloofness, Trump shows respect and even gentleness in regard to elders. More than once Granny remarked upon his graciousness, until he finally asked her, "Did you think I would behave like a savage, ma'am?" And leave it to Granny to reply, "Well, ain't you one?" He only smiled.

After the repast, Granny fetched a bucket from the wagon and declared that she was in dire need of huckleberries to make jam. She asked Harriet to go pick some for her. Harriet could not have been too pleased with this request, for it was obvious to me that she was taking great pleasure in our company, Adam's in particular. Nevertheless, she is a good, respectful girl and acquiesced. Granny, however, did not hand her over the bucket. She gave it to Adam instead.

"The little dear don't like going off on her own since that trouble at the sugar shack," she told him. "You go huntin' berries with her, Adam."

Harriet brightened up considerably when Adam agreed to accompany her, and off they went to do Granny's bidding. I spread a blanket in the shade for Grandfather, and he soon fell to dozing upon it. Trump pulled out a deck of cards from his waistcoat and started shuffling it. I know this deck well, for I found it in Trump's bloodied waistcoat, and along with the waistcoat, cleaned each and every bloody card with turpentine. I also restored the symbols I'd rubbed off with black and red paint. I am glad I took the trouble rather than throw the deck away, for Trump seems very attached to it. He has shuffled it endlessly since regaining his sensibilities and does not seem at ease without it.

"I don't countenance gamblin', young man," Granny told him right off.

Trump widened his deep, dark eyes. "Why, I would never gamble with ladies," he declared. "I merely wish to entertain you."

Which he proceeded to do, flummoxing us with his illusions. First, he vanished a card and made it reappear by plucking it from the air. Then he transformed card faces from king to queen to jack without seeming to so much as touch them. He also made the very card Granny was thinking upon levitate from the deck. "Trickster, trickster!" she cried, her old eyes shining like a child's. Then she begged him to do his tricks all over again. Trump complied, going through his repertoire a few more times, but I observed his lids drooping and suggested he rest himself awhile. He protested that he was not some old codger, giving snoozing Grandfather a haughty glance, but I cautioned him that he could have a setback if he tired himself out too much. Don't forget, I told him, that you have a hole in your skull big enough for a mouse to crawl through. That convinced him to go to the other side of the oak tree for privacy and take a nap.

A short time later, as Granny was packing up the hamper and I was sketching, we spied a tall, lanky figure striding up the pasture toward us. Thinking him to be Lyman Upson, who has taken to tracking me down wheresoever I go of late, I tightly gripped my pencil in annoyance. But as the figure neared I discerned that he was not Lyman at all. This man was elderly, carrying a staff, and a pack lay across his wide shoulders. The most proper reverend would never go about burthened thus, and he most certainly would not be dressed in a bell-crowned hat, an ancient blue coat with long tails, and yellow nankeen trousers.

"Why, 'tis the peddler Pilgrim," Granny said and waved to him. "Hain't seen the feller since summer last."

And I had not seen him for over a decade, but I still remembered him from the time I lived with my grandparents in town. Pilgrim would frequently stop in front of our picket fence and sing out his wares—*bowls and beads, clocks and calicoes, scissors and saltcellars, and dainty dolls for the little miss*—but Grandmother Walker would never open her door to him, much to the disappointment of that little miss peering out the front window.

Granny Tuttle, however, seemed on much friendlier terms with the peddler. She greeted him cordially when he reached us, and he, in turn, doffed his hat and bowed to her with the grace of a courtier, despite his back pack.

"Take that load offen your back and rest a spell," Granny told him. "Would you care fer some ginger beer of my own makin'?"

"No, thankee, Mistress Tuttle," said he. "I am a man of temperance."

She squinted at him skeptically. "Good fer you, Pilgrim. Care to show me yer wares?"

He unrolled his pack, and I was disappointed that he had so little to show—a few tin cups and plates, a jackknife, a ball of twine, a spool of black thread, and a scrap of lace. Where were all the wonders I'd imagined as a child? Where were the beads and clocks and saltcellars? And where, oh where were the dainty dolls I had so longed to inspect?

"Oh, my, ain't that pretty?" Granny said, taking up the limp piece of yellowed lace. "I'll sew it round the neck of your blue serge go-to-meetin' dress, Julia. Won't that look fine?"

I have no such dress. Nor could I imagine Granny Tuttle taking time in her busy day to work a needle on a piece of frippery for me, of all people. Besides, the lace was torn and soiled, and I would not have had it round my neck for all the tea in China. All this took but an instant to run through my mind before I caught on and replied, "It will look very fine indeed."

Granny gave me a rare smile of approval and turned to the peddler. "Can I trade you fer it, Pilgrim? I have no coins upon me, but I can give you half a loaf of bread, a chunk of cheese, and a nice slab of ham."

The peddler accepted the trade and no wonder. The piece of lace was near worthless, whereas such a generous amount of wholesome food must be priceless to a man who looks so malnourished. I used to think him quite handsome when he sang out his wares in front of the Walker house, but since then his countenance has become gaunt and coarse. Despite this, his profile remains rather noble, the high forehead and straight nose and square jaw arranged in pleasing proportions. I was tempted to make a swift sketch of him there and then but feared it might embarrass him.

Indeed, he looked embarrassed enough as he watched Granny wrap the food in a large napkin. He must have known as well as I did that it was charity she was giving him.

"Have you traveled a good distance today, sir?' I asked to put him at ease with some small talk.

"No farther than I did yesterday," he replied.

Granny laughed. "Pilgrim is as close-mouthed as a rock when it come to his travel circuit, Julia. He has appeared in these here parts every summer for at least a dozen years, but whence he came or whither he goes remains a great mystery. Nor has he ever mentioned his family name or birthplace."

"Why, I was born and bred a Green Mountain boy and care not who knows it," he said. "As for my birth name, I keep it to myself because I do not care to shame anyone who shares it."

"No one should be ashamed of his kith and kin," Granny said.

"And no one will have to be if the relationship remains my secret."

"Have it yer way, Pilgrim," Granny said.

"I did not wish to pry," said I.

"Oh, it isn't prying to inquire about my travel circuit, miss," the peddler told me, "for it is of no great mystery at all. My fellow trampers and I go south in the winter and return north in the summer, just like the birds do." He looked up at the sky. "As much as I expect to see that warbler hereabouts this time of year, I expect to see a familiar tramper." He looked back at Granny. "One I have not seen hide nor hair of this summer is a fellow called Roamer."

Granny gave a start. "Roamer?"

"So he's called. Earns his way by fixing clocks. Has a real way with them. Or used to anyway, before his hands got too shaky. Short, stocky fellow, with smarmed down hair and—"

"Oh, I know who Roamer was, all right," Granny interrupted. "I'm mighty sorry to be the one to tell you, Pilgrim, but he is dead."

"Ah." The peddler looked more resigned than surprised. "'Tis a rough life we vagabonds lead. Did the elements do poor Roamer in or was it devil drink?"

"He was hanged," Granny stated flatly. "For the murder of Mrs. Upson, the reverend's wife."

"No!" Pilgrim's long legs buckled under him, and he sat down hard on the ground.

"The sentence was harsh but just," Granny told him. "Roamer broke the poor lady's neck in her very parlor. Makes me shudder to think how many other wimmen who let him in to mend their clocks he could have kilt. Made the jury shudder too, I shouldn't wonder. They deliberated less than an hour, for the evidence was conclusive. The reverend himself, poor man, saw Roamer running from his house right before he found his wife dead. Are you ill, Peddler? You look pale as ashes."

"I would greatly appreciate that beer you so kindly offered me before, Mistress Tuttle."

"And you shall have it." She uncorked a brown bottle and handed it to him. He drank down the entire contents in one long guzzle as Granny looked at him with pity. "Better now, Pilgrim?"

He nodded and stood up shakily. I helped him arrange his pack on his back, and Granny handed him the bundle of food. Ever the gent, he gave her his heartfelt thanks and bid us Good Day. We watched him amble off, stumbling occasionally as he made his way back down the pasture and off through the newly mown fields.

"Drink has been that poor man's ruin," Granny said. "That and changin' times. Before Daggett opened his store, Pilgrim used to do a right good business selling his wares. And fine they were in those days." After a few clucks of her tongue and shakes of her head, Granny left off watching the peddler and beamed her sharp little eyes at me. "Well, missy," she said. "Let's talk turkey."

She took hold of my elbow and steered me a good three rods away from the two sleeping men under the oak tree. Turkey talk apparently required the utmost privacy. I stared out at the apple orchard and waited for her to begin. Granny Tuttle and I were never on easy chitchat terms. She did not like me much from the beginning of our acquaintance because of my city-bred ways and sharp tongue. She liked me less and less the more time Adam spent in town with me and away from Tuttle Farm. And when we ran away together she blamed me for it, as I suppose she should have.

"I know you come back here to help out the old doc, and that's to your credit," she finally said. "But how soon do you plan on leaving?" Her tone implied the sooner the better.

"When Grandfather is well enough to do without my assistance, I shall return to New York."

Granny regarded me with that squint of hers. "How do you manage there on your own?"

"At present I board with a respectable family and earn my keep by instructing young ladies to draw. But I have greater ambitions."

"Well, sure as a gun you can't pursue 'em in this little town. No, Plumford ain't the place fer the likes of you, Julia Bell. Best you go off and live your life elsewhere. You and Adam are better off apart."

"Our grandfather has already convinced me of that," I told her. "And I do not care to hear again the tragic tales regarding Walker cousins who marry. So if that was what you were intending to recount to me, ma'am, you may save your breath to cool your porridge."

"Do not be so pert with me, missy," she said. "I had no sich intention as that. The Walkers' dire family history ain't none of my business. But my grandson's happiness is. And I know for a certainty that Adam would be most happy settled right here on the farm where he belongs. Tuttles have always been farmers. They cleared this land over two hundred years ago."

"But Adam has Walker blood too," I said. "He has inherited his Grandfather Walker's doctoring skills, has he not?"

"He is a Tuttle through and through!" Granny stubbornly insisted. "But I got nothin' against his being a doctor. Why, I would sign over the land to him right off if he decided to keep on doctorin' in Plumford instead of Boston. He could manage both the farm and his practice if he has the right helpmate."

I ventured a guess as to whom she had in mind. "Would that be Harriet?"

Granny's face softened. "She is as dear to me as Adam is. And like the Bible says, I have trained her up in the way she should go. Unlike you, Julia, she would be content to be a wife and mother and wish for nothing more. She has no fancy no-tions sich as you do." A smile suddenly tilted up her thin lips as she looked over my shoulder.

I turned and saw Adam and Harriet approaching, each grasping the handle of the bucket between them. I imagined instead that they were grasping the hands of a child. A perfect, healthy child.

ADAM'S JOURNAL

Friday, August 14th

W hat has just transpired between Julia and myself leaves me most unsettled. Perhaps I should not have sought her out so late in the evening, but I missed her company. After we returned from Tuttle Farm this afternoon, she retired to her chamber and did not even come down for supper. I suppose this was understandable, considering the mountain of edibles Gran had supplied for our picknick, but neither did she sit with me in the parlor after tucking in the old doc. So when I heard her moving about her makeshift studio, I went there and told her I was at her disposal if she still wished to make a plaster cast of my undeserving countenance. Much to my surprise, she put me off, which rather irked me. Had she not requested to make a life-mask of me more than once? I confess I became rather insistent, informing her that it was now or perhaps never. In truth, I craved her attention, which she has withdrawn from me of late.

She finally relented, sat me down in a straight-backed chair, and went about her preparations, stirring a large bowl of plaster mixture until she thought it a perfect consistency to form a mold. She added bluing to it, and, when I asked why, she explained that coloring the mold plaster would distinguish it from the white plaster she would later pour into it to form the cast, thus enabling her to see one from the other when the time came to chisel the two apart. She said very little after that. She seemed preoccupied, hardly responding to my attempts at conversation, but I did not mind. I am that way myself when caught up in the preparations of my profession.

She asked me to remove my coat and vest and spread open my collar. She then draped an apron over me. When she tied the back strings her fingers brushed again my bared neck and a shudder ran down my spine. "Gran would say a rabbit just ran over my grave," I said with a laugh.

She did not laugh with me. Instead, she silently raked her fingernails through my hair like a comb, pushing it back from my forehead and making my scalp tingle. She proceeded to spread a soapy paste along my hairline.

"Good thing I do not sport a mustache," said I.

She made no response. I am not accustomed to her being so reserved with me and did not like it. Still, I found the manner in which she rubbed a thin layer of linseed oil over the surface of my face most pleasing. Her touch seemed quite affectionate, and she gazed down into my eyes so steadily and for so long that she seemed about to speak something of serious import. All she told me, however, was to breathe shallowly when she applied the plaster so as not to draw it up too far into my nostrils. She then directed me to shut my eyes and keep them shut, along with my mouth, and cease facial movement altogether.

I complied, and she began to apply the plaster with a blunt palette knife from the hairline downward, lightly coating even the outer area of my ears but taking care not to fill the auditory canals. After telling me it would take about ten minutes for the plaster to set, she fell silent again. Without the sound of her voice or her touch I suddenly felt rudderless in the stifling, all-encompassing darkness. I flexed my fingers, signaling her to take hold of my hand.

She did so, and I was content for a few moments. But soon I grew restive. I often admonish my patients to remain immobile during certain medical procedures, but I now understand how difficult that can be. I began shifting my legs about, and one of them brushed against hers. She moved slightly so that our lower limbs were no longer in contact.

"Pray still yourself, Adam," she said softly.

But I could not. I fidgeted with the restlessness of a colt until she began to stroke my hand. That quieted me. Indeed, it produced within me the blissful sensation that she and I were floating in eternity, free from all the cares in this world. Free of all its inhibitions too. Impulsively I grabbed her by the waist with my free hand and pulled her into my lap. She did not try to right herself. Perhaps she feared any sort of struggle might cause me to breathe so deeply I would inhale the plaster. For whatever reason, she stayed seated upon my knee, light and still as a fawn, as the minutes ticked by and my heart pounded in my eardrums. I longed to be free of my inhibiting mask and was at the point of ripping it off when, to my great relief, she gently tugged it away from my face.

When I opened my eyes I was so overcome by the sight of her dear face that I cupped it in my hands and pressed my lips to hers. I shall never forget how thrilling it was to kiss her on the mouth. Even more exciting was that she returned my kiss full measure. Yet as extraordinary and new as the sensation was, it was also remarkably familiar. How long our mouths and bodies melded I know not, but before my arousal made me forget prudence altogether, she drew away from me. I released her, and she rose to her feet. She stared down at me, her eyes wide and the pupils dilated. I must have looked quite a comical sight, my face mottled with bits of blue plaster and slick with oil, but she did not so much as smile. Instead, she began to weep.

Dismayed by her sudden melancholy, I stood up so quickly the chair fell over. I tried to take her back in my arms to comfort her, but she vehemently turned away from me, clutching the crushed mask to her breast.

"We have ruined it!" she said.

"I will gladly sit through the process again," I offered in a soothing tone, "and you can make another mask of me."

"I am not crying over the ruined mask, but over our ruined friendship, Adam. We can never trust ourselves to be alone together again."

And with that she left the room. I did not follow, for I did not know how to proceed with her. I still do not know. Just recalling her ardent response to my kiss makes me long to repeat the experience. Yet I know we should not indulge in such passion. No good can come of it.

JULIA'S NOTEBOOK

Saturday, 15 August

I have only myself to fault for what occurred last evening. Is it not always the woman's fault when passion overcomes prudence? Men are expected to have an ardent, impetuous nature, thus Adam was only acting in accordance with his sex. But what excuse have I? If I had immediately pulled away from him, we might have made light of his lapse in good judgment and carried forth from there. Instead, I lingered in his warm embrace, aroused by sensations far too pleasing to resist. I cannot allow such dangerous intimacy between us again! Indeed, I shall do my best to avoid being alone with Adam henceforward.

So far this forenoon I have managed to steer clear of him. I did get a brief glimpse of him, however, as he drove past me in the gig, presumably off to see a patient. He was accompanied by a stranger on horseback. And I, at the time, was accompanied by Mr. Upson. If Adam saw us walking on the Green path, he gave no sign of it.

Wherever I go in the village it seems Mr. Upson goes too. This morn he came upon me just as I was leaving Daggett's store and insisted on carrying my basket of provisions home for me. Apparently he has forgiven me for not attending his sermon Sunday last. When we stopped at the front gate he even offered to give me the latest religious tract he has written.

"I do not have a copy of it on my person," he said, "but I would be most happy to come by and read it aloud to you some evening, Miss Bell. It concerns the Doctrine of Total Depravity."

My heart sank. 'Twas the last thing I wanted to hear about. And I thought it best to be frank with him. "I would be a very poor audience, Mr. Upson," I told him, "for I do not hold to the doctrine that we are all born depraved. It simply does not ring true in my heart."

"The heart of a woman often misleads her," he responded. "Do not forget that it was a woman who caused the fall of mankind into sin."

"Ah, yes, let us blame poor Eve for every wicked deed done on earth, past, present, and future." I smiled and reached for my basket.

He kept fast hold of it. "Original Sin is nothing to smile about, Miss Bell. Because of the transgression Eve instigated in the Garden of Eden, most humans are damned to the eternal torments of hell. Only a select few have been foreordained to heaven instead. God decided who was to be saved long ago. Eons before we were born."

"But surely God takes our behavior here on earth into consideration."

"It matters not what deeds, good or bad, any of us do in this earthly realm, my dear. We are either God's chosen or we are not. And those He has chosen are His instruments, part of His unchangeable plan."

"What about our own free will?"

"For women, free will is nothing more than willfulness."

"You do not think very highly of my sex, do you, Mr. Upson?"

"On the contrary, dear Miss Bell. To earn my highest regard a woman need only possess the four cardinal virtues. Do you know what they are?"

"Well, I should think loving-kindness is the most essential one. And then intelligence. Along with integrity and good humor. Those are four virtues that have *my* highest regard in either sex."

Mr. Upson shook his head. "The cardinal virtues of true womanhood are piety, purity, submissiveness, and domesticity. Were you not taught that in school?"

I shrugged. "If so, it apparently did not make a great impression upon me."

"Perhaps you just need a better instructor." Mr. Upson gave me a rare smile.

"My days of such schooling are well behind me," I told him and made another attempt to retrieve my basket.

But he would not let go of it or the point he was trying to make. "You are still young enough to be properly trained to take on wifely duties, my dear."

"I'd sooner be trained to jump through hoops."

His smile vanished. "Such a pert remark as that is an insult to Womanhood," he admonished me.

"As a woman I do not think it is. But I do not wish to argue further with you." I was eager to go inside and read the letter from Papa that Mr. Daggett, in his role as town postmaster, had delivered into my hands at the store. It had been forwarded to Plumford from my New York address.

"Nor do I wish to argue with *you* of all people!" Mr. Upson proclaimed most fervently. "Indeed, I was hoping to find a degree of solace in your company, Miss Bell. I have been most distressed."

I gave him a closer look. There were deep shadows beneath his light gray eyes, and his fair complexion looked waxen. "What troubles you? Are you ill?"

"I pray that I am not!"

"It does not appear that you have been sleeping well, Mr. Upson."

"No, I did not sleep well at all last night. My mind was seized by thoughts of my departed wife."

I ventured to guess why. "Is the anniversary of her death nearing?"

He nodded. I waited, but he said nothing more. Knowing not what to say myself, I plucked the last blooming rose on the vine climbing along the picket fence and tucked it in the buttonhole of his black frock coat. Small as the gesture was, he seemed comforted by it. He silently handed me back my basket, shook my hand most warmly, and departed without another word spoken between us. I own that I was relieved to see him go. Yet I do so want to be kind to him. It is unkindness that is our greatest sin, I believe, and I know I am as guilty of it as anyone else. How I would like to reach a stage in my life where I am *always* loving and kind to everyone. But I fear I would have to live my life over and over again to reach such perfection.

At any rate, on to Papa's letter. He claims he has sorely missed me and begs me to return. Apparently he has been unable to find an assistant who can stretch and prime canvases, grind pigment, temper colors, or make pastel chalks as well as his drudge of a daughter. And I surmise he has fallen behind in his work again and needs me to complete a good number of his portrait commissions. Well, gone are the days when I felt honored to forge his brushstrokes. I want to sign my work with my own name. Yet I do feel a certain obligation toward him. Although he may not have been the best of fathers, when he finally took an interest in me he was the best of teachers. I have him to thank for my painting techniques and even for my innate talent, which he insists I inherited from him alone. He reminded me of all this in his letter.

Perhaps it would be best for me to go back to Paris. I cannot very well stay in Plumford after what occurred between Adam and me last night. Oh, how I regret it! No, that is a lie. For if I regret that kiss, why do I relive it over and over in my mind with such pleasure?

ADAM'S JOURNAL

Saturday, August 15th

Capt. Peck sent his house guest Lt. Finch to fetch more laudanum from me this morning. Concerned that Peck had already run through the quantity I had given him in less than a week, I told Finch I would deliver the drug personally. He asked if I had a drug for him as well, one that would overcome the vile effects he was feeling after consuming too much whiskey the night before. I mixed forty grains of powdered willow charcoal with syrup of rhubarb for him. If charcoal can combat poisoning from arsenic, why not from whiskey? Sure enough, Finch said he felt much better after downing my concoction.

He waited for me to hitch up the gig and rode alongside it like an official military escort, although he was dressed in mufti. The lieutenant sits a horse as admirably as an officer should, and I asked him if he had been long out of service. He told me he had resigned from active duty last month and was now looking for a suitable position in Boston. He had served under Capt. Peck several years ago and remarked that he saw a great change in him. He did not ask me what ailed his old commanding officer, but I expect he knew.

We found Peck lying on a couch in the library, much in need of pain relief. He readily admitted to me that he had been using the laudanum overmuch at night to find peace. I had mixed the opium with brandy in a proportion of eighteen drops to one grain of the drug and had warned him never to take more than one dose at a time and to take them no more often than every six hours or the result would be drowsiness or sickness. But his need had overcome his restraint, and now the bottle was empty. He was expecting a visit shortly from a business associate and needed to fortify himself before this man arrived. After obtaining a promise from him that he would better control his intake of laudanum, I administered a dose from the fresh bottle I had brought. He became more alert and sat up. When he noticed Finch at the other end of the room perusing an open folio upon a lectern, he smiled wanly and pushed himself to his feet.

"Come, Doctor," he said. "I wager you too will take a keen interest in the anatomy lessons the lieutenant is studying." He took my arm for support and led me to the lectern. Expecting to see medical illustrations, I saw instead engravings of women in compromising positions and lewd postures the like of which I have never beheld.

"The fellow who did these is Pierre LaFarge. Not only is he a master jeweler, but a master engraver too, perhaps the finest in Boston when it comes to work such as this," Peck said. "Being a Frenchman, he is not inhibited when he depicts the sensual pleasures of life." His smile slipped away, and his expression became brooding. "Sadly, such pleasures can lead to a life of misery if one is as misfortunate as I."

Lt. Finch closed the folio and looked away. He was clearly embarrassed, more by Peck's self-pitying, I think, than the explicit depictions. He murmured excuses about seeing to his horse and left the room.

Peck sank down on the couch again and heaved a great

sigh. "Both the Here and Now and the Hereafter trouble me greatly," he said. "Little wonder I cannot sleep." I cautioned him again about taking too much laudanum, and he waved away my concern. "I do not intend to shorten my life any more than I already have done by my indiscretions. Instead, I intend to make the remainder of my days on earth as comfortable as I can. But that will take a good deal of money, and I must therefore continue my business ventures despite my weak condition."

"Do not strain yourself," I advised. "It would be better for you to rest than to work."

"There is no rest for the wicked," he countered. "The Book of Isaiah states that more than once. I know because I was raised up on the Bible. If only I had taken its lessons to heart, I would not be so fearful of where I will end up after death. Oh, I have sinned mightily." He shook his head, and the lock of white hair that streaked through the black fell across his forehead. "I am not so much troubled by deeds I have done against heathens and such, as by those done against my fellow white Christians. I have followed your counsel and informed them of my sickness, doctor. Two of them, anyway. One more to go. It is not an easy thing to do. Nor have I been thanked for my honesty."

I would not suppose he had been. No woman could be pleased to hear her lover has syphilis. "You are doing the right thing," I assured him.

His wan smile returned. "Perchance the Devil will not roast me after all." He tilted his head to the sound of a wagon rattling up his drive. "Ah, I believe my business partner has arrived. Let us go greet him."

Using my arm for support again, he slowly made his way out to the front porch. The open wagon that serves as Plumford's stagecoach awaited, carrying not one but two passengers. Neither looked too pleased to have been transported from the

Concord railroad station by such a humble conveyance. The stage driver scrambled down from his perch and lifted out the female passenger, who appeared to be light as a butterfly. She was dressed much like one too, in colorful flounces and frills.

"Why, if it isn't Mrs. Vail," Peck said, releasing my arm and pulling back his shoulders. He made his way down the front stairs with such a spring in his step that onlookers would have thought I had revived him with a magical potion. The credit goes not to the laudanum, however, but to the pretty little lady with the pinched-in waist and bee-stung lips. Peck, reverting to the charming ways he is reputed to have with the female sex, took up her hand, clothed in a lacey black mitt, and kissed it. "What a delightful surprise, my dear lady. I had expected your husband to come alone."

"My wife insisted upon accompanying me," Mr. Vail said, clumsily climbing out of the wagon without aid from the driver, who was now devoting his attention to unloading their baggage. Vail is not much taller than his wife and homely as a stone fence. "Isn't that right, Lucy?"

The lady did not reply. Perhaps she had not even heard her husband, so intent was she on marking Capt. Peck's altered looks.

If Peck noticed her astonishment, he did not let on. "Well, it is mighty good to see you at any rate, Mrs. Vail. What a captivating pink bonnet you are wearing. You look as pretty as a picture in it."

The captain's so-called silver tongue did not much impress me, for even I could have come up with a compliment less trite than that. Still, Mrs. Vail blushed the very color of her bonnet, so it must have pleased her. "I wore it special," she murmured. "And here, I brought you this." She handed him a slender volume. "A book of verse."

The only volume I had observed in Peck's study was the

folio of obscene illustrations, and I doubt he had much interest in poetry. But he thanked her with as much enthusiasm as he could muster.

The stagecoach rattled off, Lt. Finch returned from the barn, and introductions were made all around. It is interesting to note that Peck introduced me as Mister rather than Doctor Walker. I reckon he does not want his business associate to know that he is ill. Nevertheless, his condition is hard to hide and will only become harder.

Mr. Vail again told his host that his wife had been adamant about coming to Plumford with him, even though he warned her it might be a dull time for her.

"I guess your lady cannot bear to be apart from you, Edwin," Peck drawled. "And I am sure I can come up with some sort of entertainment to amuse her." He gave Mrs. Vail a sly, sidelong look, and she got all pink again. He turned to me. "Or maybe my old friend Adam here can suggest something."

So now I was Peck's old friend. Pretty soon he would be calling me brother. "The only amusement I can suggest for this evening is a ball game on the Green," I replied.

"As I recall, the last game ended in fisticuffs," Peck said. "Such sport might be too rough for Mrs. Vail."

"Oh, I do not mind a bit of rough play," she murmured.

"I would very much like to watch a rousing ball game this evening," Lt. Finch said. "Better yet, I would like to take part in one. I have been playing town ball on the Boston Common of late and know my way around the stakes pretty good, if I do say so."

"Why, I have often played there myself," I said. "I wonder that we have not met till now, Lieutenant."

"When I say of late I mean since I came to Boston two weeks ago."

"That explains it. I have been staying here in Plumford for

near a month," I said, "playing in games on the Green whenever I can."

"And winning them," Peck said. "Adam's team is always
the crowd favorite."

"Are you in need of another player tonight?" Finch asked
me.

"All twelve are set," I said with regret, for I would have
liked a man as fit as him on my side.

"Perhaps you could replace Sergeant Badger on the opposing team," Peck suggested to Finch. "He left town yesterday,
and it is not likely he will be back tonight."

"Where did Badger go?" Mr. Vail asked sharply.

Peck shrugged. "Off somewhere to douse his rage with
liquor, no doubt."

"Ah, so you gave him the boot at long last," Vail said.

"No, I could never do that. It was hard enough for me to
tell Rufus that certain of his duties will be curtailed. He did
not take it well and lit out in a fury. But he will return with his
tail between his legs soon enough, begging for another chance.
He always does."

"But surely you cannot ever again trust him to—"

Peck raised his hand to still Vail. "We will talk about this
later." He smiled at Finch. "So what about it, Lieutenant?
Would you like to replace Sergeant Badger?"

"In the ball game, most certainly. As for your other proposal, I must think upon it."

"Of course," Peck said. He turned to me. "You may have
met your match in the lieutenant, Adam. He is much smarter
than Badger and won't be so easily fooled by those tricky
throws of yours."

That will suit me fine. Much prefer the challenge of flummoxing a sharp sportsman like Finch than a simple brute like
Badger and look forward to this evening's game.

Hope Julia comes out to watch. Have not seen much of her all day. Reckon she is avoiding me because of my imprudent behavior last evening. Meanwhile, she does not eschew the company of the dour Mr. Upson. Noticed them together as I drove past the Green on my way to Peck's. He was carrying her basket, trailing alongside her like a man a-wooing. Had the urge to stop the gig and go knock his hat off.

JULIA'S NOTEBOOK

Sunday, 16 August

The sun will be up soon, and Adam has not yet returned from his patient call. Trump has not returned either. Perhaps he never shall. Henry Thoreau continues to keep watch downstairs.

I have slept but little. Doubt Capt. Peck got much sleep last night either. If only he had not come by with his guests earlier in the evening, no one would be so distressed now. I was quite surprised to see Peck when I answered the knock on our front entry-door. Sweeping off his hat to reveal his fine head of black hair with that celebrated streak of white I have heard Plumford ladies describe more than once, he introduced himself to me, took my extended hand, and held it too long. He also held my gaze too long, as men of his ilk are apt to do, thinking we of the female gender find such ploys irresistible. He then introduced me to his party of three—Mr. and Mrs. Vail and Lt. Finch, the lanky man I had seen riding beside Adam's gig yesterday morn. Peck informed me that Adam had invited them all to come to town to watch him play in a ball game. This did not much sound like Adam, but how could I dispute it? I informed him in return that Adam had been called away to doctor a very ill child and would not be playing after all. Upon hearing this, Lt. Finch expressed disappointment, for he had looked forward to testing Adam's skill at the game. He then joined the other players on the Green.

Alas, Peck and his other two guests did not depart with Finch. Rather than go forth and mingle with the gathering townsfolk, they lingered in the door yard, remarking on what a good vantage point it offered to view the game. My inclination was to shoo them off so that I could get back to my painting, but if they were friends of Adam's I did not want to be rude to them. Putting on my best social smile, I proposed bringing out chairs so they could watch in comfort, and they accepted with such enthusiasm that I began to wonder if they might be expecting refreshments along with seats. I had little inclination to fire up the blasted cookstove on such a warm evening in order to boil water for tea and was much relieved when Capt. Peck suggested that he and Mr. Vail go to the Sun Tavern and fetch beer for the gents and Switchel for the ladies. Mrs. Vail inquired what Switchel was, and when Peck described it as a country concoction made with water, molasses, and a dash of vinegar and ginger, she wrinkled her snub nose. He informed her, with a wink, that rum could also be added if so desired, and this seemed to change her bad opinion of the drink. He promised to return shortly, and off he and Mr. Vail went down the road.

This left me alone with Mrs. Vail, and, knowing the lady not at all, I could think of nothing to discuss beyond the state of the weather, which we both agreed was fine. She kept fidgeting with her garments, as though to call my attention to them. I made no comment when she fingered her lace collar, smoothed her skirt flounces, and rearranged the paisley shawl around her narrow shoulders, but when she took such elaborate care to retie the wide silk ribbon of her bonnet beneath her weak, dimpled chin, I finally gave in and obliged her with a compliment.

"That is a very tasty bonnet, Mrs. Vail. I have not seen one as elegant since I left Paris."

"I dare say you did not see one so fine as mine even there," she replied haughtily. "A dear friend had it made for me by one of the finest milliners in Boston, as good or better, I am sure, as any in Paris."

I saw no reason to argue the point, for hers truly was a handsome bonnet, of the most voluptuous shade of pink, lined with lace frills and trimmed with a marabou plume. Indeed, it had much more character than the insipid face set in it.

Mrs. Vail gave me a careful once-over, as if searching for some article upon my person to compliment in return. Apparently she did not find it, for she remained silent. No wonder at that. I had answered the door in my paint-spattered pinafore, which must have been very off-putting to the fashionable Mrs. Vail. I told her I would bring out some chairs. She nodded but did not offer to help me. I had not expected her to.

When I went into the kitchen for the chairs I found the two recovering invalids at the table playing cards. Trump has taught Grandfather a game called poca, or something like that, and despite the old doc's long-standing aversion to any form of gambling, he is enthralled with this game. He watches Trump shuffle and deal out the cards like a cat trying to catch a fast mouse. Nevertheless, Trump has won a great many buttons and brass pins from him, for that is all they wager. At least I hope that is all they wager. For aught I know, Trump now owns the deed to this house.

I told them about our unexpected guests and suggested they come out and watch the ball game too. Trump mumbled something about having no interest in such sport, but Grandfather thought it a splendid idea. He prevailed upon Trump to assist him out to the door yard. He has been prevailing upon Trump a good deal of late, for although he is no longer bedridden, he cannot manage walking on his own. And Trump, getting stronger himself with each passing day, appears to enjoy helping the old doc get around. Or at least he does not seem to mind it much, God bless him.

Yes, I pray God blesses Trump! And protects him, wherever he is. And keeps him from doing something rash. His behavior last evening makes me fear that he will.

At first he was reluctant to join us outdoors, for he did not want to bother putting on his boots. Knowing how little he likes wearing them, I told him that it was entirely unnecessary. In the end he kindly offered to take out all the chairs for me, enough to accommodate seven people in all, for Lyman Upson and Henry Thoreau came by too. Mr. Upson took a seat beside me, and Henry went to stand in the doorway with Trump. Capt. Peck and Mr. Vail had not yet returned from the tavern, and Mrs. Vail seemed very put out about that. She paid no attention whatsoever to Grandfather, who gave up his endeavor to engage her in polite conversation.

The ball game commenced with Lt. Finch at bat—put to the test right off by Adam's teammates. He proved himself to be a fair striker, but after hitting the ball a good distance he got confused as to where the stakes were located. To confuse him even more, townsmen began pointing in different directions. Rather than take offence, the lieutenant continued to make himself the object of jest by running around in circles. Everyone laughed at his antics. Even Trump managed a smile. Henry asked him if the Cherokees took part in ball games.

"The men played a game called Anesta," he replied, more forthcoming than usual. "They were plenty earnest about it and got plenty hurt sometimes. My father was one of the best players in our Nation when he was young. He would never brag on himself about it, but Ma would. She'd tell me and my sister that when our Pa caught the ball in the cup of his stick, he would swoop across the field like a hawk, and no one could catch him. And Pa would say that she had managed to catch him easy enough, hadn't she? That would always make her laugh."

This was the first time Trump had ever spoken of his family, and I would have enjoyed hearing more about them. But Henry, intent on collecting more information about Cherokee customs, took out the notebook and pencil he always carried in his deep pocket, and began quizzing Trump on the particulars of Anesta.

"What was the ball made of?" he asked. "How long was the field?"

Trump was through reminiscing, however. "What does it matter? All that is past." He turned away and went inside the house.

I offered Henry a commiserating smile as he put his notebook back in his pocket. Despite his abiding interest in Indian customs and beliefs, he never gets much information out of Trump when he visits.

Peck and Vail returned, accompanied by a tavern boy who pushed a wheelbarrow filled with various vessels and glasses through the front gate. Grandfather gladly accepted a mug of beer, and Mrs. Vail had her Switchel with a good dose of rum in it. I thought best to have mine without any, as did Henry. Mr. Upson accepted no refreshment whatsoever and stared at Capt. Peck with such disapproval I feared a quarrel might ensue. But Peck did not meet his eyes. Neither spoke to the other all evening. I am sure they have little in common.

"High time you returned," Mrs. Vail chided Peck. She did not even glance at her husband.

Peck smiled at her. "Did you miss me?"

The insinuating manner in which he asked her this made me regard the two of them more closely. Could Peck be the

"dear friend" Mrs. Vail told me had commissioned her osten-
tatious bonnet?

Mrs. Vail did not answer his question but continued to
scold him. "Whilst you were no doubt enjoying yourself at the
tavern bar, I had a most unsettling encounter with a savage."

"Are you referring to me, ma'am?" Henry said, his tone
facetious.

"You know full well, sir, that I am referring to that red-
skinned, bare-footed fellow with his head wrapped in a bandana. I was much relieved when he went back inside for I
found his presence most disturbing."

Capt. Peck put on a face of concern. "I am sorry if you
were affrighted, my dear," he told Mrs. Vail. "I presumed the
Indian you refer to had departed from Dr. Walker's house by
now." He turned to me. "Do you not fear being under the
same roof with him, Miss Bell?"

"Certainly not, Captain. I have no reason to mind his
company."

"Do you not?" Peck eyed me slyly. "I never thought a
proper lady would welcome the company of an Indian night
after night."

This got Grandfather's attention. "What are you implying,
sir? My granddaughter is far more a lady than that one could
ever be." He gestured toward Mrs. Vail with his empty mug. I
believe the beer it once contained had gone straight to his
head.

"Now, now, Grand-dear," said I. "Let us not disparage Mrs.
Vail just because Captain Peck has disparaged me."

"That was hardly my intention, Miss Bell," Peck protested.
"I was merely registering my surprise that you could be so
trusting. Your trust, however, is most dangerously misplaced in
that redskin."

"So now you cast aspersions on a man you do not even
know," I retorted.

"I know the ways of Indians. I became very familiar with them when I was a cavalry officer posted in the south. Seminoles, Comanche, Cherokees, they are all of the same inferior race."

I looked away from Peck in disgust and noticed that Trump had come back outside. As he stood in the open doorway, listening intently to our conversation, he appeared transformed to me. The self-possessed, handsome face I had been sketching all week was contorted and ugly, and his dark eyes blazed.

"Speak no more of this," I told Peck in a low tone.

Unaware of Trump's presence behind him, he ignored my directive and went on in a commanding tone. "I *will* speak, Miss Bell, and I hope you will listen for your own good. All Indians have ungovernable appetites and treacherous natures. And they are cruel and revengeful. They are trained since boyhood to use the tomahawk and scalping knife and use them they do, without conscience or reason."

"Without reason?" Henry said. He too was unaware of Trump, his attention captured by Peck's bigoted pronouncements. "Their homelands continue to be stolen by us, they continue to die from our diseases, and all the promises made to them continue to be broken. White men kill for far less reason than that, Captain Peck."

Trump spoke out at last. "*That* white man killed for gold," he said, pointing a trembling finger at Peck. The captain whirled around, and Trump locked eyes with him. "I recognized your fiendish voice even before I saw your devil face. Both have haunted me for years."

Peck forced out a laugh. "This redskin must be drunk. When they get liquored up they hear spirits and see ghosts."

"You are the one who sees a ghost," Trump told him. "I have come back from the grave to kill you." He leapt from the doorstep and was upon Peck in an instant, his hands gripping the captain's neck.

Henry immediately intervened, grabbing Trump by the shoulders. But Trump, in a towering frenzy, seemed to have the strength of ten men, and Henry could not pull him away from Peck. Mr. Vail did not come forward to help. Nor did Mr. Upson. I suppose, as a minister, he was reluctant to use physical force against another. As a woman, so am I, but I did so anyway. I grabbed hold of Trump's left arm and Henry tugged at the other, and Trump suddenly let go his grip of Peck's neck. I do not think he was even aware of Henry or me pulling at him, however. It seemed as though he had simply changed his mind about killing Peck there and then.

We released our hold on him and he stood back, breathing hard. His expression was livid, and his entire body radiated hate as he stared at Peck. "I won't defile the home of my friends by killing you here. I will find a more suitable time and place to do it. Yours should be a slow, miserable death. And right after you die I will scalp you. Your vile spirit must perish along with your body."

Without another word, Trump walked out the front gate and through a knot of spectators who had turned their attention from the ball game to the drama in our front yard. Neither Henry nor I went after Trump, for we both felt it best to give him time alone to calm himself. We watched him disappear in the twilight as he strode past the Green and took a path that led to the river.

Peck, hand at throat, crumpled in the nearest chair. Mr. Vail suggested sending for the constable. But there was no need to do that, for Mr. Beers was standing right there on the opposite side of the picket fence along with the rest of the gawkers.

"Want I should go after him?" he asked Peck in a reluctant tone.

"No," Peck said hoarsely. "A crazed redskin is not worth

the trouble." He glared at me. "Did I not warn you about him, Miss Bell? Take care to lock your doors tonight."

I am sure Peck locked his when he went home with his guests. They and Mr. Upson, looking appalled by what had transpired, all took their leave straightaway, but Henry insisted on staying with Grandfather and me till Adam returns. I am grateful for that. It is not likely that Trump will do any of us harm should he come back to the house, yet his countenance was so fierce when he looked at Peck that I believe he is capable of almost anything.

ADAM'S JOURNAL

Sunday, August 16th

Firstly, the good news. The Fenns' two-year-old daughter Abby survived her long ordeal. This alone, of all the day's events, gives me comfort. And I hope my presence gave Abby's poor mother comfort throughout the long night. We took turns bathing the child in cool water to lower her raging fever, stroking her arms and legs to try and calm her intestinal convulsions. As the hours passed, I began to fear that her life would ebb away from sheer exhaustion. Willed myself to stay calm and composed for the mother's sake. She was hanging on my every word and expression, watching my countenance for signs of new hope or final despair. At last Abby's fever gradually eased, and she was relieved of her torment. We dried her off and put her back to bed and when she opened her eyes she looked at us both as if wondering what all the fuss was about and whispered for her doll. Mrs. Fenn collapsed in relief and sobbed in my arms. I nearly shed tears myself.

I left the Fenn farm in darkness and awoke to see the sun's first rays hitting the Meetinghouse tower. I had slept most of the way home, leaving it to Napoleon to get the gig back to town. As we came to a stop in front of the house, Henry came out and bid me good morning. I nodded back, not especially pleased to see him so early. Indeed, the only person I would have been pleased to see at that moment was Julia.

"You look mighty weary, Adam," he said. "Let me see to your horse."

"You look none too chipper yourself," I replied rather gruffly, despite his kind offer. "What brings you here at the crack of dawn, Henry?"

"I spent the night here."

Upon hearing this I felt a spurt of jealousy, immediately replaced by a rush of anxiety. "Is Julia all right?"

"Yes, and so is your grandfather. But we do not know how Trump is faring."

Before I could ask another question Julia came rushing out of the house. She looked so wan and troubled that I leapt from the gig and took her into my arms. "Pray what is wrong, dear?"

She pulled away, and we both glanced at Henry. He was studying the sky rather than us. "The kestrels are beginning to migrate," he said mildly.

And then he and Julia told me all that had transpired whilst I was away. Early last evening Peck and his guests came to watch the ball game from our door yard. When Trump espied the captain he became so enraged he tried to throttle him. His reasons for doing so remain unclear, for he did not stay around to explain himself. Concerned that he might come back to the house even more distraught than when he left, Henry did not want to leave Julia and Grandfather alone to face him and spent the night keeping watch by the front window. After thanking him I suggested we go search for Trump. I feared he might have done himself harm by wandering all night with an open head wound.

Before we could go looking for Trump, however, Constable Beers hurried toward us as fast as his excessive poundage would allow. Crossing the Green had made him so breathless I could barely understand him, but I managed to comprehend that my presence was required at Capt. Peck's immediately.

My first thought was that he had overdosed on the laudanum I had given him. "What state is Peck in?" I asked Beers.

"A most dire one," he gasped and looked askance at Julia. "Don't want to say more in front of the young lady."

"Best you go inside, Julia," I said.

Of course she did not budge. "If I faint you will not be held responsible, Mr. Beers," she assured him. "Please continue."

"Very well. Captain Peck has been murdered."

Beers then went on to relate, between pants and much mopping of the brow, how he'd been rousted out of bed by Lt. Finch, who had ridden into town to alert him of the murder. The constable then awakened Justice Phyfe, who ordered him to bring me to examine the body whilst he and Mr. Daggett collected enough men for a Coroner's Jury. Beers asked if he could ride to Peck's in my gig, for his weight made mounting a horse a trial, and I agreed on the condition that Henry could also come along. At first Henry was reluctant to do so, but when I expressed my great respect for his observational skills, he agreed. Julia beseeched us to take care, her eyes upon me alone.

Thanks to the constable's considerable bulk, we proved to be a tight threesome in the gig, and no doubt a heavy one for Napoleon to pull the short distance to Peck's house. When we reached the drive I spotted Finch beckoning to us from the far corner of the field, so we headed there instead of the house. Finch disappeared behind a stand of trees, and I recalled that was where Peck's belvedere was located. We found Finch standing at attention in front of it.

"I found him just as he lies inside," he informed us. "When I came by here on a morning ride, my horse shied, no doubt from the smell of blood. I could smell it too and dismounted to investigate. What confronted me was not a pretty sight." He did not appear over disturbed, but then he must have seen his share of bloodshed in service.

We started up the steps. Henry cautioned that we should be careful where we stepped or what we touched, but Beers disregarded him and with the authority of his office plowed ahead. What he saw caused him to immediately turn back. He did not quite make the rail before he heaved up the contents of his stomach.

Even more pungent than the smell of fresh vomit, a sweet, putrid scent drenched the close summer air. I stepped inside and saw a man's body on the white wooden floor, face up. It seemed to be floating in a pool of thick black fluid

"Tracks there, be careful," Henry cautioned, and I saw footsteps in blood about the body and leading past us to the steps.

"A number of those are mine," Finch said from behind us. "I confess I was incautious. When I saw the captain lying there, I rushed to his side, believing I might be able to assist him. But he was well past help as you see, Doctor."

What I saw shocked me. Not only did the victim have multiple wounds to the chest. He had been brutally scalped besides. The facial features were so caked in blood and so contorted in an expression of agony and fear that I had to look closely to be sure it was really Peck. His distinctive head of thick black hair with its bold white stripe was gone entirely, and only a sad rim of matted curls above the ears remained. The naked cranium, covered with bits of flesh and odd pieces of clinging membrane and tissue, glistened obscenely in the early morning light. From the copious amount of blood splattered all over the face and neck, I deduced that Peck had been scalped alive, his heart pumping blood out through the myriad number of severed arteries and veins feeding the scalp tissue.

His arms were bound tight to his torso by a length of rope to prevent him from resisting, and his eyes bulged as if they had last looked upon the Devil himself. His mouth, smeared with his own blackening blood, was agape in a silent scream of torment.

"I fear we are dealing with a madman," Henry said, his voice calm and his eyes, as always, observing all. He stood a step back, carefully studying the bloody footprints about the body.

For myself, I was stunned by the savagery before me. Death in itself is an occurrence every physician must accept with equanimity or he cannot long continue in the profession, but here was a crime of such macabre sickness that it was clearly an expression of the most base and demented evil. My heart went out to Peck, who, no matter what his faults, did not deserve such an ignominious end.

I crouched down close to the body, careful not to touch the pool of blood on which had formed a thickening skin akin to that on hot gravy that has cooled. Whoever had done the scalping had gone about it with skill, cutting a precise circle about the skull. In order to see if the body had been subjected to any other injuries I asked Henry to help me carefully raise and lean Peck's upper body forward.

He did so without hesitation and pointed to the back of the coat. There we both saw the clear dirt imprint of a boot sole. "He used his right foot," Henry said, "to press down on the center of Peck's back for leverage."

Leverage for what purpose I perceived in an instant. With his foot on Peck's upper back vertebrae, the assailant had used one or both hands to rip the scalp free from the connecting tissue of the scalp.

"So Peck must have been scalped as he lay on his stomach," I said. "Why was he then turned over to lie on his back, I wonder?"

"The better for him to look upon his own head of hair waved in front of his eyes, I conjecture," Henry said. "Last night's quarter moon and bright stars offered more than enough light for the killer to perform his operation and for Peck to clearly see its grisly results."

Hearing this, Beers groaned and leaned back over the railing. Finch burst out with several soldierly expletives of disgust.

We gently lay the body back down, and I pointed to the bloody wounds that had soaked through the shirtfront and waistcoat. "After Peck had been tormented to the murderer's satisfaction, the murderer killed him with multiple thrusts through the chest and into the heart."

Beers jolted toward us on unsteady feet, looking around through the pillars of the belvedere with round, frightened eyes. "Do you think the slayer remains in the vicinity?"

"Why linger?" I said. "This deed was done some time ago." I pointed to the pool of blood. "See how the surface has congealed? And the blood and tissue on the skull are still viscous but not fresh. That clearly indicates several hours have passed since exposure to the air." I placed my hand on the neck of the corpse. "The body has not yet cooled to air temperature." I moved the jaw open and closed. "Rigor has just begun to stiffen the joints there." I stood and took out a handkerchief, wiped my hands, and checked my pocket timepiece. "I conclude he has been dead four to eight hours. It is coming on seven now. So say between midnight and three in the morning."

"Lieutenant Finch," Henry said, "when did you last see Captain Peck alive?"

"About nine o'clock last evening," Finch said. "After we came back from town, we gathered in the parlor before retiring. Peck did not appear well. Mrs. Vail left us, and we men had a glass of port together. Mr. Vail alluded to the unpleasantness with the Indian, but Peck did not wish to discuss it. He told

Vail they had more important matters to discuss concerning their business venture, and since I had no part in it, I retired to my room. I slept most soundly and arose early to take a ride in the morning cool. The rest you know."

"Please observe, constable," Henry told Beers. "There are two sets of bloody boot prints here. The lieutenant's sharp-toed riding boots"—he pointed at them for Beers's edification— "and these." He indicated the more numerous round-toed boot prints around the body and leading away to the steps of the belvedere. Henry then looked at me. "No distinguishing marks in the right sole, unlike the boot prints we observed on the cliff."

"Therefore Peck's murderer was not Caleb's murderer," I said.

Henry shrugged. "Cannot a murderer have more than one pair of boots?"

Beers sat down on the bench below the rail where I had examined Peck less than a week ago and stared up at us defiantly. "Why waste time blathering about bloody footprints? Ain't it plain as the hand in front of your face who did this? 'Twas that damn Injun. Half the town heard him threaten to kill and scalp Peck."

"There is one problem with what you say," Henry carefully stated, studying Peck's body. "Dr. Walker has concluded that Peck was scalped before he was killed, not after."

"There you go again, counting angels on a pinhead, Mr. Thoreau," the constable said. "Before or after? After or before? What difference does it make?"

"Plenty, if you are an Indian." Henry turned to Finch. "Lieutenant, are you familiar with the Native American scalping ritual?"

"I have seen more than I care to of such barbaric brutality on the frontier," Finch replied. "Not only do those savages scalp their enemies, but they keep the scalps as hideous trophies. They paint the fleshy sides red, stretch them in hoops, attach them to poles, and present them to their sweethearts like you would give your best gal a bouquet of posies. Worse yet, the females wave 'em around like ladies' fans whilst they dance."

"God help us!" Beers cried. "How can wimmen be so wanton?"

"Never mind about that," Henry said. "It is when the victim is scalped that is of primary importance. I have read that Indians believe scalping a foe before death will not affect his immortal spirit. However, if he is scalped *after* his body dies, his spirit is extinguished and can nevermore return. The entire purpose of scalping an enemy is to kill his soul."

Finch nodded. "I have heard as much from our Indian scouts."

"And I heard as much from Trump himself," Henry said. "He told Peck he deserved first a miserable death and then a scalping so that his spirit would also perish."

"So there you are!" Beers said. "The Injun said he would do it, and he did it. We are right back to where we started, despite all your fancy talk."

"But you are missing my point," Henry said, almost out of patience. "Allow me to explain it to you again."

"Do not bother," Beers said with a dismissive wave of his hand. "Such obscure knowledge as you are spouting holds no water for me, nor will it impress the jury." He stood up at the sound of horse hooves and went forth to direct Justice Phyfe's rockaway carriage, along with a buckwagon full of men, to the belvedere. The Coroner's Jury had arrived.

The jurors concluded soon enough that murder most foul had been done, and they were sure to a man who had done it. Many had been on the Green last evening and heard with their own ears Trump threaten Peck. Henry might as well have been talking in a foreign language for all the attention they gave to his theory concerning scalping and souls. Justice Phyfe summarily announced a warrant for Trump's arrest and gave authority to Beers to form a search party. Finch and most of the men on the jury immediately volunteered to take part in the search, and Phyfe volunteered his hunting dogs and guns. He also proposed sounding the cannon to muster the town militiamen, who had muskets at the ready.

"This is not a militia matter," Henry said. "Plumford is not under attack."

"It is under the attack of a wild Indian!" Phyfe shouted back at him. "He savagely killed one of our most respected citizens, and he may claim many more white victims if we do not stop him."

"Such talk as that will only stir up fear and hate," Henry cautioned him.

"Are you siding with the enemy, sir? If so, get out of my town."

Henry did not bother to argue with him further. Instead, he urged me to leave posthaste with him. "We must find Trump before the mob does," he said as we drove off in the gig. "Many men with many guns cannot bode well for him."

"I agree, but what chance do we stand to find Trump before they do?"

"We stand a very good chance," Henry assured me. "No man in the search party, I wager, is as good a tracker as I am. The hunting dogs, however, will have an advantage over me." He tapped his nose. "Large though my scent organ may be, it is not superior to theirs. Fortunately, my intelligence is."

He speculated that the search would commence at the crime site and proposed we begin ours back in town, on the path he had seen Trump take after he'd made his threat to Peck over twelve hours ago.

Cold though his trail was, we picked up on it almost immediately. It helped that the river path was soft and Trump was barefoot. He had left the house without his shoes and as far as Henry could discern, he had not been carrying a knife upon his person.

Henry led the way upriver, sometimes stopping to kneel and bend his face close to the ground to examine it better. In the distance we heard the cannon near the old Powder House go off, calling the town militiamen to service. Neither of us bothered to remark upon it, so intent were we on tracing Trump's progress. Henry found where he had veered off the path into the woods, and we followed, climbing up the steep bank along a rivulet that was shaded by thick ferns. Here we had to proceed slowly, Henry moving from a mud smear to a bent frond to a bit of moss pulled out of place by a passing foot. Then we found Trump's red head wrap hanging from a branch.

"He is going along haphazardly," Henry said, "scarcely caring where each stride will take him. For that we are most fortunate. If he wished, I am sure he could pass along with nary a trace left behind, but he does not seem concerned about being followed."

Trump had moved in a sinuous curve up the wooded hill and so did we, first along, then away from, and finally across the now scarcely visible creek. Less than an hour later we found him. He was seated on a jumble of mossy boulders and beneath him a spring that was the source of the rivulet softly bubbled out of the cleft at the rock base.

He looked up at the sound of our tread but did not move a muscle. Nor did he speak when we sat down beside him on the rocks. I observed that he was in a state of emotional and physical exhaustion.

"You do not seem surprised to see us, Trump," I said.

"I heard you coming a good while ago."

"Are you all right?" I tried to examine his head wound, but he jerked away.

"Leave me be," he said. "I want some time alone. You shouldn't have come looking for me."

"Be thankful we found you before others did," Henry said. "There is a warrant out for your arrest, and you are being hunted down."

"For what? Crumpling a white man's starched collar? I could have gone ahead and wrung Peck's neck, but I did not. I got better plans for him."

"Peck is dead," I told Trump.

His deep, dark eyes, blank a moment before, registered astonishment. "No!" he cried. "You mean he just up and died?"

"He was murdered," Henry said.

Rage replaced astonishment. "Who killed him?"

"Most people think you did," Henry said.

Trump shook his head violently and tore at his hair. "I should have when I had the chance. How was he done in?"

"First off he was scalped alive," Henry said, "and then he was stabbed to death."

Trump swore vehemently. "Damn fool killer did it ass-backwards. "

This seemed to confirm Henry's belief that if Trump had been the killer, he would have murdered his victim before scalping him. But it was more than such esoteric proof that convinced me of the young Indian's innocence. For one thing, he was not in possession of a bloody scalp. Nor was there a trace of blood on his person. And he was barefoot, yet there had been only bloody boot prints around Peck's body.

"But I am even a bigger fool," Trump continued bitterly. "Whoever killed Peck fixed the deed on me, and now I will hang for something I got no satisfaction of doing."

Henry jumped down from the rocks and began pacing the area, deep in thought. After a few minutes he beckoned to me.

So deep was Trump's dejection that he did not even notice when I left him to join Henry a couple rods away.

"Trump is right. If he is caught, he is doomed," Henry told me. "What chance does he stand of getting a fair trial with evidence and sentiment so strongly against him? The only way out for him is to escape to Canada on the Underground Railroad, and I will see to it that he does."

His scheme surprised me. "You would break the law to help Trump?"

"Of course. I have done it in the past to help runaway slaves, and I will do it again."

"I will help you," I said.

"I thought as much. We must leave here with Trump immediately. When the searchers fail to find him in the vicinity of Peck's house, they will do as we have done and trail him from town."

Even as Henry spoke there drifted up through the trees the sound of baying hounds and men shouting from downriver. Trump must have heard them as well for he jumped to his feet, leapt from the boulder, and took off uphill through the trees. He was gone from sight in a trice, and we dared not call after him for fear we would alert the searchers.

"He is weak and has little chance," I said. "If he is caught in the excitement of the chase, he might be beaten or even killed."

"Let us try to protect him," Henry said.

We ran up the incline after Trump and came out of the woods to a freshly shorn hayfield. Just ahead Trump was running across the middle of the field toward a woodlot on a higher brow of hill. If he could reach the far woods, beyond which I knew was a swamp where he could find a place to hide, he might have a chance of escape from his pursuers.

But then a horseman came charging onto the field in pursuit of Trump, riding parallel to the group of men fast ap-

proaching from below on foot. He easily caught up to Trump
and began slashing down at him with his whip. Trump dodged
and weaved, confounding both horse and rider, but then he
began to slow down. I guessed he must be near collapse.

As Henry and I ran toward them, I saw that the man on
the horse was none other than Rufus Badger. When Trump
stumbled to the ground, Badger dismounted and began striking him with his whip. Spent though Trump must have been,
he managed to stand up again and grab the end of the whip.
He nearly threw Badger over as he wrenched at it. But Badger
kept his balance and gave Trump a powerful blow to the head
that landed him hard down on his back. Badger then drew a
coffin-handle bowie knife from his boot. The broad blade
looked to be at least a foot in length, and it curved like a nasty
smile along the top edge.

"Don't stab him!" Henry cried out, running between the
two men.

"Stand away," Badger told him. "That filthy redskin murdered my captain, and now I mean to murder him."

Trump had not moved, and a glance showed me he was
unconscious. "We cannot allow you to kill a helpless man," I
said, taking my place beside Henry.

Badger regarded me with mean little eyes that had not a
flicker of humanity in them. "I will be most happy to cut you
too, Doc. Along with your friend here."

He waved his big knife in our direction, and the blade glistened in the sunlight. Henry and I stood our ground. I do not
know if Badger would have made good his threat, but before
he could, the men with the hounds reached us. Badger lowered his knife as the dogs surrounded the fallen Indian in a
frenzy of growling and snapping. Trump opened his eyes to
their teeth-baring fury but did not seem to notice them. Instead, he sat up and stared intently at Badger, then threw back
his head and let out a howl of such chilling resonance and pain

that the dogs all drew back. Badger, looking frightened, raised his weapon again.

But now the men from the search party were all upon Trump, binding him with rope enough to secure Goliath. He lay limp and passive as they did this, as though he had given up entirely. But when I looked into his eyes I saw a hot-burning spirit in them that made his black pupils glow like coals.

JULIA'S NOTEBOOK

Monday, 17 August

Trump's Hearing was held at the Meetinghouse at nine this morning. Constable Beers, dressed in his best frock coat and highest collar, walked Trump down the aisle, keeping a hard grip on his arm. There being no jail in Plumford but for Beers's storeroom, where he confines a disorderly drunkard on occasion, Trump had spent the night locked up in the abandoned Powder House. He was dirty and disheveled, his shirt torn, his hair matted, his proud face smeared with grime. His hands were bound behind him. His bare feet were shackled. The chain between the ankle irons was short, hindering his stride, and he stumbled. Only one nitwit laughed, but nearly everyone in the packed pews glared at him as he passed. But when I glanced at Granny Tuttle, who was sitting beside me, I saw compassion rather than condemnation in her eyes.

"Shame on them that's responsible," she said to me, "for not allowin' that poor young feller to wash up before comin' to court."

"More shame on Justice Phyfe for incarcerating him in the Powder House," I replied. "That is most inhumane."

A man in the pew in front of us turned around and regarded me disdainfully. "Do not criticize your betters, missy. Justice Phyfe did right to have that wild animal securely caged."

"Pray do not refer to a fellow human being as a wild animal, sir," I told him.

"No Injun is a fellow of mine!" And with that, the man turned his back to me, which I much preferred to gaze upon instead of his ignorant face.

"He don't even belong to our congregation," Granny told me in what I suppose she considered a low voice. "Lot of folks here I never seen before, or hain't seen for a month of Sundays anyways. But I reckon a murder trial is a sight more entertainin' than a sermon."

"This isn't exactly a trial, ma'am," I explained to her. "It is a Hearing to establish if there is reason to believe Trump killed Captain Peck. If Justice Phyfe decides there is, he will order him held on suspicion of murder until the State Attorney General arrives to preside over a grand jury investigation. And if the grand jury indicts him for murder, Trump will be transferred to the county jail in Concord till the Supreme Court meets there to try the case."

"Well, ain't you sharp as a meat ax, Julia." Granny gave me one of her squint-eyed appraisals. "How come you know so much?"

"Oh, I just ask a lot of questions."

"You allus did. Whenever you came to the farm you would pester me and Mr. Tuttle with questions. If I told you once, I must've told you a dozen times that curiosity kilt the cat."

"At least a dozen times, ma'am."

Granny sniffed. "Lot good it did."

We left off talking, along with everyone else, when Justice Phyfe made his grand entrance through the red-curtained side door at the front of the Meetinghouse. He was dressed in black like a minister, and I half expected him to conduct the Hearing from the pulpit. Instead, he took a seat at the table where the deacons sit during services. Each witness he called sat across from him to give his evidence.

Trump was not allowed to sit. He stood like a statue, his expression blank, as Mr. Vail, the Rev. Mr. Upson, and Henry Thoreau testified. Grandfather was excused from testifying because of his injury, and Justice Phyfe did not require Mrs. Vail or me to bear witness because of our gender. Mr. Vail attested that he and his wife had slept soundly the night of the murder and therefore heard nothing. But both he and Mr. Upson both stated they very clearly had heard Trump threaten to kill and scalp Capt. Peck earlier that evening. When Henry was called to testify, he attempted to explain why he did not think Peck's scalping had been done by an Indian, but Justice Phyfe interrupted him.

"You are not here to lecture us about arcane rituals, Mr. Thoreau," he said. "Save that for your highfalutin Transcendentalist friends back in Concord." A few of the spectators chuckled, although I doubt they even know what a Transcendentalist is.

Adam was the next to testify, and Phyfe listened to his medical opinions concerning cause and time of death, but he grew exceedingly impatient when Adam began explaining why he believed Peck had been killed after, not before, he was scalped.

"Enough hairsplitting over scalp-splitting!" Phyfe bellowed, and that got more guffaws. "You are dismissed, Dr. Walker."

Adam looked disheartened, but when he left his seat he made his way to Trump and placed his hand on Trump's shoulder. Trump did not acknowledge this gesture of camaraderie, but I am glad Adam made it anyway.

The next witness was Lt. Finch, who described coming

upon the captain's body at dawn. Then Rufus Badger's name was called. He stomped down the aisle in his heavy, scarred boots, leaving the stink of sweat and booze in his wake, yet people regarded him with admiration. He is now considered the Town Hero for capturing Trump.

He testified that he had been in Boston till the early morning hours of Sunday, imbibing at a place called Shark's Tavern, from whence he had ridden back to Plumford, arriving in town well after sunrise. "When I learned from Lieutenant Finch that Captain Peck was dead, I swallowed down my grief and went lookin' for his murderer. I weren't about to let that damn savage git away after what he done to my captain!"

"And he did not, thanks to your swift and courageous action, Sergeant," Justice Phyfe said.

Henry stood up and cried out, "Objection, sir! The prisoner has not yet been found guilty of murder." His pew neighbors told him to sit down.

Justice Phyfe gave Henry a curt nod and proceeded with his interrogation of Badger. "Did the prisoner say anything to you after you so bravely prevented his cowardly attempt to escape?"

"He said he done did it."

"What were his exact words, Sergeant?"

"He said, 'I done killed Captain Peck, and I am glad of it.' "

A hum of disapproval wafted up from the crowd. Trump shouted over it.

"It is *you* I will kill, you pig of a man! I will cut off your snout and your ears and shove them down your lying throat. I will gut you and yank out your innards. And then I will slit your throat."

Justice Phyfe slammed his fist on the table. "Take the prisoner back to the Powder House, Constable Beers. I have heard more than enough evidence to hold him on suspicion of murder."

Beers needed the help of three men to drag Trump out of the Meetinghouse, still ranting. His speech was no longer comprehensible, and I believe he had reverted to his Native tongue.

Granny Tuttle shook her head as they hauled Trump past us. "He is going to need all our prayers, Julia," she said. "And more than prayers, he is going to need a right slick lawyer to save him from the gallows."

It will be no easy matter to find a lawyer willing to represent Trump, I fear, although Adam is determined to find him the best one he can. In the meantime I will follow Granny's advice for once and pray for Trump.

ADAM'S JOURNAL

Monday, August 17th

This morning my fear was that Trump would not get a fair Hearing, and indeed he did not. This evening my fear is that he may be hanged even before he is tried.

Had not been given the opportunity to examine Trump after his rough capture, so after the Hearing I went to the Powder House to do so. How bleak his provisional prison looked as I climbed up the hill to it. Until now I had thought this town landmark quaint and picturesque for it is built in the shape of a bee skep and capped with a pleasing domed roof. Its construction is not of wicker, however, but of solid brick, and the walls are a foot thick and windowless. It dates back to the French and Indian War and was last used to store ammunition during the War of 1812, so it is hardly fit for human habitation. To keep Trump imprisoned in such dank, dark quarters is already subjecting him to cruel and unusual punishment.

Four young men from the town militia, awkwardly holding muskets passed down to them by their fathers and grandfathers, stood guard in front of the Powder House. I demanded to see my patient, and there ensued much apprehensive discussion among the youths as to whether they dare unbolt the thick oak door. You would think there were a tribe of wild demons inside instead of one man. I had brought Trump's boots with me, and they inspected them most warily before finally allowing me to go within. The door was slammed shut behind me so fast I had to pull my frock coattail free after me.

It took a moment for my eyes to adjust to the faint light filtering through the small, barred square cut in the door. Trump was standing in the middle of the cramped enclosure, as if waiting to pounce. I would have thought being imprisoned in such a murky, musty crypt would have thrown him into a state of utter despondency, but to the contrary, I found him as alert as a hungry raptor. I soon learned that his entire being was focused upon quarry that seemed impossibly out of his range.

He thanked me for bringing his boots, but rather than put them on, he tossed them aside. He then allowed me to look at his head wound, and I was relieved to see it had completely healed shut. Nor did he have other open wounds that might become infested by creatures residing in the Powder House. I observed that his hands were caked with blood and dirt and the fingers swollen, but he did not let me examine them further. He has little patience with my medical meddling.

"I reckon it did not go well for me this morning," he said.

Such an understatement as that almost made me smile. "You did not help your case when you went into such gory detail about how you aim to kill Rufus Badger."

"And I will do it, too."

"How? Do you expect Badger to come here and hand you over his knife?" Trump glared at me and I regretted my sarcasm. "I do not mean to make light of your resentment toward the man, Trump. He is a brute and a liar."

"I have better reason than that to kill him," he said. "And it grieves me more than I can bear that I didn't kill Peck when I could have. I held myself back because Miss Julia and the old doc were present, but I shouldn't have let my regard for them stop me. *Nothing* will stop me from killing Badger."

"Why do you hate Peck and Badger so much, Trump?"

He did not speak for many long minutes, but I sensed he wanted to, so I did not speak either. Finally he said, "I never told nobody this before."

He sat down cross-legged on the dirt floor, and I did the same, despite the bat droppings. He then related the following to me in a low growl, as though the very act of putting voice to his memories caused him pain. I will set his words down as exactly as I can recall them.

The last time I seen the two of 'em was eight years ago. But I knew 'em both right off. I didn't know their names till now, but their faces were branded in my mind. When the army was rounding up Cherokees back in Georgia then, they two rode up the mountain and surprised my family. We never thought soldiers would come so high, but they must have gotten wind somehow about the gold we'd found. A while before we'd traded some of it for better tools to dig.

We were all at the mine, my father and me digging and my mother and sister outside sifting through the dirt for the flakes and nuggets. The mine was just a deep gap in the rocks where we could dig and haul out dirt with gold mixed in. For a small boy I was a strong digger. My size was to my advantage for squeezing into tight chinks between rocks, and I never lost my head when the ground fell in on me every so often.

We were working a ways in when we heard my mother and sister shouting. My father was ahead of me as we come out, and I saw my sister trying to hold onto the leather bag we kept the gold in while a man in army uniform, Badger it was, pulled at it. He was laughing. Behind him up on a fine white horse sat an officer watching. Peck. When we come out of the cut Peck holds up his hand and says, "Stop right there. It's against the law for you Cherokees to mine gold in

Georgia. So this gold is lawfully ours, and we're taking it." My father don't stop. He keeps running toward 'em, swearing up a storm and waving his pickaxe. I see Peck nod to Badger, and then I see Badger raise this big pistol. He shoots my father in the head from maybe ten feet. My father's blood and brains and part of his skull are blown clear away. My mother and sister start screaming. Maybe I do too.

Peck gets down from his horse and takes ahold of me so I can't hit or run, but I keep kicking at him. My mother is just standing still, looking down at my father, and my sister runs to her and holds her. There's maybe a minute of nothing, and then Peck says to Badger, "Well, you know what we got to do now. Can't leave the rest of 'em to run and tell." And Badger, calm as you please, raises his gun again and shoots my mother in the heart and then my pretty sister in the face. I stop fighting Peck after that. Nothing left to fight for. Badger holsters his pistol and hands the bag of gold to Peck. He hefts it and smiles. We had a year's digging in that bag. Badger comes over and grabs me and says, "This one's got to go too." Peck looks down at me and nods and says, "Go finish it." He points over to a deep gully that runs close by the mine and says, "Bury them there so no patrol will find them. We could get court-martialed for this."

Badger yanks me along with one paw and grabs my sister's foot with his other and drags us to the edge of the gully. He throws her in it and stands me on the edge and backs up maybe twenty paces to keep his self from getting splattered by my brains, I reckon. He tells me to look at him. I got nothin' to care about, so's I do. He aims his pistol and shoots me in the head, and I fall back dead in the gully, on my sister. Then they throw my father and mother down on me.

But I ain't entirely dead. Maybe an hour or a day later, I don't know, I come awake and can't move or see or breathe hardly. I reckon I am in the state betwixt living and dying as spirits go through afore they move on. But if I am a spirit, why do I hurt so much and why should I want so to breathe? I start to move around my fingers and shift my legs just a bit. Takes me a long time to figure out I am buried alive. The bullet that should have killed me only made a dent in my skull and veered off. Good thing it flat knocked me out, though. If I had thrashed about, Badger would have shot me some more till I stopped twitching.

My nose is full of dirt, but I can open my mouth just enough to get a breath. My father's body shielded me from getting completely covered by all the earth they'd shoveled over us, so even in death he sheltered and protected me like he did in life. There's still plenty of earth atop me to get through, but I been trapped before, in the mine, and I get out of this grave the same way. I make myself into a worm and start slitherin'. The worst of it is pushing away the bodies of my father and mother. My hand shoves right into the top of my father's head. When I feel the thick warm jelly that is left of his brains, I almost vomit but will myself to hold back else I might smother in my own puke. I yank free my hand, but get the other one all tangled up in my mother's long hair. No need to talk about all of that anymore, though.

I worm up slow. It's hard work, and I have to stop plenty since I can't breathe but a little. When I see light, not with my eyes open but through my eyelids, I reckon I might make it.

But then I get scared, thinking maybe Badger is standing guard waiting to shoot at any lump that moves, so I wait as long as I can. That is the hardest part of all. Finally I just go up, not being able to stand it anymore, and one hand gets out and then I work my head clear and then I take in a big dose of fresh air.

So I came out of the grave and back to life. And now I know why. I came back to avenge my family. I missed my chance with Peck, to my everlasting regret. But Badger will die by my hand, or I will die trying to kill him.

I nodded in sympathy. That Trump should want such bloody retribution was understandable. It was unfeasible, however. I cautioned him that if he wanted to ever be free again, he must keep his story to himself, for he would surely be convicted of Peck's murder on the basis of such a compelling motive. I then asked him how he had survived after extracting himself from his grave. He could not have been more than a boy of twelve.

He told me he had lived like an animal in the woods for months, snaring rabbits and shooting squirrels with a blowgun and digging roots and cattail bulbs in the swamps. He avoided all men, Indian and white, since he feared the Indians might be working for the soldiers to lure out the last of the tribe. When winter came on he began to starve and stumbled down into the camp of a family going west in a Conestoga wagon. The man didn't care a hoot if he was red or white, for he needed a hand to drive his cows behind the wagon, so the wife fed him and dressed him and treated him decently enough. Trump stayed with them, that being as good as any other prospect for a boy whose world had disappeared entirely. They got to the Mississippi, and Trump figured he'd stay with them maybe to California, but as they were ferried across the river the barge carrying them swamped, and all got swept away. He never knew what happened to the family. The men calling out the river's depth on a steamboat fished him out, and a gambler took him in to serve him and help him cheat planters out of their cash by signaling the cards they held.

He tried cards himself when he got older and eventually got so good at it he struck out on his own in New Orleans. Could be he got too good at it. To escape the wrath of a rice planter he had cleaned out, he had to stow away on a departing steamboat heading for Boston.

That's where he had met up with Caleb, a fellow stowaway. They became fast friends and had worked the North End of Boston together for the last few months, until Caleb disappeared. Trump had come to Plumford to find him. He now believes Caleb was the instrument Fate used to lead him to Peck and Badger, so that he could avenge the death of his family.

I again counseled him to keep this to himself or Fate would lead him straight to the hangman. The best I could do for him now, I said, was to try and find him a good lawyer. He scoffed at that. He said no lawyer could persuade a jury of white men that he was innocent, short of proving he was on another planet at the time of the murder.

Nevertheless, as soon as I left the Powder House I attempted to solicit the help of a lawyer for Trump. Neither of the two attorneys who practice in Plumford wanted to take on his case, nor could either of them recommend anyone in their profession who would be fool enough to represent Trump. I can only hope Henry has better luck in Concord.

That Julia continues to avoid my company has made me most fidgety, and so off I went to the Sun for an ale this evening. The tavern was abuzz about Peck's brutal murder. I was asked time and again for particulars, and time and again declined. Yet I lingered, trying to gauge the state of mind of my fellow townsmen, for some might well be jurors at Trump's trial.

There was much talk about Indian atrocities of the past and much eyeballing of a picture that has hung over the bar for decades and is usually ignored. It is a rude copy of a painting I am told is both famous and well respected, but I find the subject matter most sensational and maudlin. The rendering is of a lovely maiden on her knees in supplication, her clinging gown in disarray, her white bosom bared, as one Indian raises his tomahawk to strike her dead and another grips her golden tresses and brandishes a scalping knife. It is supposedly an historical depiction of the murder of a woman called Jane Mc-Crea by two Iroquois during the War for Independence. If this did in fact happen or it is merely folklore, I cannot say.

I do know for certain, however, that Plumford has experienced Indian violence in the past. Journals of my ancestors report the burning down of half the town by raiding Nipmuc braves in 1675, and many at the tavern tonight were eager to relate tales concerning long-gone relatives maimed or slain by savages in King Philip's War. No one bothered to mention that the vast majority of the natives in our region never raised a hand against white intruders but were wiped out anyway by their diseases or by starvation as all the game was shot out and the forests cut down.

When anecdotes about past Indian atrocities ran out, conversation turned to current newspaper reports concerning savages attacking wagon trains in our Western territories. In the midst of this talk Rufus Badger entered the tavern, and all turned to watch him make his way to the bar. He was drunk as usual, but this did not lessen admiration for the lout. A cheer rose up, and many a man hefted his glass in a toast to Badger for capturing Trump.

"Let's go lynch that dirty redskin, men!" he bellowed. "Why should he get a white Christian trial? I say hang him now and be done with it. He already confessed to me that he killed my captain."

"Don't listen to Badger. He lies," I shouted. "I was present when Trump was captured, and I heard no such confession from him."

Badger's face swelled with rage. His eyes bulged like those of one suffering from the goiter as he glared at me. "You durst call me a liar?"

"Yes, and I know you to be far worse than that." How tempted I was to proclaim him and his captain the vile murderers of Trump's defenseless family. But I cautioned myself, as I had cautioned Trump, to keep silent about it until after he is tried for Peck's murder.

"Stand up so I can knock you down, you son of a bitch," Badger told me.

I complied immediately for I was eager to fight him. In fact, my loathing for him aroused in me a great desire to do him grievous harm. I have never experienced such aggressive feelings as that toward another human being before. But at that moment I did not see Badger as human. He had lost all claim of humanity when he shot four innocent people for gold. I made my hands into fists and braced myself for his attack, eager to strike him back. He did not put up his own fists, however. Instead, he pulled his terrible knife from his boot and made his way toward me.

In the next instant more than a dozen men rose up to block Badger's path. He was shoved back from me by many hands and thrown against the wall with such force that he crashed to the floor.

Proprietor Ruggles came from behind the bar and put himself in front of Badger, no doubt one of his best customers. "That's enough, boys," he said, looking around him. "No need to dissuade the sergeant further. I expect he must have drunk a mite too much antifogmatic."

His use of the old humorous name for rum brought a few tight-lipped smiles and broke the tension. Men stepped back, and Ruggles turned his attention to Badger.

"You should have kept your knife in your boot, Rufus," he said, standing over him. "Dr. Walker is a local lad, and we will not tolerate mortal injury to him. Nor to any other unarmed Plumford citizen for that matter."

"What about Captain Peck?" Badger said, staggering to his feet. "He was a Plumford citizen, and neither should *his* mortal injuries be tolerated! Who here is willing to join me in hanging the no-good Injun who murdered him?"

No one spoke up but Ruggles. "The courts will take care of that Injun," he said. "He will be legally hanged for the captain's murder soon enough." A murmur of agreement followed.

"Or set free by the trickery of some fast-talking lawyer!" Badger yelled. "I ain't going to chance letting that happen." He looked around him and sneered. "You're all a bunch of milk-sops. I reckon I will have to find myself better men to do what needs to be done." With that, he picked up his knife from the floor and stumbled out of the tavern.

Left shortly thereafter myself, after treating the men who had prevented Badger from slashing me to ribbons to a free round of drinks. The effects of my own drinking have long worn off, but my concerns over Trump's safety have intensi-fied. Although Badger could not rile up a lynching party at the tavern tonight, he may have better luck another night. Or at another place. He is most determined to get Trump hanged before he goes to trial. Why? Does he fear that a good defense lawyer would investigate other suspects and their alibis? Could it be that Badger's own alibi is a lie? He might well have killed Peck himself. If anyone is capable of such butchery, it is Rufus Badger. God help me, I do believe he did it. And tomorrow I shall set out to prove it.

JULIA'S NOTEBOOK

Tuesday, 18 August

I attended Capt. Peck's burial today. I had not planned to, but when the sexton began tolling the bell to summon mourners to the churchyard, I found myself donning my plainest bonnet and going forth. As I stepped out the door I saw the funeral procession pass by. 'Twas not a large one—just the coffin carriage draped in reams of black crepe and pulled by a black steed, followed by a file of six men on horseback, all wearing black armbands. Sgt. Badger was on the lead horse, and Lt. Finch rode behind him, trailed by four rather rough-looking riders in shabby military jackets and caps. Vail and his wife were not in attendance.

A good number of townsfolk waited in the churchyard, though, including craftsmen who had done work on Peck's house, the tavern keeper, Mr. Ruggles, and Mr. and Mrs. Daggett from the general store.

"Captain Peck will be missed here in town," Mr. Daggett told me as we stood by the open grave. "He was very free and easy with his money."

"And his morals," Mrs. Daggett added.

"Do not speak ill of the dead," Mr. Daggett reprimanded

her. "Especially of one who died so terribly. I daresay the memory of Peck's butchered corpse will give me nightmares for the rest of my life."

"Then we shall both suffer from lack of sleep," Mrs. Daggett said. She turned to me. "When Justice Phyfe appointed my husband Town Coroner, we did not foresee that the position would put such a strain on his nerves. How could we? Murder was unheard of in Plumford until poor Mrs. Upson was killed by that horrible tramp. And now, less than a year later, yet another distressing murder to deal with. Leastways it has been good for business. Folks from all over the county been coming to the store to hear Mr. Daggett recount the details of Captain Peck's grave injuries."

This did not surprise me. I own I importuned Adam and Henry for such details myself. Henry was far more forthcoming than Adam, who seems always to fear upsetting my delicate female sensibilities. Has he forgotten how staunchly I assisted him during Trump's operation? Apparently so.

"I do not see Dr. Walker in attendance," Mrs. Daggett said, glancing around the churchyard.

"His leg still gives him difficulty getting about," I replied.

"I was referring to the young doc, not the old one."

"Adam had reason to go to Boston today."

"Did he now?" Mrs. Daggett looked at me expectantly, awaiting further explanation.

She got none. Even if I knew why Adam had taken off so early for the city, I would not have told her. But of course I do not know. Adam tells me nothing anymore. We barely speak to each other. Indeed, we avoid being in the same room together.

Our relationship has suffered most grievously since we succumbed to that kiss. Before it, we were quite comfortable in each other's company, brushing shoulders, grazing hands, leaning into each other to look at a book. We were almost (but not quite) like the familiar chums we'd been as children. I suppose we were much too free and easy with each other in those days, but our affectionate canoodling was as innocent then as it is dangerous now.

Consequently, we must endeavor to avoid even the slightest physical contact. We did share a brief hug Sunday morn, however. And I would have stayed pressed against Adam's solid frame for much longer if Henry had not been present. Whenever Adam holds me I feel I *belong* in his arms. The awkward embraces and dry, whiskery kisses from other men have felt so alien by comparison. 'Tis no wonder I have directed my passion solely to my art. Until now. Now it is *mis*directed. As right as it feels to be intimate with Adam, it cannot be right if the result of our union would be so disastrous.

The men in the funeral procession dismounted and slid Peck's coffin off the hearse. The wake at the house must have been a spirituous one, for they all seemed rather drunk as they trudged to the grave site with their burden. The coffin tilted in a precarious manner, and I do not think I was the only one who watched with bated breath, half fearing, half hoping that Peck's mutilated body would tumble out for all to see. But the bearers made it to the grave without mishap and began wrapping ropes around the oaken coffin.

"Twice the expense of a pine coffin," Mrs. Daggett remarked. "The cabinetmaker told me that when Sergeant Badger commissioned it, he could barely speak, he was so distraught. But he made clear that he wanted nothing but the best, sparing no cost. Just look how he suffers the loss of his friend and employer, Miss Bell. Is it not touching?"

I made no reply, having no sympathy for the man who had attempted to rape young Harriet. Copious tears ran down Badger's hateful, drink-flushed face as his fellow pallbearers regarded him with pity.

"They all served under Peck at one time or another," Mr. Daggett informed me. "Badger rounded them up to come help him bury their captain."

"Touching," Mrs. Daggett said again.

Most unexpectedly, the Rev. Mr. Upson came forward to conduct the burial service. "Pastor Jenkins has had a severe flare-up of gout and has asked me to take his place today," he explained.

I could not help but note how distinguished Mr. Upson looked in his dark minister's garb, the sun glinting off his spectacles and lighting up his blond hair. He balanced an open Bible in his palms, his long, white fingers gracefully splayed against the black covers. His pale eyes searched the crowd and rested a moment on me. I nodded, and he smiled back at me, ever so slightly, before he began to speak.

I did not care for his sermon, which was all about corruption and depravity, man's deceitful heart and wicked ways. I glanced around me. Most of those in attendance did not seem to be paying much mind to Mr. Upson's harsh words. But when he began reciting Scripture regarding an eye for eye, a tooth for tooth, a wound for wound, etcetera, Badger and his cronies snapped to attention and loudly voiced approval of such retribution.

After they then lowered the coffin into the grave, I went to the area of the churchyard where my mother and most of my Walker kin are buried. I know not where my father will be buried when his time comes, but I am sure it will be far, far away from here. I suppose a great distance separated my parents even when Mama was alive. Except for me, they had little in common.

As I stood at my mother's headstone, I recalled how she always told me she could not tolerate city life because of her delicate disposition. But I think now it might have been Papa's turbulent temperament she could not tolerate. That he seldom left his Boston studio to come visit us when we removed to Plumford seemed to bother her not at all. But then, Mama never complained. Hence, I never realized how very ill she really was until the day she died. And the shock of it near killed me off too. If not for Adam, I might well have followed her to the grave.

My wonderful, darling comrade! I confess thoughts of Adam as a boy, rather than thoughts my beloved mother, filled my mind as I stood there in the sunny churchyard and a light breeze tickled my neck. Adam used to tickle it with a piece of straw and make me shiver. He used to make me laugh in so many ways. I eventually recovered from the loss of my mother and found much happiness in Plumford, living with my grandparents in their fine old house on the Green and seeing my beloved cousin each and every day. I wonder even now what made my father decide to take me off to Europe with him. I suppose he was merely laying claim to what was rightfully his.

But I did not see it that way. I loved my cousin far more than I could ever love my aloof father. And Adam loved *me* more than his happy life on Tuttle Farm. The night before Papa was to come and fetch me away our plans were set in motion. Adam came to the back of the house just past midnight and softly hooted like an owl. I slid out my chamber window and climbed down the trellis, already disguised as a boy in some of his old clothes, and off we went.

A pack of vicious dogs attacked us not four hours into our journey as we walked down the moonlit Post Road. We stood back-to-back and fought them off with our sharpened walking sticks, and then sat down in the road panting like dogs ourselves until we could go on. And on we did go, hand in hand, fully expecting more adventures with wild Indians and grizzly bears and stampeding buffalo as we traveled farther and farther west. We did not get far enough to encounter any of them, but we did have a run-in with two farm boys whose intention it was to rob us of the few pennies we had. The fight that ensued

proved a bloody one, especially for Adam, who did most of the
punching and hence got punched back the most. But I managed to overcome "my delicate female sensibilities" enough to
wallop one of the bullies, albeit the smaller one, right in the
nose. So shocked was he by the gush of blood that resulted that
he ran off. Meanwhile Adam kept thumping the bigger one
until he turned tail too.

Later that day we hid in the woods. Lying together on a
mossy bank, we slept as soundly as soldiers after a successful
battle, Adam with his arm around me and me with my head
on his chest. I knew then that I wanted to be with him forever,
but what does an eleven-year-old girl know about forever?
Our freedom together lasted but five days. Always heading
west, using a compass Adam had gotten on his twelfth birthday, we went from Plumford to Concord, and then on to Sud-
bury, from there to Marlboro, and then almost to Worcester,
traveling at night, hiding in barns during the day, drinking
water from springs and eating our fill of field squash and toma-
toes and as many walnuts and hickory nuts as we could find.
We always slept twined together, breathing as one, our hearts
beating in rhythm. How could such bliss possibly last?

Once we got far enough away from home we took to walking by day instead of night to make better time of it. 'Twas
shortly after we stopped at a farm and did some chores for a hot
meal and milk that we heard a wagon come up behind us on the
road. Adam turned round and stopped in his tracks. I looked at
his face and knew our goose was cooked. Sure enough, Granny
and Grandpa Tuttle sat there in the wagon, staring at us. When
Gran yanked me up hard to sit beside her, she gave my arm a
real hard pinch for good measure.

Two days later it was good-bye Lewis, good-bye Clark.
Neither Adam nor I shed a tear in parting. What was the use?
We had done our best to stay together but all for naught. Soon
we would be separated by a vast ocean.

Lost in this reverie as I regarded my mother's headstone, I did not hear Lyman Upson approach. His voice startled me back to the present.

"You must have found today's burial most distressing, Julia," he said.

I do not recall giving Mr. Upson leave to call me by my first name but no matter. I told him that I had not known Capt. Peck well enough to grieve his loss, but of course I was sorry he had died so horribly.

"It is not his *demise* that I thought would distress you," Mr. Upson said, "but his interment in the hallowed burying ground of your ancestors."

"I am sure they shall pay him no mind," I replied, perhaps too lightly.

"It is the living who should mind," Upson said. "Peck has no right to be buried here. That he lies nearby my wife's grave offends me greatly."

"If you feel so strongly about it, Mr. Upson, why did you agree to conduct Captain Peck's requiem service?"

"As a man of God I am obligated to do many things I find difficult," he replied stiffly.

We did not have much more to say to one another after that. When I bid him Good Day he took my hand in parting and suggested most ardently that I call him Lyman. I agreed. How could I not? He seems to have so few friends in Plumford.

ADAM'S JOURNAL

Tuesday, August 18th

Glad that Henry T. decided to accompany me to Boston today. His winning ways with the whores proved most helpful. But I get ahead of myself.

Before leaving Plumford I called on Justice Phyfe, interrupting him at his breakfast. Told him why I feared for Trump's safety. With a flick of his napkin, he waived off my concern.

"I have posted guards at the Powder House door," he said, "to make sure the Indian stays in and others stay out."

"Such callow youths as that would be no match against a raging lynch mob," I said. "You must remove Trump to the secure jail in Concord."

"I will do no such thing," Phyfe said, at the end of his limited patience. "The Indian will remain imprisoned in Plumford under my jurisdiction. I shall assist the Attorney General when he arrives here to conduct his investigation."

"So you are willing to risk Trump's life for the opportunity to rub elbows with some Boston bigwig?"

Phyfe got mad as a beaver and ordered me out. The only way left to put Trump out of danger was to prove that Badger himself was Peck's murderer.

Boarded the morning stage to Concord. Had for company two girls going to visit their aunt. They began talking about the savage up in the Powder House, looking into the trees as if a pack of red fiends were about to attack them. They worked themselves into such a lather that one started sobbing and the other looked as wild-eyed as a frightened calf till I took a hand of each in mine and calmed them down. It did make me think how fear can wrest away all reason. Poor Trump will have little chance of sitting before a jury of unbiased peers if they already think him less than human.

Arrived at the Concord station with time to spare before the Boston train was due so I headed for Walden Pond, less than two miles south. A narrow footpath led to the pond, and after passing a large bean field ruled over by a fat woodchuck, I saw Henry's hut in a stand of pitch pines and hickories overlooking the greenish-blue water.

The hut is most modest, about ten by fifteen feet, with a woodshed on one side. The door was wide open, and looking in I saw it was meagerly furnished with a cot, a humble desk and table, and three plain chairs. A rough-made brick fireplace occupied the far wall, and light from two large, open windows streamed in, making the bare floor planks glow. I could not imagine a more Spartan and uncluttered existence short of living directly under the trees and was not much surprised when a phoebe flitted through one window, flew across the room and out the other, as though this was part of its habitual route.

Walked down to the pond in search of Henry. The surrounding woodlands seemed as pristine as when they were the homeland of Algonquin Indians two centuries ago, but when I reached the water's edge I espied railroad tracks running atop the opposite sand bank. They were close enough for Henry's peace to be disturbed by the clattering of train cars and the shrill whistle of the locomotive. It appears that no one, not even Henry Thoreau, can escape the progress of our times.

Gave out a holler and received one back from Henry, but he was nowhere in sight. Proceeded along the shore till I found him. He was kneeling on a bit of sandy ground, and with the enthusiasm of a boy, he had me kneel down beside him to examine a nest of mud turtle eggs. A few of the tiny turtles had just hatched and struggled sluggishly amongst bits of eggshell. Henry sat back and told me that upon awakening this morning, he had determined he would look for turtle nests. He spotted them by the slightest wavering of the surface of the sand and, placing his ear to the ground, he had detected the minute crepitation made as they broke through their shells with their beaks. He might as well have discovered the very secret to eternal life, he looked so happy.

After he had gently spread the sand back over the tiny turtles we stood and gazed out at the calm, deep pond that Henry called his liquid joy and happiness. Sun and shadow played over his quiet face as he regarded the vitreous water.

"I think of this pond as the earth's eye," he said. "It measures the depth of the beholder's own nature."

"What measure would it take of men who killed an entire family for gold?" I said and went on to tell him Trump's history with Peck and Badger.

Henry listened intently without interruption, and when I was done speaking he stared at the pond without comment.

"Badger also murdered Peck," I said after a moment.

Henry turned back at me. "Are you certain of this?"

"As certain as I can be without actual proof."

"No way of thinking can be trusted without proof," he gently chided me. "And it is hard to credit that Badger would murder his long-standing friend and benefactor."

"Well, mark this," I said. "There was recently a severe breach in their friendship. I learned of it when I had occasion to visit Peck the morning before he died. According to him,

Badger left Plumford in a rage. I think he returned to kill Peck and scalped him to cast suspicions on Trump."

Henry looked doubtful. "How would Badger know enough to incriminate Trump if he was not around to witness his run-in with Peck? He was in Boston, drinking the night away, was he not?"

"So he testified at any rate. I am going to Shark's Tavern to find out the truth of the matter."

"When?"

I pulled out my watch. "Within the hour. This cannot wait. I must interview denizens of Shark's before they forget whether he was there or not there last Saturday night."

"I doubt any of them will be disposed to talk to you, Adam."

"Oh, I can be quite insistent when the need arises, I assure you."

"Even so, I wager you will be dealing with some very rough characters if they are associates of Badger."

"It is not very likely they are refined teetotalers," I allowed.

"Then perhaps I should accompany you there."

"Do you think we would stand a better chance of getting information if we walked into Shark's together?"

Henry nodded. "And a better chance of walking out un-scathed," he added. He gave his crystalline pond a longing glance and turned back to me. "Let us go catch the cars to Boston, my friend."

I did not protest. In fact, I welcomed Henry's company and even paid for his ticket, for he had not a penny on his person. After we boarded the train and took our seats, I described to Henry the miserable conditions of Trump's imprisonment in the Powder House. I then told him about Badger's trying to stir up a lynch mob in the Sun Tavern last night.

"I am not surprised he failed," Henry said. "For all their

small-minded prejudices, the men of Plumford seem a nonviolent lot."

"But what if Badger finds men of a more bellicose nature elsewhere? Such as acquaintances from his army days or ruffians he mixes with in Boston."

"Yes, there are more than enough men ready to do outrage to their proper natures and lend themselves to perform brutal acts," Henry said. "And even the crudest of men can command those who do not command themselves."

"Then you share my apprehension that Badger is a danger to Trump?"

"I do, indeed, Adam. I also fear that Trump could be a danger to himself."

Henry proceeded to tell me about a muskrat that a Concord trapper once caught in his trap. This muskrat had evidently been caught twice before, gnawing off a leg each time to escape. Upon this, his third capture, he gnawed off his third leg, and the trapper found him lying dead by the trap, for he could not run off on just one leg.

"Now if an animal would go to such extreme measures to be free, imagine what a human being might do. Especially a young, spirited Indian like Trump," Henry said. "He might do grave harm to himself trying to escape the wretched trap they have put him in. How much better off he would be in the jail we have in Concord. I speak from experience when I say it is both clean and secure."

"I proposed exactly that to Justice Phyfe earlier this morning," I said. "But I utterly failed to convince him."

"Perhaps he will listen to Concord's most illustrious man of letters," Henry said. "I am not referring to myself, of course, but to my friend Ralph Waldo Emerson. I am also acquainted with eminent men in the law profession, namely Judge Hoar and his lawyer sons. I will attempt to recruit their aid as soon I return from Boston today. Trump must be removed from the Powder House without delay."

I was greatly relieved that Henry not only appreciated the urgency of the situation, but had come up with a possible solution. I leaned back in my seat, grateful for an hour of enforced repose till we reached Boston. I had slept but little the night before, so disturbed was I by Trump's story of his family's massacre. As we swayed along Henry pointed to a pair of shepherds on a road that ran parallel to the railway tracks. They were driving sheep with their crooks toward Boston.

"Their pastoral way of life will be gone soon enough, whirled away by the churning engines that will transport animals and goods far and wide," he said. "The railroad is not only changing the countryside but the very essence of the people who populate it. We do not ride the railroad, Adam. It rides upon us."

And off he went on an extemporaneous discourse concerning the locomotive, referring to it as a mighty iron horse that breathed fire and smoke from its nostrils as it lurched through town and country, destroying both nature and livelihoods. As Henry railed against the rails my heavy eyelids closed, and I soon found myself lying in a clover pasture. Julia was lying beside me, as she had done many times when we were children. In those days we would stare up at the clouds, pointing out the fanciful images we saw in their billowy formations, but in my dream we were as we are now, fully grown and caressing most fervently. Henry's voice suddenly intruded upon our pleasure, and I tore my lips from Julia's to shout, "Go away, Henry!"

My own voice awakened me, and I opened my eyes. Henry was smiling at me. "I would be most happy to oblige you, Adam," he said, "but we are traveling far too fast for me to leap from the car."

"Pay me no mind. I was having a dream."

"Apparently I was aggravating you mightily in it."

"The dream had little to do with you, Henry, and much to do with Julia. She fills my mind both night and day," I blurted out, still under the persuasive power of my reverie. "Yet as much as I long to be in her company, apparently she no longer wishes to be in mine."

"Really? You seem to me to be a most compatible pair."

"We used to be. We never clashed as children. We were as like as two peas in a pod in those days, a world unto ourselves. We planned a life of adventure together, intending to travel up the Missouri and across the Rockies just as Lewis and Clark had done twenty-five years before. We had read all about it in a book by Patrick Gass, who was a sergeant in the expedition."

"Ah, yes. I know of that book," Thoreau said. "I would like to peruse it myself, but copies are rather rare."

"My grandfather has one," I said. "When I was a boy he would not permit me to take it out of his study, and it is no doubt still there, on the very same shelf. I have not had the heart to look at it since . . ." I shrugged. "Well, since I grew up. As a boy, I was captivated by it though. Perhaps reading about such an adventure was a way for me to escape the pain of losing my mother. Then Julia came to Plumford. Her company was most pleasant, and she shared my enthusiasm for the book as none of my male friends had. We bonded over it, I suppose. We began writing our own expedition adventures, and she would draw illustrations more fantastical and vivid than the ones in Gass's book. She was a skillful artist even then, when she was no more than eight or nine."

Henry nodded. "We all dream of going off on adventures when we are young. But so few of us do."

"Well, Julia and I did. Her own mother died a few years after mine, and when we heard that her father intended to take her off to Europe, we took off for California instead."

"Or so you imagined," Henry said.

"No. We truly did. We lit out and got as far west as Worcester in just five days. I was but twelve and Julia eleven. That is pretty fair time for two youngsters to make, is it not? Especially since most of our walking was done at night to avoid being seen."

I saw a rare expression upon Henry's countenance. He looked impressed. "What made you turn back?"

"*Nothing* would have made us turn back. But Gran and Grandpa Tuttle tracked us down, carted us back to Plumford, and before we could even catch our breath we were abruptly separated."

"As though torn asunder by some jealous god?" Henry must have noted my blank look, for he went on to explain. "According to Aristophanes, we humans originally had four arms and legs and were so fleet and strong that Zeus became jealous and split us in half. Hence we cannot feel complete unless we find our other half again."

"It is a most compelling fancy," I said, recalling how Julia's little girl body twined into mine when we slept in haylofts or under the stars. Recalling too how her womanly body had melded so perfectly to mine when I pulled her into my lap and kissed her.

"It is more than a mere fancy," Henry said in a low, confidential tone. "I know because I have indeed found my other half. She is of me and I of her. Verily, there is such harmony when her sphere meets mine that I cannot tell where I leave off and she begins."

This surprised me, for Henry has always struck me as a man most content in his own company. I know little of his personal life, however. "Have you made plans to wed?" I made bold to ask him.

"We cannot be together as man and wife in this life," Henry

replied with sad resignation. "But I hope we will meet again in a future life and both be free."

This surprised me even more. "Surely you do not think that possible, Henry. How can you give credence to such an arcane concept as Reincarnation when you value truth based on observation?"

"Did I not observe myself as an Indian who lived over two hundred years ago?"

"Your brief experience under hypnosis convinces you that we are immortals who return to this earth time and again?" I shook my head. "Oh, Henry, I should need far more proof than that."

He did not seem the least perturbed by my declared mistrust of his conviction. "When I see Walden come back to life in the spring," he replied most calmly, "and when I see the river valley and the woods bathed in so pure and bright a light as would wake the dead, I need no stronger proof of immortality. Methinks my own soul must be a bright invisible green."

I could not help but smile. "I have never observed such a thing as a green soul during an autopsy. Nor one of any hue whatsoever."

"Some truths cannot be observed, only experienced, Adam."

"Well, I am a man of science, not metaphysics, and therefore rely on facts."

"The facts of science may dust the mind by their dryness, Doctor. Knowledge comes to us in flashes of light from heaven, and men are probably nearer the essential truth in their superstitions than in their science. There is inherent truth in most fables too."

"In some anyway," I allowed. "Such as the Aristophanes fable you just related to me. I too have found my other half, Henry. And like you, I cannot marry her."

"You refer to Julia?"

"Of course. She is the only woman I have ever loved."

"Then I do not understand. You and she are both free to wed, are you not?'

"We are neither of us married. But we are first cousins, and in our family such unions have resulted in hideously deformed offspring. As a physician I am acquainted with techniques that can hinder conception, of course, but none are infallible. To be certain we do not reproduce such a horror, Julia and I would have to forgo sexual congress entirely, and I am not sure I could endure that. Does my frankness embarrass you, Henry?"

"Not at all. I do not respect men who make the mystery of sex the subject of coarse jest, but I am always willing to speak earnestly and seriously on the subject," Henry said. "Several years ago I became acquainted with a young lady I found immensely attractive, and my yearning to have physical congress with her prompted me to propose marriage. She turned me down, however. She also turned down my brother before me, but that is neither here nor there. The point I am trying to make is this, Adam. I know what it is like to desire a woman. Yet I can assure you that it is possible to find great joy in a woman's companionship without carnal indulgence, if she is indeed your soul mate."

I nodded, as if in agreement, all the time recalling the pleasure of the kiss I had shared with Julia. Frankly, I do not think I have Henry's strength of character. Despite my high principles, my lowly desires persist. Even as I write this, I am imagining the way Julia's eyes closed and her lips parted as I drew her face to mine. But why do I continue to fan the fires of Eros with that remembrance? I must try and block it from my mind.

Back to today's events. When Henry and I arrived in Boston, we asked a goodly number of gentlemen passing through the Causeway Street Terminal if they knew where Shark's Tavern was located. One finally told us it was somewhere in the infamous Black Sea district.

We walked there directly and found ourselves in a confusion of carts, wagons, and drays rattling to and from the waterfront warehouses. Laborers, hostlers, and boisterous gangs of sailors jammed the thoroughfare. Grog shops abounded. At last we found Shark's Tavern in a side alley off Ann Street. A garish sign by the door depicted a shark with a screaming, bare-chested man caught in its bloody maw.

Inside we were assailed by the stench of stale beer, tobacco, tar, and sweat. The few early afternoon customers greeted us with scowls, and when one of them abruptly left his chair and headed toward us I became uncomfortably aware that neither Henry nor I carried a weapon of defense, not even a cane.

But the glowering galoot only yelled at us to name our poison as he went right past us and took his place behind the bar. I ordered a mug of beer to give us reason to linger, but it was abstemious Henry who eventually won the truculent barkeep over with his direct, relaxed manner. Once he got the man talking, he told us all we needed to know and more. He remembered that Badger had been there last Saturday night all right. The roughneck had gotten so drunk he had fallen backwards and shattered a stout table at which several men were enjoying plates of pigs' feet and sausages. That brought on a bit of a brawl till Badger paid for his graceful faux pas with ready and new paper notes, then lurched off.

"Do you recall what time Sergeant Badger left your establishment?" Henry asked.

"In fact I do," the barkeep said. "He often stays all night, getting uglier and drunker by the hour, but on Sadday last he left around ten."

"There we have it," I told Henry. "If Badger left here at ten, he could have easily made it back to Plumford before sunrise. It is less than a four-hour ride from Boston on horse-back."

The barkeep laughed. "Oh, Sergeant Badger didn't leave here to ride no *horse,* sir. He left for a far more pleasurable ride at Mrs. Scudder's. Her bawdy house is right around the corner. The brick house with the red door."

"Ah, yes," Henry said. "I know it."

Astounded, I gave him a sidelong look. Henry David Thoreau had never struck me as the sort of man who would patronize brothels. Yet upon leaving the tavern he suggested that we go to Mrs. Scudder's forthwith.

"I do not wish to sound disapproving, Henry," I replied, "but as a doctor I must caution you that a short time with Venus too often results in a lifetime with Mercury."

He looked puzzled for a moment and then nodded. "I be-lieve I understand your meaning. Mercury is the treatment for venereal disease, is it not?"

"Indeed it is. And a most unpleasant one."

"But I do not intend to become intimate with any Venus employed at Mrs. Scudder's, Adam. I merely want to ascertain what time Badger left there. Surely you do not take me for a whoremonger."

"Of course not, Henry," I said brusquely, sidestepping a sluggish sow that was rooting about in the gutter. "However, you did claim to the barkeep that you were familiar with Mrs. Scudder's brothel."

"And so I am. Do you not remember Trump mentioning the place? He told us that he went to Mrs. Scudder's to talk to a girl named Effie. She was the one who sent his friend Caleb to Plumford. And of all the brothels in Boston, this is the one Badger chooses to go to. It cannot be mere chance."

"No, it cannot," I agreed. "Badger and Caleb are somehow connected. I warrant Badger murdered him as well as Peck. All we need do is find out why and then prove it."

"Is that all?" Henry gave me a wry look.

We went around the corner and came upon a brick row house with a red door. Henry knocked without hesitation, and the door was opened by a girl of no more than ten years, with sallow skin and sunken eyes. She wore no pantalettes beneath her knee-length sack dress, and I noted purple spots and sores of various sizes upon her bare, skinny legs. She ushered us inside without a word, her movements slow and her attitude despondent.

By contrast, a large and lively woman bustled down the narrow hall to greet us with an effusion of energy. She introduced herself as Mrs. Scudder but did not inquire of our names. "Come into my parlor, good sirs!" she exclaimed, pulling me by the arm and giving Henry an encouraging nudge on the shoulder. We entered a small room that was crowded with stuffed seats, long wall mirrors, and three scantily attired young women.

"Look at who has come to call on you so bright and early, my dears!" our fulsome hostess told them. "A fine young gentleman"—she jerked her wigged head in my direction—"and his eager country cousin." She patted Henry's back.

Admittedly Henry did look the rustic in his dull green homespun suit and wide-brimmed hat as it had not occurred to him to change his everyday attire to go to the city. He did not look *eager*, however. But neither did he look ill at ease. He simply looked as he always did, soberly attentive yet quietly amused. If the sight of trollops wearing little more than tight corsets, lacy chemises, and black stockings made him uncomfortable, he gave no sign of it. His bright, translucent eyes scanned over them and every fixture in the room, as though recording them all to memory for future reference, as he would a phenomenon in nature.

"Being our first callers of the day, gentlemen, you will find my girls fresh as daisies," Mrs. Scudder assured us.

They did not appear so fresh to me. One had a waxy pallor, another a crooked nose that must have been fractured and not reset properly, and one poor thing had a shiner that had nearly closed her right eye. There were four parallel stripes of a mottled bluish hue on her upper arm that I surmised had been left by some brute's gripping fingers. The other two also had marks on their limbs—purpureous spots of a livid color—but I did not think they were bruises. All three women seemed lethargic to the extreme, the result of drowsiness, drugs, or perhaps a medical condition.

"Perk up, my flowers, or these gentlemen will not want to pluck you," Mrs. Scudder urged them in a tone that meant business.

Henry got right down to business too. He told Mrs. Scudder that we were neither customers nor police officers but had come to inquire about a man named Rufus Badger.

Mrs. Scudder erupted in a tornado of expletives that would put a drunken drover to shame. "Look what the bastard did to poor Lottie," she went on to say, pointing to the young woman with the black eye. "Smacked her before he even paid for her. Badger has got a mean streak running through him so deep it is unfathomable."

"When did Sergeant Badger hurt you, Lottie?" Henry asked the girl gently.

"Last Sadday night," she replied, giving him a trusting look. She was a plain enough lass who would have looked far more at home in a milkmaid's poke bonnet than the false curls framing her broad, homely face. "His favorite gal ain't here no more so he turned his attentions on me. I could not help but shrink away from him when he went to kiss me, he ascares me so. That got him all haired up, so he grabbed my arm and slugged me." She began to sob.

"Lottie is still green," Mrs. Scudder said and smiled at Henry. "I venture she might well suit you, Mr. Green Coat."

Before he could reply, the girl with the crooked nose spoke up. "I ain't ascared of that Badger," she said in a boastful tone. "Afore he could slug Lottie again, I took him off to my room."

Lottie regarded her with admiration. "And again I thank you kindly for that, Dora."

Dora shrugged. "Never you mind, Lottie. Stinker though he is, Badger allus got plenty of money. Besides which, if he took a hand to *me*, I'd have stuck him with this." She pulled out from the back of her corset a short dagger like an ice pick. "He didn't give me no trouble though. The drunken sod went to snoring like a trumpet full of spit soon as his old long Tom shot off."

"We had to haul him out of Dora's bed and into the back hall," Mrs. Scudder said, "so's he wouldn't interfere with the trade. He slept there like the pile of trash he is all night."

"All night?" Henry said.

"Well into it anyways. He waked up a little past four and took off. Good riddance to bad rubbish says I."

"Are you sure of the time he left, madam?" Henry asked her.

"Sir, I am most sure of it. The night patrolman gets off duty at four and always comes directly here to collect his tribute. He was here when Badger woke up. I was mighty glad of it too. Lord only knows what further torment that beast would have brought upon us if an officer of the law had not been on the premises."

"On me, as it so happens," boastful Dora said.

My disappointment was great, for if Badger had not left the brothel until four, he could not have ridden back to Plumford before sunrise. Hence, he could not have killed Peck.

Nevertheless, Henry plunged on with his inquiry. "Do you know a mulatto girl named Effie?" he asked Mrs. Scudder.

She suddenly got wary. "Why should I?"

"I was told she works here," Henry said.

"Well, she don't anymore. Effie run off I know not where. Nor do I care. She was trouble."

"She had a friend by the name of Caleb," Henry said.

Mrs. Scudder shrugged. "Effie had a lot of friends."

The third girl came over to us, limping slightly. As she gave Henry a searching look I noticed she had a small ecchymosis in the inner angle of each watery eye. "Do you know where Caleb is, sir?" We have been sorely worried about him."

"I am sorry to tell you this," Henry said, "but Caleb is dead."

The girl hung her head and limped away without further inquiry.

Henry looked toward the other three women. "Why were you worried about him?"

They darted glances back and forth but said nothing.

"His death was deemed an accident," Henry continued, "but we believe he was murdered."

"By that bastard Rufus Badger!" bold Dora said.

"Shut up," Mrs. Scudder ordered her between clenched teeth.

"You can't shut me up."

"Well, I can sure as hell shut you *out,* Dora dear. Would you rather be walking the streets again instead of doing business under my roof?"

The two women glared at each other. They were of equal height but not of equal power, for Mrs. Scudder won out. Dora slunk back to her chair without another word, not so fierce after all.

"Now, gentlemen, I request you very kindly to leave," Mrs. Scudder told us in a mannerly tone.

"As soon as we ask you a few more questions," Henry said.

"Get out *now!*" she shrieked, her veneer of politeness worn thin. "Else I'll call the day patrolman and have you arrested for lewd and unlawful behavior. I pay him enough that he will be most happy to oblige me."

"Your threat does not persuade me to leave," Henry told her, "but your contempt for truthfulness does. I would not believe another word that slithered out of your lips. Let us depart from this place, Adam."

"Allow me to talk to Mrs. Scudder first," I said. Both she and Henry looked rather surprised for I had not said much (or indeed anything) till now. I had seen no reason to interfere with Henry's inquiry and had been occupied with my own observations. "I would like to discuss the health of your workers with you, madam."

"Now why would you want to do that if you ain't here to use them?"

"Because I'm a doctor, and I believe they have land scurvy. That's why they are so tired and bleak. No doubt their joints ache and they suffer from muscular and lumbar pains."

"Or they are just lazy."

"Scurvy would cause those purple blotches upon their limbs," I added.

"Is that so?" Mrs. Scudder showed me more interest. "Well, those damn spots are *most* unattractive. A few gentlemen callers have remarked upon them. I suppose you are going to suggest giving my girls a good bleeding to cure 'em, doctor. How much do you charge for your services?"

"No bloodletting is necessary," I said, although I know doctors who still swear by this misconceived treatment for scurvy. "The ailment is cured most speedily with wholesome victuals. Just feed them plenty of vegetables and fruits."

"Do you take me for a wealthy woman, sir?" Mrs. Scudder said. "I can barely afford to feed 'em bread and beer."

"You do not suffer from the disease yourself," I pointed out. "Feed them what you eat."

She waved off that suggestion.

"It will be good for your business," I said to persuade her. "They will look and feel better. I beg you to follow my advice, madam. I am most concerned for the poor child who let us in. She has land scurvy to a severe degree."

Mrs. Scudder raised her double chin and stated most proudly, "I'll have you know that I do not deal in child prostitution, doctor."

"I should hope not. I am only suggesting you feed the girl better."

"But I just got through telling you I got no use for her except as a slavey. No point in making her look more presentable."

Gave up on the woman. She had the soul of a weasel. Henry and I left the house and came upon the little girl outside, scrubbing the step-stone. She gave us a timid smile, and I observed that her gums were swollen and bleeding. I told her I was a doctor and asked her to stick out her tongue. She did so with a giggle. Her tongue was livid and had a black fungus upon it. I took a closer look at the sores on her stick-like legs. They could become infected and vulnerable to gangrene if they did not heal. And heal they would not without proper diet. I gave the lass a few coins and enjoined her to buy some lemons or oranges. She promised me she would, but I am quite sure she bought sweets instead. She is, after all, just a child.

As Henry and I walked away we heard the sharp tick of high heels behind us. We turned to see Dora the Dagger Girl coming toward us, wrapped in a long shawl.

"Wait!" she said. The short walk had made her breathless, and she gasped a few times before speaking further. "I will tell you all I know and to hell with Scudder. If that old blowze darst try to kick me out of her house, I will kick her in her fat ass."

"What is it you know?" Henry asked her.

"Badger killed Caleb for sure."

"Did he admit this to you?"

"No, but I allus feared it. Last I seen the boy was about a fortnight ago, when he left to give Badger a message from that bitch hopper Effie. When Caleb didn't come back with an answer, Effie took off for parts unknown. She musta figured it had all gone wrong."

"What had gone wrong?" Henry said.

"Her scheme to get money outta Badger. She told me he left behind something in her room that she reckoned he would pay plenty to get back. I warned her he was too vicious to play with, but she had him pegged for a drunken gump."

"What did Badger leave behind?"

"Don't know. And neither did Effie."

"Then why did she think Badger valued it?"

"Well, it musta been worth something. Else why was Badger carrying it in a leather satchel with a big brass lock?"

"Did the satchel have any distinctive markings?"

"It had some letters stamped on it. And it looked mighty shabby."

"What did the letters spell out?"

She suddenly looked abashed. "I can't recall."

Henry studied her a moment. "Can you read, Dora?"

"No! And I ain't proud of it neither."

"Nor should you be ashamed of it," Henry said gently.

"I know my numbers well enough," she said, her braggadocio returning. "And I recall the number three on the satchel."

Henry nodded. "What did Effie do with satchel?"

"She hid it of course. She sent Caleb to tell Badger that she was keeping it safe for him and would give it back for a price."

"Do you know where she sent Caleb?"

"Some hick town called Plumford. Badger was allus bragging about living in a fine house there and working for a fine military gentleman. So Caleb took the cars there."

"And that was the last you saw of him?"

She swallowed hard and nodded. "But we sure as hell saw Badger soon enough. He busted into the house screaming for Effie the very next day, but she had already lit out. So he turns his anger on Hag Scudder, bellowing about wanting his satchel back. She don't know nothin' about it and starts shaking and quaking so bad I near laughed out loud. But it weren't so funny when he pulled a big knife outta his boot and threatened her with it. I don't much like Scudder, but I couldn't just stand by and see her get kilt. So I told Badger where his goddam satchel was. I'm the only one who knew Effie hid it under the floorboards 'neath her bed. Once Badger got it back and saw that the lock weren't tampered with, he settled down some. I guess he figured he couldn't kill us all like he done poor Caleb, so he just made us swear never to speak of the bag to anyone." She took a breath. "That's all I know. Now you tell me how Badger done in Caleb."

Henry explained where we had found Caleb's body and how we thought he had been pushed over the cliff after being struck from behind with a blow to the head.

"That is just like Badger to whack a man from behind," she said. "He ain't worth a pinch of shit. And Caleb was worth his weight in gold. Never mind he was a darky. He was a fine feller all the same. How he used to make us all hoot with his jokes and antics. Such a merry boy. He was but eighteen, you know. Oh, I cannot believe that he is dead!" She covered her face with her hands for a moment, but when she lowered them her eyes were dry and her expression cold. "Damn Badger to hell. I should stick him with my dagger and send him there myself."

"If you do, you will hang for it," Henry told her. "And that would be unjust, for he is the one who should hang for Caleb's murder."

"Oh, I would very much like to see Badger dance a horn pipe in the air," she said.

"If we collect enough evidence against him, we can bring him to trial," Henry said. "Will you testify?"

She gave out a bitter laugh. "Who would believe a whore?"

"I do," Henry said.

"But how many other men think like you?"

"I would no more wish them to think like me than I would wish to think like them. We need only to think for ourselves to do the right thing. It is the individual conscience that matters," Henry told her. He is by nature incapable of talking down (or up for that matter) to anyone.

If Dora understood the meaning of his words, she did not show it. I handed her some coins and told her to buy vegetables and fruit for herself and the others, taking care that the little girl got her full share. She promised me she would, but might have kept the money for herself. Or the child may be sucking on a juicy orange as I write this. That is what I hope, at any rate.

Henry and I did not tarry further in the Black Sea district, for we had fished from it all the information we could.

"It seems all we have proven for our trouble is that Badger was in Boston at the time of Peck's death," I stated glumly as we made our way back to the station. "This does not help Trump in the least."

"There are other suspects to consider," Henry said. "Such as the guests who were staying at Peck's house the night he was murdered. Do you know much about them?"

"Next to nothing. I had only a brief conversation with Lieutenant Finch and barely exchanged a word with the little banker or his wife. And Justice Phyfe saw no need to interrogate them, so convinced was he that Trump had murdered Peck." I stopped in my tracks. "I suggest we remain in town to interrogate them ourselves, Henry. I have lodgings in a house on Chestnut Street and invite you to be my guest there. My landlord and his family are spending the month at Cape Ann and have taken the maid along with them, but I am sure we can manage to fend for ourselves."

"What about Trump?"

"This *is* about him," I replied a bit impatiently. "The only way to prevent him from being sentenced to hang is to discover who really killed Peck."

"Yes, of course," Henry said. "But do not forget that Trump is in more immediate danger, Adam. He could be hanged without so much as a trial if he remains vulnerable to foes like Badger. I must go back to Concord without delay and enlist the aid of my friends to get him removed to a safer jail."

"Of course. Do what you can to help Trump in Concord. I will remain in town and interview Vail and Finch."

"The soldier seems a more likely suspect than the banker," Henry said. "I say this not because I think a banker would be too principled to commit murder. Indeed, I wager a soldier has a higher sense of honor than one who traffics in money. But soldiers sometime kill for honor, do they not? Take care, Adam. Lieutenant Finch could be dangerous."

Henry can act too much the big brother at times, but I promised I would keep up my guard. After assuring me he would inform Julia that I was staying the night in Boston, Henry continued on his way to the terminal, and I headed toward the Provident Bank on Tremont Street, where I recalled Mr. Vail had stated he was employed when he testified. Upon arriving at the bank I was informed Mr. Vail had left for the day. It was against bank policy to give out his home address, so I had little choice but to wait until the morrow to interview him at his office. I did not know where Lt. Finch resided either. My hope was that Mr. Vail might.

Rather than waste what little remained of the afternoon, I decided to go to my own office. Although Dr. Quincy had given me leave to stay in Plumford until my grandfather was fully recovered, he received me coolly. My extended absence as his assistant has clearly displeased him even though this is a slow time for the practice. Our patients, mostly ladies of the privileged class, have by and large left the city for the season. I confess I do not miss doctoring them. Their physical ailments are usually minor, brought on by assiduous dieting, tight lacing, lack of exercise, and genteel indolence. Or by sheer silliness. They swig vinegar and nibble chalk to give themselves a fashionable pallor, then come to us with stomach complaints. Dr. Quincy prescribes laudanum and morphine far too often in my opinion, and I have told him so. And he has told me that my simple prescription of robust walks in the fresh air demeans our profession. In truth, we were not getting on well before I left for Plumford.

We got on well enough today, however. That another doctor was present during our brief meeting no doubt fostered our congeniality. Upon meeting Dr. Eames, I immediately felt at ease with him. He has an infectious amiability, although I suppose infectious is a poor choice of words when referring to a doctor who specializes in venereal disease. When Dr. Eames learned that I hailed from Plumford, he spontaneously mentioned that he had recently advised a patient from that very town. He said no more than that and might have felt he had said too much as it was. His specialty requires the utmost discretion. Hence I did not inquire further, assuming that it was Peck who consulted with him. Did not blame Peck for seeking a second opinion, for mine had been dire indeed.

As I record this journal entry I can hear the city sounds of rattling carriage wheels, rumbling omnibuses, and shrill voices

coming through my open window and miss the peaceful silence of Plumford at nightfall. Mostly, though, I miss Julia.
Shall I write her a letter? It would be the next best thing to
conversing with her. We have conversed very little since we
kissed and perhaps, in this letter, I can set things right between
us again. Yes, I shall write to her.

JULIA'S NOTEBOOK

Tuesday evening, 18 August

Poor dear Molly Munger. Henceforth I shall have only kind thoughts concerning her. But as I marched toward her home this afternoon, my thoughts were anything but kind. And little wonder, for I had not seen hide nor hair of her for a week. Her father's excuse that she was indisposed with some vague ailment had worn mighty thin, and I needed to know for certain if Miss Molly had any intention of returning to work. I sorely hoped she would, for domestic helpers are hard to come by in Plumford. Most village girls prefer to work at the mills. Truth be told, so would I. And if I cannot earn my way with my art, I may well end up standing afore a loom instead of an easel.

Of course, if I so desired it, Grandfather would happily support me here in Plumford and give me leave to paint to my heart's content. But I would *not* be content merely dabbling at art whilst caring for an elderly gentleman, no matter how dear he be to me. I must strike out on my own in order to make a name for myself in my field. If I were a man that would be perfectly understandable to Grandfather, and I am sure he would encourage my ambitions, just as he encouraged his son to seek his fortune at sea and his grandson to become a doctor. But he encourages me, a mere woman, to stay by his hearth and close to his heart, where I will be safe if not satisfied.

Yet Molly was not safe in Plumford, was she? Her strong father and upright mother could not protect her from the evil she encountered right here. I pray her life is not ruined because of it. She is not yet seventeen!

As I approached the Munger house I could hear ferocious blows and pounding coming from Mr. Munger's butchery alongside it. Perchance this noise prevented Mrs. Munger from hearing my knocks upon her front door, but I do not think so. I am quite sure I glimpsed her white-capped head peeking through a downstairs window that offered a good view of me standing on the porch. I went around back where I saw a few sheep contentedly grazing in a field by the river. I knocked on the back door, and this time Mrs. Munger answered.

"Miss Bell, what a surprise," said she without a trace of a smile.

"I have come to inquire about Molly."

"Have you now?" Rather than move her large frame aside so that I could enter, she remained rigid in the doorway, arms akimbo.

"How is she faring, Mrs. Munger?"

"Molly?"

"Yes. Is she feeling any better?"

"Any better than what, pray?"

I did pray. For patience. "Better than Thursday last when your husband came to tell me she was ill, Mrs. Munger. My concern for Molly grows with each passing day she does not come back to work."

"Why, our Molly is not at all sick. I reckon Mr. Munger just didn't want to come out and tell you the truth, Miss Bell. Molly has up and quit you. She don't care to work at the doc's no more."

"Oh! And when was I to be informed of this?"

"Ain't you being informed of it now?"

I felt my cheeks burn with indignation. "I would like to discuss this with Molly herself if I may, Mrs. Munger."

She did not budge from the doorway. "My daughter has gone to work for my aunt in Ipswich. Good Day, Miss Bell."

I did not budge either. "Molly could not have gone quite yet, for I spied her looking out an upstairs window as I came up the path," I declared. In truth I had only spied Mrs. Munger's visage in a window, but I sensed she was lying and so gave her tit for tat.

We eyeballed each other in silence, neither blinking, until tears suddenly flooded Mrs. Munger's eyes. She covered her face with her apron and sobbed.

"Please tell me what is troubling you so, Mrs. Munger. Perhaps I can be of help."

She dropped her apron and considered me. "You might help at that. Molly regards you highly."

'Twas news to me that she did. During our short acquaintanceship, I have received little enough respect from the girl but more than a good share of back talk. Nevertheless, I followed Mrs. Munger up the narrow staircase and into a small, neat bed chamber. Molly was lying atop the covers staring up at the ceiling. She was barefoot and dressed in a muslin nightgown, so she did not seem to have any immediate intention of going out. Yet a bright pink bonnet adorned her head. She stared at me blankly but did not move a muscle. She seemed to be waiting for me to speak first, and so I did.

"What a pretty bonnet, Molly. May I ask why you are wearing it in bed?"

Mrs. Munger sighed and said, "She has not taken the fool thing off for a good three days."

Without uttering a word, Molly turned away to face the wall, giving me the back of her bonnet to regard. Regard it I did, for it looked mighty familiar, right down to the marabou feather trimming. Why, it could have been the very bonnet I had seen on the empty little head of the banker's wife! Had she given it to Molly before she left town? That did not seem likely. Mrs. Vail had made it clear to me that she prized her bonnet too highly to ever part with it. Besides, she did not even know Molly. Perchance she'd left her bonnet behind accidentally and Molly had come upon it somehow. Or could it be that the bonnet Molly was wearing was not Mrs. Vail's after all, but her very own? How could she have acquired it? Mrs. Vail told me that a "dear friend" had ordered her bonnet from an exclusive Boston milliner. Could Molly have the same dear friend? Someone with a penchant for women decked out in pink bonnets? I recalled the sly smile I had seen Capt. Peck give Mrs. Vail. Could it be possible . . . ?

"Were you well acquainted with Captain Peck, Molly?" I ventured to ask.

After a long moment of silence, I saw the marabou plume on Molly's hat bob up and down as she nodded yes.

"He seduced my girl with that blasphemous bonnet," Mrs. Munger said, confirming my suspicions.

"His murder must have been a great shock to her. Is that why she has taken to bed?"

"She took to bed from the shock of what he told her a few days before he died," Mrs. Munger said. "And she miscarried because of it too."

"Good Lord! She was with child?"

"The fetus had not yet stirred when she lost it, and she is as good as recovered from the ordeal."

"Are you sure she is going to be all right, Mrs. Munger?"

"Yes, I know a good deal about birthing. But I know *nothing* about . . ." She clapped her mouth shut and turned her eyes from me.

I waited for her to continue, and when she did not, I sat

myself on the edge of the bed and patted Molly's back. "I am very sorry," I told her. "I know this is a mighty bleak time for you. Nevertheless, you have your whole life ahead of you. A full, happy life, I am sure, for you still have your health and—"

"What if she don't?" Mrs. Munger bawled. "What if she caught the pox from that villain? He told her he had it for sure."

I was stunned silent by Peck's vileness but only for a moment. "I will send Dr. Adam to examine Molly as soon as he returns from Boston."

She looked relieved yet cautious. "No one but you and Doc Adam must know about this."

"What about Molly's father?"

"Oh, Ira knows." Mrs. Munger sank down on the bed beside me. "I wish he didn't, but it couldn't be helped. He was home when Molly miscarried, just back from playing town ball. In her upset state, she confessed all to him, even that she might have caught the pox from Peck. He listened real quiet and did not so much as raise his voice, much less his hand, to our daughter. He just went out to the butchery and stayed there all night. He has not spoken a word of it since."

"And neither shall I speak a word of this to anyone but my cousin," I assured Mrs. Munger. "This whole affair will be as dead and buried as Peck."

"I pray that be so. But what if Molly got the pox from him? Do you know what the signs are, Miss Bell?"

"Like most women, I have been kept in the dark about such things. But Dr. Adam will know. And I am sure he can prescribe remedies if she did. She is young and resilient. In time she will forget this sad episode in her life."

"I do not want to forget!" Molly sat up and stared at me with tear-glazed eyes. "That's why I will always wear this bonnet."

"To remember the heartless man who gave it to you?"

"No, to repent that I gave myself to such a man as that." She turned to her mother. "Bury me in this bonnet, Ma. That is my final wish."

This morbid directive caused Mrs. Munger to start sobbing again. I sat quietly on the bed and contemplated what Molly had said. Her belief that the bonnet was a symbol of her disgrace and that she should wear it in shame forevermore—or even for another minute!—seemed absurd to me.

"Allow me, dear," I said, and before she could lift a hand to prevent me I yanked the hateful thing off her head.

I tossed it to the floor and trampled upon it till it was flattened. I was breathing rather hard when I was done. I looked at Molly. She looked back at me with an expression of pure relief.

Mrs. Munger gingerly picked up the destroyed bonnet by a frayed ribbon, as one would pick up a rat by its tail. "I will burn it," she said.

Molly insisted on watching it burn and went downstairs with us. Her mother opened the oven door of the cookstove, removed the johnnycake baking on a tin, and added some wood sticks to spruce up the fire. She tossed the bonnet onto the flames, and we all watched it blacken and shrivel to nothing. Then we ate the johnnycake and drank some tea. I was pleased to see that Molly's appetite was as keen as ever.

I left the house shortly thereafter and saw Ira Munger walking toward the grazing sheep. He was wearing a leather apron stained black with blood and grease. I waved to him. He solemnly nodded back to me, then gripped one of the sheep by the nape of the neck and began pulling it toward the butchery. It did not so much as let out a single bleat of protest, for it did not know its fate. Alas, I did. I looked away and hurried home.

There I impatiently awaited Adam's return from Boston, anxious to tell him about Molly. When I heard the stage pull up in front of the house I hurried out, expecting Adam to be on it. He was not, and the note the driver handed me was not from him, but from Henry Thoreau, who had dispatched the driver to deliver it to me from the Concord station. Scrawled in pencil on a sheet torn from his notebook, Henry's terse message informed me that Adam would be spending the night in the city. How could Henry know this? Had he taken the cars to Boston with Adam this morning? If so, why had Henry returned without him? What is keeping Adam in the city tonight? And what made him decide to go there in the first place?

So many questions! And the biggest one of all is this: Will Adam ever confide in me again? How paradoxical it is that our moment of intimacy has rendered us strangers. I long to be his closest friend again, his trusted companion and fellow traveler through life. But now that we are adults this can no longer be possible unless . . . No! We *cannot* marry!

ADAM'S JOURNAL

Wednesday, August 19th

Can it be that I shall discover Peck's killer this evening? Perhaps I already have.

I interviewed Edwin Vail at the Provident Bank on Tremont this morning. For such an unremarkable little man, he has a rather grand office, with tall windows and an enormous ornate desk. Behind the desk, built right into the wall, is some sort of vault, the steel door of which was shut tight.

As Vail was greeting me with cool civility, a nervous young man carrying a metal case hurried in. "You were due here twenty minutes ago," Vail told him in a severe tone. "I came near to sending a guard after you."

The young man winced. "Please forgive my being tardy, sir." He hefted the case onto a solid side table. "I left the printer posthaste, but my hack got held up in traffic."

"Why did you not disembark from the conveyance and continue on foot?"

"These bank plates are heavy, sir! And I feared I would be too vulnerable to thieves."

"You are chock-full of excuses, aren't you? If you are so much as five minutes late in future, I will see you never work at this bank or any other as long as you live. Now get back to work."

The browbeaten bank clerk slinked out, closing the door behind him. Vail turned his glare toward me, as if seeking another target upon which to further vent his anger. But he must have thought better of it, for he only motioned for me to sit and took his own seat behind his desk. Its massiveness dwarfed him. "So what is it you want, Dr. Walker?" he asked with impatient bluntness.

Here I admit to being caught inexcusably unprepared. I had thought we would exchange pleasantries and eventually get around to Peck's demise, but I saw that would not wash. Thought fast and saved my bacon by pulling my gold watch out of my waistcoat pocket.

"This timepiece," I said, "was found in the front yard of my grandfather's house the evening you were there, Mr. Vail. Given its quality, I presumed it yours. You left Plumford before I had opportunity to return it to you, and I came here to do so now."

Vail's eyes lit up at the sight of the embossed gold watch-case. "Let me see it."

He extended his hand, rising slightly to reach across the broad expanse of his desk, and I had no choice but to unhitch the chain and drop my timepiece into his soft, open palm. My heart also dropped as I watched him examine it with a covetous eye. He nodded and smiled as if recognizing it and grasped it in his hand as if it had found its way home again. Then he looked hard at me and frowned. "No, no, it is not mine." He handed my watch back to me. The case felt oily from his touch. "No doubt its owner will soon enough claim it."

"Well, neither Mr. Thoreau nor Mr. Upson has done so. And the only other guests in the yard that evening were you and Captain Peck."

"Do not forget the Indian was also present. Perhaps the

watch is his." He smiled at his own ludicrous suggestion. "Though it is doubtful such a savage as he can even tell time."

"Mr. Trump is no more a savage than I am," I replied.

Vail widened his eyes to feign fear. "Then I beseech you not to scalp me the way Trump scalped Peck!" He smiled again.

"You do not seem much distressed over your friend's demise."

"Peck was not my friend. Why, I barely knew the man."

"Oh? You were not his business partner?" I voiced this in perhaps too inquisitorial a manner, but snooping into the affairs of others is all new to me.

"I have no idea what you're talking about," Vail said, looking at me as if I were insane. "I cannot imagine how you made such a preposterous assumption."

I considered telling Vail that Peck himself had told me but thought better of it. It was obvious that if I confronted him further in such a direct manner I would get nowhere. "I beg your pardon, Mr. Vail. I did not mean to offend you by that question."

"Your offence, sir, is that you are wasting my time." His stood abruptly. "Good day."

Such a rude dismissal left me far less inclined to be polite. I reckoned I had nothing to lose (and perhaps something to gain) if I riled him again.

So I remained seated and said, "Then it was only your wife who had a close friendship with the captain."

I had not forgotten the way Mrs. Vail had looked so intensely at Peck upon her arrival. And I hoped my impertinence might trigger an outburst from Vail that would reveal more than he wanted me to know.

His face grew red, and his eyes bulged like a rabbit's. Unfortunately, his anger left him speechless.

Tried again. "I came to that conclusion because she brought him a volume of poetry when you visited. And I heard you yourself proclaim to Captain Peck that your wife—Lucy, is it?—insisted on accompanying you to Plumford."

"How dare you presume to call my wife by her Christian name?" he sputtered.

I had clearly presumed far worse than that, yet he was calling me on a point of etiquette. That made me think he had plenty to hide. "Again I apologize," I said. "I was only trying to remind you of what you said when—"

"Enough!" He straightened his waistcoat over the bulge of his belly. "Only to stifle your ill-mannered prying do I tell you my wife suggested we take up Peck's offer to visit him for the simple reason that she wanted to get some fresh country air. As for the book Mrs. Vail brought him, it was merely a formal gift a guest gives a host. She went to no great trouble to obtain it, for we reside directly across the street from a fine bookseller. Now that I think upon it, I recall that it was my idea to bring Captain Peck a book. Mrs. Vail did not *know* the man well, and for you to imply she did comes perilously close to a brazen insult."

I declared I wished to cause no offence. However, I remained firmly ensconced in my chair, ignoring his movements toward the door. He waited by it, and I waited him out until he reluctantly spoke again.

"Such a dreadful business it was," he muttered, eyeing me closely as though to gauge the effect of his words on me. "All my dear wife and I want to do is forget our perilous proximity to such a heinous crime as that. Why, that wild Indian could have slaughtered us as well as Peck as we lay asleep and defenseless in our bed! It is all too horrible to contemplate, and I do not wish to speak of it further."

I could hardly force him to. Nor could I come right out and call him a liar for denying he had any business dealings with Peck. I would have to find out about them from another. How relieved he looked when I rose from my seat and made my way to the door. Before I left I asked him if he knew of Lt. Finch's whereabouts. I was not surprised when he replied that he knew nothing of the man and had barely exchanged two words altogether with him during their brief acquaintanceship. Vail and I did not shake hands in parting.

As I stood outside the bank wondering how to go about finding Finch, I recalled the man's newfound devotion to town ball. With no other avenue of inquiry open to me, I walked to the Common where he had told me he played.

Once there I abandoned the promenades and struck out across the rolling grass. As I passed the Great Elm I paused to regard it. That this fine specimen, over two hundred years old, is still standing never fails to inspire me. When its very core started rotting away a century ago, the large cavity was filled with clay and the exterior swathed with a canvas bandage. The tree healed! And when four limbs were torn from it in a gale ten years ago, they were bolted back in place with iron bands and appear to have knitted back to the trunk! My hope is that advancements in medical science will some day make it possible for doctors to perform such curative feats upon humans.

This morning, however, I had less uplifting thoughts concerning the Great Elm. My first recollection was that the son of an Indian sachem had been hanged from it. Like Trump, he had been accused of murdering a white man, and although there were no witnesses to the crime, the young brave's insolent manner toward the governing body of Puritans was considered proof enough of his guilt. I fear that will be Trump's fate too if I fail to find Peck's true murderer.

I had yet another dark recollection regarding the Great Elm's history as a gallows. Two centuries ago brave Mary Dyer was also hanged from a stout bough for daring to preach her Quaker faith. That she had given birth to a deformed stillborn child was considered confirmation of her union with the Devil. Governor Winthrop went so far as to have the infant corpse exhumed and gives a detailed description of it in his journal of 1638. Among other grotesqueries it had four horns over the eyes, and instead of toes, claws with sharp talons. Today I could not help but wonder if my ancestor Hezekiah Walker had attended the public exhumation to see if the babe looked like the one he had sired with his cousin back in England.

Thoughts of my own cousin filled my mind. The letter I had written Julia last night was tucked in my waistcoat and lay heavy on my heart. I could not decide whether to burn it or send it to her.

Strode on toward the Smoker's Circle over the knoll. As always, there were a dozen or so men gathered there, puffing away on their pipes and cigars in the only area of the Common where such indulgence is allowed. Pulled my short clay traveling pipe from my coat pocket and offered around my tobacco pouch of the latest blend. That earned me a seat on the bench betwixt two old-timers, and as we smoked I steered the subject away from the weather to that of town ball. Turns out both oldsters were keen spectators of the sport, and when I described the lanky Finch to them they well knew the fellow I meant. But they had no idea where he resided. They suggested I return that evening, when men came to the Common to form teams and play. Perhaps Finch would be amongst them. Or others would know how to locate him.

I noticed a group of rough urchins playing catch nearby. Boys such as they were always hanging about the men who played town ball, begging for the honor of carrying their sticks and bags. Some of those I approached might well have performed this service for me in games past, but now they all eyed me warily. No doubt my high silk hat put them in mind of the day watchmen. Fearing they might bolt rather than deal with me, I scooped up a ball that had bounced near and began a game of catch and toss with them. One boy had a glove, so I smoked a few overhand tosses at him, which he failed to catch, and they all gathered around to see how I gripped the ball to make it curve so. There is nothing better to form trust between members of the male species than a shared sport, and I confess I threw myself into the impromptu fun of pitching and catching. Perhaps I have too much boy in me yet but no matter. Would regret losing the simple joy of play. And if one day I should be blessed with fine, healthy boys of my own to play ball with, it would fill my heart to its full measure.

Remembered my purpose, stopped tossing the ball, and called the boys around me again. But rather than give them more pointers, I inquired about Lt. Finch. They not only knew who he was, but could appraise his strengths and weaknesses as a striker and runner in exacting detail. One boy mentioned he had seen the lieutenant just an hour ago, marching alone on the Mill Dam roadway. So there I went.

Halfway across the long dam I spotted Finch staring at the boats bringing goods downriver. I strode toward him, and upon my approach he greeted me forthrightly. He told me he walked across the dam to Brookline and back most days as he had little else to do in his present state of unemployment. And it helped him stay fit.

Fit the man certainly is. He is also trained as a soldier in the ways of killing and even knows the particulars of Indian scalping. If I had not been so prejudiced against Badger, I might have considered the lieutenant the prime suspect of Peck's murder right off. Yet I liked the lieutenant and was still reluctant to see him as a murderer.

He marveled over the chance occurrence of us meeting on the dam roadway, and I told him I often walked there for I had rooms nearby. He inquired if I could suggest places in the area where a single man could get cheap but wholesome meals, for he couldn't stomach the slop served up at his boardinghouse and was near close to starving. I recommended an oyster house on Union Street, but he said he could not afford it. So I offered to treat him to dinner there forthwith. I too was near starving.

In less than ten minutes we were being greeted by one of the establishment's proprietors, Mr. Atwood, who ushered us toward the bar where I recognized Daniel Webster gulping down oysters. But I wished to engage Finch in private conversation and suggested a table in a quiet corner instead. We started off with a mound of raw oysters the size of plates, come direct from the harbor mudflats. I went at them with the shucking knife the waiter supplied, but Finch tossed his aside, declaring it too dull.

"Request another," I said.

"No need." He took from the inside of his coat sleeve what looked like a flat piece of horn. He snapped his wrist and a long, thin blade sprang out of it. "My flick knife shall do the job handily."

He proceeded to slip the blade between top and bottom shell and run it around the mollusk hemispheres with practiced precision. I could not help but imagine such a blade running around the top of poor Peck's skull with the same smooth skill and ease. This did not dampen my appetite, however, and I did my best to match Finch oyster for oyster. But my shucking utensil was no match for his killer knife, which made his work so quick he beat me at least three to one. He really was a marvel to watch, slipping his blade into each oyster, slitting it open, severing the flesh from the shell, scooping it up with the tip of the knife and popping it into his mouth, all with the swiftness of a bird on the wing gulping an insect. After dispatching with heaps of oysters in the raw we went on to consume piles of them fried in batter, along with bowls of steamed Ipswich clams and roasted quahogs. All this washed down with sarsaparilla by me and with tumblers of brandy and water by Finch. 'Twas the brandy that loosened his tongue.

"You did not attend Captain Peck's funeral yesterday," he commented to me.

"No, I had business to see to here in Boston. And I was not his comrade as you were."

"We were comrades in arms only. Never friends. I served briefly under Captain Peck at Fort Cass, but I was transferred out west before the Cherokee removal. Peck came west later, and we got on well enough at Fort Laramie. We hunted buffalo together when the herds swung near the fort. Peck was a fine horseman but only a passing shot. Rumor was that he had profited mightily during his posting in Georgia, something to do with a gold mine but nothing specific. He acted at Laramie like he was now in the Army more for amusement than his having to make a career. Always had the best horse and latest repeating rifle and pistols and paid extra for comfortable quarters. He got too uppity to follow orders he didn't like and resigned one day, Badger with him, as always."

"How long ago was that?"

"Four years or thereabouts. His going was nothing to me till I decided to muster out myself and head back east. Upon arriving in Boston I met up with some soldiers at Fort Independence. They told me Peck had a fine place out in Plumford and looked to be making money hand over fist. So I rented me a horse and rode out there to see if my old captain might be in need of my services."

"What sort of services?" I asked.

"I was willing to leave that up to Peck. When a man is making money hand over fist, he can surely afford to hire someone like me to help him take care of it."

"Do you know how Peck was making all this money?"

"You ask a lot of questions, doctor." Finch gave me a wolfish smile. "Do you expect to buy the answers with clam shells?"

"I'll buy you another brandy."

"I accept your kind offer." After he was served he said, "As to how Peck made his money, all I know is that it had something to do with a Frenchy jeweler in Boston, same one who made those fine engravings we goggled in Peck's study. Where did he find such limber ladies to model for him, I wonder."

"They were far too anatomically supple," I said, "to be anything but figments of the artist's imagination."

"Do you speak from medical or personal knowledge, Doctor?"

"We are getting off the subject of Peck."

"Well, if anyone would know where to find such women, it would be him. Peck was always seeking out novel enticements. I expect that's why the poor devil ended up with the pox."

"He told you of his ailment?"

"He didn't have to. I saw right off he had it bad and that it would do him no good to caterwaul about it. But caterwaul he did. You'd think he was the first man ever to perish from the pox."

"So you knew he was dying of it."

"I guessed as much. He looked god-awful, and he was suffering mightily." Finch shrugged. "Could be his killer did him a favor by cutting short his torment."

"No," I said. "I believe Peck's killer wanted to torment him as much as possible. He scalped him *alive* and then dangled the scalp in front of his face!"

"A pretty sight that must have been." Finch laughed, and when I did not join him he said, "Come now, Dr. Walker. Surely a macabre sense of humor helps a man in your profession as well as in mine. Both soldiers and doctors see too much of death to be in awe of it."

"It is life I am in awe of," I said. "And no one has the right to play God by cutting short the life of another, even to end his suffering."

"You think not?" Finch took a long sip from his tumbler. "Well, I will admit here and now that I have done so."

"Are you telling me you killed Peck?"

He laughed again, turned his tumbler upside down, and arched an eyebrow. I got him another drink, and he continued. "No, I am not confessing to Peck's murder, Doctor. The man I killed was a soldier out of Fort Laramie name of Jamie James. The young fool was in my patrol party and managed to get himself captured by crazy redskins during the night, most likely when he roamed off to relieve himself. We were awakened by his horrible screams in the distance, and my men wanted to rush off half-cocked to try and save him. Fearing an ambush, I ordered them to stay put and went out alone with my buffalo gun. It was real easy for me to find the redskins, and I am sure that was their intention. They had made camp not far from us, but it was across a deep ravine more than two hundred yards wide. Knowing we couldn't get at 'em there, the devils felt safe to light a big bonfire and put on a show to taunt us. With much whooping and dancing, they were flaying poor Jamie alive. That's right, Doctor. They were stripping flesh off his arms and legs like you'd peel the hide off a deer. I never doubted for a moment what I had to do. Laid down, steadied the long barrel of my gun on a stump, and shot a bullet across the ravine. It took off half Jamie's head and gave him instant peace. Those damn savages scattered afore I could get off another shot, but leastways I'd put an end to their fun."

"That's a horrible tale, Lieutenant."

"And a true one, I swear! Indians are the greatest of tormentors. Torture is an art with them, although Captain Peck was not so artfully dispatched."

"What could possibly be gained by such cruelty as that?"

"Nothing by me," Finch said. "Peck was worth far more to me alive than dead. He told me he was involved in a very lucrative enterprise and would cut me in on it if his business partner agreed. I was to replace Badger, who had mucked up somehow."

"Replace Badger doing what?"

Finch shook his head. "Never got the chance to find out, which vexes me still. After Peck was murdered, I hoped to talk to the little banker about it, but he lit out before I could."

"I just saw Vail, and he claimed he knew nothing of Peck's business affairs.

"Well, he is a lying little buffalo chip. He and Peck were thick as thieves."

"You think they were involved in something unlawful?"

"Peck told me as much."

"And you were still interested in working for him?"

"Oh, I had some misgiving about it. I came east aiming to find honest work. But beggars cannot be choosers, and I learned in the Army that you must do what is most expedient for your survival." He stared at me with cold hawk eyes but smiled as friendly as you please. "If you have any more questions I could do with more refreshment."

Once again I had his tumbler refilled to keep his tongue well-lubricated.

"What did you think of the banker's wife?" I asked him.

He looked most pleased to tell me. "I thought her a very tasty piece of goods indeed. What a little darling she looked in all her silken ruffles and fine gold jewelry. I reckon it took both men to keep her in such grand style."

"Both men?"

"Well, sure. Peck was as familiar with her charms as her husband. I could see that from twenty feet away, when I spied them in that little summerhouse of Peck's. What did he call it?"

"A belvedere. Perhaps he was simply showing Mrs. Vail the view it commanded."

"No, it was she who was showing him a view—that of her two snowy hillocks. She had unbuttoned her bodice for his delectation, yet Peck kept his hands to himself. He said they must refrain from such intimacy for he had something important to tell her. Then he bowed his head and fell silent. She urged him to go on, but all he did was hum and haw. When she buttoned up her bodice, I lost interest and went on."

"Do you think Peck was trying to tell Mrs. Vail that he had syphilis?"

"I shouldn't wonder that was his intention. Doubt he ever got his nerve up though. Ain't an easy thing to tell a lady."

"She should know for her own good."

"Well, that's not my concern." Finch leaned back in his chair and stretched out his long legs beneath the table. He looked drowsy and no wonder. His belly was full of food and drink. "That belvedere was quite the stage, come to think of it, for I witnessed yet another scene that took place there."

"You are not referring to Peck's murder, are you?"

"Of course not. I would not have remained a mere on-looker if I had seen that nasty act unfold. What I saw and heard occurred the night before. If you would like, I will recount the scene to you, but my throat is somewhat dry."

I was beginning to wonder if he was just fabricating stories to keep me buying drinks for him, but the brandy at the Oyster House was cheap enough, and I had time enough to listen. So I ordered him yet another, and he began spouting off again.

"When I showed up at Peck's house, he did not seem too pleased to see me. And I was quite shocked at the sorry sight of him. But once we got drinking and talking of old skirmishes, we warmed up to each other again. Peck could no longer consume as much whiskey as he once did, though, and he cut short our reminiscences. He told me he was expecting another visitor. The more the merrier, said I. But he claimed he had a private matter to discuss with the other man and excused himself. Left alone in his parlor, I had nothing better to do than continue drinking, and soon enough the entire contents of the whiskey bottle had gone down my hatch. So I left the room to find either Peck or more drink in the house. Finding neither, I stumbled outside. It was a fine night, and I decided to take a little stroll. Ended up at that damn belvedere. I heard Peck's voice coming forth from it, along with another man's. Peck's voice was pleading. The other's was cold and angry."

"What did the other man look like?"

"I could not make him out in the shadows."

"Well, what were they saying to each other?"

"That I cannot recall. I believe I was more than a little drunk, you see."

"I see you are more than a little drunk now, Lieutenant. Perhaps you will not recall this conversation either."

He straightened up immediately and looked offended. "I hold my liquor far better than most men and can remember anything I choose to. But I am not in the habit of eavesdropping on private conversations, Doctor. So I paid little mind to the one taking place in the belvedere."

"Yet it might have been between Peck and his future killer. What was the captain pleading for? And why was the other man so angry?"

Finch rubbed his temples. "It is all at the edge of my mind, but I cannot get at it. I confess I was moon-eyed as a loon."

I wanted to reach across and shake the memory out of his brain. Then an idea blossomed in my head. "Will you allow me to hypnotize you, Lieutenant Finch?"

He narrowed his eyes. "That depends."

"On what?"

"On what the blazes I would be allowing you to do exactly."

I realized he did not know what hypnotism was, and I explained the process to him as simply as possible.

He still looked dubious. "You mean to say that by putting

me to sleep you can get me to recall things I have no recollection of awake?"

"More or less. I may at least be able to bring forth a memory fragment that could identify the man Peck was talking to so fervently. This mysterious visitor might have asked Peck to meet him again at the belvedere the next evening in order to kill him there."

Finch thought about it a moment. "If Peck's killer is hiding in my head, I suppose I owe it to my old captain to try and flush him out. But I do not care to let my guard down in a public place such as this."

"I can hypnotize you in the privacy of my rooms. The family I board with is away this month, along with the help."

"So the house would be empty except for us?"

I assured him it would be, and he offered to go there directly. But as we strode out of the restaurant he slipped on some clamshells strewn upon the sawdusted planks and, although his quick reflexes saved him from falling flat on his face, I realized he was far too inebriated to hypnotize. It might even do him harm. I told him as much and suggested we try the experiment the next day.

"I plan to leave Boston tomorrow," he told me. "But I will sleep off the brandy this afternoon and be sobered up by nightfall."

Hence it was agreed he would come to my rooms at eight this evening. Before we parted on the street I asked if he by any chance knew where the Vails lived.

Finch gave me a wink. "So you mean to visit the missus. Need I remind you that she most likely had relations with Captain Pox?"

"Need I remind you that I am a doctor?" I retorted. "Mrs. Vail should be informed that she might be infected, and I suppose I am the one left to do it."

He nodded, swayed a bit, and said, "I recall her mentioning to Peck that she and her husband had recently removed to a most prestigious boardinghouse."

"There are more than a few of those in Boston," I said.

"Near Parson's Corner or some such place," Finch added, then went on his way, spine ramrod straight, and only the slightest drunken swagger in his step.

Although I am familiar with just about every neighborhood in our dear City on a Hill, I had never heard of Parson's Corner and knew not where to go forth. I could not very well return to the bank and ask Mr. Vail where his wife and he resided, but I recalled that he had told me they lived directly across from a bookseller. There are more than a few of those in Boston too. One that immediately came to mind was the Old Corner Bookstore, situated where School and Washington Streets meet, and known, because intellectuals and muses congregate there, as *Parnassus* Corner! Off I went in the hope of finding Mrs. Vail thereabouts.

As always, Washington Street was teeming with coupes and coaches, phaetons and buggies, wagons, omnibuses, and shays. The brick sidewalks were clogged with all manner of pedestrians, from genteel shoppers carrying bandboxes and parasols, to ragamuffin newsboys hawking penny papers and Irish crones selling apples. When I paused to watch the antics of an organ monkey, the bright pink bonnet of another bystander caught my eye. Unfortunately, it also caught the eye of the monkey, and he made a leap to snatch it off her head. The organ grinder jerked the monkey back by its chain before it could touch her person, but still she screamed and ran off. I took chase and managed to reach her side just as she was about to blindly cross the street in front of a fast-moving dray loaded with timber.

"Watch out, Mrs. Vail!" I enjoined, taking her arm and pulling her back to the sidewalk.

"Thank you, sir," she said, looking up at me with dazed eyes. "Pray, how do you know my name?"

"I am Adam Walker. You met me briefly in Plumford. We were introduced by Captain Peck."

The very name caused her to start weeping. She was clothed in black mourning, except for the pink hat, and this incongruity, along with her overwrought demeanor, made me fear she might have lost hold of her senses. But after a moment she collected herself, accepted the handkerchief I proffered, and daintily blotted her eyes with it.

"Yes, now I recognize you," she told me. "You were the captain's closest friend in Plumford."

I did not contradict her. Instead, I told her that I wished to relate something of a very private nature regarding Capt. Peck.

"Oh!" She pressed her hand to her breast. "Please go on."

"Not here on a public street, Mrs. Vail. Might we go back to your residence?"

She shook her head vehemently. "There is no privacy *there*. Mr. Vail comes home shortly after three. Let us go to a coffee house."

I did not think that a suitable place. "I share consultation offices with another doctor on Beacon Street. We can go there."

"No," she said. "I cannot wait to hear what you wish me to tell me. Mrs. Abner's shop is only a few steps away."

In fact, it was right next door to the Old Corner Bookstore. We settled at a small table a good distance from the few other coffee imbibers in the establishment.

After we were served, Mrs. Vail pushed aside her coffee cup and leaned toward me, tugging at a slender chain round her neck. "Let us gaze upon his beloved features whilst we speak of him," she said, bringing forth from beneath her bodice a richly engraved gold locket. She opened it with trembling fingers, and I beheld Peck's daguerreotype likeness in one compartment and coiled strands of his silver and black hair in the opposite one. I drew back slightly, reminded of how horribly Peck had been scalped.

Apparently Mrs. Vail had much happier associations concerning Peck's hair for she softly smiled as she regarded it. "Is it not lovely?" she asked me.

Unable to come up with a response, I merely nodded.

Realized she was referring to the locket rather than the lock of hair when she went on to say, "Gideon had it specially made for me out of Georgia gold, which he said was the finest gold there is. It is the work of the jeweler Pierre LaFarge."

A vivid depiction of lovemaking sprang to my mind. It was not the fair Mrs. Vail's proximity that roused it, however, but the name LaFarge, for I recalled Peck stating that the artist who produced his erotica engravings was named thus.

"I wish I could display such a fine piece of jewelry on my person rather than keep it hidden beneath my bodice," Mrs. Vail continued, "but I do not wish to provoke Mr. Vail. He cannot bear it if I even mention Gideon's name."

"Your husband knows that you and Captain Peck were . . . ?"

"Lovers? He does indeed."

"How long has he known?"

"Since our visit to Plumford. My tongue was loosened by a rum concoction I drank during the ball game on the Green, and I told him everything. It was a great relief!"

"Did you tell him before or after the captain was murdered?"

"Before of course. What point would there have been to tell my husband after my darling Gideon was forever lost to me?"

I had no answer to such a riddle as that and remained silent.

She continued, almost breathless in her eagerness to talk about Peck. "Gideon was too kindhearted to tell my husband himself. You see, they got on rather well. They had even formed a successful business together."

"What sort of business exactly?"

"How should I know? Business is not a woman's sphere. But I do take credit for bringing the two together. And a good thing too, for my husband and I had accumulated a great deal of debt before Gideon came into our lives. He was like a heaven-sent angel. Is it no wonder I fell in love with him?" She did not wait for my reply. "Now you must tell me what you wish to relate concerning Gideon."

Stalling for time, I took a sip of coffee. This would not be easy.

"Well, go on," she prodded. "I think I already know what you are about to say, so you need not hesitate. I can bear it, I assure you."

But I did hesitate. For if she really did know, why would she be smiling so wistfully? "What is it you think I want to tell you, Mrs. Vail?"

"The same thing Gideon tried to tell me the afternoon before he died. But just as he was about to, that ill-mannered Lieutenant Finch came slinking around the belvedere, disturbing our privacy, and Gideon was obliged to postpone his confession. Yet he had already confessed to you, his good friend, had he not?"

"He took me into his confidence because I am a doctor."

She frowned. "He never mentioned you were a doctor, only that he had divulged his deepest secret to you."

I nodded. "A secret he should have shared with you."

"Yes, of course. But he never got a chance to, poor love! No matter. I guessed it the moment I laid eyes on him in Plumford. It was clear he was in pain, and I knew why."

"Ah, you recognized the symptoms."

"How could I not, doctor? I was suffering from the same thing."

"I am very sorry to hear it, Mrs. Vail. How long have you experienced pain?"

"Oh, my poor heart started aching weeks ago."

I had expected her to relate pain from a different area of her anatomy. "Only your heart?"

"Not only mine, but his! Although Gideon was the one who ended our relationship for the sake of my marriage, he could not endure being apart any more than I could. How ill he looked!"

"Yes, he was very ill, Mrs. Vail." Obviously she did not know why, and the time had come to tell her. "His condition was irreversible."

She sighed. "Love such as ours is indeed an irreversible condition. That is why I know Gideon wanted to ask me to leave my husband and remove to Plumford to live with him. Was that not the secret he shared with you?"

"No."

She blinked a few times, as though waking up from a dream. "No?"

I glanced around the shop. A group of men at a table across the room were arguing vociferously about Manifest Destiny, and I knew I would not be overheard. "He had syphilis, Mrs. Vail. Do you know what that is?"

The horror and disgust transforming her pretty face made it clear that she did. "You lie!"

"What reason would I have to lie?"

"To punish me."

"I do not even know you, Mrs. Vail. Why would I want to punish you?"

"My husband wants to. He put you up to this, didn't he? He paid you to tell me this scurrilous lie to make me hate Gideon. But I shall love him to my death!" She stood up so vehemently that the table tilted. The coffee cups fell off it and crashed to the floor. Customers stopped talking and turned to look our way.

"Calm yourself, madam," I cautioned softly. "Please sit down and listen to me."

Instead, she ran out of the shop. I had no choice but to go after her, for I did not want her love for Peck to be the death of her. I took her arm once again as she waited to cross School Street.

"Unhand me, sir."

"Please, Mrs. Vail. Allow me to examine you in my office."

"I will not!"

"At least allow me to question you in private."

"No!"

Having no choice, I proceeded to pose extremely personal questions to her on the busy sidewalk as people jostled past us. Did she have fever? Muscle aches? Hair loss? A rash on the palms of her hands or soles of her feet? Lesions on her mouth, or any other parts of her body? She kept shaking her head vehemently, and I hoped it was in response to my queries rather than my persistent presence. As determined as she was to tug her arm free from my hold, I was determined to delay her until she had heard me out.

"Even if you have not noticed the symptoms I have mentioned, you must see a doctor to be sure you did not contract the disease from Captain Peck," I told her. "If you will not allow me to examine you, I suggest you go to Dr. Eames here in Boston."

As I was spelling out his name for her a police officer came down the street, and Mrs. Vail called out to him. "Officer, this man is spewing the most vile questions into my ear and will not let me go!"

"Release that lady at once!" the patrolman ordered me with as much authority as he could muster. As an officer in the daytime police force, rather than the night watch, he was most likely more accustomed to helping pedestrians cross streets than dealing with any sort of trouble.

I immediately let go Mrs. Vail's arm, and she immediately ran off. The officer clamped a beefy hand on my shoulder and called me a scoundrel and worse. Mrs. Abner bustled forth from the coffee house and informed him that I had caused the breakage of two fine cups and then run out of her establishment without recompensing her for either them or the beverages they had contained. I sputtered my apology for this oversight and settled my small debt, but neither she nor the officer seemed of a very forgiving nature. Indeed, I believe I was at the point of being arrested when a past medical school professor of mine appeared on the scene and vouched for my good character. When Oliver Wendell Holmes speaks, others listen. The officer released his grip, and Mrs. Abner showed more clemency. Dr. Holmes kindly invited me to join him in the coffee house, but I declined, for I had hopes of catching up to Mrs. Vail again. The crowded street had swallowed her up, however, and she was lost to me. I pray she takes my advice and visits a doctor. No matter that she has the character of a canary and the depth of a puddle, I feel sorry for her.

Posted my letter to Julia and felt better for it. What is wrong in letting her know how highly I regard her? Went back to my rooms and thought about her for the rest of the day.

Now it is well past eight. Lt. Finch is late in arriving, and I am beginning to doubt he will keep our appointment. Does he have misgivings about divulging too much to me as it is? Why should he unless he really is Peck's murderer? It is hard to credit the crime to him, for he had no motive that I can perceive. The cuckold banker had far greater cause to kill Peck. He does not seem mentally or physically capable of carrying out such a grisly murder, however. Finch, on the other hand, could manage it with ease. No *motive,* though. Unless . . .

could Vail have paid him to do it? Finch is both in need of money and handy with a knife. He even justified murdering Peck by declaring that his death put an end to his suffering. Yes, he might well be the murderer after all.

Hear someone knocking on the front entrance. Must be Finch. If indeed he is a vicious killer, I am rather reluctant to go downstairs and open the door to him. A voice I recognize to be his now calls my name. T'would be prudent for me to ignore him until he goes away, I reckon. But curiosity compels me to let him in. Who knows what discoveries I will make once I hypnotize him? So if I am murdered tonight, here are my last recorded words: *Lt. Finch most likely did it.*

JULIA'S NOTEBOOK

Wednesday, 19 August

Today I received a marriage proposal from the Reverend Lyman Upson. Lors me! I would suit him even less than a hare would suit a tortoise. Two of God's creatures could not be more poorly matched than Lyman and I. Yet he is determined to have me as his wife.

He came by this afternoon and found me contentedly sketching in the garden. I wish I had remained there. But when he told me it was his birthday I did not have the heart to refuse his offer to go for a ride. I put aside my sketchbook and we set out, at his suggestion, for Devil's Perch. Small wonder he is drawn to that spot. Legend has it a minister of his ilk did indeed see the Devil there during a horrific lightning storm nearly two centuries ago. Hence the name. Along the way Lyman pointed out his fine house, set far back from the road on a quiet lane. He said he was happy he had no close neighbors to bother him. He asked me if I would like to view the house interior, and I told him I would prefer to keep to the carriage.

We continued up the road. I did not much care for his driving. He kept such a tight rein on his little bay mare that she had not the slightest liberty of movement. And he occasionally gave her a sharp cut of his whip for no reason I could discern. Napoleon is a far more obstinate horse, yet Adam manages him quite well with words of encouragement and a relaxed rein, keeping his whip in the holder. Not so Lyman. His whip is ever ready in his hand.

When I suggested he fold down the hood of his chaise so we could enjoy the fine day, he rebuked me for wanting to call attention to myself, and we continued onward shrouded from sunlight and eyesight. We came upon a dead raccoon lying in the middle of the road, and Lyman yanked back hard on the reins to halt his poor horse. "My lucky day," he declared. He leapt out of the chaise, picked up the coon by the tail, and deposited the furry corpse right behind my seat. The smell of it was rather pungent. Alas, 'twas not *my* lucky day.

"Are you going to have made a coonskin cap like Benjamin Franklin's?" I asked him.

He adjusted the narrow brim of his proper silk stovepipe and told me he had no intention of doing any such thing. He was going to skin the animal and preserve the pelt for future use in the making of fishing lures. I recalled him mentioning this hobby once before, when he showed me a leather sack stuffed full of dead birds he had shot. At least he had not shot the raccoon. If I glanced over my left shoulder I could just see one of its tiny black hands curled in the most graceful of attitudes. I could not keep myself from looking back at it.

When we arrived at the top of the cliff I suggested we get out of the carriage to better take in the view. This time Lyman acquiesced, perhaps because nobody was about. Together we went to the edge of the precipice and looked down at the river below, where we had both seen the body of the young black man lying on the rocky shore two weeks ago. I waited for Lyman to propose a prayer in his memory, and when he did not, I did.

"He cannot be saved with our prayers," Lyman replied.

"God foreordained his soul to hell even before he was born, and there it now writhes in agony."

"No! I do not believe that."

"Surely you do not believe God would foreordain a Negro to heaven, Julia."

"I believe we are all equal in God's eyes. And I do not believe God would decide beforehand where our souls will go when we die. Predestination makes no sense to me, Lyman. It is how we conduct ourselves in this life that should ordain our fate in the next one."

"Only those God has already chosen for heaven will conduct themselves correctly on earth," Lyman explained to me in a most patient tone. "As for us all being equal in His eyes, I am afraid you have misspoken, my dear. Such a statement implies that woman was created equal to man. Do not forget the Bible doth tell us that man was made *first,* in God's very image. God later took from man's side the material for woman's creation, and by the institution of matrimony she is restored to the side of man. They become one flesh and one being. Hence, in the eyes of the law, they are one person."

"That person being the husband," I said wryly.

"Of course. Man rules over woman as God rules over man. What reason is there for a wife to have a separate identity from her husband's, Julia? Is it not his duty to support and protect her? In return, she will rise to his requirements and satisfy him in every possible way." Lyman smiled at me. Although his teeth are good, his smile lacks charm. "In every possible way," he repeated.

I did not care for the turn our conversation had taken, and without further comment I strolled away.

Lyman followed me and continued talking. "A man should deliberate long and hard before making a woman his wife. He must consider whether her soul is worthy to hold communion with his."

He waited for my response to that. I had none.

"Your reticence is to your credit, Julia," he said. "It conveys to me that you have doubts concerning your own worthiness. But do not fear, my dear. Despite your youthful errors of belief, which I believe can be corrected in good time, I find you most worthy indeed."

I realized he intended to propose to me and attempted to discourage him before he did. "You do not know me well at all, Lyman, and if you did you would see me in a different light."

"I see you suffused in sunlight now, and you are flawless in appearance, dearest girl. Does not outward beauty reflect inward spirit? Are not angels beautiful?"

"I am no angel, I assure you. And such talk as this embarrasses me. Pray let us discuss something less personal."

But he would not desist. "I feel an intense attraction toward you, Julia. And having been a widower for now a year, I am in great need of a wife." He took off his high-crowned hat and his own high crown and mane of golden hair glowed in the bright sun. "Give me your hand in marriage, and let us become one flesh as soon as possible."

Such a direct proposition as that left me no choice but to be equally direct in my rejection. "I cannot give my hand unaccompanied by my heart, Lyman. I do not love you."

This seemed to perplex him. "Do you love another?"

I did not reply.

"I hope it is not Henry Thoreau who you are foolish enough to care for, Julia. After seeing you alone with him up here, I made inquiries concerning him in Concord. He has spent time in jail, you know."

"Yes, I do know. He was jailed for one night because, on principle, he would not pay his poll tax."

"And did he burn down a man's forest land on principle?"

"This I know nothing of, but I am sure Henry would never do such a thing deliberately."

"Henry is it? So you are on familiar terms with him."

"He is a good friend, but I am not in love with him, Lyman."

"I will take your word on that. In truth, I cannot conceive of you giving your heart to such a homely bumpkin as Henry David Thoreau. Yet I have seen you in the company of no other men except for your close kin. Does the man you love reside in New York then? Or in Europe?"

"Stop interrogating me, Lyman. I have not told you I am in love with anyone, only that I do not love *you!*"

Even though the sun shined directly upon it, Lyman's countenance grew dark. "Jezebel!" he shouted, raising his hand. For an instant I feared he would strike me. Of course he did no such thing. He only brought his hand to his own cheek and stroked his closely trimmed muttonchop whiskers. "If you do not want me for a husband, why have you so cruelly played with my affections, Julia?"

"Pray give me but one example when I have done so."

His response was to unbutton his black serge frock coat and silk waistcoat to reveal his linen shirt. Upon it, pinned in the area of his heart, was a shriveled red flower. I stared at it in bewilderment.

"Do you not recognize the rose you gave me, Julia? Four days ago you picked it from a vine that grew on your grandfather's picket fence and tucked it into the buttonhole of my coat. I took it to be a symbol of your love for me and have not been parted from it since."

How I regretted my impulsive gesture! "I gave you that rose because you looked so despondent that morning, Lyman. I hoped it might cheer you up somewhat. That was all there was to it."

I turned away and began walking back to the carriage.

Lyman yanked me by the arm to halt my progress, much as he had yanked the reins on his little mare. I glared up at him, hot anger coursing through me, and demanded he let go of me.

Instead, he grabbed my other arm too, pulled me to him, and lowered his face to mine. I twisted my head away so he could not kiss me on the lips.

"Good Day to you!" a male voice called out.

Lyman released me at once, and we swiveled around to see the peddler Pilgrim coming up the cart path. He tipped his hat to me and then regarded Lyman. They were of the same height, and their eyes locked.

"I know you," the peddler said. "You are the Reverend Mr. Upson."

"And I know you to be a tramp of no account."

"True enough, sir. I am a man of little consequence. Yet I am neither blind nor deaf. I see and hear much as I tramp around, and I remember all of it." Keeping his steely stare directed at Lyman, he then addressed me. "I am on my way to town, miss. Would you care to walk there with me?"

I could not accept without grossly offending Lyman, and I did not think he would attempt further familiarities with me. "Thank you, Mr. Pilgrim, but I will ride home with Mr. Upson. We were just going, were we not?"

Lyman nodded, picked up his shiny black hat, which he had dropped in order to lay hands on me, and placed it firmly on his head. Pilgrim watched us walk back to the carriage and waited as still as a sentinel till we drove away.

On the way back to town Lyman begged my forgiveness for his untoward behavior. Of course I gave it to him. Less harm had been done to me, after all, than to his own self-esteem. And it was partly my fault! At three and twenty I should be old enough to know better than to give a lonely widower a flower.

"I am comfortably well situated, you know," he told me after we had traveled in silence for a mile or so. "Although I was forced to resign my pulpit in Plumford a few years ago, I do not need the support of a congregation to get by. I write tracts and treatises that are well received by right-thinking believers, and I am occasionally asked to lecture at Yale and Andover, if not at that den of iniquity called Harvard. I intend to write books that I believe might be as influential as John Calvin's works, so I do not lack ambition, Julia. Nor do I lack money. My first wife was left a small fortune by her father, which of course became mine when we wed. It is more than enough to support us, my dear, if you become one with me."

He was renewing his suit! I stared at him with wide-eyed disbelief.

He smiled back at me. "I am not yet forty years old, Julia. I have more than enough vigor to take on a young wife, I assure you." He slashed his whip across his little horse's rump. "And I am without any disease whatsoever. I recently had a thorough examination by a Boston specialist who assured me of that."

"I am happy to hear you are in good health, Lyman," I managed to reply. "And I hope you will find a suitable wife. But I am not—"

"No! Do not refuse me again today, Julia. My poor heart could not bear it. As for your own heart, I believe I know it better than you do. Although you do not yet realize it, you love me. I see it in your present distress. You are overcome by my declaration and need time to collect yourself. After your emotions become settled, I am confident you will be able to deliver the correct reply to my offer."

Exhausted by his misdirected fervor, I did not protest further. All I wished to do was vacate the carriage, which I attempted to do as soon as Lyman stopped it in front of the gate. But he halted me by taking hold of my arm once again—more gently this time.

"Wait but a moment, Julia," he commanded in a low voice.

"I would like to call on you next Monday afternoon and receive a more considered answer from you. I promise I will stay
away till then."

That was at least a small reprieve. I nodded assent, and he
allowed me to disembark from the chaise.

Of course my answer shall be the same one I gave him
today. The only correct assumption he made was that his declaration had upset me. To calm myself before attending to Grandfather, I returned to the garden and picked up my sketchbook. I
soon became lost in my work, drawing the intricate tangles of
sorrel, calendula, and horehound in the style of Dürer. Suddenly
I caught movement at the corner of my eye. A tall man stepped
into the garden, and at first glance I thought him to be Lyman.
When I realized it was the peddler, I smiled with relief.

"You came to town fast enough on foot, Mr. Pilgrim."

"I trotted behind the reverend's carriage. I wanted to be
sure you arrived home safely, miss."

"Why would you doubt that I would?"

"Do you forget that I saw you struggle with him?"

"Struggle is far too strong a word. I am sure I am not the
only female who ever resisted being kissed. I have forgiven the
reverend his indiscretion. Indeed, I have dismissed it from my
mind and wish you would do the same, Mr. Pilgrim. Pray forget what you witnessed regarding Mr. Upson's behavior."

The peddler looked down at the ground and shook his
head. "If only I could, Miss Walker."

"My last name is Bell."

"Is not young Dr. Walker your brother?"

This annoyed me far more than it should have. "He most
certainly is not. We are merely cousins. I must go now and
make tea for my grandfather. It is getting late in the day."

"I beg your pardon for imposing on your time, young
lady."

I had not meant to sound so dismissive. "I have time enough to make you a cup of tea too," I quickly told him, "and would be most happy to do so."

He refused my offer with a genteel bow. "Your kindheartedness is to your credit, Miss Bell. But it could also be to your detriment if it induces you to forgive and forget Mr. Upson's conduct toward you."

"You are making far too much of the incident!"

"Just heed my words. I will say no more." He pressed a grubby finger to his lips, bowed again, and took his leave. I fear he might be a bit addle-pated.

So that was my day. Far more interesting than most. Yet somewhat disturbing too. A long, lonely evening awaits me, for Grandfather is already asleep and it is not yet nine. If Adam were here I would ask him to play his guitar for me. He is not very accomplished at it, but I do so enjoy singing along as he strums. I am not very accomplished musically either. Indeed, I am quite tone deaf. But Adam does not seem to mind my false notes. I miss him! I had expected him back this evening, but apparently he has been delayed in Boston yet another night.

ADAM'S JOURNAL

Thursday, August 20th

Well, Finch did not kill me after all, although he did act mighty suspicious when first he came inside. I suggested that he remove his coat because the evening was very warm, but he insisted he was more comfortable keeping it on. I was not so comfortable, however, knowing he kept a flick knife up his coat sleeve. He then insisted on looking all around the downstairs of the house, claiming he needed to feel secure from prying eyes and ears before going into a trance. Or before doing away with me, I thought, not feeling at all secure myself. But I finally got him settled down on a chair in the front parlor and told him to try and relax.

"That goes against my grain," he said. "As a soldier I have been well trained to always keep up my guard."

Began to doubt he would be susceptible to hypnosis. But I took out my timepiece anyway. "Please follow the watch's movement," I told Finch, gently swinging it back and forth.

Although this method had worked well with Julia and Henry, Finch claimed it was making him more dizzy than calm. I recalled that instead of a moving object, Dr. Braid had used his own lancet case as the bright object to focus on. Not being in the habit of carrying a lancet, I considered asking Finch for his flick knife to focus on but decided that handing it over to me would only increase his apprehension. Tried my watch again, this time holding it steady in front of him. Finch said the ticking annoyed him. Suggested he liken the sound to the beat of a distant Indian drum and soon perceived a gradual relaxation in his posture as he listened. His hands on his lap unclenched, his brow went smooth, and his breathing eased from short and irregular breaths to a deeper, softer, and more even rhythm. When his pupils dilated I extended the fore and middle fingers of my free hand to his eyes. Rather than close involuntarily, his orbs widened, and he drew back his head.

"Hey, watch it, doc. You near poked out my eyeball."

"I assure you that was not my intention."

"This ain't going to work," he said.

Recalling my failure with Molly Munger, I almost agreed with him. But my stubborn nature would not let me. "I am no quitter, Lieutenant Finch, and I do not believe you are one, either."

"You are right. As I soldier, I have been trained to persevere. Let us give it another try."

And so we did. We went through the same procedure once again, but this time I assured Finch he would awaken to the sound of my clap and recall everything he said or did in a hypnotic state. This put him more at ease. Eventually his eyelids began to quiver, and after a moment they firmly closed.

Although he appeared to be in the state of waking sleep I sought, I confess that I briefly considered trying to test the depth of his trance by telling him he would feel no pain and then pricking his finger with a needle. Indeed, I almost reached into the sewing basket on the table beside me for one. But I did not do so for two reasons. First, the man was a soldier, and if he was tricking me, he would no doubt be able to endure more pain in an unflinching manner than I was willing to subject him to. Secondly, if he wasn't tricking me, such an action would violate his trust in me. So I proceeded with my examination, never at any moment being certain whether Finch was perpetrating an elaborate ruse or if he was in fact recalling what his conscious mind could not reach.

"Go back to the night you arrived at Captain Peck's home in Plumford," I said.

After a moment he said, "I am there."

"What are you doing?"

"The captain and I are drinking whiskey together in his parlor. He can't keep up with me like he used to, though. He excuses himself, claiming he has to go meet someone outside."

"When he leaves, do you follow him?"

"No reason to. Have a bottle of whiskey for company. But when it is empty I go looking about the house for more. Come up empty-handed and wander outside to catch the cooler air. Drinking makes me heat up like coke in a forge."

"You are outdoors now. What do you see?"

"The moon in its last quarter. Such a clear night. How the stars do shimmer! Makes me giddy, and I lose my balance. Land down so hard on the porch step that I am sure I have put another crack in my arse. And damn if I have not bitten my lip." At that he licked at the corner of his mouth.

"Do you hear anything?"

"Voices. I get up and wander toward them. Get caught up in a thicket and scare up a grouse. It thunders off so loud that I fall back on my arse again. Get up and dust myself off. Feel a fool for getting scared like that by a damn bird. Mightily glad no one is around to witness it."

"What about those you hear?"

"They are a good distance off."

"Continue toward the sound of their voices, Lieutenant."

"I am closer now. They are up yonder in a little open structure with a round roof."

"Who are they?"

"Can't make 'em out in the shadows. Two silhouettes, one taller than the other. Recognize Peck's voice. Not the other one's."

"Which is the taller one. Peck or his visitor?"

"Can't rightly know for sure. Can't see their mouths moving. But I twig they are talking private, and so I move into the bushes. Step onto a dead frog or toad or something, and the slick mess under my boot sends me down hard on a stump. Hurts like the devil. Not a peep out of me though."

"Can you hear what Peck and the other man are talking about?"

"Peck is the one doing all the yammering. The other one is just listening now."

"And what is Peck saying?" I asked as patiently as I could.

"Not so very much. He just keeps repeating how sorry he is."

"For what?"

Finch yawned mightily. "I'm getting sleepy out here in the dark. I will lay myself down upon the ground for a bit." He started snoring.

"Lieutenant Finch, wake up!" I hoped my demand would not pull him out of hypnosis, but it was of little purpose to allow him to reenact his slumber.

He snuffled and sat up straighter. "Those stars sure do sparkle tonight."

"Good. You are awake. Now please listen again to the two men in the belvedere."

"Oh, they are long gone. Must have left whilst I was dozing. Best I get up off this damp ground and go to my bed-chamber. Very fine house Peck has. With all the refinements. My mattress is stuffed with feathers instead of straw, and I make sure to take off my boots before getting into such a fine bed as that."

"Before you climb in and fall asleep, I ask you once again if you saw the face of the man who met with Peck at the belvedere."

"Never got close enough. And he stayed in deep shadow."

So that was it. I learned no more from Finch under hypnosis than I had over our noon repast. I clapped my hands sharply, and his eyes immediately opened. He stood and stretched his long limbs. "Sorry I could not help you further concerning Peck's mysterious visitor, Doctor."

"I am very sorry too. It might have helped save an innocent man."

"You really think that young Cherokee is innocent?"

"I would not be so determined to help him if I did not."

"Well, I wish you luck. I am doubtful myself that he murdered Captain Peck. No Indian would scalp a man in such a sloppy manner. They take too much pride in their tortures."

We shook hands good-bye. Finch told me he has family Down East near the Canadian border and may take up an uncle's offer to go into the timber trade. I considered advising him to reenlist instead, for he seems a military man through and through. Yet I do not know him well enough to give him such advice. He must have his reasons for leaving the Army. For aught I know, he was asked to. He impresses me as a dodgy, albeit amiable man. If he is Peck's killer, though, he has fooled me mightily.

This morning I awoke eager to get back to Plumford and back in Julia's good graces. But decided to take an afternoon train and interview one last person this morning—Pierre La-Farge. I have been most curious about him ever since Mrs. Vail informed me that he makes jewelry out of Georgia gold. I was almost certain it was the ill-gotten gold that Peck stole from Trump's family and wanted to find out more.

Had to inquire at a good many Washington Street jewelry

establishments before I came upon anyone who knew where I could find the Frenchman. His little shop on Province Street is a good distance from the fashionable commercial district. Although alerted of my entrance into his shop by the bell above the door, the stocky, broad-shouldered fellow in the adjacent room kept his back to me as he worked at a high table. I looked at the fine engravings depicting landscapes and sentimental scenes covering the walls, then gazed into the glass case displaying lockets, bracelets, pendants, and earbobs. Even my inexperienced eye could discern that they were of unique design and superior craftsmanship.

I cleared my throat a few times, and the fellow finally shrugged out of his blue work smock, took his time getting into a frock coat of an even brighter blue hue, and came forward to assist me. He had a high forehead, broad nose, and unwashed hair tied back in a tail.

"*Bonjour, monsieur.* How may I help you?"

The first thing that came into my head was to tell him I was in the market for a piece of gold jewelry.

"Jewelry for a young lady?"

"Perhaps."

He laughed. "Perhaps she is young? Or perhaps she is a lady?"

"She is both," I said most definitely as Julia's image appeared in my mind's eye. "And I would like to buy her a present." Although that had not been my intention upon entering the shop, I now wished to do so very much.

"Is this young lady your betrothed, *monsieur?*"

"No, no. We have made no plans to marry."

He gave me a wink, opened the case, and took out an oval pendant. "No need to marry when you can encourage a woman's most intimate embraces with a gift such as this, eh?" He placed the pendant on a piece of black velvet cloth for my delectation. It was rather small but sublimely etched with interwoven leaves surrounding two clasped hands. I imagined how it would look resting upon Julia's bosom. "Go ahead and cup it in your hand," he urged me.

And so I did. The pendant warmed in my palm, and I could not stop staring at it. "Who is the craftsman of this excellent piece?"

"*C'est moi!*" the jeweler said. His blunt but not unhandsome face glowed with pride. "I am Pierre LaFarge, *artisan extraordinaire!*"

"Tell me, Mr. LaFarge. Is this pendant fashioned from Georgia gold? I hear that is the best gold there is."

"What you hear is correct, young man. And that is indeed Georgia gold you caress in your hand. The trace of copper alloy lends it the rose tint that makes it unique in the world. I alone have a supply provided by a former officer of your Army. He obtained it directly from the miners in the mountains of that wild and uncivilized place."

I made an effort to keep my expression disinterested. "The man who told me about Georgia gold was also in the Army. Captain Gideon Peck served in that region during the Cherokee removal."

LaFarge stepped back and studied my face warily. "Is this Captain Peck you mention a friend of yours?"

"We knew each other well enough. He recently died, you know."

"How would I know that, *monsieur?*"

"Well, if you do not, I am sorry to be the one to tell you."

"You presume I was acquainted with Captain Peck?"

"Were you not?"

LaFarge shook his head so vehemently his tail of hair swayed.

If he would not admit to knowing Peck, I could get no

further information from him. I looked around the shop a moment, taking in the framed scenes on the wall, and recalled the far more vivid depictions of LaFarge's work I had seen.

"In truth, the reason I came here, Mr. LaFarge, has nothing to do with gold," I said. "I am far more interested in the paper impressions you produced for Captain Peck."

He paled. "I do not know what you are talking about."

I could understand his obvious nervousness. Men in Boston had been imprisoned for writing about sexual behavior much milder than what LaFarge so vividly depicted in his engravings. "Have no fear," I said. "I am an admirer, not a censor. Captain Peck showed me his collection of erotica and informed me you were the artist."

He immediately relaxed. "Ah, *those* impressions." Color returned to his face, and a glimmer lit his eye. "Are you a collector yourself?"

"I would like to be. Have you anything to show me?"

"*Mais bien sûr!*"

He led me to the adjoining room where the smell of copper, ink, and acid competed with the scent of ripe cheese. I spied a big wedge of it upon the worktable, along with a small brown mouse taking nibbles from it. The little creature regarded us without fear, but it must have had its fill of cheese, for a moment later it leapt down and scurried across the room. As my glance idly followed its movements, I noticed it had no tail. I also noticed a satchel with a large brass lock in the corner of the room. The worn leather bore the faded lettering "U. S. Army, 3rd Infantry" on its side. The sight of that snagged at my memory like a cat's claw on silk, but soon more vivid sights captured my attention.

After hurriedly clearing his worktable of copper sheets, engraving tools, food, and a half-empty wine bottle, LaFarge unfurled upon it a sheaf of finely drawn, graphic scenes of lovemaking. Most exceeded in sheer lubricious wantonness what I had seen at Peck's. Naked men embraced naked women in both familiar and quite unique postures of congress, and their expressions conveyed a passionate joy free from any sense of guilt, sin, or embarrassment. The artistry was superb if absolutely pagan.

"And I have others of a far less tender character in my private studio," he said, his lantern chin jutting in the direction of a closed door. "Depictions that include whips and animals and such, if you are so inclined."

I was not. "These are quite impressive enough," I said. "Such vivid detail."

"*Oui*. I am a masterful draftsman. But the quality comes not only from my drawing and etching. It is impossible to convey from plate to paper such exquisite details without a good printing press. I have an excellent press in there." Again the chin wag toward the closed door. "I brought it with me from France at great expense and trouble. But heavy as it is, it has turned out to be worth its weight in gold." He boomed out a laugh. "Indeed, it has!"

"Yes, I suppose such . . . explicit art as this fetches a fine price here in Boston."

"For you, a special price, *mon jeune ami*," he said. "Which prints would you care to purchase today?"

"I must think about it."

His heavy face fell. "You will purchase nothing today then?"

"Oh, yes." I opened my palm to show him the pendant I had been clutching as we talked. "I want to buy this."

His small eyes lit up with a conspiratorial glint. "For that *demoiselle* you have no plans to marry, eh? *Très bien*. Such a fine gift as this is sure to open her heart and her limbs, and you will soon be enacting some of these very scenes with her." He pointed to his lascivious depictions.

I felt my face heat and looked down at the pendant. La-Farge's insinuating words should have cast a taint upon it, but the purity of the gold still delighted me. And I still wanted it for Julia. I took out my wallet and asked him how much it was. When he told me, I realized I could not meet his price.

"I am afraid I do not have that amount on my person," I said.

"Perhaps you do." He peered at the gold chain on my waistcoat. "If we include your watch in the trade. Take it out, and let me have a look at it."

"I would prefer to come back with more money if you will only hold the pendant for me."

He smiled but shook his head. "And I would prefer to be paid for it now. Or I shall sell it to the next person who comes in and wants it."

I had made up my mind to have the pendant and could not abide the thought of someone else getting it. So I let the jeweler have my timepiece, which I had almost lost to the banker anyway. I could always buy another one for myself, but never another pendant so suited for Julia.

LaFarge examined the watch, nodded, and slipped it in his pocket. When I gave him all the notes I had in my wallet, he examined each one more carefully than he had the watch.

Left the shop with my purchase, looking forward to giving it to Julia this afternoon. But as I strolled through the Common on my way to the station, the number three snagged at my memory again. Suddenly it struck me that three was the number the brothel girl Dora had seen imprinted on Badger's satchel. She had also said it had a big brass lock. Surely it was the same satchel I had seen in LaFarge's back room!

Sat down on a bench by the Frog Pond and puzzled out

the rest of it. I had learned during my visit to Vail's office yesterday that he has easy access to the plates his bank uses to print notes. Saw for myself that his clerk brought some back to him direct from the printer's. Later that day Vail's wife informed me that her husband and Peck had formed a business venture together. Could that venture be a counterfeiting operation? It was surely a possibility. Vail had access to bank plates, LaFarge had access to a printing press, and Peck had an acquaintance with both men. So he had brought them together. And used his minion Badger as a courier to transport the plates. But one evening Badger got so drunk that he forgot the old military satchel he carried them in at Mrs. Scudder's brothel. When Caleb came to Plumford to demand money for the satchel, Badger killed him to try and cover up his mistake. But who killed Peck? Most likely it was the mysterious visitor Lt. Finch had spied talking to Peck in the belvedere the evening before he was killed. Was it LaFarge?

Yes! True, I had not seen the Frenchman when I brought medication to Peck. But his association with the captain was a covert one, so it would make sense that LaFarge would keep out of sight. Then Vail came to Plumford and, after overhearing Trump threaten to kill Peck, cooked up a murder scheme with LaFarge to kill Peck themselves. By incriminating Trump, they would be free of all suspicion.

But why did LaFarge and Vail want to do away with Peck, who was the mastermind of their operation? Because he was no longer needed, of course. Why continue to give him a cut of the proceeds when they were the ones carrying out the operation and taking all the risks? That Peck was fornicating with Vail's wife would be another potent reason for the banker to want to get rid of him.

Of course I must somehow prove what is only a series of logical deductions on my part. Without such proof the police will never arrest a respectable banker like Vail. And if he or La-Farge is alerted that they are now under suspicion, they will be sure to conceal all evidence of the counterfeit scheme. Consequently, it is up to me to return to Province Street in the hope that I can find such evidence myself, be it actual plates or false banknotes printed from them in the back room of LaFarge's shop.

JULIA'S NOTEBOOK

Thursday, 20 August

A letter from Adam was waiting for me at Daggett's store this afternoon. It was dated Tuesday, and although I have read it at least twenty times, it perplexes me more with each reading. *Dear Kindred Spirit,* he begins. This salutation alone puzzles me. Is he simply referring to our relationship as kin, or does he mean we have like natures? He goes on to write that he is most appreciative of a recovered intimacy with his dearest friend. I shall assume that I am the friend he alludes to, but what means he by intimacy? Our long-standing friendship? Or the intimacy we shared when we kissed? We most certainly never kissed like that as children, so it could hardly be called a *recovered* intimacy. In point of fact, he does not mention the kiss even once in the entire letter. Has he forgotten about it then? Alas, I have not.

He writes that he wants to be open and frank with me and wishes us to share a free and mutual confidence. Yet he continues to keep much from me concerning his investigation of Peck's murder, just as he did in regard to the suspicious death of the young Negro. Indeed, Henry Thoreau is Adam's only confidant in these matters, and if it were not for dear Henry, I would not know what Adam has been up to in Boston. All he tells me in his letter is that he is looking for evidence that would exonerate Trump.

And then, in the very first sentence of the next paragraph, he declares me to be the most perfect and satisfying woman he has ever known! I like this sentence very much. Nevertheless, I cannot help but wonder how many women he has known well enough to compare me with. Perhaps I parse too much. But I cannot help it. Every word in Adam's missive has become indelible in my heart. "Regard me as one with yourself," he writes. What am I to understand that to *mean?* He goes on to claim that everything in life seems insipid and flat without me, and that he thinks about me wherever he goes and whatever he does (which he continues to keep to himself). After informing me he intends to return to Plumford no later than Thursday, he closes: "I long to be again united with thee." He then signs himself "Your affectionate cousin." By thus calling attention to our consanguinity, is he not also calling attention to our ill-fated family history and the impossibility of us ever being truly united?

I cannot conceive of myself as any other man's wife though. Most certainly not Mr. Upson's! I know not what Lyman sees in me, for I see nothing in him. I had hoped he would come to his good senses after we parted yesterday, but apparently he has not. Although he is keeping his promise not to call on me, I believe he left me a present this morning. Henry Thoreau handed it over to me when I opened the front door to his knock.

"Why, thank you very much, Henry," I said, taking the package he proffered. The brown paper wrapping had my name written on it. I could not help but think Henry was giving me the box of Thoreau pencils he had once offered and I had so foolishly refused.

He hastily disabused me of that happy notion. "The package is not from me, Julia. I found it here on your doorstep."

I invited him to join my grandfather and me at breakfast, and when we went into the kitchen I placed the package on the table. Grandfather hobbled in and looked rather surprised to see Henry.

"What brings you to Plumford so early?" he inquired.

"My own two feet brought me, sir," Henry replied in that quietly humorous way of his. "An early-morning walk is a blessing for the whole day."

"So it is!" Grandfather agreed. "And I hope to be partaking in such walks soon myself. My grandson is of the opinion that I should keep off my broken limb for another week, but I am eager to test it out. Indeed, if Adam doesn't return from Boston today, I will take off these damn splints myself and toss them aside."

"Adam has not come back yet?" Henry said.

"No, and we have heard nary a word from him," I replied in an injured tone. (This was before I received Adam's letter.)

A look of concern crossed Henry's countenance. "He must be quite busy."

"Doing what, pray?"

"He told me he planned to interview the banker Vail and the soldier Finch when we parted the day before yesterday."

Appreciating Henry's direct response to my question, I asked him another. "And what did the two of you do whilst together in Boston?"

"We went to a waterfront tavern and a brothel."

This time Henry's directness took me aback. "Well! I suppose you had good reason to visit such places as that."

"Good or not, men do have their reasons," Grandfather said, doing his best to sound the worldly old doctor. But he too looked rather astonished.

Henry explained to us that he and Adam had been investigating the veracity of Sgt. Badger's testimony that he was at Shark's Tavern the night Capt. Peck was murdered. This, in turn, led them to Mrs. Scudder's bawdy house, where Badger, they discovered, had spent most of the night. The girls who worked there had confirmed this, disproving Adam's theory that Badger was back in Plumford in time to kill Peck. I was most curious to hear more about these bawdy girls, but Henry was not inclined to discuss them further.

"I came by to inform Adam of the progress I was making on Trump's behalf," he said. "I am sorry to say it has been slight. My mission is to get him transferred from the Powder House to our jail in Concord, but I have found little support from my fellow townsmen, with the exception of Mr. Emerson. He too is enraged by the way the Indian is being treated and has written a letter of protest to the State's Attorney General. Let us hope it is more influential than the last letter he wrote on behalf of Cherokees to President Van Buren. Meanwhile, Trump remains at risk in the Powder House. Has Rufus Badger made further attempts to incite the men in town to hang the poor Indian?"

"Badger has not shown his face in town since the captain's funeral," I told Henry. "From what we hear, he and his army pals are having themselves a grand time at Peck's house, drinking up his ample supply of liquor."

"A drinking party can easily become a lynching party," Henry said.

It was decided that right after breakfast he would go to the Powder House to see how Trump was faring, although it was doubtful he would be granted an interview with the prisoner. I cut him a big wedge of the apple pie Granny Tuttle had sent over, and as he and Grandfather ate, I turned my attention to the package I had left on the table.

"What is it?" Grandfather asked.

"We shall soon see." Pulling back the brown wrapping paper, I gasped. "It's a dead bird!"

"Many dead birds," Henry said, staring bleakly at the contents.

Grandfather craned his neck for a better look. "Why, I see no bird carcasses at all. Merely feathers sewn onto a long strip of cloth."

I lifted the strip from the wrapping. "It is a pelerine. Narrow capes such as this used to be quite fashionable."

Henry reached across the table to run his hand lightly over the myriad of feathers arranged on the cloth in triangles and half-moon patterns. They were predominately in shades of brown and white, with accents of blue and red. "Mostly quail and grouse feathers," he said. "Wrens and warblers too. And bright plumage from bluebirds and cardinals."

I turned the pelerine over and examined the back. Each feather had been attached to the cotton buckram with coarse stitching. It looked more the handiwork of a man than a woman.

"Drape it over your shoulders, Julia," my grandfather urged. "Let us see how it suits you."

"It does not suit me at all. And I shan't put it on."

"It will please you more in the winter, I warrant," Grandfather said. "Think of the warmth it will afford you around your neck and bosom, my dear. Why, I would not mind having such a practical adornment myself come December."

"You may have this one, Grand-dear."

"I do not think it was intended for the likes of me. Who sent it?"

"There is no card," I replied, but I was sure it had come from Lyman. I was glad Grandfather knew nothing of his marriage proposal. Losing interest in the pelerine, he went back to eating his piece of pie.

Henry consumed his in short order and refused a second

helping. He was anxious to go to the Powder House. He promised he would return with a report of the young Indian's mood and condition if he managed to see him.

But Henry did not return, so he must have been refused a visit. Adam has not returned either. It is well past ten p.m., so I do not expect to see him until the morrow. Pray that I shall!

For now I have his letter to keep me company. And his meerschaum pipe. I removed it from his desk this evening and placed it upon mine. As I write I occasionally take up the pipe and touch the tip of the curved stem to my lips. I imagine Adam's own lips there. I imagine his lips upon mine. This must stop!

JULIA'S NOTEBOOK

Friday, 21 August

I decided to pay Granny Tuttle a visit today to thank her for all the delicious provisions she has been sending our way of late. The dry grass crunched underfoot as I walked through the meadows to the farm, and the sun beat down on my shoulders and neck. I had neglected, as is my wont, to take a parasol, thinking Grandfather's tattered straw hat would sufficiently shield me from the mid-morning rays. It did not, and I was quite flushed by the time I got to the farm. Granny was not in the kitchen, but I found little Harriet outside. She was sitting in the shade of the grape arbor and looked cool as a cucumber even though she had a big duck in her lap. Its feet were bound together with strips of cloth, its head was tucked under Harriet's arm, and she was plucking feathers off its upper back and depositing them into a sack. She left off cooing a soothing lullaby to the duck as I approached.

"Good Day, Miss Bell," she said.

That vexed me somewhat. Although I have oft requested that she call me Julia, she insists upon treating me as a visiting stranger. I made some vague comment in regard to the poor duck.

"Look-a-here, Miss Bell. You got no reason to call this duck *poor*. Picking its feathers does not hurt it. Why, it would have shed them anyway." Harriet's tone indicated to me that I had ruffled *her* feathers. "Indeed, it will be cooler without them."

"As I would be without my petticoats. I am tempted to shed every last one of them in this heat!" My small jest got no smile from Harriet, nor did I get an offer for something cooling to drink.

"Their feathers grow back quickly, you know," she told me, still determined to rectify my obvious ignorance concerning duck plucking. "Six weeks hence I shall be picking this one again."

"And how long does it take you to collect enough feathers to stuff a pillow?"

"That depends on how many ducks I pick, doesn't it?"

"Right. I hadn't considered that." I shook my head over my own slow-wittedness.

Harriet, who has a sweet nature despite her sour manner toward me, relented. "If you really care to know, Miss Bell, it has taken me about three months and four ducks to collect almost enough feathers to make a nice pair of plump pillows."

"And I am sure Granny Tuttle will be very pleased to have them."

"Oh, but I am not making the pillows for her. Granny thinks it is high time I start amassing my own store of household linens and such."

"Ah. So the pillows are for your trousseau."

She frowned at the foreign word. "They are for when I get married."

"And who will you be marrying, Harriet?"

She turned red as a poppy. "I am sure I do not know yet!"

And I am sure she has spent many a night imagining Adam's head upon one of those nice plump pillows. "Well, whoever he turns out to be, he will be fortunate to have you for a wife, Harriet." I said this most sincerely, for she is a good, hard-working, and able girl. And quite pretty to boot.

Still blushing, she lowered her face and untied the duck's legs. It fluttered off her lap and waddled off, looking a little raggedy and quacking very loudly. After Harriet informed me that Granny was in the dairy room beneath the kitchen, I waddled off toward the back of the house, also quacking loudly. My antics were rewarded by a laugh from Harriet.

I descended a steep staircase into the cool stone and brick dairy room. Granny was ladling off the cream floating in a shallow pan of milk. "You are my second visitor this morn," she stated, making it sound like I was one too many. But she did at least kindly tell me to get myself a drink from the well.

"And who was your first visitor?" I asked, dipping the wooden cup into the bucket.

"Pilgrim."

I drank a deep draught. Tuttle well water is just as sweet and cold as I remembered from childhood, and Granny just as taciturn. Without another word, she turned her attention back to her ladling. The thin milk ran through the holes in her tin spoon and back into the pan, but the thicker cream did not, and as she plopped spoonful after spoonful of captured cream into an earthenware jar I waited for her to say more about Pilgrim's visit.

When the jar was filled, she put it aside. "Cream needs to ripen fer a few days afore it be ready to churn," she said and pointed to a wooden barrel. "Cream in there has already turned. And I best get to churnin' it afore it curdles."

"Allow me to do it for you," I offered.

Granny looked doubtful. "Could you?"

"Why ever not?" I took a seat on the stool beside the barrel, but I was not quite sure what to do next.

"Just start pumpin' the dasher," Granny said.

I took hold of the long handle sticking out of the hole in the cover of the barrel and moved it up and down. "Like this?"

"Put a bit more elbow grease into it."

I went at it most energetically. Granny silently watched for what seemed a good long while before she spoke. "You ain't well suited fer farm work, are you, Julia?" she said.

"I am quite fit," I replied huffily, for I thought I had been doing a fine job of churning despite being hindered by my tight-fitting bodice.

Turns out 'twas my bodice, not my physical condition, that Granny was alluding to. "Don't see how you can breathe, much less work, dressed in them fine city clothes of yours."

"I am afraid they are all I have to wear. And they are not so fine, either."

Granny gave me one of her dismissive sniffs and went over to a wooden cheese press that was a good foot taller than she is. She loosened the screws, hauled out the heavy wooden mold, removed the cover, and salted the cheese. After she put the mold back in the press and tightened up the screws again, she looked back at me with a knowing little smile.

"Pilgrim tells me the Reverend Mr. Upson is courtin' you, Julia."

"I swear! Men tattle more than women."

"Pilgrim don't tattle. More often than not, he's as silent as a tomb. He only spoke of it to me so I would speak to you."

"I see no reason for *anyone* to speak about it. Whatever interest Mr. Upson has in me will come to nothing."

"Pilgrim will be relieved to hear it."

"What has he against the reverend? "

"He would not say. But I myself do not care fer Mr. Upson. As much as I would like to see you married off, Julia, I would not wish you chained fer life to the likes of him. Fine lookin' though he may be, he is a mighty stiff stick of a man."

I continued to churn without comment.

"Then again, you never know," Granny said in that sly voice of hers. "Some sticks are just waitin' to be set afire. The colder they are on the outside, the hotter they heat up." She squinted at me appraisingly. "Could be the reverend just needs his passion ignited. What say you to that, Julia?"

I stopped churning. "I do not wish to say anything. Nor hear any more of such talk, ma'am."

"Gracious me, have I offended you, Julia? I did not suppose you were one to mind frank talk."

"I appreciate frankness when it is called for, but in this case it is not. You presume an intimacy between Mr. Upson and me that does not exist."

"Pilgrim claims to have witnessed Upson takin' liberties with you on Devil's Perch."

"In truth he did attempt to kiss me. But I would not allow it. Pilgrim came upon us at that brief instant. His lack of discretion disappoints me exceedingly."

"Now, now, missy. No need to get all haired up. Pilgrim would never go gabbin' about it to anyone exceptin' me."

"Why you, of all people?"

"He supposes I am your grandmother as well as Adam's. I tried to set him straight on that score, but he still thinks you will listen to me better'n him regarding the reverend."

"I cannot fathom why he has such an interest in my personal business."

"He has taken a likin' to you fer some reason, Julia. And he does not think Mr. Upson would make you a good husband."

"Well, neither do I. But how would a vagabond who traipses through Plumford but once a year know anything about Mr. Upson?"

"Oh, Pilgrim is very sharp-eyed. I am sure he knows more about most folks hereabouts than they would want him to."

"He sounds even more a busybody than you, ma'am."

Granny laughed. "You got that butter churned yet, Miss Saucy?"

We removed the barrel cover and took a look. It appeared that I had. But my job was not yet done. Granny scooped the solidified cream out of the barrel, plopped it into a chinaware basin, handed me a small wooden paddle, and told me to work out the buttermilk, else the butter would go rancid. As I slid the soft, silky mass back and forth against the sides of the basin, I told Granny how much my grandfather and I had enjoyed the cheeses and breads and pies her foreman had been dropping off at our door.

"Well, I know you can't cook to save your dear life, Julia," she said, "and when I heard your hired girl was laid up, I feared you and the old doc might starve to death. Adam usually gets his nourishment here, but he ain't been around all week. Still in Boston, is he?"

"I expect he shall return today."

"Little Harriet will be most pleased. She misses Adam's kind attentions."

"As we all do," I said.

"Well, I reckon you better git accustomed to missin' Adam's kind attentions, Julia. You still aim to go away soon as your grandfather can manage without you, don't you?" I responded with a weak nod, and she gave me a gimlet-eyed gaze. "You ain't waverin', are you? What about all your fine ambitions to be a limner?"

"I could paint portraits in Boston as well as New York."

"Wouldn't you and Adam be too close fer comfort?"

She was right of course. "I suppose the wisest thing for me to do is put an ocean between us," I said.

"Up and do it then!" Granny urged. "No sense lingerin' around here when there ain't no future in it. You told me yerself that Walker cousins should not marry, did you not?"

"Yes, but the tales I have heard concerning the dire consequences may have been exaggerated over the years."

"You are grasping at straws, foolish girl," Granny said, sorely vexed. "Ask anyone who knew poor Eugenia Walker, and they will set you straight."

"Did you know her?"

"I was but a mere girl at the time," Granny said, "but I recall Miss Eugenia well enough. She had much the same golden coloring you do, Julia, and I wager she could have married any young man in the county. Instead she went and married her own Walker cousin. And you know as well as I what resulted."

"A child that was born . . . disfigured."

"Born a *monster*. The congregation would not brook havin' it put in the church buryin' ground, and the shame of it forced the poor couple to leave town."

"What happened to them? Did they have other children?"

Granny looked shocked. "Of course not. They durst not share a bed again! Even so, they were still bound to each other till death did them part. That happened soon enough, when the husband up and kilt himself."

"What?"

"You heard me right," Granny said. "Some in your family claim he drowned by accident, but most Walkers acknowledge there were rocks in that young man's coat pockets when he jumped out of his boat. He did it to free Eugenia, so's she could marry again and have a proper life and family. But she never married again, and 'twas all fer naught the poor boy doomed himself to hell."

"Such a selfless soul as his does not belong in hell!"

"Self-murder is the greatest sin there is aside from murdering another, Julia. If there be a hell, he is surely in it."

"Then I do not believe there is such a place." I turned away so Granny would not see my tears.

Nothing eludes those beady eyes of hers, however. She

pulled a rough linen hankie out of her apron pocket and handed it to me. "What I just told you happened more than fifty years ago, and there is no need to blubber over it now, my girl."

I dried my eyes and went on with the task of paddling the butter, then rinsing it until the water ran clear. When Granny was satisfied all the buttermilk had been expunged, she salted the butter and packed it in a small stoneware jar for me to take back to Grandfather's house, along with a basket of food.

"I am sorry if my speakin' of yer family history caused you sich distress, dearie," she told me in parting.

But I do not think she was sorry. Like Grandfather, she wants me to understand and accept that Adam and I cannot have a happy future together.

JULIA'S NOTEBOOK

Saturday, 22 August

Adam did not return to Plumford yesterday. His last communication was four days ago. I know something bad has happened to him. I can feel it in my bones, in my heart, in the pit of my stomach. I must *go* to him. I shall set off for Concord as soon as day breaks and take the earliest morning train to Boston. If I cannot find Adam at the house where he boards, I will go to Dr. Quincy. If that proves futile, I do not know where else in the city to search for him. How helpless I feel. I pray for guidance.

To pass the time and calm myself as I await sunrise, I shall record an astounding event that took place yesterday. Trump escaped from the Powder House! Whilst imprisoned there, he was so feared by his guards that they would not set foot inside, giving him ample opportunity to excavate a tunnel beneath the brick wall. He dug and burrowed his way out to freedom sometime last evening. No one knows exactly when, but it was before midnight, when a guard shined a lantern through the small door window and discovered him gone. Constable Beers, with a group of townsmen acting as his deputies, came to the house to inform us. Grandfather was asleep, but I had not yet retired, and when I opened the door they all looked much relieved. They had half a notion that Trump might have returned to our house to rob and scalp us. This shows how ill they think of him, and how little they know him. Although it may be wrong of me, I hope he makes good his escape and re‐ mains free.

The sun has at last risen. Time to go. My prayer for guid‐ ance has been answered. A voice within has directed me to go straight to Walden Pond and ask Henry Thoreau to aid me in finding Adam.

ADAM'S JOURNAL

Sunday, August 23rd

That I am alive and fit enough to record the events of the last two days fills me with the deepest gratitude. Here is what happened to the best of my recollection.

Last Friday morn, hoping to acquire concrete evidence that LaFarge and Vail were involved in a counterfeiting scheme, I set out for the jeweler's shop again. My goal was to get into the room where he kept his printing press. When I arrived at nine a sign stating that the shop was closed hung in the window. I tried the door anyway, but it was locked. I spent the rest of the morning loitering at a bookseller's close by, making forays back to LaFarge's shop every hour or so. When I went to LaFarge's shop for the third time I was most happy to see a broom lying across the stoop. Surely that was a sign that LaFarge was about. The sign proclaiming the place closed for business was still in place, but I tried the door again anyway. This time it opened, but when I stepped inside LaFarge was nowhere to be seen.

Did not call out for him. Instead, I quietly made my way to the adjoining room. The tail-less mouse was perched on the worktable as before, this time nibbling bread crusts left on a plate beside an empty wine bottle. The creature regarded me complacently, then went back to its repast. Observed an open trapdoor in the floor and could hear LaFarge's voice below. He was singing a French ditty. Hastily crossed the room to the door LaFarge had gestured to when he mentioned his printing press. It was locked. As I was about to kneel down to peer through the keyhole, LaFarge popped up through the floor opening like a Jack-in-the-box, a wine bottle tucked under each armpit and one in each fist.

"*Sacrebleu!*" he shouted. "How did you get in here?"

"The shop door was open," I said.

He thought for a moment. "Ah, yes. So it was. I am getting *négligent.*" He placed the wine bottles on the worktable and addressed the little rodent, who had not bothered to budge. "Why did you not alert me we had a customer, Mademoiselle Souris?" Miss Mouse squeaked, and LaFarge laughed. "*Voilà!* I have trained her to speak. And I speak back to her." He made a clicking sound with his tongue, and the mouse responded by climbing up his arm and perching on his shoulder. He gently brushed her off, and she took the same arm pathway down to the table to resume eating. LaFarge turned his attention on me. "I knew you would return, *mon jeune ami*. Few men who have gazed upon *mes représentations de l'amour* can resist coming back to see more."

"Did you not say you say kept depictions of a wilder nature in another room?" I drawled, doing my best to sound like a jaded rake.

He wagged his finger at me. "You are not as *naïf* as you look. *Très bien*. I will show you images that will please your *nature sauvage.*"

Just as I had hoped, he took a key from the deep pocket of his work smock and unlocked the door I had just tried. Unfortunately, he did not invite me to enter the room with him. All I got was a brief glimpse of a printing press when he swung open the door, then promptly closed it behind him. He reemerged a moment later with a leather case and took care to lock the door after him. After returning the key to his pocket, he shooed Mademoiselle Souris off the worktable and placed the portfolio upon it. He rubbed his palms together and smiled at me.

"Are you prepared to be scandalized, *mon ami?*"

Gritted my teeth and nodded. Just then the bell above the shop door tinkled, and we both looked toward the front room. Two very proper ladies entered. Heaving a sigh, LaFarge shrugged out of his smock, hung it on a wall hook, and got into his frock coat.

"I will attend to them," he told me softly, "and leave you to attend to your *goût dépravé* alone. Perhaps you prefer it that way, eh?" He winked, patted the supple leather portfolio, and departed, drawing a curtain across the doorway to insure my privacy.

It was the locked door, not the portfolio, I wanted to open, and I dug into the pocket of LaFarge's work smock for the key. A moment later I was inside a small room with long windows. A printing press took up most of the space. Beside it stood a table draped with a piece of sailcloth. Lifted up the cloth and uncovered stacks of Provident Bank notes tied in neat bundles. They were in ten, twenty, and fifty-dollar denominations. Stowed a packet of each amount into my pockets, intending to make my excuses to LaFarge and hurry off to the bank to alert officials there. Considered my investigation a grand success.

But I had reached that conclusion too hastily, for in the next moment I was hit over the head so hard I crumpled to the floor. Looked up to see LaFarge hovering over me, a wine bottle in his hand. Attempted to get to my feet, and he clubbed me with the bottle once again, stunning me to near oblivion. Remained conscious enough to realize he was dragging me toward the open trapdoor. As I struggled most feebly in protest, he easily managed to pull me down a steep, narrow flight of stairs, and my poor, battered pate hit each and every one of them during my long descent. By the time I reached the bottom I was insensible.

Awoke bound to a chair in a deep-dug, cluttered cellar that looked to have been excavated at the time of the initial settlement of the city. The foundation stones were enormous, rough-hewn boulders, and the ceiling beams were huge, half trunks of trees. It was silent as a tomb down there, not a sound from the streets penetrating the stones and ancient timbers. LaFarge had lit a hanging lamp and was sitting on a three-legged stool beside me, patting the blood dripping from my head with a rag. Saw that he had emptied my pockets. Displayed upon the large, rough table under the lamp were my wallet, the pendant I had acquired for Julia, and the counterfeit money I had taken.

"You are nothing but a common thief," LaFarge said. "And I thought you were a gentleman." He seemed genuinely offended and disappointed.

"I have fallen on hard times," I told him in the saddest tone I could manage. "When I saw the notes I could not help myself. Please forgive me."

LaFarge looked inclined to do just that. "I know how it is, *mon jeune ami*. I too have gone through hard times in this heartless country of yours. I never would have stooped to counterfeiting if I had not. I am an artist, not a criminal."

"I will never say a word if you let me go."

"I would like to. But I cannot. It is not up to me to decide what to do with you."

"Who is it up to?"

Before he could reply a man's voice rang out from the room above. "LaFarge! Where the dickens are you?"

LaFarge rose from the stool and went to the stairway. "Down here," he called up. "Come quickly."

Two short legs in striped trousers appeared as the man descended, followed by a small, round torso clothed in a black frock coat, white shirt, and carefully tied gray cravat. Next appeared a jowly face beneath a very high black silk hat. The banker Vail.

"Why did you summon me here?" he demanded of La-Farge. "What is the emergency?" When he saw me his eyes stuck out like a lobster's, and his face got as red. "Dr. Walker!" he screeched.

"You are acquainted with this young man?" LaFarge sounded most surprised.

"I know him well enough to wish I didn't," Vail said. "Dr. Walker has been investigating Peck's murder."

LaFarge shrugged. "We had nothing to do with that sorry business."

"Even so," Peck said, "he is still a danger to us if he knows *our* business. Does he, LaFarge?"

"I caught him in the press room stuffing banknotes in his pockets."

"How the hell did he get in there?"

LaFarge hung his large head. "He somehow got hold of my key."

"You careless cheese-eater," Vail muttered.

"Buy my silence, gentlemen," I said, hoping yet to talk my way free. "It will come cheap, I assure you. I am not a greedy man, just a needy one."

"I am for it," LaFarge told Vail. "What is the cost to us but paper and ink?"

"No, he cannot be bought off. He is hoaxing us."

"*Tout le monde* can be bought off," the jeweler insisted.

"Not everyone," Vail said. "Some men are too damn honorable. But even if Dr. Walker were the dishonorable sort, it would be just as ruinous to us. A man whose silence can be bought cannot be trusted to keep it for long without another payment. And another and another. There would never be an end to it until he was silenced for good."

As LaFarge considered this, I saw his thoughts move across his expressive face like cloud shadows. The glint in his eyes dimmed, and his mobile mouth stiffened when he reached the unavoidable conclusion. "There is only one way to silence a man for good."

"You do it," Vail told him.

LaFarge looked aghast. "*Moi?*"

"Who else?"

"Why not you?"

Vail put up his clean, plump hands in protest. "Don't be ridiculous, LaFarge. I have never killed anyone."

"*Moi non plus!* I don't even own a weapon."

"Use whatever you thwacked him with."

"I cannot very well cudgel him to death with a bottle of *vin Bourgogne!* That would be *atroce!*"

Vail thought a moment and came up with a better suggestion. "Choke him to death," he said, pointing to a length of rope on the floor.

"You would have to remove my corpse up the stairs," I hurriedly pointed out. "And then dispose of it. Murder is a nasty, complicated business, gentlemen. And since neither of you have experience in it, you will never get away with it."

"He is right! *Mon Dieu*, we will hang for it!" LaFarge said.

"Yes. Dr. Walker is indeed right," Vail conceded. Relief coursed through me, for I assumed that now that they had seen reason, they would just leave me tied up and abscond. But that frail hope shriveled as Vail continued speaking. "We do not have experience in murder and need the services of someone who does." He then he uttered a name that filled me with dread. "Rufus Badger."

"Badger?" LaFarge's tone expressed dread too.

"Of course. He will be most happy to accommodate us, I am sure."

"Peck told us never to trust him again after he left those bank plates at a *bordel.*"

"Well, Peck is dead, and I am the one making decisions now," Vail said. "Badger may be an idiot, but he excels at one thing. Killing."

LaFarge clutched his hands in dismay. "But he is so *brutal.* So *dérangé.* This young man does not deserve such a *destin horrible* as that."

"Dr. Walker has sealed his own fate," Vail declared, glaring at me with pure hate in his bulging eyes. I sensed that he wanted me dead for two reasons. Not only had I discovered his counterfeiting operation. I had also discovered that his wife had been unfaithful to him, and for that I was to be punished most cruelly. "I will summon Badger straightaway."

"Tant pis, mon jeune ami," LaFarge said, his expression resigned as he regarded me. "If I had more courage I would kill you myself, but I do not want to live with such a deed on my conscience."

His fine moral sense left me desolate.

My fate decided, the two men went on to discuss matters relating to it. LaFarge said he would close up shop and clear out until Badger had accomplished his task and disposed of the evidence. Vail declared that it would be most improvident to leave stacks of counterfeit banknotes in the press room. Badger would have little trouble breaking down the locked door to get at them. He directed LaFarge to pack up the notes in a crate whilst he brought around a conveyance to transfer them to his place for safekeeping. He also directed LaFarge to gag me before they left the cellar.

"Pourquoi? No one can hear him shout for help from down here."

"How can you be so sure, LaFarge? Gag him, I say!"

Demonstrating his regret with a deep sigh, the Frenchman shoved the rag he had used to mop blood off my brow against my mouth and bound it in place with my neck cloth. That done, he plucked Julia's pendant from the table and slipped it into his pocket, along with my wallet and the counterfeit notes I had taken, then followed Vail up the stairs without so much as a glance back at me.

But a short time later, LaFarge returned to the cellar alone, and my heart rose with the hope that he had come to save me. Alas, he had just come to save precious whale oil. After lighting a candle to illumine his way out, he reached up to extinguish the overhead lantern. "You can just as well wait for Badger in the dark, eh?"

I yowled in protest.

And he relented. "*D'accord, mon jeune ami.* If the light gives you comfort, I will not snuff it out."

As if such munificence absolved him of any guilt whatsoever regarding my fate, he gave me a fond farewell pat on the back and once more departed without looking back. When he reached the top of the stairs, he dropped the trapdoor with a bang of finality, and I heard something heavy being pulled over it to further ensure my imprisonment.

Looked up at the lantern and estimated I had little more than a few hours of light before the oil burned out. Strained and worked my wrists bloody against the ropes, but it did me no good. As dark thoughts of my impending doom began to creep into my mind, who should creep into my sight but Mademoiselle Souris as she made her way across the tabletop. When she spotted me she stopped in her tracks, right under the lamp, and regarded me with her bright black eyes. Grateful for the distraction, I looked back at her with an unexpected degree of affection. Despite the deformity of a missing tail, she was a pretty little thing as mice go, with a healthy brown pelt tinged pink around her delicate feet and inside her petal-shaped ears. No more than three inches long, she emanated such a great degree of energy that her long, silvery whiskers seemed to vibrate with it. What life there was in her! Indeed, upon closer examination I observed that her belly was beginning to bulge with pups. So it was Madame Souris, not Mademoiselle.

She began squeaking, no doubt expecting to be rewarded with food, and when she was not, she started to scurry away. I clicked my tongue as LaFarge had done to call her back, but the sound was so stifled by my gag that I doubted she could hear it. When she jumped off the tabletop, I was sure I would never see her again, but in the next moment I felt her scampering up my pant leg. She perched on my knee as I continued to make a clicking sound, tilting her head from side to side as though to get the measure of me. I must have passed muster, for she proceeded to tiptoe up my torso and perch on the ledge of my shoulder. She took in the view from there for a time, then curled herself up against my neck. There she stayed. I assume she fell asleep.

Giving peace and comfort to another creature made me feel less helpless. Told myself that I would somehow find a way out of my woeful predicament, being far too young and hearty to die. Such optimism dimmed considerably when I recalled the Negro called Caleb lying at the base of Devil's Perch. He too had been young and robust, yet his life had been snuffed out prematurely by the same brute who was now coming to murder me. How it galled me that a man I so scorned would end my existence.

Could not allow that ugly notion to take hold of my mind. To blot it out, I conjured up the most lovely images I could—the Tuttle apple orchard in bloom, a trout's stippled flank, swallows dipping over waving hay. Then I saw before my eyes the most lovely image of all—Julia Bell. Recalled every detail I could of her face and form, from the sweep of her lashes to the graceful movements of her limbs. Reviewed every expression I had observed upon her mobile countenance these last few weeks, especially the upward tilt of her mouth when I made her smile.

Next I began to envision what I had never seen of Julia— her unclothed body. Reveries of conjugal intimacy between us followed. Could not control such imaginings. Nor did I want to. Their compelling vividness made me consider the possibility that we had experienced such intimacies many times before, in a hundred or a thousand lives we had shared going as far back as the Egyptians and even farther, to a time when we twined together under thick mastodon robes by a fire in a cave. These were just fancies, not actual remembrances, and I did not come to believe in Reincarnation during my long wait in the cellar. But I did arrive at a greater certainty of conviction that Julia and I were meant to spend this present life on earth together. Pledged there and then to marry my cousin, despite the Walker curse, if I survived this ordeal.

Began to twist against my bonds with renewed energy. The only result my strenuous efforts produced was pain as the rope cut ever deeper into my flesh. Even more painful was the dawning realization that I would never see Julia again, much less have her as my wife. My poor soaring heart came crashing down. The mouse, disturbed by my futile gyrations, skittered off my shoulder, down my body, and into the darkness beyond the small pool of lamplight. All I had left was the light.

And then I didn't. It seemed I merely blinked, but I must have dozed, for the next time I opened my eyes all was darkness. It covered me like a suffocating shroud, and my breaths came short and shallow. Because my limbs were bound so tightly, my entire body had grown numb, and the only sound I heard was the pounding of my own heart. As time passed sensory deprivation caused me to lose all sense of my own selfhood, and I felt that my very soul had been cast into oblivion.

Despair overwhelmed me. I hung my head and gave myself up to it. Never had I experienced such an anguished state. To lose hope is to lose everything.

But suddenly I felt a presence penetrate the blackness. As it came toward me, a sweet, familiar scent infused the musty cellar atmosphere. 'Twas the scent of honey. The gentle touch of a hand on my cheek convinced me that this unseen yet deeply felt presence was my dear, departed mother.

"*All shall be well,*" she communed to me.

"But how can that be so, Mother?" I silently responded. "I am going to die soon!"

"*All shall be well,*" she again communed.

From whence had she come to deliver this simple message to me? From heaven, from another time and place, from my own imaginings? It did not matter. What mattered was that I believed what she told me. All *would* be well in the end, even if I should die most miserably, for my soul could never be hurt or destroyed. The moment I acknowledged this everlasting truth, I felt my mother's spirit depart and my own spirit return full force. I no longer despaired. I merely waited.

Did not know if it was night or day when I heard the object over the trapdoor being slid aside. A square of light appeared when the door was raised, and I could not help but welcome the sight of it even though I knew my death could soon follow. Heard heavy boots descending. Then saw a swaying lantern. Before I saw the man who carried it, I knew for sure it was Badger. I could smell him.

He ignored me at first and went about the cellar lighting lamps, a little smile on his bristly, rough-hewn countenance. "There. Ain't that better?" he said, finally turning his full attention to me. "Got to see what I'm doing, don't I?" His gravelly voice expressed a devilish glee. "If I'm not careful with my sport I just might knock out your brains too quick. Got to show some restraint. That's the word the captain used to caution me more than once. Restraint. Well, never did get the hang of that, but I do intend to try. Why cut short my fun?"

But before he could begin his fun, the tail-less mouse distracted him. Scampering onto the table again, she began squeaking at this new visitor to her domain, expecting a treat, no doubt. Poor, trusting creature. Badger snaked out his thick hand, grabbed her in his fist, and laughing with delight over his own speed and nimbleness, he yanked off her head. He threw it at me, and as it bounced off my cheek I felt a trickle of warm blood slide down my cheek like a teardrop. Then Badger slapped my face so hard he near wrenched my jaw off its sockets.

"That's for making me look a fool at town ball," he said. His next slap was even harder. "And that's for stopping my fun with that little trick of a farm girl." He struck again, an open hand to my ear that almost split my eardrum. "That's pay back for the lucky clout you gave me in the sugar shed." He then hammered a fist into my stomach so deep it felt like his knuckles drove clear back to my spine. "That's for keeping me from killing the Injun." He paused as if reviewing his list of grievances against me. "And here's for calling me a liar at the tavern." He punched my stomach again. Bile rose up my throat, and I prayed I would not choke on it. Even knowing more pain lay ahead for me, I did not want to die quite yet.

He stepped back toward the stairs to study his handiwork, and I saw he was full of joy, his smile now wide across his face. "How I do so like to hit a man," he needlessly declared. "But we's just started. Yes, we have."

He proceeded to extract his bowie knife from his boot, and fear raced through me like an inferno, igniting every cell in my body. He saw the panic in my eyes and snickered. I told myself that I must not be afraid or it would go worse for me. *All shall be well in the end.*

At that moment I saw an apparition descend from above and silently inch its way down the stairs. But this was not my mother's spirit returning. This was the figure of a man. Was I hallucinating? Or was I actually staring at Trump the Indian? How could that be? Trump was locked up in the Powder House back in Plumford. Or had he died and become a specter? Gaunt, shrouded in torn, filthy raiment, his dirt-caked face a rigid mask, he did indeed look as though he had just risen from a fresh grave. His eyes gleamed coal-red with hate as he stared at Badger's broad back. Midway down the stairs, he suddenly leapt off them with a powerful push and landed on Badger's shoulders.

I knew then that he was no apparition, for his flesh and blood weight slammed Badger off balance, and he crashed to the floor. Staying atop him, Trump wrapped his arms around Badger's head and twisted it with enough force to break a normal man's neck. But not Badger's. He violently threw Trump off his back and rose up like a mountain, bowie knife still in hand. Trump, armed with nothing but rage, cast about for a weapon of his own. For want of anything better, he picked up the three-legged stool beside my chair. Badger snorted in derision and went at him. Trump held the stool in front of him as Badger slashed away at its legs, sending slivers of wood in every direction, and it looked like he would just whittle it down to nothing and have his man. It took but one careless thrust, however, for Trump to entangle Badger's forearm between the legs of the stool and thereby force the blade from Badger's grasp. Badger howled in surprise and pulled his arm back, yanking the stool from Trump.

Trump reached down for the knife on the floor, but before he could get hold of it, Badger threw the stool at him with such force Trump was knocked off his feet. Badger lurched at him and tried to kick him in the head, but Trump rolled away under the table and came up on the other side. Badger retrieved his knife and headed round the table to get at Trump. Trump vaulted over the top of it, and then feinted as if to run toward the stairs. When Badger rushed after him, Trump suddenly wheeled and kicked his boot up into the bigger man's face. His heel met Badger's nose with a crack so clear and loud I knew the cartilage was crushed flat. Badger's nostrils burst gouts of blood, and he staggered back. Trump kicked again, this time aiming at the hand gripping the knife, but Badger, despite the stunning kick to his face, reacted quickly enough to grab Trump's ankle with his other hand and yank him off balance. As Trump went down, Badger slashed at him. Trump twisted away, just eluding the blade before it sliced into his chest. He sprang to his feet again, clutching a piece of rope he'd found on the floor. He wrapped one end of it around his hand and whipped the other end at Badger's face, cutting open his cheek and forehead but missing his eyes. Demonstrating the same dexterity he had shown when he captured the mouse, Badger captured the whistling end of the rope in his grip and began pulling Trump to him. Trump, unable to free his hand from the taut rope wrapped around it, pulled back in the opposite direction. But he was no match in size for Badger, and he struggled like a fish caught at the end of a line as Badger stepped back with one leg and yanked with all his might to bring Trump to his waiting knife.

It was when Badger took that step back in my direction that I saw my opportunity. Flung myself sideways in my chair with all the force I could call forth, and despite being constrained in a crouch by my bonds, managed to pitch myself against the back of Badger's knees. This caused him to fall backwards and tumble on top of me as my chair tipped over and crashed to the floor. He landed on his back, with his legs tangled over my lower half, our torsos side by side. He twisted to face me, his small eyes red with rage, and raised his knife to thrust it into my chest. Trump jumped forward, kicked the knife from Badger's fist, and bent down to get it. Just as he got hold of the knife, Badger reached up and grabbed him by the throat. His enormous hand near encircling the Indian's neck, Badger began to choke the life out of him. As he gasped for air, Trump slashed the knife deep into the muscles of Badger's arm, and his grip gave way. Trump then plunged the knife into Badger's opposite shoulder, making his other arm useless too.

My face was close enough to Badger's so that I could smell his fetid expulsion of breath and see fear creep into his eyes. He knew he was done for now, flat on his back with both arms useless. I looked up at Trump and saw no mercy in his countenance. I had not expected to. But neither had I expected the savagery that followed.

Trump straddled Badger's chest, grabbed hold of his thick, greasy hair, and yanked back his head to expose his neck. His eyes never leaving Badger's, he placed the cruelly curved tip of the bowie knife below his enemy's left ear, sank it in deep, and very slowly sliced his way toward the other ear. I could feel Badger's legs, still draped over mine, kick out in a death dance. I could smell the blood spewing out of his mouth and pouring from his neck. And I could see Trump watching with the rapt attention of a hawk as the light dimmed from his prey's eyes.

When Badger gurgled out his last breath, however, Trump was not done with him. Still grasping the dead man's hair in one hand and his knife in the other, Trump stood and yanked the half-decapitated head upright. As he made a deep incision in the forehead, I guessed what was going to follow and bellowed a protest through my gag. Trump paid me no mind. All that existed for him at that moment was his vanquished enemy. Perchance the ghosts of his murdered family and his ancestors were also present as he chanted softly and cut round Badger's head. Knife work completed, he dropped the bowie and got a good hold of Badger's hair with both hands. He wrenched upward, and the scalp came off with a sucking sound as a viscous slither of blood and tissue flowed forth. He held it up, regarded it for a moment, then wiped it on the dead man's shirt and tucked it inside his own shirt.

He then pulled me from under the bloody corpse's legs and set my chair upright. When he untied my gag I said nothing, for what I'd just witnessed left me speechless. Trump did not speak either. We just stared at each other. I saw no remorse in his eyes. No gladness either. Only exhaustion and relief. And he could not have seen censure in my own eyes, for all I felt was gratitude. Trump had saved my life, after all, and if he believed that it had been his right, his duty, and his destiny to avenge the deaths of his family members, then so too did I.

He reached over Badger's body, reclaimed the bowie knife, and started to cut through the ropes that bound me to the chair. But before he could free me we heard footsteps coming down the stairs. Had Vail sent another henchman? Trump leaped behind the stairway and crouched in the shadows, knife raised.

"Adam?" a man called out as he descended.

"It's Henry Thoreau!" I told Trump.

He lowered the knife just as Henry's torso came within striking distance. Henry did not even notice him lurking in the gloom.

"Yes, it is I, Adam," he replied. "And I am glad I have found you. But why are you sitting all alone down here?" He smiled, not yet discerning that I was tied to the chair rather than taking my ease in it. Then his lips twisted into an expression of revulsion, and I knew he had espied the mutilated corpse behind me.

"That is Rufus Badger," I told him. "He came here to kill me."

Trump stepped into the light. "And I came here to kill Rufus Badger," he said.

If Henry was shaken by the sight of Trump holding a bloody knife, he did not show it. "Did you scalp him alive or dead?" he inquired most calmly.

"Dead of course." Trump slid the knife into his boot. "To kill his spirit."

Henry nodded. His theory had been confirmed. He walked to the corpse and studied it, then turned back to Trump. "You must flee before a police officer arrives. Julia has gone to fetch one."

"Julia?" I cried, glaring at Henry. "Why did you involve her?"

"She was the one who involved me. She came to—"

"Police! Is there anyone below?" a booming voice interrupted from the top of the stairs.

Trump desperately looked around for an avenue of escape, but there was no way out but the stairs.

"Up there!" Henry told him, pointing to the rafters.

Trump vaulted onto the table, took hold of a ceiling joist, and pulled himself up. He folded himself between two thick beams, straining to keep his balance. I knew he could not remain in that precarious position long before his muscles gave out and he tumbled down.

"Is there anyone below?" the policeman inquired again.

"Blindfold me, Henry," I said in a hushed tone.

He did not question my odd request but quickly plucked up my neck cloth from the floor and covered my eyes with it. He then called out to the policeman. I heard his footsteps descend and an eruption of high-pitched expletives when he saw the body.

"I just now came upon that horrible sight myself, officer," Henry said. "Found Dr. Walker here bound and blindfolded."

"Remove the cloth from his eyes," the policeman ordered.

Henry complied, and I saw a young man with a badge pinned to his top hat standing before me. There was a billy club in his hand and panic in his eyes. "Is the murderer still about?" he asked me in a quavering voice.

"I heard him depart a good time ago," I assured him.

The officer looked much relieved. "What did he look like?"

"As you observed, I was blindfolded," I replied.

Before he could interrogate me further, Julia rushed down the stairs, calling out my name. The officer ordered her to turn back, but not even the sight of a mutilated corpse could make her do that. She wavered for only an instant before continuing to my side. Tears streamed down her face as she caressed my face with trembling fingers. I assured her that I was all right.

"Thank God!" she said, turning her eyes heavenward. They widened. She had espied Trump in the rafters.

"He saved my life," I told her softly.

"What did you say?" the officer demanded, turning his attention from the grisly body to me.

"I said that I prayed for my life."

"And the Good Lord must have heard you," the officer said, peering into the dark recesses of the cellar, as if trying to steel himself to go forth and investigate. Before he could muster the courage to do so, Julia pitched herself forward, and he caught her in his arms. "Do you feel faint, miss?"

"Yes! Please take me away from this gruesome place, officer."

He accepted this new duty with alacrity. "I will help the young lady upstairs," he told Henry and me, "and then go to the police office to report this heinous crime. I have never dealt with a murder before and require assistance."

"Yes, go straightaway," Henry urged him. "I will untie Dr. Walker."

The policeman guided Julia up the stairs, and just as his boots disappeared from sight, Trump slipped down from his precarious perch and landed in a heap beside Henry and me.

Henry helped him stand up. "Can you manage to walk away from here?"

"I'd sooner ride away," Trump said. "Left a horse unteth-ered out back but don't know if it's still there."

"I observed two saddled horses in the alleyway," Henry in-formed him. "Yours and Badger's, I surmise."

"Stole mine from Peck's place," Trump said. "Went there after I dug myself out of the Powder House, hoping to find Badger. He was there all right, holed up with his cronies. Couldn't take them all on at once, so I waited around for bet-ter odds. When I saw Badger ride out alone, I took a horse from the barn and trailed him here. I had good reason to kill him."

"I know," Henry said. "Adam told me he murdered your family." He went back to the corpse for another look. "And it appears that he murdered your friend Caleb too. The cuts on the heel of his right boot match prints Adam and I found on the top of Devil's Perch, proving it was Badger who tossed the body down from there."

Trump pulled out the bowie knife and stepped toward the body. "I vowed to carve Caleb's name in the chest of his mur-derer."

"You have no time for that." Henry put a restraining hand on his arm.

Trump shrugged it off and bent over the corpse he had de-faced, determined to deface it further.

"Forget about Badger!" I shouted. "Just go!"

He ignored me and cut open Badger's shirt.

"Please stop, Trump!" Julia called from the foot of the stairs.

This time he paid attention. He turned and regarded her.

"You have done what you set out to do, and now it is over," she told him. "Further vengeance is needless. It will only get you caught. Is it worth it?"

As he considered this, all anger seemed to drain from him, and an expression of peacefulness suffused his countenance. In the next moment he brushed past Julia, bounded up the stairs and out the back door. We heard the faint sound of horse hooves on the cobblestones as he rode away.

Henry untied me, and a short time later the police officer returned with his sergeant and two additional officers. All three were impressed at the sight of Badger's mutilated corpse. Julia, Henry, and I were escorted to police headquarters, and the initial officer on the scene testified that I had been found bound and blindfolded, therefore unable to identify Badger's murderer.

That a no-account scoundrel such as Badger had been slain did not much concern the newly appointed City Marshal, Francis Tukey. What peaked his interest were my allegations against the banker and a jeweler. Proclaiming intolerance for swindlers in his fine city, he assured me he would investigate the matter thoroughly.

Unfortunately, this investigation has not amounted to much so far. By the time Marshal Tukey sent officers to Vail's boardinghouse, the banker and his wife were long gone, with nary a counterfeit note left behind as evidence. As for LaFarge, he never returned to his shop, and he too still remains at large. I cannot help but wonder why they had taken the trouble to have me murdered if they intended to make a run for it.

So far Trump has evaded capture as well. Even though he has not been implicated in Badger's death, he will remain a fugitive for the rest of his life unless Peck's true murderer is discovered.

My face is still swollen, my abdomen still sore, my wrists still raw, but I have come away from this horrendous experience relatively unscathed. Not unchanged, however, for what I came to realize when I was so close to death is that life, no matter how precious, will be incomplete for me without Julia.

JULIA'S NOTEBOOK

Sunday, 23 August

Oh, his poor, dear, battered face! I cannot bear to think of the torment he must have endured in that tomb of a cellar. He will not speak of it to me. Not yet anyway.

How grateful I am to Henry Thoreau for helping me find Adam in Boston. 'Tis doubtful he would have allowed me to accompany him there if I had not caught him at a most awkward moment. I was far too worried about Adam to find the situation amusing at the time, but recalling it now makes me smile. What surprise and distress upon Henry's countenance when he saw me walking toward Walden Pond in the wan morning light whilst he was bathing. Plunging neck-deep in the water to hide his nakedness, he demanded to know why I had come to visit him so early in the day. When I told him of my concerns regarding Adam, he immediately volunteered to go look for him. Alone, he insisted most adamantly. I, just as adamant, did not budge from the shore until he agreed to let me come with him. Only then did I turn my back so that he could emerge from his pond unobserved by female eyes and go back to his hut to dress.

As we walked to the Concord station I informed Henry of Trump's escape. He looked greatly relieved.

"May that young Indian remain free for the rest of his life. He has suffered enough," he said. "For Trump to have set eyes upon the men who murdered his family after all these years must have pained him greatly. And although Peck met with a terrible death, his henchman still thrives. That Badger shall never pay for his monstrous crime must rankle the depths of Trump's being."

I stopped in my tracks. "Peck and Badger murdered Trump's family?"

"Yes. In Georgia during the Cherokee removal. Adam did not tell you this, Julia?"

"He tells me nothing!"

"Then I will say no more about it. Best you get the whole story from Adam, who heard it directly from Trump's lips."

We left it at that, but I needed no further details to have complete compassion for poor Trump. I was more glad than ever that he had escaped.

Upon arriving in Boston, we went directly to the house on Chestnut Street where Adam boards. No one responded to our knocks, and the house appeared empty of inhabitants. All doors were locked. I recalled a trick a concierge in Paris, weary of Papa forever losing the key to his studio, once taught me and pulled out a hairpin. When I poked it into the back door lock hole and began probing and twisting, Henry was most impressed by my ingenuity. Alas, the lock was too sophisticated to succumb to my amateurish efforts.

We espied an open window on the third floor but could find no ladder to get to it. Henry turned his attention to an ivy plant climbing up the building's brick façade alongside a copper downspout. He examined the thick stem at the plant's base and pulled at the tendrils fastened to the brick. I knew of his great interest in florae but did not think this an appropriate time to indulge in it.

"I don't need a ladder," he finally announced.

And with that he reached over his head, gripped the ivy by the stem, and hoisted himself upward. He next grabbed the spout with his other hand, and pulled himself up a foot more. In this manner he slowly ascended the side of the house, displaying the agility of an acrobat. The old spout shook and rattled from his weight, and at times the ivy tendrils adhering to the brick broke free. When that happened he swayed out from the building, and I sent up fervent prayers that he would not plummet down onto the flagstones below. At last he attained the level of the open window, but it was a good three feet away. He let go the downspout, hung his full weight on the ivy for a terrifying moment, then kicked out against the building and swung himself toward the window ledge. His maneuver was more than the ivy plant could bear, and all the vines ripped loose from the façade and tumbled down to the ground like frayed rope. I swallowed a scream, expecting Henry to tumble too. But he had succeeded in getting hold of the window ledge with one hand and hung off it for a terrifying moment before getting hold with the other hand too and pulling himself up and through the window.

He let me in by the back door, and we proceeded to search the house until we found chambers containing Adam's belongings. Upon a desk lay an open journal. Henry refused to read it for he regards a person's private writings as sacred. I overcame my own reluctance to invade Adam's privacy and read enough of the last few pages to ascertain that he was going to investigate a counterfeiting operation taking place at a jeweler's shop on Province Street. Such a solo undertaking seemed most imprudent, and Henry and I hurried forth to the shop.

We found it shuttered up and went around to the alleyway, where we discovered two saddled horses and the back door to the shop ajar. Henry directed me to go fetch a police officer whilst he kept watch. Off I fled and found a young officer stationed at a crossing a few streets away. When I brought him to the alleyway, Henry was nowhere to be seen. I should have known he would throw caution to the wind and go inside the shop before I returned with help. The officer ordered me to wait outside, but I followed after him anyway, and when I heard Adam's voice below nothing could stop me from descending the cellar stairs.

A descent into hell! As much as I wish I could forget what I witnessed in that cellar, I am sure I shall be able to draw every detail of it for as long as I live. But I do not wish to write about it. May God forgive Trump for what he did. I suppose Adam, Henry, and I should ask God's forgiveness too, for we have allowed a murderer to go free. Yet as I write this I feel no regret. As brutal as the murder was, the victim was a brute himself, and by killing him Trump saved Adam's life.

ADAM'S JOURNAL

Monday, August 24th

I try to remain tolerant and charitable toward all my patients, both living and dead, but I must make an exception regarding Capt. Gideon Peck. My loathing for him increases with each revelation concerning his conduct here on earth. Today Julia informed me of his relationship with Molly Munger, her subsequent pregnancy and miscarriage, and the resulting sorrow and apprehension brought upon the entire Munger family.

Went forthwith to examine Molly at her home, and to my great relief found no signs whatever of Peck's disease upon her body, nor did she have any symptoms. Molly told me she and Peck had performed the act of coition three times only, when he still looked to be in good health. My belief is that the sickness in him had been somnolent during those times with Molly and then come on with such speed it reduced his desire, sparing Molly further exposure. She expressed her relief with such a Niagara of tears I had to blink away a few of my own.

When I came out of the Munger house, I saw swirls of dense smoke issuing from Ira's butchery next door and hurried to it, expecting to help quench a fire. The sharp stench of burning hair and singed flesh assaulted me through the open door. Through the semidarkness I made out the carcass of a monster hog, hair singed clean off, hanging by its back legs from a rafter. Wondered why it was slaughtered in August, when blowflies can quickly corrupt the flesh with maggots.

"Come in, Adam, if you be inclined to," Ira said, glancing around the pig at me. "A hog butchering in the summer heat is no place for them that has a delicate nose."

"I have smelled far worse in the dissecting rooms at medical school," I assured him, coming forward for a closer look.

The mature pig was of enormous weight, no less than four hundred pounds, and it was clearly evident that the poor beast had been stomped, battered, and stabbed to death in a most grisly fashion.

Ira, holding a heavy cleaver, came around the carcass, his eyes red-rimmed from the smoke. His countenance was a mask of worry. "You just come from examining our Molly?"

Aware that he had been informed of the danger his daughter had encountered with her liaison with Peck, I spoke frankly. "She did not become infected with that man's disease."

Overcome with relief, he leaned against the burnt flank of the dead hog and muttered a prayer of thanks. Then he straightened to his full great height, cursed Peck to damnation, and swung the cleaver into the flank of the dead hog with such force it plunged into the side of the animal and disappeared from sight. His face was so contorted with rage that he was hardly recognizable as the man I had long known.

I took a step back from his anger. "Peck is dead and gone from Molly's life, Ira. That is all that matters now."

"No, what matters is that he suffered greatly before he died. This alone comforts me, for we cannot be sure there really is a hell."

That said, Ira's fury subsided as quickly as it had erupted. He sliced off the hog's ears that had been crisped right through with the burning off of the hair and offered me one. The thin, clean flesh, with a bit of smoke for spice, was most delicious, and we chewed in silence for a moment.

"How did the hog come to such a gory end?" I eventually asked Ira.

"Killed by the same bull that attacked your Indian," he said.

"Farmer Herd is still letting that mad bull of his roam free?"

"Oh, Sultan never left his pen. 'Twas the fool hog that got *in* it. The greedy porker smelled the grain in the bull's feed tray, rooted his way under and threw up the boards to get at it. As you can see from the evidence, the bull was not inclined to share his victuals. Gored his uninvited dinner guest full of holes like an old pincushion. Then the ornery cuss picked the fool pig up with his horns, slammed it against the walls of the pen, and stomped it on the stone floor. All that at least bled the beast out for me pretty fairly, which in this heat was good fortune. Herd wanted to save what he could of the pork and so sledded it over an hour ago. I'm keeping the smoke up in here to keep out the pestiferous flies."

"That bull's more trouble than he's worth."

"No, no, he's a fine breeder," Ira said. "Herd makes a tidy sum mounting Sultan atop cows all around the county."

Not one for too much conversation, he went back to work. He yanked the cleaver out of the hog's flank and cut deep across the back of its neck, continuing around to slice through the gullet and sever the spine. The head dropped to the brick floor. My training in surgery gave me an appreciation of his skill in butchery. And *his* training, I suddenly realized, would give him the wherewithal to butcher a man with the same ease as he would a hog.

If anyone had an unadulterated motive to kill Peck, it was surely Ira Munger. According to Julia, he had learned of

Molly's liaison with the captain when he returned from playing town ball the very evening the man was murdered. He'd been so upset that he'd spent the night brooding in his butchery, so neither his wife nor anyone else could verify his whereabouts at the time of Peck's murder. I watched Ira toss the pig's head into a vat and then slice off its pizzle. Yes, he was fully capable of butchering the man who had defiled and perhaps diseased his daughter. But had he?

I was almost certain of it. Not only could he have scalped Peck with ease, but he had been on the Green when Trump had threatened to do just that to Peck. Ira could have easily overheard Trump. My only reservation was that I knew Ira to be an honest man. Would he frame another for his crime?

"I was astonished when I heard the Indian had escaped the Powder House," I said, hoping to ascertain Ira's attitude regarding Trump.

"Everyone in town was," Ira said. "And a few were mightily pleased to hear it. Me being one."

"So you do not think he deserved to be hanged?"

"No, I do not." Ira reached deep into the carcass and split the pelvic girdle with a resounding snap. "No one should be hanged for killing a low animal such as Peck."

"But it is almost certain that Trump would have been executed for Peck's murder," I said.

Ira took a firm grip on the viscera, rolled the mass out toward him, and dropped the entire, dripping innards into the vat. Then he looked at me. "Maybe, if he'd been brought to trial, he would have been found innocent."

"Not very likely, Ira." I looked intently back at him. "All the evidence, especially the scalping, pointed to him as Peck's killer."

"But if he didn't do the deed," Ira said, "the real killer might have come forth and confessed in time to spare the Injun's life."

Is that what Ira had intended to do? Or had he just deluded himself into thinking he would? As I stared at him, I could not fathom his thoughts, much less what lay deep in his heart. He held my gaze without blinking, big arms crossed over a leather apron caked with gore. Had he worn that apron when he slaughtered Peck? Was he waiting for me to accuse him?

I did not. It is unlikely he would have confessed to me if I had. And in truth I did not want him to, for I might then have felt obligated to notify the authorities. I feel no such obligation now, for as certain as I am that Ira killed Peck, I have no way of proving it. All I have are suppositions that would not stand up in court, and the only thing I would accomplish would be the ruin of the Munger family's reputation. Peck's time on earth was quickly nearing an end, with or without Ira's intervention, and it is up to God, not me, to judge both men.

JULIA'S NOTEBOOK

Monday, 24 August

It seems I have managed to offend two men this afternoon. I am sorry for that, but if either of them had truly listened to me, none of us would be so distressed now.

And to think it all started with such good news from Adam. He found me in the garden and told me that he had examined Molly and found her to be free of Peck's dreadful affliction.

"Now she can get on with her life as before," I said. "Unless, that is, her father holds her unfortunate indiscretion against her, as men are wont to do. Molly might have behaved with naïve imprudence, but it was Peck's behavior that was deplorable beyond measure. Mr. Munger should blame him alone."

"I believe he does," Adam said.

"Did he tell you so?"

"Not in so many words." He turned his gaze from mine.

"Are you keeping something from me, Adam?"

"Why would you think it?" he said, still avoiding my eyes.

"Because you are always keeping things from me."

"Only to shield you from the unsavory side of life. Other than that, I am most open with you."

"You are not," I insisted. "You shield your deepest feelings from me too."

"How can you say that? Did you not receive my letter from Boston?"

"Oh, yes. And I have read it so many times that I can recite it verbatim. Yet I still do not understand why you wrote to me in such a manner."

"I suppose I did not understand myself at the time. But now I do." Adam hesitated. "Will you allow me to speak frankly to you, Julia?"

"It is what I most wish you to do!"

He took my hand and led me to the little stone bench behind the tall phlox. There we sat in silence for a while, breathing in the scent of mint and lavender wafting in the light breeze, until he spoke again.

"Here is what I now know to be true, Julia. You are absolutely necessary to my happiness, and a separate existence from you would not be worth living. I realized this as I awaited my death in the cellar."

"Do not remind me how close I came to losing you!" I said as tears sprang to my eyes.

Adam took me in his arms to comfort me. I relaxed in his embrace, and he began to kiss my cheeks and temples and throat. I soaked up his kisses like a thirsty flower and could not make myself tell him to stop. But he suddenly released me and rose from the bench.

"You should have announced your presence, sir," he said.

I looked over my shoulder and saw Lyman Upson standing behind the row of swaying phlox, ashen-faced as he stared at us. "I could not announce my presence," he replied, "for I was struck speechless by such blatant impropriety."

"Leave immediately," Adam commanded. "You have no business here."

"I was under the assumption I had an appointment with

Miss Bell today," Lyman said without looking at me. "But now I will gladly leave her to you, sir." And with that he abruptly turned his back to us and marched rigidly to the gate. The latch caught when he tried to open it so he kicked the gate open instead, leaving it swinging forlornly on a broken hinge in the wake of his departure.

Adam started to go after him, but I quickly rose from the bench and took hold of his arm to stop him. "Let the poor man go," I said. "He has reason to be upset. I forgot he was coming today for my answer."

Adam frowned at me most ferociously. "Your answer to *what?*"

"His marriage proposal. Of course I had no intention of accepting his offer, but—"

"Upson proposed marriage to you? When and where?"

"Wednesday last on Devil's Perch. He seems to have a great affinity for that place. I refused him right off, but he insisted that I take some time to reconsider and—"

Adam interrupted me again. "And you obliged him."

"Well, yes. That is, no. I mean, I did not reconsider his offer for even a moment, but I did consent to allow him to make it one final time for the sake of his pride."

"Hah! So much for his pride. What could be more mortifying than to find the woman he hoped to marry being kissed by another man?"

"You are not *another* man, Adam. You are the only one in my life. I have always loved you."

"Yet you have been considering marriage to another."

"I have not considered it! How many times must I tell you?"

"Once would have been sufficient," he replied coldly. "But you had no intention of ever telling me of Upson's proposal, did you?"

"In truth I did not."

"I cannot help but wonder what other secrets you have held back from me, Julia."

"Are you implying that I have been deceitful?" I asked him in horror.

Without answering me, he left the garden and strode off down the road. It is now suppertime, and he has not yet returned. Most likely he went to the Tuttle farm to be fed and fawned over by Granny and little Harriet.

I imagine the cozy trio round the big kitchen table heaped high with food, Granny and Harriet beaming with delight at Adam. And then I imagine one, two, three little beings more round the table, all with Adam's dear blue eyes and Harriet's curly hair. Such a wholesome family. Such a happy picture.

I blink it away. I want Adam to be mine, not Harriet's. Even during all those years apart, he filled my heart so completely that there was no room left in it for another. Yet the image of Adam I carried with me for the last ten years was that of a boy, not a man. It is only now that I know him full-grown that I want him most carnally and selfishly. Oh, Julia, you poor miserable creature! Do not impose your wanton desires upon that pretty picture of domestic bliss in Granny's kitchen. It is all for the best that Adam has gone off in a sulk. March away from me, my beloved cousin. And do not look back.

ADAM'S JOURNAL

Tuesday, August 25th

Sultan has struck again. Young Hiram discovered the battered body when he went out to the barn at sunrise to milk the cows. He immediately rode to town to notify me and went on to alert Constable Beers.

Drove to the Herd farm, went straight to the barn, and found the peddler Pilgrim's body lying outside the bull pen. The elder Herd was standing over it.

"He was dead when Hiram and me dragged him out," Herd informed me.

"Was his skin cold to the touch?"

"Didn't want to touch him, doctor. Just pulled him by his boots."

"Were his limbs stiff as you dragged him?"

"Can't say I noticed. Could barely look at him, being he was so bloodied and stomped."

"Was the blood dry on him? I am trying to ascertain time of death."

"Dry. And Sultan was calm as a millpond over in his favorite corner by the window. So it weren't like he just done it. When he gets riled up he rolls his eyes, shakes that big head of his, and drools." Herd shook his own big head in bewilderment. "Why in tarnation did Pilgrim go into Sultan's pen? Never would have tolerated him sleeping in my barn iffen I'd known he was that crazy."

I crouched over the mangled corpse, which gave off a strong smell of whiskey. The head was severely smashed up. The jaw, hands, and arms had begun to show signs of rigor mortis. So death had occurred late last night. Had difficulty removing the clothes. A dead body often seems quite reluctant to surrender its modesty. Observed the neck vertebrae had been fractured in two places. The right arm was wrenched from its socket, three ribs broken on the left and two on the right side, the pelvis shattered, and the left femur had suffered two separate fractures. Noted multiple and deep puncture wounds to the chest and abdomen similar to those the pig had endured. Attributed these to the bull's horns.

"Be it pig or man, Sultan don't like company," Herd remarked unnecessarily.

I looked over at the beast standing by his water trough, nose dripping, eyes glaring balefully at us. "That animal is a killer, Mr. Herd."

"Well, I ain't accountable for his actions."

"Of course you are. It is your bull. And you allowed Pilgrim to sleep in your barn."

"I never allowed no such a thing! Just never stopped him from doing so. Can't stop rats comin' in here, neither."

"A human being lies here, Mr. Herd. Show him some respect."

Instead he stomped out of the barn, leaving me alone with the bull and its victim until the younger Herd came back with Constable Beers. Soon the Coroner's Jury assembled in the barn, led by Coroner Daggett, but controlled by Justice Phyfe. After Hiram was questioned in a cursory manner about discovering the body, he was allowed to get on with his milking.

I reported the injuries I had observed on poor Pilgrim's mauled body, and we all went over to Sultan's pen to examine the scene of the crime. The bull paid us no mind. There was blood on his hooves and spattered all over the hay.

Justice Phyfe pointed to a half-empty whiskey bottle lying on its side in the corner. He ventured that Pilgrim must have accidentally dropped it through the boards and then, with a drunkard's temerity, gone into the pen to retrieve it. I remarked that it was odd the bull had not shattered the bottle along with Pilgrim's body during his rampage.

Coroner Daggett reminded me that my only role was to give medical testimony, not to attempt to complicate the investigation as I had with the Negro. But he took up a hay rake, gingerly poked it through the boards, and retrieved the bottle as evidence. A pocketknife was revealed in the displaced straw, and he raked that out too. It was passed from one man to another. Its ivory handle was engraved with the graceful image of a leaping trout. We all agreed it was a fine-looking piece, most likely the only thing of value the tramp owned, and it was suggested that his pocketknife should be buried with him.

The undertaker, Mr. Jackson, then inquired as to whom was going to assume the cost of the burial. Pilgrim had no kin that anyone knew of. No one even knew his true name. I volunteered to go ask Farmer Herd if he would pay for it, being of the strong opinion that he should.

Walked over to the little farmhouse beyond the big barn. The kitchen door was open. I knocked on the jamb, and Mrs. Herd looked up from the mound of dough she was kneading on the table and invited me in. She asked if my grandfather was still keeled up with his broken leg, and I told her he was much improved and moving about now. She said she was glad to hear it and offered to heat up some coffee for me. Refused her kind offer and asked to speak to her husband. Didn't tell her why. Her prosy manner made me wonder if she knew a dead man lay in the barn. Mr. Herd and his son might well have kept the sorry news from her. Else how could she be carrying on with her bread-making as though nothing were amiss?

"Albion, young Doc Walker wants yer!" she called out. She then wiped her flour-dusted hands on her apron and gave me a teary-eyed look. "How Pilgrim did relish my bread. Wish I could have given him one last piece, God rest his soul." So she did know.

Herd came in from the back room, and as I was telling him he should pay for the burial he rolled his eyes just as he'd described Sultan's doing when riled.

"Why should I?" he bellowed. "Weren't my fault the old drunkard got hisself kilt."

"Albion means no disrespect to the dead," Mrs. Herd told me, dabbing her eyes with her apron string. "Pain is what causes his meanness. He has been in great discomfort for near two weeks."

"What is the trouble?" I asked Herd.

He stuffed his left hand into the pocket of his overalls and winced. "Never you mind," he replied. "It will take care of itself by and by."

I did not pursue the matter, for at that moment Coroner Daggett came to the kitchen door. "Our verdict is Death by Bovine Assault," he announced. "And we strongly recommend execution of the bull."

"And I strongly refuse to do it," Herd replied. "Sultan is too fine a breeder."

"I'd like to pickle that prodigious pizzle of his," Mrs. Herd muttered, punching her fists into the dough. Her husband gave her a wary look. "You heard me right," she told him. "And here's another thing I have to say, Albion. You must do the decent thing and give Pilgrim a proper burial. Go tell Mr. Jackson you will pay whatever it costs."

Much to my astonishment, he nodded his assent and went back to the barn with us to do his wife's bidding. The undertaker covered Pilgrim's body with a shroud from his wagon, and we carried him out on a plank. Soon as Mr. Jackson took off with his pitiful cargo and the jury disbanded, Herd bid me a curt Good Day. I told him I would now like to accept his wife's earlier offer of coffee. He grunted assent, and we went back to the house.

But it wasn't coffee that I wanted. I wished to get a look at Herd's hand in the presence of his wife. He reluctantly took it out of hiding in his pocket and extended it toward me. The second finger was a bright purple and swollen so tight it could not be bent. "Got it caught twixt two milk cans I was unloading at the Concord depot. The train to Boston was comin' in, and I had to work fast."

"In haste is error," Mrs. Herd said.

He ignored her. "Well, Doc? It will be all right soon enough, will it not?"

I shook my head. "It will have to come off, Mr. Herd." Although I felt sorry for the man, I kept my tone firm. "You have waited too long as it is, and if I don't operate soon the infection will spread, and you'll lose more than one finger. Your whole hand most likely. Possibly your arm. Or your life, if it comes to that."

Mrs. Herd gripped her husband's shoulder. "You hear that, Albion?"

"I ain't deaf." He scowled at her, but then his expression softened. I waited as they silently communicated with each other. After a moment Herd looked back at me. "Chop it off now and be done with it."

"I'll take you back to the office to do it."

"I ain't got time to go into town. Take the dang thing off now or not at all."

Knew it would be useless to argue with him. The important thing was to get the job done before the obstinate old coot changed his mind. "Let's go outside where there is better light," I said.

Got my surgical kit from the rig and laid a saw and scalpel on a splitting block out in the sun. "I suggest a good dose of spirits before I start," I said to Herd.

"He took the Pledge," his wife said.

"But this would be for medicinal purposes," I said. "To help ease the pain."

Herd shook his head most adamantly. "Gave my word to man, God, and the missus that I would not ever take a drink again."

"Then let me hypnotize you," I said. Herd listened most impatiently as I explained my method of inducing nervous sleep.

"I ain't got time to *sleep*, doctor. Just get on with it."

So I did. Sat Herd on the ground and laid his hand on the block. Told his wife to hold down his arm to keep the hand steady. Tied a tight tourniquet above the first joint in the swollen finger whilst Herd stared out at his cornfields with a stony countenance.

"I'm starting now," I said.

Mrs. Herd scrunched her eyes tight, gritted her teeth, and pressed down hard on her husband's forearm. Herd only blinked.

Used a short, curved amputation knife to cut cleanly to the bone right around the finger. Hoped Mrs. Herd still had her eyes closed as a gout of blood and fluid flowed onto the ground. Eased back skin and muscle so I would have a flap to cover and tie off the wound. Put down the knife and picked up my metacarpal saw. Glanced at Herd, pale now but still rock-steady, and brought the saw blade to the finger bone. Cut through it in three clean strokes. Let the finger drop to the ground and teased out the main artery and nerves of the stump that remained with my tenaculum. Tied them off with catgut ligatures.

Mr. Herd never uttered a sound, although he shifted his legs a bit, but no more than he would have done under the kitchen table. He looked at his wife. "You can open your eyes now, missus," he said.

Squinting, she watched me finish the job. I washed out the wound with a dipper of well water, pulled down the skin and muscle, and closed the blunt end of the finger stump with a plaster of rubber dissolved in turpentine and spread on a tightly wound bit of linen.

"That should do it," I said, feeling right proud, I must admit, of accomplishing a clean amputation and a good, tight dressing in just a few minutes.

Mrs. Herd picked up the finger from the ground and tucked it in her apron pocket.

"Feed it to the pigs," Herd suggested.

"I got more regard for it than that. I'll bury it in my flower garden. Good fertilizer."

She headed for the garden, and Herd and I went back inside to settle up. He took down a pewter mug from the chimney shelf and upended it on the table. Coins fell out in a jumble and rolled into the flour—American silver dollars, old English shillings and pence, and even a Spanish coin cut into pieces of eight. "Take what I owe you, doc."

Picked out far less than I should have charged, but money doesn't matter as much to me as it does to him. Felt a real sense of accomplishment as I drove back to town, sure I had saved a life.

Surprised and pleased to find a bright-eyed Molly Munger in the kitchen. She assured me she felt well enough to resume her household duties, and she did indeed look the picture of health. She seems to have put her recent troubles well behind her, and I have no intention of causing her or her family further grief. I shall take the secret of who killed Capt. Peck to my grave.

JULIA'S NOTEBOOK

Tuesday, 25 August

Am I the foolish female Adam obviously thinks me? I shall enumerate the observations that have led me to the conclusion he finds so absurd, and if I am still convinced I am right, I shall have to do something about it, with or without his help.

Arising at cockcrow this morning, I took a walk along the river path. When I glimpsed Lyman Upson fishing out in the current, I decided to attempt a conciliation with him. He was so intent on his sport that he did not notice my approach down the bank, and the closer I came, the more reluctant I became to disturb his peaceful pleasure. Instead, I leaned against an aspen and watched him fish.

I had never seen Lyman so at ease with himself and the world around him. Moreover, I had rarely seen him without his tall black hat and never without his proper black frock coat. His blond hair gleamed in the morning light, and the full sleeves of his white linen shirt shimmered like angel wings as he raised his long bamboo rod, whisked his line into the air and over his shoulder, then reversed the direction forward with the flexing of his forearm. It amazed me how far such a simple, controlled motion made the line unfurl over the foamy current before descending into it. After a while he would lift the line off the water and go through the same movements again. As I watched I yearned for my pencil and pad in order to sketch such grace in action.

He suddenly raised the tip of his rod and pulled in line. I surmised he had hooked a fish, and sure enough, a struggle commenced. The fish leapt out of the water in a silvery arc a few times but could not regain its freedom. Lyman reeled it away from the weedy shallows and soon had it in hand. He slipped the unfortunate creature into a wicker creel hanging from his side and smiled with satisfaction. I believe that was the first sincere smile I have ever seen upon Lyman's visage, but when he looked up and saw me, it disappeared.

"Are you spying on me?" he demanded.

I forced a laugh. "Of course not, Lyman. You caught my attention as I was walking along the river path. No one else is about this early."

"That is why I come here every day at both sunrise and sunset," he said. "I consider this part of the river my private sanctuary."

"I did not mean to intrude. I was merely observing your fishing skills."

His expression became more amiable. "It is true that I am a most competent angler. And I am always happy to discuss my sport with anyone who professes an interest in it. Come closer and I will show you my fine tackle."

I complied, reassured by his friendly attitude. Indeed, he was so amiable as he discussed the superior attributes of his nine-foot bamboo rod and brass reel that he seemed to have forgotten all about the unfortunate incident in the garden yesterday.

"I have already caught five trout this morning," he boasted.

"You will eat well today," I said.

His countenance registered disgust. "I never consume fish."

"But trout are so delicious!"

"So my late wife Urena claimed. I cannot abide the smell of fish cooking, however, so I never brought home my catch."

"Well, what do you do with all the fish you catch, Lyman?"

"Throw them away, of course."

"What a pity to have them die for naught," I could not help but remark.

"Not for naught," he said. "They die for my pleasure in catching them. Doth not the Bible state that God gave man dominion over the fish of the sea, and over the fowl of the air, and over every creeping thing that creepeth upon the earth?"

I did not argue this point with him, for my objective was to be conciliatory, not provocative. "Lyman, I am most sorry about yesterday," I began.

He held up his hand to halt me from speaking further. "It is over and done with, Julia Bell. You are not the virtuous young woman I thought you to be, and I am thankful God made me see it in time. My only regret is sending you that cape. I used many fine feathers from my collection to make it, and they could have been put to far better use in the making of flies."

"I shall return the cape to you forthwith!" I said, glad to soon be rid of the dreadful thing. "Could you not use the feathers again?"

"I suppose I could at that," he said, mildly mollified. "Tying flies is a craft I excel in. Here. Allow me to show you." He pulled a leather book from his satchel and opened it. The book was lined with shearling, and attached to its felt pages were fishing flies in a variety of sizes and shapes. "I imitate insects and amphibians by using bits of animal hair and feathers to trick the fish," he explained, turning the pages. "See how these small ones resemble mosquitoes and gnats. And these larger ones duplicate minnows and tadpoles."

"Yes, the resemblance is quite remarkable," I said, feigning interest. Lyman was being so affable that I began to believe it possible that we would shake hands at the end of this tedious conversation and part friends. I pointed to a particularly gaudy fly that was comprised of black and white hair, pink wispy feathers, and ribbon. It held center stage on a page all its own. "What creature on God's earth is that supposed to resemble?"

"Oh, that one is not meant to resemble any earthly creature *God* made. No, no, it is entirely one of my own creation, and I have an ample supply of materials to fashion many more like it," Lyman replied. "It is called an attractor fly, and fish strike at it out of curiosity."

"What is it made of?"

"The hair comes from a skunk," Lyman said, smiling slyly. His expression then became dour. "And the feathers and ribbon come from a garish pink bonnet I found hidden deep in Urena's wardrobe chest."

"Your wife owned a pink bonnet?"

He nodded grimly "A bonnet fit for a whore. How apt to combine fragments of it with the hair of that skunk."

It took me but a moment to realize what I was looking at, and as the sickening realization overwhelmed me, I thought I might faint. I reached for a tree limb to regain my balance, catching my sleeve on the sharp prongs of a branch. I could not dislodge it, and panic seized me by the throat. All I wanted to do was flee.

"Let me assist you," Lyman calmly offered. "I'll cut you free with my pocketknife." He reached for his satchel and peered into it. "Where is my knife?" he said, looking alarmed.

I most certainly did not want to wait for him to find it! I yanked hard and welcomed the sound of ripping silk. A torn sleeve was a small enough price to pay for my freedom.

"I must go at once," I told Lyman.

"Well, go then," he said without even bothering to look up at me as he continued to anxiously search his satchel.

I ran all the way back to town and burst through the back door to the kitchen just as Molly was pouring coffee for Grandfather and Adam. I managed to catch enough breath to ask Adam if I could talk with him privately. He instantly rose from the table and stepped out to the garden with me.

"What is wrong? What has happened?" he asked, taking hold of my elbows to steady me as I near swooned from exertion and shock.

"I know who killed Captain Peck," I gasped.

He nodded. "So you guessed it."

"Not a guess. A certainty. I saw the captain's hair on his hook."

"Calm yourself," Adam told me. "You are making no sense."

"Do the actions of a madman make sense? Lyman Upson scalped his wife's lover and made a fishing fly from his hair and the pink bonnet Peck had given her!"

Adam said nothing. He just stared at me.

"Don't you believe me?"

"What you say is rather hard to believe."

"I saw this fly from hell with my own eyes, Adam! Just a short while ago. Lyman is probably using it for bait as we speak!"

Adam scowled. "You had an assignation with Upson this morning?"

"No, I came upon him fishing."

"You just came upon him?"

"Yes, by happenstance."

"You did not arrange to meet him?"

"No, I say! Adam, please pay heed to what I am telling you. The Reverend Mr. Upson murdered Captain Peck."

"No, Julia. He did not."

"How can you be so sure?"

"Never mind. Just trust me."

"No, it is you who must trust me, Adam. Listen closely. Peck was Mrs. Upson's lover, and that is why Upson murdered him."

"How could you possibly know this?"

"The bonnet! Peck gave a pink bonnet to each of his mistresses. He even gave one to Molly. Mrs. Upson had one too that she kept hidden from her husband. But Lyman found it."

"You base your evidence on a mere *bonnet?*"

"No, on the fly!"

"A *fly* then. Do you not realize how flimsy your evidence is?"

Tears of frustration flooded my eyes. "Why is your mind so closed to what I am telling you, Adam?"

"Because I know more than you do."

"Hah!"

"I truly do, Julia. I know more about Peck's murder than you do, and I cannot accept your absurd supposition. Your emotions have gotten the better of your good sense."

"My emotions?"

"Obviously your meeting with Upson has caused you great agitation. That he can disturb your sensibilities in such a manner makes me wonder if you have a deeper regard for him than you are willing to admit to me."

"And you accuse *me* of making an absurd supposition! You are way off the mark, Adam."

"Am I? Why would Upson ask you to marry him if he had not seen at least a glimmer of tenderness in your gaze? And why would you keep his proposal a secret unless you had an inclination to accept it?"

"Oh, Adam, you have hurt me most painfully with such

accusations." I sank to the garden bench and buried my face in my hands.

After a long moment of silence he finally said, "Perhaps I have spoken too rashly."

Perhaps? That word alone kept me from accepting his apology, if indeed that is what it was. I remained with my face in my hands until I heard him walk away.

I did not join him at the breakfast table, nor have I seen him since. He will never believe me, I fear, unless I produce Peck's scalp as evidence.

Of course that is impossible. Lord only knows where Lyman has buried it. Or *has* he buried it? He asserted that he could make many more of his horrific, hooked creations, so that must mean he has preserved not only his poor wife's bonnet but also the captain's scalp. Now where would he keep handy such a nasty thing as that? Same place he keeps all his other skins and pelts, I reckon.

ADAM'S JOURNAL

Wednesday, August 26th

Looked all about the house and garden for Julia as soon as I returned from patient calls yesterday. Wanted to beg her pardon. Not for discounting her wild speculation that Upson scalped Peck, but for spouting wild speculations of my own concerning her relationship with him. Jealousy truly is the green-eyed monster and the great exaggerator. Did not find Julia at home, and Grandfather could not account for her whereabouts. Went and looked for her on the Green, where she often strolls at sunset, but no sign of her there either. Returned to the house to find Henry in the parlor chewing the rag with Grandfather. He had brought a box of Thoreau pencils for Julia. Told him she should be along shortly. We heard a wagon come barreling down the road, and I looked out the window to see Granny pull up at the gate. Went out and helped her get down from the buckboard. She looked mighty worried.

"I come to see Julia," she said.

That rather surprised me. They had never been very budge. "Julia isn't here right now. She could be at the store."

"It's past six. Store's closed."

"Well then, she's out walking somewhere."

"You know where?"

"No. What's wrong, Gran?"

"Well, Pilgrim is dead for one thing."

"Ah, so you know. I intended to come by later to tell you."

"I just heard about it from one of the farmhands." Gran pulled a letter from her apron pocket. "And I just read this letter Pilgrim gave me last I saw him. Now you read it, Adam." She thrust the letter into my hand.

I hesitated before unfolding it for upon the address fold, written in a most elegant hand, was this caveat: *To be entrusted to and held in strictest confidence by Mistress Elizabeth Tuttle of Tuttle Farm and opened only upon the death of the peddler known as Pilgrim.*

"Go on. Open it," Granny urged me impatiently.

"But it is marked private."

"If you care a whit about Julia you will read the dang letter *now*, Adam!"

And so I did. I copied its contents before turning it over to the authorities.

> *My Dear Madame -*
>
> *If you have opened this letter then I am dead. Only that certainty permits me to share my fears with another. I have chosen to share them with you because you are close to the one I believe to be in most danger at present. Pray ignore what you have oftentimes seen of my overindulgence in spirits to the detriment of mind and body and take to heart the facts and grave warning contained herein.*
>
> *You know me as Pilgrim, but my true Christian name is Nathan and surname Upson, born in Bennington, Vermont, now three score and two years past. I am the natural father, unbeknownst to him all these years, of the Reverend Lyman Upson. My sad history is this.*

I was a law student with great promise when my sweet-heart and I found ourselves in necessity to wed. We did so, and I soon had a baby boy to provide for. Without the means to support a family whilst continuing my studies, I abandoned them with great regret and found work in a wire mill. Such labor did not suit me and most regrettably I took to the bottle. My otherwise mild temperament had always been subject to bouts of uncontrollable temper, which became even more severe under the influence of drink. May God forgive me, but I began to frequently beat my wife. This was followed by a state of near insufferable regret and then yet more indulgence in the bottle. One night I took to her hard with my bare knuckles. Little Lyman screamed so at her piteous sobbing that I turned and kicked his cradle with an inhuman impatience and cruelty, knocking it over and throwing him out and into the fire-place. I staggered to him and yanked him out within a few seconds, but the poor babe had fallen directly upon the bars of the red-hot andirons. His bare little chest was seared by two deep burns—lasting marks of his own father's Sinfulness.

That day I acknowledged I could neither abstain from drink nor control my insensible rages. To spare their very lives I abandoned my wife and son and took to peddling as an un-demanding path by which to earn what I needed to continue to indulge my weakness for liquor. The rages have faded away these past years, but liquor will hold me tight in a devil's embrace until I breathe no more.

Despite my decision to foreswear my family, I always kept myself, at a discreet distance, abreast of my son's progress in life, following him through his schooling, then his choice of a severe Calvinist ministry, which eventually led him to Plumford. That was the reason I commenced to include the town in my round of summer peddling twelve years ago, arriving here each year at the time of my son's birthday. Over this time I have had the temerity to attend several of his fiery sermons and even appear at his back door, secure he could not recognize me, to offer my humble wares to his wife and observe him, if he happened to grace me with his presence, for at least a few precious moments. On such rare occasions he regarded me always with the unconcealed scorn he showed to his lessers; by that I mean those he perceived to be not preordained by God to stand at his side for Eternity in the Hereafter.

Last summer I tramped into town with a fellow wanderer and imbiber you know, or did know, as Roamer. He was a fine fellow of meek temperament who supported himself by most cleverly repairing clocks and small mechanical devices of any and all sort. We worked house to house about town and then moved on to more secluded abodes beyond the Green. We came to the Upson back door, as I had planned, on the date of my son's birth. We found the door wide open, for it was a day of sulfurous heat. I was about to call out when we were assailed by an outburst of rage directed by my son at his wife. We both stood in silent shock and mortified embarrassment as Lyman chastised her, in the most vicious tone, as an immoral female of the lowest order—an unfaithful wife—and repeatedly demanded that she name her lover, which she refused to do. I motioned my friend to come away from there, anxious not to be found listening. Later Roamer told me that, as I ran ahead of him round the corner of the house, he paused to look back and glimpsed the preacher glaring after him from the doorway, clutching a bonnet as deep a pink as his angry face.

We departed Plumford, and having earned enough to meet our modest needs, we retreated upriver to a farmhouse deserted by a family gone westering, where we drank and dawdled, fishing in the heat.

Roamer and I parted ways three days later, he never leaving my presence until then, and I set my feet south toward Connecticut to continue my yearly round. You can imagine my astonishment when I returned again to Plumford this year and was informed by you that Roamer had been hanged for the murder of Mrs. Upson. He must have gone back to Plumford after parting with me, but I could not for an instant believe him capable of perpetrating such a deed. Then to my utter shock I learned the murder had taken place on Lyman's birthday, the very day of our visit the year before! Being with me then and several days after, Roamer could not have done it. Upon reading the transcripts of the murder trial at the Concord courthouse, I learned my son had testified he had seen Roamer running from the house as he returned home from a walk and then found his beloved wife dead in the kitchen, her neck snapped. This testimony alone sent Roamer to the gallows. I can only conclude that my son killed his wife in a jealous rage and then caused poor Roamer to hang for it.

I do not ever intend to inform the authorities of this most horrible injustice. Roamer is dead, and I will not be the instrument in my own son's destruction. Yet I fear that Lyman, after so easily escaping punishment for murdering his wife, might be capable of killing again.

I have seen him courting Julia Bell. I have even seen him lay angry hands on her. And I am certain that if she were to marry him, she would be in grave danger. My attempt to warn her about Lyman was a sorry failure, for I could not tell her what I knew. I shall have to tell Lyman himself. I intend to seek him out this very day and entreat him to confess his crime to save his soul or at the very least leave off his pursuit of Julia Bell. I cannot tell him I am his father, for I am ashamed of my tawdry existence and know such a revelation would revolt him. I am even more ashamed that I have passed on to him such a vile, uncontrollable temper.

Bad blood! Bad blood! I was not fit to sire a child. Look what has come of it. My son is a Wife Murderer.

I pray my death was swift and with my maker I now find
a peace unknown to me here on this earth.
                    The Wastrel known as Pilgrim, born
                                Nathan Upson

After reading the letter I tucked it in my waistcoat pocket. "I will go to Upson's house directly," I told Gran, "and see if Julia is with him."

"Yes, go!" she urged. "But pray take care."

"Better yet, I will take Henry Thoreau."

Stuck my head inside the door and called him. When he came out I told him that Julia might be in dangerous company, keeping my voice low so that Grandfather would not over-hear. Leaving it to Gran to make our excuses inside, Henry and I took off down the road. On our way to Upson's house I quickly repeated the contents of Pilgrim's letter. Then I told Henry about Julia's speculation that Upson had scalped and murdered Peck. It did not seem so outlandish anymore. If Upson had managed to get a tramp blamed for his wife's mur-der, why would he not try to get an Indian blamed for the murder of his wife's lover?

"And the peddler is dead now too?" Henry said.

"Yes, I examined his body just this morning. Sometime last night he was accidentally trampled to death by a vicious bull, the same one that gored Trump." I suddenly recalled the pocketknife in Sultan's pen—the kind of knife an avid fisherman, more than a destitute vagabond, would own. "No!"

"No to what?" Henry said.

"To the assumption that he was trampled to death acciden-tally. I submit that Upson dragged Pilgrim into the bull pen al-ready dead, or at least unconscious."

"If Upson is the cold-blooded killer you believe him to be, we must make haste!" Henry said.

Knowing that Gran's old nag pulling a wagon could not

match us in speed, we ran as fast as we could through the Green and up the road to Upson's house. I pounded against the locked front door, but no one answered. We went around the house, found the back door unlatched, and went inside. A kettle lay on its side in the middle of the kitchen floor, but other than that nothing looked amiss. The parlor too looked in good order. The study, however, was in disarray, with hooks and feathers and bits of animal pelts scattered upon the carpet. To my horror the largest pelt looked to be of black and white human hair, and on closer inspection I determined that it was most likely Peck's scalp. Even more horrifying was the discovery of a lady's gray kid slipper by the threshold. Recognizing it as Julia's, I picked it up, pressed it to my chest, and cried out her name. No response. After searching the rest of the house in vain we went to the barn and saw that Upson's horse and carriage were gone.

"We must conclude," Henry said, "that he has taken Julia away against her will."

"But where?" I choked out, fear contracting my throat.

Henry pointed to the tracks the carriage wheels had left in the ground. "We will follow his trail."

We trotted along the dusty road, heading upriver, until the tracks left by Upson's gig became hopelessly confused with a multitude of other wagon and buggy wheel marks.

"He could have taken her up to Devil's Perch," I said. "Julia told me he proposed to her there and is much attracted to the spot." My heart clenched. "He would be safe from prying eyes to do with her as he wishes there."

We ran another half mile or so and proceeded up a steep path that cut directly through the woods to Devil's Perch, a much shorter route than the cart path. When the slope leveled out, we regained sight of the carriage tracks not a hundred yards from the cliff.

"To better our chances," Henry said, "we should approach

from different directions. I know the cliff face from when we found Caleb and will come up from that side. Upson will not expect it."

With that he slipped away through the bushes and began to work his way round to where the slope sharply steepened and became a rocky precipice.

I continued forward and soon saw Upson's horse and chaise through the trees. Just beyond was the clearing by the cliff where Julia and Henry had made their plaster casts. As I came closer I saw Julia's lithe figure silhouetted against the dusky sky. Upson was pointing his fowling piece at her. My only hope was to creep close enough to surprise him before he had a chance to do her harm. As fast and as silently as I could manage I stalked through the undergrowth toward them.

As I neared I heard Upson tell Julia to kneel before him. She complied. He then told her to beg forgiveness.

"God forgive me," she sang out in a clear, brave voice.

"Not *His* forgiveness! Do you think God listens to harlots? He did not listen to my wanton wife when she begged Him to save her, did He? He allowed me to keep shaking Urena until her neck snapped. How frail your sex is. How polluted your souls. Beg *my* forgiveness, Julia Bell. I am God's Avenging Angel and you have offended me most grievously with your whorish ways."

She did not respond. He drew closer to her and put the barrel of his gun to her breast. A twitch of his finger would bring her instant death! I could wait no longer and silently sprinted from cover. Above my head a crow, no doubt af-frighted by my sudden charge, cawed a raucous alarm. Upson looked over his shoulder at the sound and saw me. He spun around and pointed his gun at me, and I noticed numerous small cuts on his face.

"Stop or you die!" he shouted.

Continued to charge forward with all the speed my legs

could deliver. His firearm held only enough buckshot for one shot, and I wanted him to fire it at me instead of Julia. Hoped to drop to the ground before I was hit. But then he swung the muzzle away from me and back at Julia.

"Stop or *she* dies!"

That made me skid to a halt not ten feet from them. Knowing how many he had killed already, not for an instant did I think him incapable of acting on his threat.

Upson ordered Julia to stand up, and then he motioned me to come stand beside her. He backed away twenty feet, and from that range his barrel of buckshot could well kill us both.

"I was going to throw Julia over the cliff," he told me. "But God intervened by sending you here. He has a far better plan."

"That's right," I said, speaking to him in the soothing tone I use with distraught patients. "God does not want you to harm Julia. He sent me here to take her away."

Upson shook his head. "No, God sent you here to die with her. You are both foul sinners. Did I not witness your lascivious embrace in the garden? God wants you and your paramour to leap to your death together and plummet to hell."

Julia and I stared at him, aghast.

"Go forth," he urged us, waving his gun barrel in the direction of the cliff edge. "And when I give the command, you must jump."

"We won't do it," I said.

"Then I will shoot you instead. Either way you will die."

"But if you shoot us, it won't look like suicide," I said, still hoping I could get him to see reason. "You cannot get away with murdering us outright, Upson."

"God will provide me a scapegoat. He always has."

"You are using God as *your* scapegoat," I told him, "when you kill in His name."

His madness had no tolerance for the truth. He pointed his gun directly at me, and a murderous expression contorted his face. Sure he was going to pull the trigger, my only thought was that I would now take the brunt of the buckshot and Julia might manage to run away.

But she fell to her knees again and cried, "Have mercy on us, Angel Lyman!"

Addressing him in that manner seemed to appease him somewhat. Leastways he did not shoot me. He lowered the gun slightly as he seemed to consider the possibility of granting Julia's plea for mercy. But then he sighed and said, "No. I cannot spare your lives. You know too much." He frowned and looked confused. "But that is not the reason I must kill you. I must kill you because it is God's will that I do. I am His instrument of justice here on earth."

"Yes, you are God's mighty avenger," Julia said. "Adam and I have no doubt that you are. But pray tell us, Angel Lyman, when you came to know that you were so chosen."

"God marked me when I was but a babe. He reached down from heaven and touched me in my cradle, searing my flesh. My blessed mother witnessed it."

"Hallelujah!" Julia sang out, clutching her hands in prayer and staring up at him as though in awe. Her hair was loose and wild around her pale face, and I must say she appeared as mad as Upson. He smiled down upon her, but I doubted she could cajole him for much longer and gathered myself to jump at him.

Did not have to risk such a dangerous maneuver, however, for at that moment I saw Henry Thoreau climb up and over the rocky edge of the cliff. He looked about him, picked up a rock the size of a melon, and as Julia kept Upson distracted with her babble about his being a seraph incarnate, Henry crept up behind him. When he was within reach of the crazed minister he brought the rock down upon the back of his head. Upson pitched forward, and as he fell I raced to him and pulled the gun from his grasp. I kept it pointed at him as he lay on the ground groaning.

Henry tossed away the rock. "It was necessary to cause him injury, and I do not regret it," he told us. "All the same, I am glad I did not kill him."

"Well, he was glad enough to kill Peck," Julia said. "I found the poor captain's scalp in his study. He killed his wife too. His own wife!"

"And his own father," Henry told her. "The peddler Pilgrim."

"You lie!" Upson shouted, sitting up. "My father was a sainted missionary lost in darkest Africa before I was born. The man I killed was nothing but a dirty, worthless tramp."

"Then you admit you did it," I said.

"I had no choice. He could have ruined me."

"The man you murdered last night sired you, Upson," Henry said. "Show him the letter, Adam."

I took the peddler's letter from my waistcoat and threw it down to Upson. He did not deign to look at it.

"What was your father's name?" Henry asked him. He did not reply. "Was it Nathan?"

Upson's mouth went agape. "How do you know that?"

"Nathan Upson is the name of the man who wrote that letter. Look for yourself."

Upson picked up the letter and read it with care. As he did so he was transformed before us. His sense of superiority drained away, and his face fell into lines of painful dejection. Indeed, he looked much like his father when I'd last seen him alive. He folded the letter, put it aside, and staggered to his feet. I raised the gun.

"We are taking you to the constable," I said.

He did not even look at me. His gaze was inward, as though he was peering deep into his very soul. Suddenly he ripped open his vest and shirt, and there for us to see were the long black marks the hot andirons had burned into his flesh when he was a babe. He opened wide his arms and looked up at the darkening sky.

"Father!" he screamed.

And then he turned and broke into a run, heading for the cliff edge. Grasping his intention, Henry and I raced to catch him, but before we could, he leaped out and away from the cliff. Being a mere mortal man rather than an angel, he plunged to his death.

JULIA'S NOTEBOOK

Wednesday, 26 August

All yesterday afternoon I paced and fretted, waiting for Adam to return from his rounds. I hoped that I could finally convince him that Lyman had killed Peck and that he would agree to help me find proof of it. When the sun began to sink, I could wait no longer. Lyman had told me he went fishing every day at sundown, and I wanted to take advantage of his absence to search his house for Peck's scalp. Just in case he was home, however, I brought with me the horrid feather cape I'd promised to return as an excuse for my visit. I knocked on his front door and waited with bated breath. Much to my relief, Lyman did not answer. I tried the door and found it locked, as was the back door. This I had not expected, for locked doors are rare in Plumford. I took out a hairpin, and this time it worked like a charm. The simple catch gave way, and the back door eased open before me.

I prowled the first-floor rooms and detected a rank odor in Lyman's study when I entered. His beloved gun lay on a long bench, and beside it were cups and tins of shot and gunpowder. One corner of the room was cluttered with fishing paraphernalia, rods and reels and creels and such. By a window stood a big desk.

A snub-nosed vise was mounted upon it. It held a bare fish hook awaiting adornment. There were plenty more hooks in a box beside the vise, along with spools of colored threads, bundles of feathers, and strips of hides with the fur still clinging to them. I recognized hair from a woodchuck, a raccoon, a rabbit, and a squirrel, but none from a skunk, either animal or human.

The faint stink I had discerned upon my entrance was much stronger in the area of the desk, yet when I took a good sniff of the animal pelts they did not smell all that offensive. The more powerful smell seemed to be emanating from beneath the desk. I peered into the knee well and spotted a small wooden chest. I crouched down, took a good whiff, and nearly fell back on my heels in a swoon when the odor of decay hit my nostrils. But that did not stop me from retrieving the chest from the knee well and placing it on the desk. It was padlocked. That did not stop me either. I pulled out another hairpin and went to work on the small lock until the bow slid out of the bolt.

Holding my breath, I opened the chest. Inside lay a scalp that most certainly looked to be Capt. Peck's thick black mane with its distinctive streak of white. It still bore bits of sticky flesh and membrane, and I had to use all the power of my will to keep from retching. I turned away from the gory sight and saw another sight far more alarming. Lyman was standing in the doorway, regarding me with his cold, silvery gray eyes. Panic seized me, but once again I used all the power of my will to remain calm.

"Lyman, you are home at last," I said and hoped he did not notice the tremble in my voice. "I returned the lovely cape you made. Did you see it on the porch?"

He said nothing, just looked at me. His opalescent eyes, I noticed for the first time, were as blank of humanity as a ram's.

"I was disappointed you were not here," I continued, "and

when I discovered your back door was open, I let myself in and decided to wait for you here."

He did not respond, and so I rattled on in a rush. "Well, Lyman, I must say I noticed a pungent odor in this room, and you know how women are when they smell something amiss. I set out to investigate where the scent was coming from and lo! I found this skunk pelt." I gestured toward the open chest on the desk. "I am sure it is the pelt of a skunk for it stinks to high heaven!" My attempt at a laugh sounded more like a squeal.

In three long strides he came across the room and hovered over me. I looked up at him and attempted a coquettish expression.

"But do not fear," I went on as calmly as possible. "I will tell no one about what I found. It shall remain our secret. Rather, I shall forget all about it. Your lackadaisical housekeeping habits are certainly none of my concern. Indeed, I am not much of a housekeeper myself and—"

My babble was cut short when he slapped me across the face so hard I lost my balance and crashed against the desk. The chest atop it fell to the floor, and the scalp tumbled out, but he paid it no mind. His attention was concentrated solely on me. "You snooping she-devil!" he shouted, gripping my neck with both his hands.

Sure he would throttle the life out of me, I felt around the desk behind me for some kind of weapon to defend myself. Feathers would not help me, nor would the soft hides. When my hand found the open box of fish hooks, I grabbed it and smashed the contents into Lyman's face, thereby sinking the barbed points deep into his flesh.

He roared in pain, letting go my neck as he attempted to brush the hooks from his face, only managing to give himself more pain. I dashed away from him, losing one slipper as I scurried out of the room and headed toward the front door. I had forgotten that it was locked! As I tugged on the handle in vain, Lyman came up behind me and caught me by the arm with such force he almost tore it out of its socket. He twisted me around to face him and began slapping my face again, as though keeping beat to some mad music in his head. Through my tears I could see hooks dangling from his eyebrows, and several were caught in his upper lip.

That gave me the idea to yank the horn comb from my hair and thrust it deep into the hand clutching my arm. Blood spurted out, and he immediately released his hold on me to pull out the comb. I raced through the kitchen, heading now for the back door.

If my freed hair had not been streaming down my back, I might have made it. But Lyman managed to get hold of a hank of it and began reeling me in. No helpless flapping fish was I, however. I grabbed the heavy kettle off the cookstove and struck him on the head with it. He let go of my tresses, stumbled backward, and fell. I turned toward the door again, but Lyman, although supine, still had a long reach. He caught the edge of my skirt to halt me, took hold of my ankles, and pulled my legs out from under me. My head struck the cookstove, and my world instantly went black.

When I awakened I found myself sitting beside Lyman in his chaise, propped up by his arm around my waist as we traveled along a country road at a smart clip. The carriage hood was up, and we were as secluded from prying eyes as any courting couple could hope to be.

"Surely you do not intend to kill me, Lyman," I said.

"Ah, you are conscious," he said. His handsome face was dotted with puncture wounds from the hooks I'd sunk into his flesh. A bump rose from the spot on his high forehead where I'd whacked him with the kettle. But he smiled at me as though all was forgiven. "No, I will not kill you, Julia. I think it better that you kill yourself. Do you know where we are heading?"

I looked around, and when I recognized the road, my heart sank. "Devil's Perch."

He nodded. "The very place I proposed to you. But I had a change of heart, you see. I withdrew my offer of marriage today when you came to visit me. You became very distraught, Julia. You told me you could not live without me. Indeed, you threatened to go to Devil's Perch and throw yourself off the precipice. Alas, I did not take you seriously. How remorseful I shall be when I hear that your body has been found at the base of the cliff."

"It won't wash, Lyman. No one will believe you."

"There you are wrong, Julia. People always believe me. Did not the jury believe me when I told them I saw the tramp Roamer run from my house after killing my wife? Did not the vile sinner Peck, who confessed to me he might have infected my wife with the pox, believe me when I told him to meet me again at his belvedere so that we might pray together for his salvation? Did not the wretch called Pilgrim, who presumed to tell me how to save my soul, believe me when I told him I would do him no harm after I followed him into Herd's barn? And will not the entire town of Plumford believe me when I profess that your unrequited love for me drove you to commit suicide? Poor, disconsolate, rejected Julia Bell! How I shall weep over your lost soul."

That did it. I screamed with rage. And with the hope that someone might hear me. Lyman's little mare did at any rate. Startled by my shrieking, she pulled back her ears and reared up on her hind legs. When Lyman let go of me to take the reins in both hands to control her, I jumped out of the chaise and sprinted into the field beside the road, heading for a farmhouse I saw in the distance.

The field was too overgrown for a carriage to get through,

so Lyman set out after me on foot. I doubted he could catch me before I reached my goal. He was near twenty years my senior for one thing. And for another, I am an exceptional runner, taught by Adam in my youth to race like a boy. I had lost a shoe, however, and I was wearing five layers of petticoats. To my further detriment, the field was thick with blackberry bushes, and their noxious brambles kept getting caught on my skirts like tiny claws grabbing at me from every direction. This slowed me down considerably, and I could hear Lyman's heavy pants as he gained on me. I ran all the harder, still sure I could reach the farmhouse before he reached me. But as I got closer to it, I saw there were gaping holes where there should have been windows and half the roof had tumbled down. The place was abandoned! Nothing remained of its former inhabitants but pieces of a broken, rusty sickle lying on the ground.

I glanced over my shoulder to see Lyman looming. I picked up a sickle piece and threw it at him with all my might. Regrettably, it missed his head (although by no more than a hair), and he was upon me. He hit me again, this time with his fist, and my knees buckled under me. He half-carried, half-dragged me back to the carriage, hauling me off to my death.

I never gave up though. Even when we reached the top of Devil's Perch and Lyman took his gun out of the carriage, I did not lose heart. I was still determined to save myself, and if I could not, I maintained the belief that I would be saved in some other way. I was also certain I would see Adam again—how or when I did not know.

Alas, when I did see Adam again he was charging toward the gun Lyman pointed at him, and I feared we would both end up dead. But thanks to Henry Thoreau we did not. He saved us by bashing Lyman with a rock. And Lyman saved the state of Massachusetts the trouble of hanging him by choosing to take his own life.

There is no room in my heart to pity Lyman. It is too filled with compassion for his victims—his poor wife Urena, the blameless Roamer, and the flawed yet well-intentioned Pilgrim. As for Capt. Peck, I cannot help but think his own actions brought on his miserable demise. Not only had he seduced Lyman's wife, he might have infected her. Consequently, Lyman too could have been infected. And for that outrageous sin against his most precious being, the Avenging Angel that Lyman considered himself to be tortured Peck most horribly before slaying him.

Ah, well, it is over and done with, and life in Plumford will go on as before. As for Adam and me, can we go on as before? If only it were possible for us to dwell here together as we once did when this town was the innocent Eden of our childhood. I cannot help but wish it.

JULIA'S NOTEBOOK

Friday, 28 August

As I write in my cabin the ship is pulling away from the East Boston dock. That I was able to book passage convinces me that the Fates intervened to get me far away from Adam as fast as possible. He will know I have departed when he receives my letter by messenger this evening. In six weeks I shall be landing in Liverpool, with the great expanse of the Atlantic Ocean separating us. Our proximity of blood makes proximity of place too perilous for us, and I pray Adam will understand this is why I had to leave so abruptly. After what happened between us last evening, he should.

He found me in front of my easel, putting the finishing touches on my portrait of Grandfather. It was well past midnight.

"So you cannot sleep either," he said. "I have been walking in the Green, wishing you were beside me."

And I had been lying in my bed, wishing he was beside me, but of course I did not tell him that.

"Come out with me now, and we can gaze at the stars together," he said.

"Dressed as I am?" I was wearing only my muslin night-gown, with my painting pinafore wrapped around it.

"You are most modestly covered."

"But not properly so. You do not seem to appreciate that I am no longer a child, Adam. I am a full-grown woman who must behave with a certain amount of decorum."

"I fully appreciate that you are a woman now, Julia," he replied, regarding me intently. "Your features and form please me in every way it is possible to please a man." He took a step toward me.

I took a step back. "Adam, such talk as that can lead us nowhere."

"I am hoping it will lead to marriage."

"You know that is impossible. Was it not you who first told me it was?"

"Nothing is impossible if we want it enough, Julia."

"Do we want offspring who are born so deformed they cannot sustain life?"

"There are methods to prevent conception."

"But is not conception the primary function of the marriage act?"

"Conjugal passion is an expression of love, Julia. It need not result in procreation to be justified."

"I allow that to be true. But I cannot allow us to chance creating a being that will only suffer and die. As far as those preventive methods you mention go, can you promise me they will never fail us? Or that we will never fail to use them?"

He took a moment before replying, and when he spoke his voice was strained. "All I can promise you is this, my beloved. If the fear of possible conception is what prevents you from agreeing to be my wife, I will be willing to practice marital continence with you. That is how dearest above all things you are to me."

"You are proposing a platonic marriage?" I asked in disbe-lief.

"Does not love, when platonic, express its most perfect form?"

I pressed my hands to my cheeks, quite moved by his obvi-ous sincerity. All the same, I did not think either of us could keep such a promise unless we lived completely apart. To prove this to him would be simple enough.

I put down my paintbrush, untied my pinafore, and slipped it off. He did not turn his eyes from me as I removed the pins in my hair and let it fall around my face and shoulders. I slowly walked toward him, raising the hem of my nightgown so that my bare feet and ankles were visible.

"If you became my husband, Adam, this is how you would see me every night." I smiled up at him. "Would we not share a home together?"

"Your home would always be here," he said in a low-pitched voice, opening his arms to me.

I stepped into his embrace and lay my head upon his solid bosom. How his heart did beat! And how I loved him! I loved him because he was so pleasing to look at, so good-hearted, so brave, so intelligent and skilled. But mostly I loved him be-cause *I could not help it.* Our hearts had knit together in bonds of sympathy and companionship long ago. And as he held me against him, my body yearned to knit with his too. I could feel, through the thin layer of muslin covering me, that he too was excited by our bodily contact. We pressed against each other in silence for as long as we both could bear it, and when I pulled away my nightgown stuck to my burning flesh.

He did not suggest marital continence again. He did not say anything at all. I picked up the lamp and made my way up-stairs. He did not follow me, and for that alone I am grateful. I do not think I could have resisted him if he had.

I took the first stage out of Plumford this morning, then

the first train out of Concord. Before I departed I placed a note on Grandfather's pillow whilst he slept. As much as I longed to gaze upon Adam's dear face one last time, I dared not enter his bedchamber. But I am sure I shall be able to recall each and every detail of his countenance for the rest of my years.

I am quite sure Adam will never forget me, either. Still, I pray his desire to have me as his wife will eventually dim. One day he will start to notice that Harriet is no longer a child. Or he will meet an elegant young lady at a Boston soirée. It comforts me to think that in due course my beloved cousin will find happiness with another and have healthy children with her. Truly it does. Even so, I shall allow myself a very long cry.

ADAM'S JOURNAL

Saturday, August 29th

I have been reborn a new man! Yesterday I was sorrowing over Julia's sudden departure. Today I attended Henry's melon party in the highest of spirits. As I drove to Walden Pond the tang of autumn spiced the air, and the thick golden light made everything I beheld most pleasing. Noted that in the water-meadows the hay was being got in. Men were raking it up and heaping it atop their carts to form great gilded towers as their patient oxen bent their massive heads to munch at forkfuls that fell beside them. Up on dryer ground farmers topped their corn and dug out potatoes and onions for the Boston market, and clouds of dust issued out of the wide doors of barns as grain was being flailed. Had to slow down and walk Napoleon through herds of cows being driven homewards from their summer gorging on the rich grass up on the Vermont hills. I beamed a foolish smile at all and sundry as Gran's words echoed in my mind. *You was born on the wrong side of the blanket, Adam.*

When I reached Henry's cabin, I saw that long tables of sawn boards had been arranged under the pines, laden with many varieties of sliced melons. And as many varieties of guests—young and old, refined and rough, dour and jovial—were helping themselves to succulent portions. In addition to the melons, there were baskets of ripe huckleberries and whortleberries, plates of bread, jars of jam, and bowls of thick cream. Artfully arranged about them were leafy vines, bouquets of squash blossoms, and sunflowers.

I did not spot Henry in the crowd, but a friendly fellow came forward to warmly welcome me. He introduced himself as Ellery Channing and declared himself to be a close friend of Henry's. He took me round to meet other guests, and I shook hand with the famous Ralph Waldo Emerson and his regal wife Lidian. Can't recall the names of half the other folks I met, but one I do remember is Bronson Alcott. Quite the windbag, he railed against the Mexican War longer than I cared to listen, even though I was in agreement with him. To change the subject I expressed my admiration of Henry's neat, efficient abode. Mr. Alcott told me he had lent Henry the ax he used to build it, which Henry returned even sharper than he had received it.

As we regarded the cabin, Henry came out the open door, a yellow flute in hand. A tall girl shouted, "There be our dear hermit!" and ran to him, dark hair and white petticoats flying.

Mr. Alcott sighed. "That is my wild child, Louisa," he said. "My three other daughters conduct themselves with far more decorum, I assure you."

As Louisa pranced around Henry, enjoining him to play his flute, he smiled at her indulgently but put her off to come greet me.

"How do you like the world today, Adam?" he said.

"I would like it far better if only Julia were beside me."

"She did not come with you?" The invitation to Henry's spur-of-the-moment party had been addressed to us both.

"She sailed for Europe yesterday."

Henry looked much put out. "She might have bid her friends adieu before she left."

"Do not feel slighted, Henry. Julia did not say good-bye

even to me. When I awoke she was gone with the morning dew."

"Just like the fairy princess," young Louisa Alcott piped in. She was standing right behind Henry, blatantly eavesdropping.

"Small pitchers have wide ears," he told her, looking more amused than stern. "Why don't you go join your playmates, Lou?"

She glared at him with lovely dark eyes. "I am near fifteen, far too old to have playmates," she said and flounced off to converse with Mr. Emerson.

Henry turned back to me. "Pray, how long does Julia intend to stay in Europe?"

"Forevermore, according to the letter she sent me before her ship left the dock. But I shall be on the first available vessel in pursuit of her. I assume her destination is Paris, for that is where her father abides. And if she is not there he will know how I can find her."

"That you have to *find* her, Adam, makes me conjecture that Julia wishes to elude you."

"Indeed she does. In her letter she stated that she does not wish to be anywhere near me, much less marry me."

Henry regarded me with pity in his eyes. "If she feels such a strong aversion as that, perhaps you should leave her be, my friend."

I smiled back at him. "You do not understand. It is not because Julia loves me so little that she has fled, but because she loves me so much. She thinks it is in my best interest for her to go away, but I know better than she does."

"Some women cannot accept that men know better," Henry said. "Margaret Fuller, for one, always made that extremely clear to me whenever we conversed."

"But I have intelligence Julia does not have."

"Again, some women, such as the aforementioned Miss Fuller, cannot accept that men are more intelligent."

"You are not getting my meaning, Henry, but it is of no matter. Suffice it to say that there is no longer anything keeping my soul mate and me apart."

"Then you are far more fortunate than me," Henry said, looking toward a lone female figure standing at the water's edge. She turned, as if feeling Henry's eyes upon her. 'Twas Mrs. Emerson! She and Henry stared at each other across the chattering crowd for a moment, and then she turned back to gaze at the pond.

"There is no remedy for love but to love more," Henry said softly.

Nodding in agreement, I pulled out from my pocket the gold locket I hope never to lose sight of again. "I shall put this around Julia's neck when we are reunited," I told Henry. "It arrived by post with a note from that brigand LaFarge. He apologized most eloquently for leaving me to await my death and expressed the fervent hope I would forgive him." I laughed. "The gall of that Gaul!"

"How did LaFarge know Badger failed to kill you?"

"He was heading back to his shop the next morning when he saw me exit from it with you and Julia and a band of police officers. So off he skedaddled to warn his partner Vail, and they both cleared out of town straightaway."

"It is most regretful they were not captured," Henry said. "But the laws of karma insure that they will pay for their sins in a life to come."

"I would prefer they pay in this one," said I, "for we have no proof there will be others."

"Perhaps we can obtain proof," Henry said.

"Of Reincarnation?"

He nodded. "I made an amazing discovery this morning. If you can wait until my other guests depart, I will tell you about it."

I agreed to stay and spent the rest of the afternoon being astonished at how social Henry can be when he so chooses.

He entertained us by playing old-time ballads on his flute, occasionally breaking into a vigorous jig at the same time, and we sang along as the sun poured down upon us. A subtle energy seemed to rise from the sparkling pond and pervade the atmosphere, and despite all the horrors I had witnessed these last days, I had the positive sense that the Universe wishes no evil upon us. We bring it upon ourselves by supplanting the Divinity within us with egoism and selfishness. Was it not egoism and selfishness that spawned the evil carried out by Peck and Badger and Upson?

After Henry's guests had trundled off by wagon or foot back to town, he and I sat silent in our chairs outside the cabin. I began to wonder why he had asked me to linger. When he was ready to, he told me.

"As I walked this morning on Bartlett's Hill," he began, "I faintly smelt a flower I did not recognize but somehow believed I knew. I could not find it, but when I returned home my mind could not let go of that scent. Then all of a sudden, as my guests began to arrive, it came on me that I had last smelt that flower when I was running to warn my tribe of an imminent attack." Henry paused for my reaction.

It was rather slow in coming. "Are you telling me that you recall the scent from the time you were in a hypnotic state?"

"Yes, from the time I was an Indian!"

"Or *believed* yourself to be one."

He disregarded my qualification. "Methinks I killed those two braves on Bartlett's Hill, Adam."

"Might you not smell the same flower elsewhere?"

"I never have, Adam. So it cannot be a common variety. And the scent brought back the memory of the terrain in my retrogression. It resembled Bartlett's Hill in every detail. Even the feel of the slope under my moccasins was familiar. I know in my bones that the incident occurred there, and I am determined to find evidence of it. Will you help me?"

I was excited and yet wary of somehow meddling in matters of time and space. "More than two hundred years have passed, Henry. Even if you are correct as to the location, what evidence would be left to find?"

"Bones. The bones of the warrior who fell between the boulders when I smote him with my ax."

"But how can we locate those particular boulders in such a large area as that?"

"Why, the scent of the flower will lead us to it."

I shook my head. "This is a wild goose chase if ever there was one."

"Oh, come, Adam. What have you better to do on such a fine afternoon than accompany a friend on a walk up a hill?"

"Pack for one thing. I intend to set sail for Europe next week."

"And I am off to Maine to climb Katahdin on Monday. So this is our only opportunity. Pray accompany me, Adam. I need a witness with clear eyes to see what I hope to see. And what better witness than the man who sent me back into the past in the first place?"

In truth I was almost as excited as he was over the possibility of proving his experience under hypnosis had really happened. And so I accompanied Henry around the pond and up Bartlett's Hill. On a slope below the brow of the hill he slowed and sniffed to either side of the path like a hound trailing a fox. "I smell a fragrance of checkerberry and mayflower combined," he said.

I could smell it too, a sweet but evanescent scent that seemed to fade away as I turned toward the direction from whence I thought it emanated. We rustled about in the grass and leaves, and of course Henry's preternaturally sharp eyes were the ones to spot the flower. It was a most inconspicuous, compact plant with narrow leaves and pale flower heads that looked more like burrs than blossoms. Henry knelt down and gazed upon it as one would some long lost friend.

"Polygala cruciata," he said. "Very rare. Why, this discovery alone would be enough." He sat for some time over the limp little bit of greenery. I wondered if he had altogether forgotten our momentous purpose, but he soon rose to his feet. "However, we seek an even rarer prize this day." He pointed up the hill. "This is the slope," he said softly. "I feel it underfoot as I did then. And yonder the boulders."

He ran up to the heap of rocks and quick as a squirrel climbed atop two boulders that leaned close against each other.

"There," he shouted down into the mossy space between them. "There is where he fell."

I climbed up beside him, peered down into the wide crevasse, and despaired, for the space between the rocks narrowed with no bottom in sight. "As good a place to grab hold of a copperhead or rattler as any I ever laid eyes on," I said.

"Never seen either hereabouts," Henry said, most clearly not discouraged. "I will drop downward headfirst and see if I can reach bottom whilst you remain wedged above holding me by my feet."

Addressing him as I would a deranged patient, I tried to convey to him how very unwise was his proposition. "What if I let you go and you become jammed down there? Or I slip, tumble in with you, and the both of us become trapped? That would be a fine pickle for two grown men to find ourselves in."

"If we were lucky," he placidly answered, "Waldo Emerson might hear our shouts, for he walks in these woods on occasion. And if we were not so lucky, he or some other wayfarer would eventually smell us."

"That does not assuage my misgivings," said I.

But no one can be more persuasive than Henry when his mind is set upon a thing, and before I knew it we went into the crevasse. I found purchase for my boots on each opposing boulder face where the split between them narrowed just enough for a man of Henry's slight build to squeeze through. He slid down headfirst as I held him by his ankles. He kept urging me to lower him deeper down, and I bent over as far as I could, my arms extended to their limit.

"I am at bottom!" Henry shouted. Dust began to rise as he pawed his way through the remains of whatever had tumbled down there over the centuries. Just as I was about to tell him I could hold on no longer, he shouted, "Haul me up!"

Did so, my arms trembling, and soon had him up beside me. He had not returned empty-handed. He was grasping a big, heavy ball of earth and leaves. He gave it to me, heaved himself out, took his prize back, and I vaulted out beside him. We lay atop the boulder taking in the air with bellow breaths like a pair of winded horses. Henry's face was streaked with sweat and dust, and ancient cobwebs clung around his nose and mouth. I swept several generous-sized spiders from his hair and off his coat and used my sleeve to sweep filth from his eyes so he could see. I never saw him happier. He hung onto his ball of earth like a boy clutching a new puppy.

We scaled down the rocks and found a clear space atop the hill overlooking Walden Pond. After we had caught our breath, he said, "Your hands gripped my ankles like a pair of vises, and I am most grateful for your fortitude and strength, Adam."

"And I am most grateful you did not require me to dangle you a moment longer, Henry, for I swear I could not have," I replied gruffly, although his heartfelt words had pleased me. "Was this big clump of dirt worth such risk and effort?"

"We shall soon see," he said calmly, but his eyes glowed bright with expectation.

He laid the dirt ball down, and from it we pried loose clots of dark, dried earth mixed with leaves. It was like peeling an onion as we slowly revealed a human skull. A wedge of stone was deeply imbedded in the cracked frontal bone. Thoreau spit on the stone and rubbed away the dirt, revealing the pink blush of quartz crystal.

Speechless, we stared at each other with wide eyes for a moment, and then got to work spitting and rubbing some more, until a jagged blaze of black stone running through the pink quartz was revealed.

We sat back and gaped at the ax head Henry had described during his hypnotic trance. The handle once attached to it by sinew or leather had long ago dropped away.

Henry brushed away more dirt from the face of the skull, fully revealing the eye sockets, strong jaw line, and a full set of teeth that any modern man in Massachusetts would be most proud to own.

"He died a good, honorable death," Henry said. "And I must have died that day too, for I did not go back to retrieve my treasured ax."

We sat in the skull's company for a good long piece of time as a breeze cooled us and the wavelets on the pond reflected sunlight back at us. We heard the whistle of the steam engine and the rattle of cars shunted along from Boston toward Concord station past the west end of the pond.

"I have the proof now," Henry stated serenely. "I have lived before."

The realization that Julia's recollection of a past life with me was most likely also true overwhelmed me, and I could not reply. We sat in silence for a good quarter hour more, staring at the split skull and then out at the sky and down at the curving green shores of Walden Pond.

Henry broke the silence with a surprising directive. "We cannot speak of this to anyone, Adam."

"Why in heaven's name not? Why not tell the world? It is joyous news!"

"Only if it is believed," Henry said. "But it will not be. And we will forever be puppets in an endless whirlwind of claims and dismissals concerning what we have found here today. We will be portrayed as charlatans promoting a fantastical theory to hoodwink the gullible for fame and profit. It will be just too easy for folks to conclude we planted the skull down there for the purpose of making this claim."

I had to agree with Henry's assessment of the situation. As much as he wants to return to his cabin and write in peace, I want to practice medicine and live in peace with Julia. Therefore, no one can hear about this.

"The skull is yours if you want it," Henry told me.

Knowing how much he treasured Indian artifacts, I was most surprised. "Don't you want it, Henry?"

"No. Explaining how I came to acquire it would involve lying, which I am loath to do. And now that it has been proven to me that I existed as an Indian in another life, I need consider it no further. It is my present life that delights me. I am content to experience one world at a time."

I felt much the same way, and we decided the most respectful thing we could do was to return the skull with its ax to its grave. So we cast our great discovery back into the crevice and went on our way. At Henry's cabin we shook hands in parting.

"Have a good trip," I said. "Take care in the wilds of Maine."

"In wildness is the preservation of the world, yet one must travel farther and farther to experience it," he replied, staring dolefully at the railroad tracks on the opposite bank of Walden Pond. He looked back at me and managed a smile. "Should I bid you to take care too, Adam? No, I think not. Instead I bid you to go confidently in the direction of your dreams and live the life you imagine."

And so I will. For I shall soon be heading in the direction of Julia, to tell her that we can now live the life we have only dared imagine. We can embrace without caution or restraint. We can enjoy each other completely without fearing the results of our conjugal bliss.

When I returned to the house I paused at the office doorway to watch Grandfather apply leeches to Justice Phyfe's leg veins to assuage the pain of his gout. Phyfe sighed with relief, evidence of the power of suggestion upon the body rather than the efficacy of bleeding as far as I am concerned. Even so, I was happy to see that Grandfather felt fit enough to practice his own brand of medicine again.

I went to the kitchen and devoured most of the apple pandowdy Gran had brought by earlier. As I masticated I ruminated on my conversation with her this morning. She had come by to inquire how Julia was faring after her horrible ordeal with Upson, and when I informed her that Julia had sailed off to Europe, Gran looked stunned.

"For *good?*" she asked me.

"There's no good in it, but yes, that is her intention. I frightened her off by proposing marriage."

Gran regarded me somberly. "You look mighty bleak, dearie. Mighty bleak indeed."

"I am desolate. My heart urges me to pursue Julia, yet my conscience cautions me that I should let her go. As much as it pains me to admit it, I know she would be better off marrying somebody else."

Gran took umbrage. "Ain't nobody better than you, my boy. You come from good strong Tuttle stock."

"Do not forget I am also half Walker and so is Julia. Therefore, our future happiness together is cursed."

"No, it ain't," Gran said in a dismissive, flat tone.

"But surely you realize that we cannot have a natural marital relationship, Gran. Because of the bloodline we share, engendering children would be wickedly reckless."

" 'Twas yer ma who was reckless," Gran muttered.

"How?"

"Never you mind," Gran said and made her way toward the door.

I walked out to the back porch with her. "How was my mother reckless?" I persisted.

"When she climbed that consarn tree to catch a swarm of wild bees, was that not reckless? If she had taken more care, you would not have been left a bereft orphan."

"I am grateful I had you and Grandpa Tuttle to raise me up, Gran. I had a happy childhood."

"I want you to be happy *now*, Adam."

I shook my head. "I cannot be. Not without Julia as my wife."

"Well, if spunk and gumption are what yer lookin' fer in a mate, I reckon she's got plenty enough to suit you. She acted most bravely up on Devil's Perch. And she acted most unselfishly by leaving you yesterday. It has always been clear to me that she loves you. But I did not think she would make you a good wife, what with her ambitions and independent ways."

"She is the only woman I will ever want."

"Then I reckon it was mighty wrong of me to deceive her." Gran lowered her eyes and stared at her clenched, boney hands. "I encouraged Julia's belief in a falsehood, Adam. Now it grieves me to see you so miserable without her. But the truth can set things right."

"The truth about what?"

"Yer father." Gran heaved a sigh and continued. "You was born on the wrong side of the blanket, my boy. You don't have a drop of Walker blood in you." She waited for my reaction. All she got was a puzzled frown. "Owen Walker did not sire you, Adam. You was begotten whilst he was off whalin'."

"Are you sure of this, Gran?"

"Sure as shootin' Oh, how we prayed together, my Sarah and me, that Owen's ship would come in early so she could claim the babe growin' in her belly as his. And his ship did land early enough, thank the Lord, to pass you off as a legitimate Walker. 'Nuff said."

Hardly enough said to satisfy me. "But who *is* my father, Gran?"

"Another mariner. Not a whaler though. A riverboat captain. Yer Ma met him when she went out to visit my sister Hattie in St. Louis. Fool that I was, I urged her to go to cheer her up. She was so sad when Owen was gone. And he was gone far too often, Adam, and for far too long at a time. I ain't claimin' it was his fault, mind you. Yet I cannot fault my daughter entirely. She was very young and lonely. And like I said, she was reckless, God bless her."

"Why did you not tell me this sooner?"

"I promised yer ma I would never tell you. Or tell anyone. Even yer Grandpa Tuttle didn't know. Nor yer Walker grandparents, of course."

"Doc Silas has always claimed I am the spitting image of his son."

"You don't look nothin' at all like Owen Walker, Adam. But we only see what we want to see, and the old doc wants to see his lost son in you. You gonna tell him the truth?"

"I don't know," I said. And I still do not know. My mind is too filled with joyous thoughts of reuniting with Julia to consider much else.

"Do you forgive me for not speakin' up sooner?" Gran asked me, clenching her hands again.

My response was to wrap my arms around her and lift her

off her feet in a hearty hug. "You have made me the happiest man in the world."

"So you don't mind about not being a Walker?"

"I am still who I was before you told me, Gran. Nothing has changed about me except my determination to marry Julia as soon as I can."

I shall start preparing for my voyage directly. Before long I will be with Julia again, and, as my dear, reckless mother's spirit whispered to me when I was in such dire straits, *all shall be well.*